"I wish you could see the island the way I see it, Aiden."

"Seashell Bay is such a beautiful place and the people are just so damn decent, despite their faults. I hate it that your father took that away from you."

Aiden pressed his lips together, his tangled emotions keeping him silent.

"There's so much good here," Lily said as she gazed up at him. "So much that's right for the soul. You just have to be able to see it."

He wanted to. He really did, but he could still see his dad, whose contempt and bitterness had colored everything about the place. There was too much ugliness in his past, too much darkness to ever make the island right for him again.

But he couldn't say that. Not all of it, anyway.

"The only good thing I see in Seashell Bay is you, Lily, just like always," he said, briefly cupping her soft cheek. "Because you're right, nothing's changed for me."

When Lily's pretty mouth pursed in dismay, it was all Aiden could do not to grab her and kiss her...

Meet Me at the Beach

V. K. SYKES

FOREVER

NEW YORK   BOSTON

Copyright © 2015 by Vanessa Kelly and Randall Sykes
Excerpt from *Summer at the Shore* copyright © 2015 by Vanessa Kelly and Randall Sykes

Forever
Hachette Book Group
1290 Avenue of the Americas
New York, NY 10104

www.HachetteBookGroup.com

Printed in the United States of America

First Edition: February 2015
10 9 8 7 6 5 4 3 2 1

OPM

Forever is an imprint of Grand Central Publishing.
The Forever name and logo are trademarks of Hachette Book Group, Inc.

The Hachette Speakers Bureau provides a wide range of authors for speaking events. To find out more, go to www.hachettespeakersbureau.com or call (866) 376-6591.

The publisher is not responsible for websites (or their content) that are not owned by the publisher.

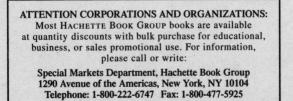

*For Phil and Anne Kelly, who showed
us the way to Seashell Bay.*

Acknowledgments

Seashell Bay is a fictional place, of course. But there is certainly a Casco Bay, and it provided us with much inspiration for our series. Grateful thanks go to the residents of one small island in particular, especially Bob Stack, Liz and Robin Walker, and Harriet Davis and her two wonderful girls, Claire and Annie (thanks for the finding the missing angel, Claire!). We'd also like to thank our agent, Evan Marshall, and our editor, Alex Logan, for working so hard on our behalf and keeping us on track. Thanks are also due to all the exceptional, dedicated staff at Grand Central Publishing.

Many thanks to Dan, Naoko, Liz, and Beryl for their love and support. And an infinite debt of gratitude goes to Debbie Mason, talented writer and critique partner and a truly wonderful friend. Every conversation is enlightening, fun, and well worth the insane number of hours we spend on the phone!

Meet Me at the Beach

Chapter 1

Home.

The word normally conjured all sorts of good feelings like Mom, apple pie, and "The Star-Spangled Banner." But not to Aiden Flynn. To him, home meant a slug to the jaw from his drunken father and ugly memories of long days on a lobster boat, covered in slime as he hauled and set lobster traps in freezing cold water. It meant a mother's tears when Aiden told her he was leaving forever and a brother's disappointment that he'd eventually be left to carry on the family business by himself. It meant struggling every minute of every day to escape the life that fate and heritage had tried to map out for him.

But Aiden couldn't dodge the tortured walk down memory lane any longer, which accounted for his lousy mood despite the warm sunshine reflecting off the sparkling waters that surrounded him on the ferry. In just a few minutes, the boat would dock at Seashell Bay Island, where he grew up. Like so many other islands in Maine, it was accessible only by ferry or private boat.

A tangy ocean breeze tempered the hot, clear day in

August. It was the kind of day that made a man happy to be alive. It was also a perfect day for baseball, a game Aiden would have still have been playing if not for his screwed-up knees.

As if on cue, his agent's ringtone, "For the Love of Money," blared out from the pocket of his Phillies windbreaker. Turning his back on the view of Great Diamond Island, with its shoreline homes perched high on the rocky cliffs, he answered his phone just as the captain blasted the horn at a sister ferry.

"What the hell was that?" Paul Johnson yelped over the phone. "Are you trying to make me go deaf?"

"Sounds of the bay, man. Out here it's boats, lobster, booze, and not much else."

"Well, I like booze, and I love lobster, but I'll give the boats a pass, if you don't mind."

Aiden felt the same way. "Please tell me you have some good news."

"Hey, you just left Philly yesterday. I'm good, pal, but I'm not that good. I just wanted to let you know I put out some more feelers this morning—this time to the Orioles and the Royals."

Aiden nodded when a middle-aged woman leading an enormously fat black Labrador gave him a friendly smile before taking the stairs to the lower deck. He thought she might be from Seashell Bay, but since he'd been home only once in the last fourteen years, it would have been a miracle if he recognized anybody but his father and brother and maybe a few others.

"That's good," Aiden said as he headed toward the bow, searching for some privacy. "Keep working the phones, Paul. Someone's got to need a DH." Realistically, the designated hitter position was all his knees were up to anymore.

When Paul remained silent for several seconds, Aiden had to clamp down hard on the stab of dismay knifing through his chest. Dammit, he was only thirty-two. He refused to believe his career in major-league baseball had already flamed out.

"I'm still hopeful," Paul responded cautiously, "but you need to be thinking about a backup plan."

Aiden stalked to the front of the boat, ignoring the screech of seagulls wheeling overhead. "Screw that. This *is* my backup plan. Latch on to another team, take a salary cut if necessary. I can still hit, Paul. You know that."

"Yeah, you can. I'll keep working and keep you posted. But try to enjoy the time off, will ya? You should be relaxing and having some fun, not just waiting for the phone to ring."

"Easy for you to say," Aiden said. It had been more than two weeks since the Phillies released him, and he still felt mired in disbelief.

"I know," his agent said in a sympathetic voice. "Hang in there, buddy."

Aiden stowed the phone and grabbed the rail, automatically bracing himself as the ferry rocked through the swell of a passing boat. Sucking in a breath of the cleansing sea air, he told himself an opportunity *would* come up. Aiden had never been a superstar, but he'd had a solid career and could still get on base and drive in runs. This had to be just a temporary hiatus, because any other outcome was unthinkable. Any other *life* than the one he'd fought so hard to create was unthinkable.

The ferry made the turn past Diamond Cove and

headed directly toward Seashell Bay, dodging the colorful lobster buoys dotting the blue water. Happy-looking vacationers and island residents, most loaded down with various shopping bags and coolers, gathered up their gear as the boat steamed toward the public dock. The downward spiral of Aiden's mood didn't fit the cheerful scene, but who the hell could blame him? Not only was he returning to the one place in the world he truly hated, his career was hanging on by a frigging thread. It would take more than a sunny day and an ice-cold bottle of Corona to dispel his emotional nor'easter.

As he turned his gaze away from the dock, he caught a flash of color out in the bay, a fiery red that reflected the sunlight. Aiden lifted the brim of his ball cap, narrowing his eyes against the shimmering light off the water. Less than a hundred yards away, a green-and-white lobster boat bobbed on the waves. A slender woman dressed in jeans, rubber boots, and a tight white T-shirt, her bright auburn hair gleaming in the sunshine, leaned over the gunwale of the boat as the pot hauler brought a lobster trap to the surface. When she tilted her head briefly to smile and wave at the passing ferry, recognition seared through Aiden with a jolt that lit up every synapse in his brain.

Lily Doyle.

The most beautiful girl on Seashell Bay Island and the only one who'd ever stopped him dead in his tracks. He'd spent his last two years in high school lusting after her, but she'd been off-limits thanks to the insane, multigenerational feud that had smoldered between their families for decades. Off-limits except for one memorable night near the end of his senior year, when he and Lily finally gave in to mutual temptation after a school dance in Portland. They crossed some boundaries that night and broke more than a few family taboos. But sanity had prevailed with the coming of dawn, and they'd both had the smarts to go their separate ways. Aiden had always wondered how Lily had fared over the years. Now, he guessed he had his answer.

She was as gorgeous as ever, even in clunky rubber boots and a dirty T-shirt that couldn't hide the gentle swell of her breasts.

As he stared at her, Lily froze, one gloved hand on her trap line. Then she whipped her other hand up, shoving her sunglasses onto her forehead to peer straight at him. When their gazes caught and locked, Aiden could feel the impact of her eyes with all the force of a baseball screaming at him at ninety miles an hour.

Sweet Mother of God.

A moment later, another swell hit her boat, and Lily snapped back to life, dragging her trap onto the rail. The ferry sailed past, making its final turn to line up with the dock. Aiden leaned out, but all he could see was the lobster boat's dark green stern, its name blazoned in big white letters.

Miss Annie.

He couldn't hold back a smile. Hard-working Lily had always wanted her own boat and had obviously made it happen. She'd even named it after her beloved granny, Annie Letellier. For some reason, the fact that Lily was still on the island and following her dream boosted his mood. She'd been one of the few things he'd cared about in Seashell Bay, and he'd like to think she got everything she truly deserved.

The ferry's horn blasted out a final note as it nudged up against the dock. Aiden headed down the stairs to the lower deck, retrieving his computer case and small sports bag from the corner where he'd stashed them. He didn't worry about anyone lifting his stuff, because no one ever stole anything around the islands. Well, except for Daisy Whipple, Seashell Bay's kleptomaniac. If an item went missing from someone's porch or deck, you headed to Daisy's house. Since she usually just smiled when you retrieved whatever it was she'd pilfered, islanders chose not to make a fuss about the old gal's bizarre habit.

When it came to their own, the people of Seashell Bay were remarkably tolerant. Outsiders...that was another story.

He joined the crowd of families, young couples, and dogs—there were always a lot of dogs on the ferry—waiting patiently for the deckhands to tie off the anchoring lines and secure the metal gangway. When the exit cleared, Aiden joined the throng surging onto the dock to the sounds of barking dogs and children's voices pitched high with excitement. Most locals headed directly to the parking lot at the end of the long pier, but other passengers milled around in the bright sunshine, greeting loved ones or waiting for their luggage or supplies to be rolled out in metal carts from the bow of the boat.

It was all as weirdly familiar as Aiden expected. Seashell Bay actively resisted change. Depending on your point of view, it was either the island's greatest asset or its biggest flaw, and he knew exactly which camp he belonged to.

As he waited for his luggage, a set of brawny arms clamped him from behind, lifting him in a bear hug. There were very few people who could lift Aiden straight off the ground, so that meant his little brother—who topped him by two inches—was indulging in one of his outsized displays of emotion.

"Yo, man, put me down," Aiden said in a mock growl, giving his brother an elbow to the ribs.

"Oof." Bram dropped him to his feet.

Aiden turned to greet his grinning brother.

"Man, it's great to see you, bro," Bram enthused. "I've missed you."

"But I saw you six weeks ago, remember? At Fenway? Ring a bell?"

Bram waved a dismissive hand. "Doesn't mean I can't still miss you." He grabbed Aiden's sports bag. "It's good to have you home. You look fucking great."

A family of tourists marched by and the mother, wearing a floppy bright-red beach hat, glowered at Bram with disapproval. Aiden gave her an apologetic smile. Bram had a deep and abiding love for profanity, laying the f-bomb down with dependable regularity, regardless of his surroundings.

"I wish I could say the same for you," Aiden replied, giving him a once-over.

Bram looked like crap. His stubbled excuse of a beard was scruffy, his dark hair long and unkempt, and his shorts and sleeveless tee rumpled and none too clean. And he'd added yet another tattoo to his impressive display of ink—a character from the video game *Halo* in lurid colors on the inside of his forearm. Not that Aiden had any problems with ink—he had a few nice examples of body art himself—but he'd figured out over the years that Bram added a tattoo whenever he was in a deep funk.

His brother shrugged. "Sorry I don't meet your exacting standards, Mr. Baseball, but I had a long night. Some of us have to work for a living, you know."

"Since when did you start working again?"

Bram had been more or less out of work these last two years after a pot hauler miscue on their father's boat had trashed the nerves in his left hand. Aiden had paid for two operations by the best hand surgeon in Boston, but Bram would never regain full use, and that meant his lobstering days were over. And unlike Aiden, Bram had always loved lobster fishing. Ever since the accident, he'd struggled with a toxic mixture of partial disability, depression, and alcohol.

"I get by," Bram said, his gaze sliding away.

Aiden didn't press him, instead hauling his large duffel out of one of the carts that had come off the boat. With his computer case over one shoulder and the duffel over the other, he started down the dock as the ferry, with its cheery combination of yellow and red paint glinting in the sun, started to load cargo for the return trip to Portland.

"So I guess the old man couldn't be bothered to come meet me," Aiden said, confronting the emotional elephant lumbering along beside them.

Bram shot him a startled glance. "You didn't really think he would, did you?"

"No."

Why the hell Aiden would expect—or want—his father to meet him was a complete mystery. He and Sean Flynn hadn't spoken in the two years since Aiden's mom's funeral. That was the only time that Aiden had returned to the island. It had been a grim, tragic exercise in every way, and he and his father had barely exchanged a handful of words.

But at least his dad hadn't gotten drunk and tried to belt him. He'd given up that habit when Aiden turned sixteen, finally big enough and strong enough to hit back. That day had been one of the best of Aiden's life. Knowing that his oldest son could and would stand up to him, his father had stopped pounding on Bram too.

"Look, I know you didn't want to come," Bram said, "but we really need you, man. *I* really need you. If we don't pull off this land deal, the old man and me are going to be in deep shit."

Aiden and Bram crossed the parking lot in front of the gray clapboard building that served as Seashell Bay's Town Hall. His brother's rusted-out old pickup, which had once been Aiden's, was parked toward the back of the lot in one of two spaces unofficially reserved for the Flynns.

"I'm here, aren't I?" Aiden pitched his duffel into the back of the truck. Bram dumped the sports bag beside it, and they climbed into the cab.

"So, what's the latest on the deal with this development company anyway?" Aiden asked as he put his computer between his feet and reached for his seat belt. It took him a moment to remember that most of the old beaters on Seashell Bay Island didn't even have seat belts, or other necessities like air bags or mufflers. "They want to go full steam ahead with building a big-ass resort on our property, right?"

The Flynn family owned 270 acres of prime coastal land, a considerable piece of it bordered by bluffs overlooking the ocean. It had passed down to his mother through her family, and on her death Rebecca Flynn had divided it between her husband and two sons. Sean now owned 70 percent of the parcel, while Aiden and Bram had the remaining 30 percent roughly split between them. The previous year, a high-end real estate developer from Portland had expressed quiet interest in buying them out. The offer had eventually led to this—Aiden's reluctant return to Seashell Bay.

"Not just a resort, but over a hundred luxury houses, too," Bram said, as they drove up the incline to the main road that circled the island. "They're getting serious about putting an offer on the table, but they say they need all our land. Since your piece is right in the middle of mine and Dad's, that means you gotta buy into the deal, bro."

Before Aiden could respond, Bram yanked the wheel to the right, swerving to the side of the road. A four-person golf cart blasted past them in the opposite direction, an old guy at the wheel.

Aiden cursed as he slid across the cracked vinyl seat into the door, banging his elbow hard. "Jesus, who the hell was that?"

Bram wrestled the ancient truck back in a straight line. "That was Roy Mayo. You remember him, don't you? Miss Annie's Roy?"

"I thought he'd be dead by now," Aiden said drily. "The guy has to be ninety, if he's a day."

"He turned ninety last March. Miss Annie threw a big party for him down at the Rec Center. It was a really good time."

"No doubt. And I take it old Roy still likes fixing up golf carts."

Fixing up was a nice way of putting it. Roy's specialty was adding extras to the small engines that made them run way faster than they were ever designed for—or safe for.

"Yep. Down at Josh Bryson's motor shop. Makes a few bucks at it too."

As far as Aiden was concerned, one of the most irritating traits of some of the older islanders was their preference for driving golf carts instead of cars. There was nothing more frustrating than getting stuck behind one of the geezers as they tootled down the middle of the island's narrow, winding roads, often refusing to pull over to let other vehicles pass. Not that Roy fell into that category. No, Roy was more likely to blast by, pretty much running your vehicle into the ditch while doing it.

"Well, enough about the local color," Aiden said. "Tell me more about the development deal."

Bram shrugged. "Not much more to tell. They made it clear they won't make a binding offer until it's for all three parcels of Flynn land."

Aiden could practically hear his mother spinning in her coffin. That land was her legacy, one she'd wanted to remain in the family for many generations of future Flynns to cherish and enjoy.

"Any other conditions?" he asked.

"Yeah, they want a dock for a car ferry, built and paid for by the town. Mr. Dunnagan, the company's liaison, said the island has to get into the twenty-first century if it's going to attract new homeowners and resort guests. We need a car ferry to bring new people and business to the island."

"Well, good luck with that," Aiden said.

Seashell Bay residents had beaten back more than one proposal for a car ferry service, believing it would draw too many tourists and day-trippers and ruin the island's sleepy, old-fashioned way of life. Only one neighboring island had a car ferry, and it had a much bigger year-round population and residents who commuted to work on the mainland. For Seashell Bay folk, the only way to get a car or any other vehicle larger than a golf cart over to the island was to hire a company to transport it by barge.

"Things are changing," Bram said. "Lobster prices have sucked for a while, and the cost of fuel and bait is always going up. Some folks are thinking it's time to get some development onto the island to bring some more bucks into town." His brother cut him a sideways glance. "We sure as hell could use more money around here, man."

Aiden frowned, hoping his brother wasn't talking about him. Ever since he signed his first pro ball contract, he'd been sending money home to his family. And it wasn't like he was some superstar with a fat salary. Sure, he made a good living, but he'd been careful to save and invest as much as he could. He knew his days of making real money were limited, and Bram knew it too.

He chewed his thoughts in silence for a few minutes as his brother drove them to his cottage—mostly built with Aiden's money—on the south shore of the island. Bram took the longer route that wound up and down the rocky coast, affording spectacular views of the Atlantic whenever the dense woods opened up. At this time of year, the island's roses were in full bloom, both in the wild and in the garden plots that surrounded so many homes. Their heavy scent wafted through the open windows of the truck, carried on the soft breeze of the fading summer afternoon.

"A decision on a new dock has to go to a town referendum, right?" Aiden said. "And the land deal can't happen unless people vote yes?"

Bram turned into the narrow lane that led to his cottage overlooking the bluffs. "Right. That's all in the works, but Dad says we need to hammer things out among the three of us beforehand. And since you had some free time anyway..."

Aiden waved an impatient hand. "Yeah, I got it. And I'll think about it."

"Okay, but Dad—"

"I said I'd think about it," Aiden repeated firmly. He'd be damned if his father or anyone else was going to force his hand.

Bram cast him a wary look before returning his attention to the rocky lane.

Aiden was glad for the silence. Truthfully, he didn't know what he wanted to do with the land his mother had left him. He'd never thought it would be worth much, but now it looked like it was. It should be easy to make the decision. He should say yes and hope that the car ferry vote went through so he could walk away from Seashell Bay once and for all, knowing that his brother and father were set for life.

But it wasn't easy. Aiden had loved his mother more than anyone. He'd respected her strength and decency, and he'd watched in sorrow and anger as his father gradually bled the joy out of her. At the end, all Rebecca Flynn had to love was her boys and the island and the land that had been in her family for generations. She'd never given up on the dream that someday her sons would build their own homes in Seashell Bay and raise their families there, loving it as much as she did.

Aiden would never do that, but he wasn't yet ready to turn his back on his mother's dream. The fact that the sale was something his father wanted, in defiance of his wife's last wishes, added to his reluctance.

The truck bottomed out through a final series of brutal ruts, and then the lane opened into a grassy clearing dotted with wildflowers. Massive evergreens rimmed the perimeter, reaching feathered branches to the sky. At the far end of the clearing, Bram's cottage perched on a cliff with the beach fifty feet below. It was built in the style of a log cabin, rustic and appealing despite its owner's obvious neglect.

Bram killed the engine at the side of the cottage. Aiden got out and trudged in his brother's wake, climbing the few steps onto the narrow deck that ringed the cottage on three sides. Rounding the corner, he stopped in his tracks at the sight of the gray-haired, grim-looking man in one of the old rocking chairs by the front door.

"Hey, Dad," he said. "Nice of you to come over to say hello."

Sean Flynn hauled himself out of the chair, narrowing his gaze on his eldest son. Then he flicked his attention to Bram.

"So?" He barked the word out in a voice roughened by years of cigarettes and cheap whiskey.

Glancing uneasily between the two of them, Bram shifted his feet like the scrawny kid he'd been so many years ago. "Aiden wants a little more time to think about it, Dad."

Their father let out a foul curse and stomped into the cottage, slamming the screen door behind him. Bram gave Aiden an apologetic grimace then trailed in after their father. A moment later, Aiden could hear ice cubes rattle and a drink being poured.

Sighing, he took a long look at the serene ocean view before going inside.

Yeah, dude. Welcome home.

Chapter 2

As his crew hauled a half-empty lobster barrel onto the bait smack's floating platform, Billy Paine gave Lily one of his trademark roguish grins.

Roguish wasn't a word Lily would ever use, but Billy had said it one night at the Lobster Pot, bragging about his success with *the ladies*. The annoying thing about Billy was that he did have a fair amount of success in servicing not just the lobster boats of these islands but the women too. Lily had never been able to figure it out. While he was good looking in a vaguely dangerous, offbeat kind of way, his prehistoric view of women left her cold.

"Sure I can't interest you in dinner and drinks in Portland tonight, Lil?" Billy called over. "Aren't you tired of hanging out with the losers at the Pot?"

As Lily turned to answer, she winced at the twinge of pain in her lower back. She still had a lot of heavy cleanup work ahead of her when she got back to her mooring, and her back was already protesting. If she didn't find a new sternman soon, she could really trash it—or worse yet, have a bad accident. Fishing alone wasn't a great idea, but what choice did she have now that her idiot crewman, Johnny Leblanc, had jumped bail after his third DUI and disappeared?

"Billy, when have I ever said yes to your repeated and very lame attempts to ask me out on a date?"

"Can't blame me for trying, Lil. You're one hot piece of—"

"Don't say it," she interrupted, holding up a gloved hand.

Billy laughed as he deftly tossed her one of the lines anchoring *Miss Annie* to the floating platform. His bait smack was based out of Portland and owned by one of the big co-ops that supplied the lobster boats with fresh bait in the morning and bought their catch at the end of the day. Lily had known Billy for years. Despite his annoying banter, he was a competent and honest seaman. That was why she put up with his crap instead of dumping a bucket of slimy seawater over his head.

"All kidding aside, Lil," Billy said, "you look pretty beat. Still no luck finding a new sternman?"

She shook her head. "All the guys with any experience are already working."

Billy rested one rubber-booted foot on his gunwale, a frown pulling his dark brows together. "Try harder, Lil. What'll happen if you're out there alone and a trapline catches your foot? I'd hate to think of you as fish food."

She flashed him a tired smile. One of the great things about life on the water was that even obnoxious guys like Billy had your back. Good fishermen never took the job lightly or underestimated the danger, and they always looked out for each other. Coming from a long line of lobstermen, Lily knew that better than anyone.

Lily pulled her Droid out of her jeans pocket. "I always have my trusty cell phone close at hand."

Billy shook his head impatiently. "If you get your hand or foot caught in a line, you know it'll drag you straight to the bottom. And last I heard, cell phones don't work underwater."

"Of course I know it's dangerous, Billy," she said with frustration. "But I have to do it. You know how much bait and fuel cost now. I can't afford to lose any time on the water—if I do, I won't make the payments on my boat." After all, without a sternman's help, there were only so many traps she could haul in a day before exhaustion did her in.

Billy shot her a worried frown as he stepped away from *Miss Annie*. But when he opened his mouth to argue, Lily held up a hand. "I'll keep looking, Billy. I promise."

"See that you do. Oh, and if you get tired of the yahoos at the Pot, you know where to find me." He gave her a comic book leer over his shoulder as he strode across the floating platform.

"In your dreams, dude," Lily called back, trying not laugh. Hell would freeze over before she dated Billy Paine.

Not that there was much dating material on the island. Most of the single guys she knew were nonstarters because she'd grown up with them. Obviously, she'd dated some over the years, but none had panned out. There was no mystery, no spark, no excitement. Just the decent guys she'd known forever. Familiar, safe, and as boring as a pair of old slippers.

Except for Aiden Flynn.

Lily clamped down on that thought, but her hand

actually shook on the wheel as she eased *Miss Annie* away from the platform. Aiden freaking Flynn, a delicious blast from the past. When she recognized him staring at her from the ferry's upper deck, she'd almost fallen overboard. Their gazes had locked for only a few seconds, but it had been long enough to bring up a rush of memories she'd worked hard to forget. But dammit, one searing look from him had been enough to get her nerves dancing like dragonflies over the water.

Only the rocking of her boat in the ferry's swell and her uncharacteristic loss of balance had kicked her back to her senses. She'd spent the rest of the afternoon trying not to think about that wild night all those years ago, when they'd gone just shy of the point of no return. And after she'd managed to wrestle those distracting memories under control—barely—she started to worry about the reason he was returning home. Aiden avoided Seashell Bay like it was Devil's Island. Lily knew why, so she'd never blamed him. If her dad had been anything like Sean Flynn, she'd have bolted long ago too.

So Aiden's return could only mean one thing—the Flynns weren't just thinking about selling their land, they were actually going to do it.

Over my dead body.

Grimly, she guided her boat through the narrow channel that separated Seashell Bay Island from neighboring Long Island. There had been rumors, of course, ever since those damn developers had shown up, sniffing around the south shore properties. Then some of the newer residents, as well as a few business owners and some folks worried about their jobs and livelihoods, had started a push to resurrect the car ferry issue, vocal enough to prompt the town selectmen to schedule a vote on funding a new dock.

With Aiden back in town, things would go from merely anxiety provoking to truly problematic. If the car ferry won approval and the developers moved in, Seashell Bay would never be the same. The quiet, close-knit community would be smothered by a wave of affluent mainlanders who wouldn't give a damn about the island's heritage or the unique Seashell Bay way of life. They'd tear up blooming meadows and virgin timber and build monster houses and ugly condos on the craggy bluffs overlooking the ocean, destroying the rural beauty that made the island unique.

Picturing that future made her gut churn.

Lily steered up to her mooring off Foley Point and tied up. She still had at least an hour's work cleaning the boat and stowing gear, and she was already both exhausted and ravenous. She hadn't had a bite to eat for hours, which no doubt helped account for her rotten mood.

She heard a cheerful hail and turned to see her grandfather motoring out in his skiff. Preston Doyle had once been one of the best fishermen on the bay and still liked to keep his hand in when he could, even though he was eighty-six. He'd often come down to help her with the cleanup, and for that, Lily was profoundly grateful. Her father used to help her, but his arthritis made it hard for him to do much physical work these days.

"Ahoy, Sweet Pea," Gramps said as she threw him a rope. "Catch any bugs?" To most islanders, lobsters were *bugs* whenever the catch was poor.

Lily tied her end of the rope to a cleat. "About enough

to pay for bait and fuel for the day and maybe buy a loaf of bread."

"Well, when you're fishing lobster, any day you can make more than a penny in profit is a good day, I always say."

Lily smiled. Her gramps had a million sayings, stowed up over years of working in the merchant marine and then hauling traps in these very waters. Preston was the wisest, kindest man she knew, and she thanked God every day that he was her grandfather.

He climbed aboard with surprising agility for a man his age, and they worked easily together to hose out the boat and stow gear. They mostly just listened to the sounds of the day—the gentle slap of water against the side of the boat and the calls of the sea birds wheeling overhead. Thanks to Gramps, she was finishing early enough to have some time to hit the island's general store before heading home. For once, she might even have time to cook herself a decent meal before the start of the weekly Darts Night at the Pot.

Lily helped her grandfather back into his skiff and then followed him to the town dock in her seventeen-footer.

"I saw that no-good Flynn boy get off the three o'clock boat," Gramps said, as they tied up next to each other at one of the landing's floating docks. He said *no-good Flynn boy* in the same tone of voice he would use for commenting on the price of milk. Her grandfather no longer wasted energy on the feud between the Flynn and Doyle families, although he would forever loathe Sean Flynn. It had become habit more than anything else to refer to the Flynns in disparaging terms, and no one truly took it all that seriously—except for her hardheaded father and Sean.

Still, Lily's heart skipped a beat at the very mention of Aiden. For some reason, she didn't want to admit that she'd already seen him. "Bram? Nothing special about that."

Gramps snorted. "You don't fool me, missy. You know exactly which Flynn I'm talking about."

She cut him an exasperated glance. "Okay, you saw Aiden Flynn get off the boat."

He shook his head in disgust. "That no-good Bram met him. I expect their father couldn't be bothered to rouse himself to meet his own son."

Gramps had always had a soft spot for Aiden, though he would never admit it. When Aiden played high school baseball in Portland, Gramps had made a point of going to many of the games. Unlike Aiden's own father.

"No surprise there." She followed her grandfather up the ramp to the parking lot. "Want a ride home? I have to stop at the store first."

"That'd be nice," he said as he climbed into her red Jeep. "Don't get to spend nearly enough time with my favorite girl."

"I thought Grandma was your favorite girl," she teased. "Better not let her hear you say that."

"Your grandma is so busy these days she barely notices I'm still on the right side of the dirt. Now that she's taking those yoga classes at the Rec Center, she's home even less. And forget about cooking dinner. If I didn't do it, I swear we'd both starve to death."

Lily laughed as she started the ancient but reliable Jeep. Despite his grumblings, she heard the pride in her grandfather's voice. Grandma Doyle was a dynamo, looking and acting years younger than eighty-three. She was devoted to her family but had always made it known that she had her own life and had no intention of "drudging away like a house slave." She was an accomplished gardener and potter and an avid devotee of whatever current exercise rage hit the island. This month it was hot yoga, of all things.

"But you like to cook, so what's the problem, Gramps?"

"That's beside the point, young lady. Cooking is supposed to be a woman's job, just like it's a man's job to catch the bugs."

She knew he was yanking her chain. Gramps had always supported her dream, even loaning her money to help with the down payment on her boat. "If that's the case, then why did you help me buy *Miss Annie*?"

"Couldn't stop you. You're a girl, but you're a Doyle through and through. What else could make you happy but fishing?"

Lily shifted into a lower gear as the Jeep rumbled up the hill onto Island Road. "You got that right, Gramps."

"Lily, you know what it means that Aiden's come back, don't you?" he asked.

She sighed, absently waving to Peggy Fogg, who was riding her bike to her shift at the Lobster Pot. Although most everyone on the island sported shorts or jeans with sneakers in the summer, Peggy insisted on wearing a starched, old-fashioned waitress uniform to work. It was endearing in a throwback kind of way. "Yes. It means the Flynns are trying to move ahead with their plans to sell their land to the developers."

Gramps scowled. "I expected it from Sean and Bram, but I had higher hopes for Aiden. That boy has a powerful load of resentment stored up toward Seashell Bay. But he's his mother's son for all that, and Rebecca would never have wanted him to sell her inheritance."

"We don't know whether Aiden's agreed to sell. And if he refuses, I bet the whole thing will be dead in its tracks."

Her grandfather's faded blue eyes gave her a shrewd inspection. "So I guess the first thing we have to do is find out where the boy stands. Got any ideas how to do that?"

Lily stared grimly ahead as they came around a bend in the road that afforded a spectacular view of the bay, with its bobbing lobster boats and a yellow-and-black-hulled ferry steaming in from Diamond Cove.

"I'm working on it, Gramps," she finally said.

"See that you do, before this island goes to hell in a handcart."

The number of cars in the lot where Aiden parked suggested the Lobster Pot was packed, as did the sounds of rock music and laughter drifting out through its rustic-looking front door.

The bar he remembered was a dumpy, old-fashioned hangout for fishermen trying to escape wives and kids. He'd only agreed to take Bram to Darts Night because his idiot brother had pounded back several beers over dinner. In his condition, Aiden had no intention of letting him drive anywhere. But he sure as hell hadn't expected the good old Pot to be rocking it to the rafters.

Bram's teeth flashed a ghoulish white in the glow of a giant red neon lobster that appeared to be crawling along the roof of the bar. "The place is a lot better since Laura Vickers bought it from old man Merrifield."

Another surprise. Laura Vickers had been one of Aiden's best friends in high school. She was ambitious, so he'd figured she wouldn't stay on the island either. Obviously, she'd decided to stick around.

"The food's pretty good too," Bram added. "We probably should have eaten here tonight instead of cooking in."

Aiden made a noncommittal grunt by way of reply. Naturally, their father had pulled his usual crap. After belting down a couple of fast shots of scotch, Sean had demanded to know exactly where Aiden stood on the sale of the land. When Aiden told him he hadn't yet made up his mind, his father had gone nuts, attacking him for disloyalty to the family and even insulting his baseball skills. That had been too much for Bram, who had stepped in to defend his brother. Their father had then stormed out, flinging back the threat that Aiden had better come aboard or he would wash his hands of him.

Pretty empty threat, since the old man had washed his hands of Aiden years ago.

After that charming little scene, he'd retreated to the spare bedroom while Bram grilled up some steaks and vegetables. And when Aiden saw the gruesome state of the bathroom, he'd dug out some aging cleaning supplies and did some scrubbing. Yeah, he was a guy, but even he had his limits.

Given how grimly the evening had started, the Lobster Pot had to be an improvement.

"So, Darts Night," he said. "All I remember is a bunch of old guys three-quarters in the bag and barely able to hit the board."

Bram shook his head. "Not anymore. You'd be surprised at how cutthroat it can be. And don't think you can stroll in and wipe everybody out, Mr. Big Shot Athlete. I bet I could take you."

"We'll see," Aiden said, giving his brother a friendly punch on the shoulder. As competitive as he was, he'd always found darts pretty boring.

They shoved each other a couple of times, like idiot kids, before heading inside. Instead of the scuffed pine floor and battered tables and chairs that Aiden remembered from his childhood, he saw an English-style pub, warmly lit by the glow of imitation gas lamps, with a padded oak bar that stretched along one side of the room. There were nooks with comfortable chairs and a couple of love seats, as well as some booths and a few larger groupings of tables in the middle of the room. Framed posters of London decorated the walls. There was a pool table and a shuffleboard table, and three dartboards hung from the wall opposite the door. The boards were already in play, and the action was lively.

Then his gaze went to the big flatscreen TV that was silently carrying the game between the Phillies and the Mets. It took a minute to choke down that bitter pill before he could drag his attention back to the crowded room.

Surprisingly, about half the people were his age or younger. The bar was obviously no longer a second home for ornery old lobstermen who could only agree on two things—the price of bait was too high and the price of lobster was too low.

His brother jerked his head in the direction of the bar. "Let's say hi to Laura."

Aiden wove through the crowd, greeting people he hadn't seen in years. Some seemed genuinely happy that Seashell Bay's *celebrity*—as one young woman called him, batting her eyes—had come home. That label made his skin crawl, as did the fact that he had to repeatedly deflect questions about his absence from baseball.

When he and Bram finally reached the bar, a short, curvy woman with long blond hair ducked out from behind it to greet Aiden with a wide grin. Laura Vickers wore dark jeans and a red T-shirt with a black graphic of a lobster brandishing a beer glass in his crusher claw.

"Well, all hail our baseball hero." Laura grabbed Aiden in a fierce hug. "Welcome home, prodigal son."

Aiden returned the hug with genuine enthusiasm. "I have to say I'm surprised to see you here, Laura. You always had your sights set on Boston."

"Oh, we can't all be stars, Aiden. When Cal Merrifield decided to sell, I gambled on the potential for a make-over and stayed." She gazed around the pub with evident pride. "And I think I've done pretty damn well with the place."

"It looks terrific, Laura. You always wanted to own a restaurant, and I'm really glad you're able to make a go of it."

"How about a beer?" she asked.

"A Corona would be great, thanks."

A tall guy with a buzz cut who looked vaguely familiar ambled up to them, slinging a possessive arm around Laura's shoulders. "Hey, Aiden." He stuck out his hand. "Remember me? Brett Clayton? I'm Laura's boyfriend."

"Sure. Hi, Brett." Aiden shook his hand. Clayton had been a couple of years behind him in school.

It didn't take long for Brett to point out most of the people in the bar and remind him of the complex web of relationships that made up life on the island. People were still inspecting Aiden with more than casual interest. Some nodded in friendly fashion when they caught his eye, but others definitely looked wary.

Just how upset were people with the Flynns these days anyway?

When Brett took a call on his cell, Aiden turned back to the bar. Laura finished serving a customer and came over.

"Ready for another?" she asked.

"Better not. I'm the designated driver," Aiden glanced over at his brother. Bram was laughing it up with some friends at the pool table.

Laura followed Aiden's gaze. "You need to be, with that one."

When Aiden shot her a startled glance, she winced. "Sorry, I shouldn't have said that."

He shook his head. "No, it's okay. I'm glad you did."

From what he'd seen so far, Laura was probably right. Bram's drinking had gotten worse.

She began stacking dirty glasses into the sink under the bar. "Dare I ask how it went with your dad?"

"The usual." He leaned a forearm on the leather bumper. "Is Bram in here a lot?"

"More than he should be, but not as much as some."

"Thanks for that incisive analysis," he said drily.

"You're welcome," she replied with a grin. "So tell me if I'm being too nosy, but how are the negotiations going between your family and the development company, anyway? I'm assuming that's why you're here instead of playing baseball in Philadelphia. Are you in sync with your dad and Bram?"

She obviously hadn't heard that he'd been released from his contract. "Maybe, but I want to know what people on the island think about the development. Bram said a lot of folks are in favor, but the Doyles are leading the charge against it."

Laura looked grim. "It's a mess, that's what it is. A lot of islanders are dead set against it, but times aren't great right now because the crappy lobster price hurts everybody. More and more people are saying the development would bring money and jobs to the island, and I guess it would."

Aiden put his bottle down on a cardboard coaster shaped like a lobster. "Are you in favor of it?"

"Honestly, I'm still on the fence. Business has been pretty decent here, but I'm worried about young people leaving the island if there aren't some more opportunities."

"Yo, Laura," some drunk yelled from down the bar. "Another round down here, sweet thing."

"You mind your manners, Boone Cleary, or I'll call your wife and tell her you're acting like an asshat again," Laura yelled back.

That set off a round of laughs. Laura flashed Aiden an apologetic smile. "I'd better take care of business."

He nodded. "And I'd better go mingle."

"Aiden, wait a second." Laura leaned over the bar again. "I meant what I said about people being tense. A lot of folks aren't happy with the Flynns."

"Enough to be worried about it?"

"Just be aware that not everyone is going to be friendly."

He managed a smile. "Well, they can't be any worse than my own father, right?"

She left, and Aiden started through the crowd toward Bram. A few people stopped him to chat, and a woman he didn't know asked for his opinion on the development.

He managed to deflect the question, and she let him. They were having a vague chat about changes to the island when Aiden heard raised voices behind him.

He turned and saw Bram in what looked like a full-blown argument with Miss Annie Letellier. Bram was looming over the elderly, gray-haired lady, his face an angry scowl. The line of empty beer bottles along the edge of the pool table told Aiden his brother was probably blitzed.

Aiden practically leaped across the space between them and grabbed his brother's arm, pulling him back. "Jesus, Bram, what the hell are you doing?"

Bleary-eyed, his brother tried to jerk out of Aiden's grip. "I'm just talking to Miss Annie." He glared past Aiden's shoulder. "Hell, she was stabbing her finger into my chest and yelling, not me. She's the one you should be holding back."

Aiden turned to face the five-foot-zero, one-hundred-pounds-dripping-wet dynamo who had more or less run Seashell Bay for as long as he could remember. Annie Letellier was an eighty-three-year-old member by marriage of the Doyle clan. And Lily's grandmother.

"Good evening, Miss Annie," he said. "It's a pleasure to see you looking so well."

In khaki pants and a starched blue shirt, Miss Annie propped her hands on her hips and tilted her head back to glare up at him. "Don't you try to sweet-talk me, Aiden Flynn. Your brother is acting like a pure horse's ass."

Bram made a garbled sound of protest that Aiden silenced with a sharp elbow.

"I'm sorry," Aiden said politely. "You know better than anyone that Bram was pretty much born that way."

There were a few snickers from the peanut gallery, and Miss Annie let out a delicate snort. "You've got that right, son."

Aiden knew Miss Annie was actually fond of Bram. She'd often babysat both brothers when they were snotty little runts, despite their father's objections about a Doyle looking after his sons. Aiden's mother had ignored his protests, because Miss Annie was her dear friend. Like most of the women in the Flynn and Doyle families, they steered clear of the feud that was carried on by the *damn fool men*.

"Can I buy you a drink?" he asked, trying to defuse the tension.

Miss Annie's gaze coasted over the crowd that watched with undisguised anticipation. Then her eagle-eyed gaze snapped back to him. "I'll not be drinking with any Flynn until I get my answer."

What the hell? When had Miss Annie started playing Hatfields and McCoys? "What answer would that be, ma'am?"

She jabbed a gnarly finger at Aiden. "I asked that brother of yours why your father was spreading rumors about the car ferry. That's when you barged in on us."

"They're not rumors," Bram interjected hotly.

Aiden glared at his brother. "Shut. Up." Then he turned back to Miss Annie. "Exactly what rumors?"

"Sean's been claiming that the developer won't buy his land unless the town builds a car ferry dock. And he says if the Doyles convince people to vote against it, there'll be no development at all."

"Well, I think that's the case. If the town won't build the dock, the developer isn't interested in going ahead with the project." Aiden glanced over his shoulder at Bram. "Don't people know that already?"

When the onlookers started jabbering at once, Aiden had his answer.

Miss Annie sidestepped him to resume her rant at Bram. "It's pure blackmail, if you ask me. Why are you and your father in bed with those greedy mainlanders? Shame on you, Bram Flynn!"

Bram loomed over the old woman, looking furious. "You can't talk to me like that, Miss Annie. Not even you!"

Swallowing a curse, Aiden figured he'd better pull Bram out of the bar before Miss Annie started whacking him upside the head. He grabbed his brother's arm again just as the door opened and the deputy sheriff strode in. Deputy Micah Lancaster, Aiden's sworn rival in high school and just what he didn't need right now.

When his idiot brother tried to push him out of the way so he could continue arguing with Miss Annie, Aiden grabbed him by the shoulders to manhandle him out the door. But then a slender, feminine figure popped out of the crowd and gently eased Miss Annie away from Bram.

Sweet Mother of God, it was Lily Doyle, up close and personal.

The tumult around him faded as Aiden drank her in, starting at her pretty, gold-painted toenails showcased by matching sparkly flip-flops, and then traveling all the way up to her gorgeous face. She was wearing a denim skirt short enough to show off a fair amount of spectacular leg and a slim-fitting, sleeveless, white polo shirt that showcased her tan. Her auburn hair fell in soft waves around her shoulders, and her emerald eyes sparkled with amusement. Her Irish-fair complexion seemed devoid of makeup, and he could see the freckles tossed lightly across the bridge of her nose and cheeks. Yeah, he remembered kissing those freckles, and that luscious mouth too. Lily was the embodiment of a sweet, all-American girl—a girl who was as smart as a whip and a lobster boat captain who held her own in a rugged man's world. Not to mention she was also the island's reigning darts champion, which definitely meant something in Seashell Bay.

She was one hell of a sexy package, and she rocked Aiden right back on his heels. A quizzical look pulled Lily's eyebrows together and made him realize he was gaping at her.

Dork.

He shook himself free. "Good to see you, Lily. I hope you're going to help me get these two wildcats under control." He glanced around the rowdy bar. "Along with the rest of the knuckleheads in this place."

Her lush lips—oh, yeah, he definitely remembered those lips—parted in an easy smile. Lily had always had a way about her, a low-key charm that could defuse just about any situation. He'd take care of Bram, but he had to hope she'd exercise her personal magic to pull Miss Annie off the ledge.

Lily flashed a knowing look around. "Granny, I think we can trust Micah to take care of the others. As for you," she said, keeping a gentle grip on her grandmother, "why don't you go on over to the bar and catch up with Laura? I know she's got a bottle of Harvey's Bristol Cream back there with your name on it."

Miss Annie's wrinkled lips flattened into a grim line. "I'm not done with these two boys yet. This is serious, Lily."

"I'll take care of it," her granddaughter replied softly. "I promise."

It seemed to Aiden that the two of them held an unspoken debate. The tiny, old lady and the tall, vibrant young woman could not have looked more different. But then you looked at their eyes and saw the connection, one that spoke of a heritage deeper than the cold North Atlantic. Both pairs of eyes were vividly green, bright with the determination and the strong will that had been a hallmark of the women in Lily's family for decades.

Aiden shot a quick glance around the bar. Things seemed to be settling, thanks to Micah's law-and-order intervention. He'd clearly told people to calm the hell down and get back to enjoying their evening, and since he was a hulking, mean-looking dude in uniform, everyone seemed pretty much down with the plan. Unfortunately, Micah was now staring at Aiden with an expression bordering on loathing, which didn't bode well. He and Micah Lancaster had never seen eye to eye, and Aiden guessed that the passing of fourteen years hadn't altered the other man's ill will.

Sighing, Aiden switched his attention back to Lily, if for no other reason than she was the best-looking thing he'd seen in a very long time. She and her grandmother had obviously come to some sort of silent agreement that resulted in Miss Annie's ire cooling down. And since Bram was still sitting, the crisis appeared to be averted— for now.

Miss Annie cut Aiden a sharp glance. "You behave yourself, young man. I don't want any more trouble out of you."

Before Aiden could protest that he hadn't done anything, Miss Annie startled him by wrapping her wiry arms around his waist, giving him a tight hug. "It's good to have you back, boy," she said, finally letting him go. "I hope you're planning on staying awhile."

"Uh, yeah. Awhile," he said, sounding like a moron.

"Good. Now why don't you spend some time with my granddaughter? And try to remember that your blessed mama raised you to be a gentleman."

"Yes, ma'am," he said.

Miss Annie marched off to the bar, leaving him alone with Lily. Things were definitely looking up, but Aiden couldn't help feeling he'd stepped into an alternate universe. "What the hell just happened?"

When Lily tilted her head to look at him, her long hair spilled down her back, exposing her slender shoulders in the sleeveless top. Her skin looked smooth as peach ice cream and just as tasty. Aiden felt every muscle in his body tighten with instinctive, good old-fashioned lust.

"That's Granny for you," she said. "Always a little hard to predict, remember?"

"I guess I should be used to that." He dragged his attention away from her gorgeous body up to her equally gorgeous face. "But I was talking about that thing with the car ferry."

Lily's expression turned oddly speculative for a moment, but then she leveled him with a sultry smile that ramped up his lust into the red zone.

"You don't really want to talk about that right now, do you?" she said in a voice that sounded like it might lead him into a garden of earthly delights.

"Kind of." Aiden found it both interesting and a bit alarming that she was trying to manage him.

"Really? Because I can think of something a lot more entertaining to do," she purred.

Okay, maybe he *was* in favor of a program change after all. He took a step forward, crowding her a bit, letting her know he knew how to play the game too. "What do you have in mind?"

Her lush lips parted in a seductive smile. "How about a game of darts?"

Chapter 3

*A*iden stared down into emerald eyes just as bewitching as he remembered—eyes that now also held a depth and maturity that sucked him right in. As much as he might have liked to deny it, he felt the pull toward Lily as strongly as he ever had, and he'd be willing to bet his parcel of land she felt the same.

But frigging darts...really? If Lily had no intention—sadly—of leaping his bones, he would have expected her to get down to business right away, pumping him for info about his position on the development project.

He glanced away from her challenging, amused stare to take in the avid gazes of the crowd, waiting with bated breath for his answer. And his destruction, he suspected, given the nasty smiles of anticipation that lit the faces of at least half the people in the bar. It was Thunderdome, Seashell Bay style, with Aiden tagged as the loser.

Just swell. Nothing like a little ritual humiliation to cap off his fabulous homecoming.

Lily Doyle had always had a touch with darts, just like Aiden had the God-given ability to hit baseballs. Most people thought it was simply a matter of natural coordination, but there was more to it than that. Lots of people had great coordination. Damn few, though, could hit a ninety-five-mile-per-hour fastball or throw a dart with perfect precision.

Lily had coordination in spades and a sweet, sweet form.

Aiden clapped a hand to his chest, trying to look like a wounded puppy. "Such a coldhearted way to welcome a native son back to the island. Since you're the top dog in these parts, I reckon you have some ulterior motive for wanting to whip my ass in front of the entire damn town."

Her gaze cut off to the side for a few seconds, surprising him. Lily was never one to dodge a question or a direct challenge. But then she looked back, dazzling him with a glorious smile that fried the logic part of his brain.

"Oh, I don't know," she replied with a throaty purr that made Aiden want to lift her over his shoulder and haul her out to his truck. "I guess I'm pretty good, but you're a *professional athlete*, after all. You're not afraid of a little old game of darts, are you, Aiden Flynn?"

"You tell him, Lil," Boone Cleary said, leaving his bar stool long enough to weave over and see what the fuss was all about. "Nobody walks away from a challenge on Darts Night. Not on this island, anyway." He belched as if to emphasize his weighty intervention, which prompted a whack to the back of his head from Miss Annie and a lecture on minding one's manners in public.

Bram whispered into Aiden's ear, "He's right, bro. Look, just keep saying stuff that'll get her rattled. You can start by reminding her of that time when you and me tailed her down to Bunny Tail Trail and saw—"

"Shut up," Aiden said through gritted teeth.

Lily had crossed to the dartboard but now came back to Aiden, still giving him that sexy smile that said, *What are you afraid of, big boy?* His brain might have been addled by waves of hot lust, but he couldn't shake the feeling she was somehow trying to manipulate him.

"Well?" She held her palm out, daring him to take the three darts that lay there.

Instinctively, he reached out, his hand swallowing hers and the red-tailed darts. Her skin felt hot and almost as smooth as he remembered from that long-ago night, when her hands had been all over him. That surprised him, given the work she did. Of course she wore gloves on the boat, but she set and hauled traps all day long. Both his dad and Bram had always suffered from unending cuts, scrapes, and chewed-up hands from snapping lobster claws.

He froze for a few seconds, her small hand trapped in his, and his mind became swamped with images of the battle-hardened warriors who fought the cold sea and the unforgiving elements to eke out their living. He could only imagine what Lily had gone through all these years he'd been away. While he'd been playing and partying in the glamor of big-city pro baseball, the slender, fine-boned woman before him had toiled long and hard on her lobster boat, facing down the dangers—and the dangers were real and ever-present—of a brutally unforgiving family trade.

When Lily tilted her head, her half-smile curving with an unspoken question, he released her.

"You go first," he said, sliding his hand across the swell of her hip to gently turn her toward the throw line.

"You are such a gentleman, sir," Lily said over her shoulder, flashing him a mocking yet heated smile that went straight to his dick. "Okay, we play the usual rules here—501, straight start, double finish."

In that sultry voice, even the scoring rules sounded like an invitation to bed boogie. "Fine. Say, who's that girl keeping score?"

He nodded toward a tall, young woman at the side of the board who was staring intently at him as she gripped a black marker. She had cropped, dark hair and wore a black T-shirt and leggings so tight she couldn't possibly have been wearing a scrap of fabric underneath them. Though he didn't recognize her, she sure seemed to know him.

Lily swung around and shot him a look somewhere between puzzlement and annoyance. "That's Jessie Jameson."

Aiden couldn't hold back a disbelieving laugh. He remembered Jessie as a scrawny, preteen tomboy who hung around the boatyard. It was yet another lesson that not everything on Seashell Bay Island had stayed the same.

As Lily turned into the throw line, positioning her flip-flops at a slight angle, Aiden's eyes automatically locked onto the way her beautifully rounded ass filled out the little denim skirt. *Nice*, his libido muttered, imagining how easy it would be to slide his hands underneath that well-worn fabric and—

"Good one, Lily!" a blond woman said from a table near the board. "You give him holy hell!"

He jerked his attention away from Lily's very fine ass to the board. Her first dart had landed in the double twenty ring, no doubt exactly where she'd aimed it. She didn't turn around and gloat, though, instead giving her arm a little shake as she set up for her next throw.

Aiden glanced at the woman who'd shouted out the encouragement. "I know that blonde's a friend of Lily's, but I can't dredge up her name," he said to Bram at his side. It was starting to piss him off that he couldn't remember the names of people he'd known all his life.

"That's Morgan Merrifield," Bram said. "She's a teacher up the coast now, but she comes back every summer to help her dad at the B&B. Hell, she and Lily are so freaking close they might as well be married."

Aiden's mind went blank. "You don't mean that they're…"

Before he even finished his sentence, Bram looked at him like he was a freak. "What the fuck, bro? Did you get hit in the head with a baseball and not tell me? Lily isn't gay, and neither is Morgan."

"Nothing wrong about it if they were," Aiden said defensively. He didn't give a shit one way or another about anyone's sexuality, except for Lily's. That seemed to matter a lot to him at the moment, way more than it should.

Mumbling something that sounded like *fucking bonehead* under his breath, Bram turned to watch Lily while Aiden glanced discretely at Morgan. Now he remembered her. She, like Lily, had been a couple of years behind him in school. The girls had been close back then too. He probably hadn't recognized Morgan right off because she was thinner than she'd been in high school and because she'd worn wire-rimmed glasses back then.

Aiden returned his focus to Lily and watched as her dart just missed the double ring. A couple of seconds later, she sent her last one on a perfect arc into the double twenty ring again. Scoring one hundred on her first set was pretty sweet.

"Woo-hoo!" Morgan yelled. "Let's see you top that start, Mr. Big Shot."

Aiden ignored the taunt, just as he'd learned to ignore far worse from opposing teams' fans as he patrolled the outfield. Morgan was trying to rattle him, just as Bram had wanted him to do with Lily. But Lily's easy mastery of the game made it plain he was in over his head.

Story of his life, when it came to Lily Doyle.

"Let's go, Aiden! You can do it!"

He glanced to the bar where Laura was pumping her fist. He grinned at her, thankful that he had at least two supporters in the bar tonight.

Aiden held his first dart lightly in the pencil grip he favored. *Don't think, man. Visualize the tip of the dart hitting the target and just let it go.* He repeated that mantra twice and let the dart fly, a part of his mind jeering that he was taking a darts game so seriously. But it was Lily and it was Seashell Bay, so it mattered.

The dart headed straight for the top of the twenty but clanked against the double ring and dropped to the floor. *Bounce-out.*

Amid hoots from the crowd, Lily made a little shrug that held a lot more mockery than sympathy. Undaunted, Aiden launched his second dart. This time it angled perfectly between the wires for a double twenty.

Lily's eyes narrowed as she gave him a golf clap in response—all motion and almost no sound. Her cheering squad suddenly went quiet. Apparently the game mattered to them too.

Aiden took a deep breath and held it as he threw his last dart, this time aiming for the more difficult triple ring. How better to set sweet Lily Doyle back on her heels than to score a triple twenty the first time he was up?

And...*thunk*.

He did it. To the sounds of breath being sucked in from all sides, Aiden casually strolled over to the board, plucked out the two darts, and then bent to pick up the bounce-out. When he straightened, he gave Lily a deep, exaggerated bow. Damned if he didn't feel as good as if he'd just thrown out a runner at the plate.

"Jackass," Morgan Merrifield muttered from behind him.

Lily simply tilted her head, looking more intrigued than worried. "Decent," she finally said, then eased up to the throw line for her second turn.

Aiden moved in close, practically whispering in her ear. "Not to blow your concentration or anything, but why the hell was Miss Annie so freaked out just now? It's not like the stuff with the developer and the car ferry vote is a big secret."

Okay, maybe he *was* trying to blow her concentration, but as he inhaled her scent, the years melted away. He swore her hair smelled exactly the same as it had that last night in his car, when his lips were trailing kisses over her long, perfect neck and his hands were exploring the gentle swells of her breasts and ass. Her gleaming auburn hair was as sweetly fragrant as the roses that bloomed all over the island.

He couldn't hold back a smile. Yes, Lily had changed, had grown up. But she'd also remained essentially the same, and he found that incredibly appealing.

Clearly unfazed by his comment—or by the fact that he'd crowded her sweet bod—Lily launched her dart and then turned to face him. "I'm sorry about that. Granny's memory isn't what it used to be, and she sometimes thinks people are keeping her in the dark. You remember how much she hates not being in the know about absolutely everything that's happening on the island."

"Got it. But she sure still looks and sounds sharp to me." Annie Letellier might be in her eighties, but she looked like the same fireball he remembered from when he was a kid. He hated to think it might be otherwise.

Lily shook her head, her hair gently brushing over her bare shoulders. "She's definitely still our Miss Annie, but you'll notice some differences in her, for sure." For a nanosecond she looked sad, but then she lifted an eyebrow. "If you stick around long enough, that is."

She was probing for clues again, but he wasn't ready yet to give up that kind of info. "I don't know how long I'll be here. Depends on a lot of things," he said.

But after seeing you, babe, I may not be out of here quite as quick as I'd thought.

Lily let out a derisive little snort and turned to throw again, scoring a twenty.

"This match could be close," she said over a shoulder that Aiden wanted to caress.

"Don't count on it," he replied absently, letting his gaze drift down to her shapely ass.

She turned to him and blinked, as if startled that he stood so close. A faint blush washed over her cheekbones, but then she put her hands on her hips. "Then maybe we should make a little wager before we get too far in. What do you think, city boy? You up for the challenge?"

The gentle taunt in her voice tweaked his competitive instincts. "Name it," he said.

Lily tapped an index finger on her chin, as if pondering a weighty question. "Let's say if I win, my tab tonight is on you. If you win—like that's going to happen—I pick up yours."

"Even if I stay and close the place down?"

"Even if. In fact, be my guest. On Darts Night, I usually don't go home too early."

Which means you do every other night? He liked that idea. Lily tucked up in her bed safe and alone—preferably in a skimpy nightie that only he would ever see.

"You're on, then," he said.

Lily thought she'd done a fairly respectable job preventing Darts Night from deteriorating into full-blown war. Not that Bram would ever lay a hand on a woman, much less one almost three times his age, but Granny had lots of supporters in the Pot. Any one of them would have been more than willing to throw a punch on her behalf.

Aiden had done his bit to keep the situation under control too. He'd reacted calmly and decisively, keeping his stupid brother locked down and treating Granny with a sweet, old-fashioned respect.

And she had to admit that his understated confidence turned her on a little too.

Okay, he was pretty much melting her panties.

Once a high school hunk, Aiden had now matured into an incredibly sexy man with a laid-back assurance and masculinity that vacuumed up the attention of every woman in the bar but Granny. Every cell in Lily's overheated body was telling her that he felt the pull between them too, and that he was more than willing to act on it. Should she use that attraction to get closer to him and probe for info? She hated the idea of using such sleazy tactics, no matter how just the cause, and the idea of getting involved with Aiden was even more anxiety provoking. She felt pretty certain that would be a one-way boat ride to a whole lot of heartache.

But Gramps had made her mission crystal clear—find out where *the boy* stood on Seashell Bay's future. Would he honor his mother's inheritance, or would he side with his jerkwad of a father? From the few clues Aiden had dropped, she sensed that he had yet to make up his mind. Aiden wasn't the kind of guy to let his father—or anyone else—force him to make a decision before he was ready.

So there was time to push back, especially if he hung around for a while. And if he did, Aiden just might be a temporary fix for the other problem that was keeping her awake at nights.

If she could get him to agree to it, and that was a very big if.

She flashed him a bright smile when he hit the double ring to score another twenty-six points with the third dart of his turn. "Very nice."

Lily didn't need to fake her compliment—he was damn good. Now it would come down to the first person to hit the double needed in order to check out.

He casually rested his hand on the base of her spine as she took up her position. His hand, big enough to nearly span her lower back, sent heat through to her skin. The sensation forced her to lock her knees to hold her stance.

"Feeling the pressure yet?" His deep voice made her

want to press her thighs together. "You must really hate the thought of losing in front of the home crowd."

"Lose? In your dreams." She mentally winced at the squeaky note to her voice.

He was teasing, but his words contained an element of truth. Lily hated losing, and there were a few people watching who would find pleasure in rubbing it in. Folks in Seashell Bay took their darts seriously, and she'd been whipping their asses for years. Still, she'd developed a game plan, and she had to stick to it.

Think big picture and get over yourself, girl.

"Put him away, Lily," Morgan shouted, her face lit up with loyal enthusiasm.

"She's gonna bust," Bram retorted.

Lily shut everything out and threw three straight darts just outside the double nine, scoring zero for her turn. Perspiration prickled along her spine where Aiden's hand had rested only moments ago. It took skill to throw a game and not look suspicious.

"Ah, so close," Aiden said with a mock sigh as he moved up to the line.

"Let's see you do better, pal," Lily shot back, secretly hoping he'd put his first dart straight into the double seven to check out.

Deputy Micah moved in close, just off to her right beside Morgan's table. He scowled at the board like he wanted to pull out his gun and blast it. Given Micah's long-standing antipathy to the Flynns, she knew he was going to be pissed when Aiden won the match. Lily and Micah were old friends, and he wouldn't take kindly to Aiden beating her.

Despite the noise and catcalls, Aiden's hand was steady as he tossed his dart to score the double he needed. Just like that, the match was over, and Lily was on the hook for his beer tab.

Small price to pay.

"Yes!" Bram leaped out of his chair, knocking it to the floor. Once he finished pummeling his brother on the back, he swung around to sneer at Morgan and Micah. "How about that, huh? A Flynn wins!"

Aiden hauled him back. "It could have gone either way, bro. Lily just missed by an eyelash. She's a great player." Then he flashed her a seductive smile, turning her brain to fish bait. "Want to go again, Lily? Get your revenge on the city slicker?"

Morgan jumped up from her chair and whispered urgently in Micah's ear. Clearly, she'd figured out that Lily had tossed the game and wanted to keep Micah from acting like a bull-headed deputy.

"What? Now you want to stick me with Bram's beer too?" Lily said, struggling to find a light note.

Aiden shook his head. "No, and you don't need to buy mine either. I just like spending time with you. I always did." His voice was deep and sincere, a quiet undertone cutting through the raucous bar.

Lily was afraid she might melt on the spot, just when she most needed to focus.

"If you really want to give me a chance to get even, I just got another idea," she replied, trying not to sound breathless. She told herself the tight feeling in her chest was only about the crazy plan she was about to drop on him. "Are you up for a *real* challenge?"

He gave her a lazy grin that curled its way right down between her thighs.

Lord, the man could smile.

"Lily, have you ever known me to back down from any kind of challenge?" he asked.

She'd been counting on that, but not on the predatory heat in his gorgeous, dark eyes. He looked as if he was hoping she would suggest a wild night of strip poker as her next challenge. Now *that* would be a disaster. Getting a look at Aiden Flynn's naked body would be as dangerous as going out on the *Miss Annie* in a winter gale.

Bram was practically standing on his tiptoes behind his brother as he strained to eavesdrop. Micah started to move forward and Morgan scrambled after him, ready to run a little interference.

"You always loved watching the lobster boat races, right, Aiden?" Lily asked.

Every summer, up and down the Maine coast, various harbors hosted the races. Aiden's father had often raced his boat, though never once had the bastard allowed either of his boys to go with him. He'd been determined, she suspected, to keep any glory to himself.

"Sure," Aiden said, suddenly wary. "Who doesn't?"

Lily gave him an easy smile. "Well, the Seashell Bay races are this weekend, and I'll be racing my boat."

When Aiden's jaw tightened, she knew he'd caught her drift. "So?" he said.

"So, even though it hasn't raced in a while, I figure your dad's boat might still be one of the fastest out there. Right, Bram?"

Bram looked as stunned as a deer caught in headlights. "Uh, you know Dad can't race anymore, and neither can I."

"No, but this big, strong *professional athlete* surely can," Lily said, pouring on the sugar. "Do you think you could beat me, Aiden? Could you outrace a girl?"

Aiden let his thoughtful gaze roam over her. As always, he wouldn't rush to answer. "Let's just say for a moment that I agree to this little idea of yours," he finally said. "What kind of bet are we talking about? What would I win when I whip your butt?"

Oh, I think you'd like to spank my butt, wouldn't you?

Lily forced that too-enticing image from her mind. "Well, I was thinking the loser could grant the winner a wish. Say, something that involved a *personal service.*" She tried for as much sexual innuendo as she could without going completely hot with embarrassment, hoping he would take the bait.

"Come on, Flynn. You're going to take that bet, right?" Micah needled, taking an aggressive, wide-legged stance. "Or has the Boy Wonder just come home to sign away his heritage and hustle back to the big city again?"

Crap. Lily had to repress the urge to smack Micah upside the head. If the well-intentioned loyalist of the Doyle clan managed to mess up her plans, she'd kill him. "Micah, come on. You know that's not the way we do things in Seashell Bay," she said in a firm voice. "Aiden will always be one of us."

Her friend grimaced but remained silent as he glared at Aiden.

Aiden's balled fists slowly opened, and he turned his gaze from Micah to Lily. He let the silence between them drag on for too long but then nodded. "I appreciate that, Lily. And if you want me to take a shot at the races, fine. As long as *Irish Lady* is up to it." He glanced back at his brother. "Can we get the old girl in shape by the weekend?"

If there was one thing the Flynns had in quantity it was

pride, so it was no surprise when Bram started to look enthusiastic. "It'll take some work, but damn right we can, bro. And it'll be great to kick some Doyle ass again, even one as sweet as Lil's."

Though Aiden was still looking wary and skeptical, Lily had been right in thinking he couldn't refuse the challenge. Especially from a girl, and worse yet, a Doyle.

But Mr. Aiden Flynn had no idea what he was getting himself into. After all, she'd won her class in the Seashell Bay boat races for the past two years.

And he'd be in for an even bigger surprise when she finally laid out the penalty for losing.

Chapter 4

*E*ven with his legs firmly braced and one hand propped against the dash, Aiden bounced up and down in the old truck as Bram sped along the potholed goat track that was a sorry excuse for a road. He struggled to remember the name of the curving east-end road, but he couldn't quite pull it from his brain. The houses were certainly familiar, since little had physically changed on Seashell Bay Island for decades. After all, the last building boom was during World War II, after the navy built a fuel depot on the island.

As much as Aiden held no sentimentality toward the island, it didn't seem right that simple things like the names of the roads he'd walked, cycled, and driven on all through his youth would be so difficult to recall. It looked as if his subconscious mind was as eager to erase childhood memories as his conscious mind was, and that kind of sucked.

When Bram hit another pothole at full speed, Aiden banged his elbow against the door handle yet again.

"Jesus, man, you're gonna kill the old beater if you

keep driving like you're in frigging NASCAR," Aiden growled. "And I doubt the old man's about to spring for a new one."

Not when you're blowing what little money you've got on booze and online gambling, little brother.

"He couldn't, even if he wanted to," Bram retorted. "That's why we need to sell all that useless land. Dad's running through his money fast, not that he ever gave me much anyway. We've got nothing now that we can't fish anymore. Nothing but the land."

Aiden was sorry he'd opened his mouth. He'd been back on the island less than twenty-four hours, and it already felt like he was in a pressure cooker. That hot-button argument between Bram and Miss Annie last night—plus the nasty-ass scene with his dad—had provided a full-color snapshot of how bad things might still get.

"At least the old man didn't blow a gasket over this bet," Aiden said, wanting to change the subject.

When the three of them met for a late breakfast at Bram's this morning, their father had risen to Lily's bait even faster than Aiden and Bram. Fueled by the beer he'd put away before they even sat down to eat, he'd cursed Lily's lineage right back to her great-great-grandfather Seamus.

"You'd better whip her skinny little ass," Sean had ordered. "But, hell, she's got a damn fast boat, so I've got a phone call to make." With that cryptic sentence, Sean had bolted from the table muttering something about *Roy's magic.*

"I knew he'd be pissed off at her for doing that to you," Bram said now, braking at the last minute before swerving onto Island Road.

At least Aiden had no difficulty remembering the name
of the road that wound around the perimeter of Seashell
Bay Island. O'Hanlon's Boatyard was straight ahead.
"Yeah, pissed off enough to agree to a challenge we're
probably going to lose," he said.

In the sane light of day, he couldn't come up with one
good reason why he'd agreed to the ridiculous bet. Most
likely it was a combination of pride and sheer stubbornness in the face of a challenge from sweet Lily Doyle, who
could be every bit as pigheaded as he was. And it hadn't
helped that half the population of Seashell Bay had wit-
nessed their little scene.

Bram flashed him a crooked grin. "Lose? Maybe. But
when you've got Roy Mayo in your corner, anything can
happen."

"You really think a ninety-year-old dude is going to
sprinkle fairy dust and turn *Irish Lady* into a speedboat?
You said the old tub hasn't been raced in years."

Bram made a hard left into the boatyard, bouncing down yet another rutted track until he stopped in
front of a red building that looked like a cross between a
dairy barn and an airplane hangar. "I don't care whether
Roy's ninety or a hundred and ninety. Nobody can tune
a diesel—or any engine—like Roy Mayo. He's the damn
engine whisperer."

"He'd better hope Miss Annie doesn't put cyanide
in his lobster stew," Aiden said in a dry voice as he followed his brother from the truck. "You know she's going
to be madder than hell if he helps the Flynns beat her
granddaughter."

Bram simply snorted a cynical laugh.

Inside, owner Mike O'Hanlon was hunched over a

battered reception counter where wire baskets were stuffed with untidy piles of receipts and envelopes, the Portland daily paper spread open in front of him. Mike had been a senior in high school when Aiden was a freshman, and he now ran the boatyard with his semiretired father.

Aiden couldn't help noticing that some of the same posters from decades ago still hung on the walls, along with decrepit, outdated calendars from marine suppliers. He even recognized the broken-down couch and banged-up metal chairs for the customers. It was like stepping into Mr. Peabody's Wayback Machine and yet another example of how most residents of Seashell Bay insisted on living in the past.

Mike greeted them with firm handshakes but didn't waste time with small talk. He led them into the cavernous repair shop in the rear, where Aiden spotted *Irish Lady* up on a metal trolley.

Aiden stopped dead, as if someone had rammed a fist into his chest. The last time he'd stood on her deck, he'd vowed never to return. And yet, here he was, ready to climb back on board as if nothing had ever happened. As if he hadn't spent the most miserable hours of his life on *Irish Lady*, helplessly stuck in his father's ugly-ass, bitter world.

He took a deep breath, shoved down the unwelcome memories, and focused on the job at hand. He was good at doing that. Every pro athlete was. You either learned to control your emotions or you washed out at the first sign of trouble.

Old Roy, coffee in hand, leaned on the boat's black-and-white hull—a hull that desperately needed a new paint job. Roy looked unbelievable for his age—tall, tanned, and apparently fit, despite his thoroughly wrinkled face. His white hair was a little long and a lot wild, as if he'd just gotten out of bed. He wore jeans and a white T-shirt that revealed surprisingly sinewy arms.

Aiden blinked when he saw Jessie Jameson. She was dressed in a tube top and overalls and looked more like a grease monkey than the pretty girl he'd seen in the bar last night. Jessie crouched beside Roy, working a metal scraper over the hull as she talked to the old guy.

"Aiden, you know everybody, right?" Mike asked.

"It's been a long time, Mr. Mayo," Aiden said, sticking out his hand. "You probably don't remember me."

Roy grabbed his hand in a crushing grip. "Hell, boy, you think I got Alzheimer's or something? Of course I remember Sean Flynn's oldest son. You hit three home runs to win the high school regionals back in...was it 'ninety-nine? Anyway, I remember Lily got so excited that night I thought Annie and I were going to have to call 911 if she didn't calm down," he said with a toothy grin.

That gave Aiden a little jolt, since he hadn't even known Lily was at that particular game. She'd only been a freshman then, a nice girl from his hometown and just one of the kids he rode the ferry with every day to school on the mainland.

"And call me Roy, for God's sake," the old guy added.

In light of the hostility over the development deal, it was nice to see that not everyone in the Doyle camp hated the Flynns. Well, Lily didn't hate him, although Aiden was beginning to think she wasn't ready to welcome him with open arms either. Not if this crazy bet was any indication.

"Aiden, I'm Jessie." The dark-haired girl offered him a slender hand topped with purple fingernails. "I was your scorer last night. I'm sure you don't remember me from before, since you were so much *older*."

Jessie's emphasis on *older* was obviously a little payback for his gaffe about Roy's memory. He replied with a polite smile and a murmur that of course he remembered her. And he certainly would have said hello to her last night if he hadn't been so focused on trying to get Lily alone. In the end, that hadn't worked out because Morgan Merrifield had never once left Lily's side, and Micah Lancaster had hung close too. Both had given off the distinct vibe of being on a mission to protect Lily, as if Aiden were some kind of pirate intent on having his evil way with their island princess.

Mike slapped *Irish Lady*'s bow and looked at Bram. "You brought her in last week for antifouling paint and an upgrade to the GPS, but now you want to tune her up for racing too?" He raised skeptical brows at Aiden. "You're serious?"

"She's that bad, huh?" Aiden sighed.

Mike and Jessie exchanged meaningful glances before Mike said, "Look, that old diesel is fine for trips back and forth into Portland, which is about all your father and Bram use it for anymore. But for racing? No way."

"Shee-it, Michael O'Hanlon, since when did you start talking like a pussy?" Roy scoffed. "If these boys are set on racing this old bag of hammers, let's you and me try to give them a chance to win." He shifted his gaze, his faded blue eyes zeroing in on Aiden. "Sean already told me you'd be footing the bill for this work, son. So, if you give me the go-ahead, I can tune this engine, all right.

It'll cost you, but I'll find you some extra horsepower. Guaranteed."

"You're on your own with that, boys," Mike said, shaking his head. "We'll get the hull shipshape, but any diesel modifications are all Roy's. And Aiden," he added, "remember that Roy Mayo doesn't work for O'Hanlon's, so whatever happens with the engine, my company's not on the hook for it."

"Got it," Aiden said drily.

Mike obviously thought they were nuts to let Roy anywhere near *Irish Lady*. Not that money was an issue. He hadn't become rich playing baseball, unlike some of the superstars he'd played with. But spending a little on the boat to try to measure up to Lily's challenge wouldn't put a dent in his healthy bank account. Maybe it was just a crazy waste of time and money, but he couldn't back down now.

"Do what you need to do, Roy," he said. "Give me all the power you can squeeze out of the old girl because I sure don't want to be bouncing around in Lily Doyle's wake."

Or have to find out what she's got in mind for me if I lose.

What was Lily's idea of *a personal service*, anyway? It had to involve some kind of humiliation, maybe something to do with the feud between their clans or the crap going down over the development deal.

Or maybe she just wanted to take the piss out of the guy who had abandoned Seashell Bay. Lily had never wanted anything but a life on the island, which was one of the reasons they'd both known a relationship between them would never work.

But that didn't mean things couldn't work between them in the short term, at least on the physical level. With that in mind, Aiden had a *very* good idea of what he'd demand from Lily Doyle—if, that is, Roy could perform a miracle and give him a fighting chance.

"Are you sure you know what you're doing?" Holly Tyler tucked a few loose strands of her silky auburn hair behind her ears as she peered at Lily. "You've never entirely gotten over Aiden Flynn, and don't even try to deny it."

Holly had been a year behind Lily and Morgan in school. Despite that, the three of them had been almost inseparable until the day Holly left for college in Boston, where she now lived and worked as a marketing consultant. An orphan, she'd been raised by her aunts, Florence and Beatrice Jenkins, sisters who'd owned the island's general store for decades. Fortunately, Holly had always returned to her island roots for an August vacation, even when she'd still been married.

The three friends sat in white rocking chairs on the porch of Lily's cottage, sipping the fresh lemonade she'd squeezed after a full day on the water. The lobsters were plentiful this August, and she had to take advantage while it lasted. Soon enough, the pickings would be slim, forcing her to move offshore to catch anything worthwhile.

Exhaustion and aching muscles weighed Lily down. Though she was supposed to have dinner with her parents tonight, she longed to curl up under a comforter and go to sleep. Lobstering without a sternman was just about killing her.

"I can handle Aiden," she said, trying to sound like she

meant it. "He might be some big baseball hero, but he still puts his pants on one leg at a time, as my dad always says."

Morgan glanced at Holly. "Lily thinks that if she wins the race, Aiden will be honor bound to work sternman for her until she finds somebody else for the rest of the season."

The dubious expression on Holly's face told Lily what her friend thought of that plan.

"Even a couple of weeks would give me a breather," Lily argued. "I've tried hard to replace Johnny, but guys have all the work they need these days. And then there are the ones who don't want to take orders from a woman." It might be the twenty-first century, but some of the men in these islands still didn't think women belonged in a working lobster boat and sure not as captain. She tried not to feel bitter, but her career—heck, her entire life—was on the line.

Holly grimaced. "I'm not buying it, sweetie. And did you really flirt with Aiden last night? You know he's not going to be here for long. What if he sucks you into his web again and then scoots back to Philadelphia without so much as a wave from the boat?"

Lily avoided Holly's worried gaze by tracing a curving line down the mist on her frosted glass. But if she were in Holly's position, she'd be asking the same questions, determined to protect her friend from heartache.

But Lily was no longer the not-quite-seventeen-year-old girl who'd had a deranged, forbidden-fruit crush on Aiden Flynn ever since she could remember. So what if he was probably the hottest guy Seashell Bay had ever seen? Holly didn't have to tell *her* that he'd be getting back on the ferry and heading home as soon as his business here was done. Lily knew she'd probably never see Aiden again after this summer, and that was fine with her.

Because it had to be fine, didn't it?

She forced a smile, determined to make the best of a bad situation. "Aiden might be a big old spider, but, darlin', I assure you that I'm no fly. And may I remind you both that I do have some experience escaping his evil web of sin."

Morgan laughed. "We know, but that was a long time ago. And he *is* Aiden Flynn, after all."

"I'm hoping to find out more about what he's thinking in terms of selling his land," Lily said, changing tack. "I thought about asking him straight out last night but just couldn't do it. It felt like coming at it that way might bring all the old, stupid feud stuff right out in the open, especially with Bram and Granny almost getting into it."

Morgan flashed Holly a cockeyed grin. "The way Aiden was looking at her when they were playing darts, I figured I'd better hustle her out of the Pot as soon as I could if I wanted to preserve her virtue. I swear he had visions of laying Lily out on the pool table and—"

Lily thrust up a hand, palm out. "And we are *not* going there. I refuse to have that particular image rolling around in my head."

Morgan laughed. "Rolling around, huh? A lot of women wouldn't mind doing some rolling around with Aiden Flynn. There were more than a few ready to climb all over him last night—as you would have realized if you ever thought about something else besides your boat and Seashell Bay."

Lily grabbed the lemonade pitcher as if to pour it over her best friend's head. "Can we please talk about something else? And what's wrong with worrying about Seashell Bay? Somebody's got to do something, or pretty soon those idiot developers will end up destroying the island."

Both Holly and Morgan turned serious.

"It's getting clearer every day how much this development is dividing people," Holly said in a worried voice. "My aunts say it's pretty much all anybody's been talking about at the store since Bay Island Properties started sniffing around. And all the rumors flying around lately have just made it worse. I'm not around much so I'm not sure what's true and what isn't."

"Dividing us is right," Morgan said. "A lot of the full-time residents are worried as hell about the impact on the island, though others want the business it would bring in. The people with vacation homes aren't crazy about an influx of newcomers, but most are keen on having a car ferry, so you can't depend on them to hold the line. At the B&B, our regular guests seem to be more or less split. Some like the island just the way it is and some think it would be great to have more development because it would bring some more stores and restaurants. According to that crowd, quaint is cute for a few days but a big bore after that."

Morgan had summed up the situation pretty accurately. Just thinking of big-city developers ripping up their beautiful, serene island made Lily sick, almost as sick as seeing the nasty fractures that had started to form among the residents.

"That's exactly what I worry about," Holly said. "What would happen to our general store if the population doubles or triples? Would it bring more business for my aunts?" She shook her head. "Maybe, but you can also bet that some mainland retailer will want to set up a bigger store here at some point. Florence and Beatrice always put on a brave face, but they're not making much money. It's hard to imagine them having to compete with a chain store that would undercut their prices."

"A bigger population and a car ferry could be good for the B&B," Morgan said. "Dad thinks so, anyway."

Holly shook her head. "Maybe, but a big resort with all the amenities could hurt your business too, couldn't it?"

"Yeah, I worry about that," Morgan admitted. "I've always thought our clientele prefers our home-style atmosphere to that of a resort, but who knows how it would all shake out in the end?"

In silence, the three friends contemplated what a big development on the Flynn lands could do to Seashell Bay. Every soul on the island would be deeply affected, some possibly for the better, but others definitely for the worse. It sure didn't seem worth the risk to Lily, not with all the unknowns.

"I know it's not as clear-cut for your families as it is for mine," Lily said, "but you know how strongly we feel about that proposal. I'm going to keep fighting it with everything I've got, because I don't have a choice. If the Flynns and Bay Island get their way, we won't recognize this place in five years. It could even end up as some junior version of Martha's Vineyard or Nantucket. The Seashell Bay Island we grew up in will basically cease to exist."

By the time she finished, she was starting to choke up. It made her feel sort of stupid, so she stared out over the trap lot toward the rocky shoreline until she regained control.

Morgan reached over and squeezed her hand. "You know I'm there for you, Lily, no matter what. Even if I have to go toe-to-toe with my dad, though I sure hope it doesn't have to come to that. I've been working on him a little every day to come out for the no vote."

Lily grasped her friend's hand. It felt like a lifeline in a frigid, storm-tossed sea. "Thanks, sweetie. You know how much I appreciate it."

She did, too, because she also knew how much Morgan hated disagreeing with her father. Ever since his wife's death two years ago from ovarian cancer, Cal Merrifield had come to emotionally depend on his eldest daughter more and more. Cal continued to do everything he could to convince her to move back home, and Morgan felt tremendous guilt over her refusal to give up her teaching job on the mainland.

Morgan gave her hand one more squeeze and then let go. "But let's forget about that depressing stuff for a while. It's the Flynns I'm worried about and how they're going to cheat to win the boat race. Aiden was always a stand-up guy, but Bram has been getting a little weird the last few years. And their no-good father..." Her mouth curled into a sneer, which expressed how they all felt about Sean Flynn.

Holly put her empty glass down on the wicker table beside her chair. "How the heck do you cheat in a boat race? Don't the captains just open their throttles wide and blast straight down the channel to the finish line?"

Lily waggled a hand. "You'd be surprised at the lengths some guys will go to win, and there's not much that can be done about it. The organizers here don't go in for heavy-duty regulations and engine inspections, like they do in the bigger races along the coast. It's more of a friendly match atmosphere. The nine-hundred-horsepower superboats don't bother with our little Blueberry Festival races."

"If the Flynns want to soup up that old tub of theirs, Aiden's got the money to do it," Morgan said in a dramatically dark voice.

Lily had thought of that factor *after* she'd thrown out her challenge to Aiden. For all she knew, Aiden and Bram could even be on the mainland buying a powerful new engine for *Irish Lady*. Or contracting for some structural modifications, though they wouldn't have time for anything major. Still, something like that might give them the edge they needed to win.

"They could," she acknowledged. "But I haven't exactly been resting on my laurels since I won my class last year. My boat's in great shape. I had Josh do some fine-tuning last week, and he's going to be at it again tomorrow."

Morgan wagged a finger at her. "Fine-tuning, as in squeezing out every last ounce of horsepower your diesel's got?"

"You know Josh," Lily said, keeping it vague.

Josh Bryson wasn't a marine mechanic—his specialty was motorcycles—but he could work miracles with almost any kind of engine from lawn mowers to big truck diesels. He worked on a few boat engines around the island, but most captains kept their business with O'Hanlon's Boatyard. Lily, on the other hand, was happy to support Josh. The island certainly didn't need to lose another young man to the mainland due to lack of work.

She leaned forward in her rocker. "Let's just say that I have no intention of losing the race to Aiden Flynn. Besides, the poor guy probably couldn't run a boat on a straight course to save his soul. You know how much he hated going anywhere near *Irish Lady*."

Holly and Morgan exchanged knowing glances.

"We all know why too," Morgan said. "So it's a pretty gutsy thing for him to be doing, if you ask me. There's more than just his ego at stake, which is why he'll probably do anything to win."

Lily knew that all too well. For Aiden, stepping on board *Irish Lady* would bring back bitter memories of his father's abuse.

To Lily, and to everyone else she knew, the island and its people were one in blood and bone, and neither distance nor time could erase the bonds that had grown over the generations. She had no intention of ever leaving, but if something were to force her away, everything about Seashell Bay would stay with her until the end of her days, always cherished and always missed.

But with Aiden it was different. To him, island life was something to leave far behind, to wipe from his memory as much as possible. And yet here she was, shoving it all right in his face.

Chapter 5

$\mathscr{A}$iden pounded along the asphalt, slowing his pace as he took the sharp bend where Island Road abruptly shifted direction, bringing the sun around to his back. A few minutes earlier, as he'd headed east from Bram's cottage, it had crept over the Atlantic's horizon in a perfect sphere, tinting the calm ocean a glowing orange. The reflection had skipped across the dark water straight at him, stirring up memories of other sunrises on the island. The cool, damp stillness of dawn, with only a few squawks from seagulls to keep him company, seemed to reach deep inside to unleash a flood of memories. Unfortunately, most of them were ones he'd rather have kept buried, far from the light of day.

Sunrises spoke to the soul, and crisp dawns could invigorate mind and body. Or so he'd been told a thousand freaking times by lobster fishermen, who liked nothing better than freezing their asses off while they gripped a mug of coffee in one hand and steered their boats out into the channel with the other. But Aiden never got it. For him, the sunrises of his youth had preceded long days of work on his father's boat, and there had been no pleasure on *Irish Lady*. Just backbreaking work and more than the occasional backhand across the face or slap to the head from his father's ham-sized fists.

Aiden had never hated the work itself, as tough as it was, because it was an honest way to make a living, and he enjoyed physical labor. But nothing he did was ever right in his old man's eyes. No matter how hard he'd sweated to keep up, he almost always fell behind the punishing rhythm enforced by his father. In those days, even a half-drunk Sean Flynn could haul a trap and clean it out in seconds before impatiently shoving it at Aiden to load new bait.

To this day, Aiden still didn't much like either dawns or boats, so how ironic was it that he hadn't been on the island even six hours when Lily Doyle had challenged him to a boat race? The universe could be a fickle bitch.

After stewing most of the night, he'd been glad to abandon his restless sleep and throw on a sleeveless jersey and sweat shorts. Running had always been a sort of mental therapy for him, a way to slow down his racing brain and bring a semblance of order to his thoughts. And right now he really needed to get those thoughts in order.

Yesterday, after they'd turned the fate of *Irish Lady* over to Rocket Roy Mayo, Aiden and Bram had sat down at the cottage, cracked a couple of beers, and reviewed the developer's preliminary plans for their land. Bram had wanted to bring their father into the discussion but Aiden had balked. Another shouting match was not on the agenda if he could help it. He'd wanted to carefully study the plans with Bram and ask questions that would be met with answers, not tirades and threats.

The sketches and descriptions his brother had laid out on the battered kitchen table had knocked Aiden off-kilter. Months ago, when Bram had first contacted him about the possibility of a land sale, the only project he'd mentioned had been the construction of a resort overlooking the bluffs—a hotel complex that stretched from the eastern portion of their father's property across Aiden's entire acreage to the western third of Bram's land. Though Bram had been full of regret that the proposal would eliminate the possibility of Aiden having an oceanfront house of his own, Aiden had assured him that he had no intention of ever building such a home—or any other home—on Seashell Bay Island.

But the new plans clearly showed that Bay Island Properties had their sights set on clear-cutting three-quarters of the Flynn lands. In addition to the resort, over a hundred luxury homes would be constructed, most of them on their father's huge parcel between Island Road and the sea. If the full project went forward, something much like a city suburb would rise up on the Atlantic side of the low hill that bisected the island.

Aiden could barely imagine it. The historic little town on one side, with its old Victorians, its seaside cottages, and its quirky local businesses, and a weird slice of suburbia on the other. No wonder the developer was now insisting on the car ferry as a precondition. Those swathes of oversized, high-end homes would have to be filled by people who would commute to the mainland for work, along with well-heeled mainlanders who would use them as vacation homes.

He got it that his father and Bram were anxious—even desperate—to give the developer confirmation that all three of them were fully committed to the sale. That way the lawyers could get started on the paperwork, and Bay Island could be comfortable getting their architects and engineers working on detailed plans. Aiden understood all that, but he had no intention of caving in to their demand that he do it on their schedule and not his. There was simply too much at stake, for his family and for the entire island.

With his mind finally settling down into the rhythm of the run, Aiden swung off Island Road onto Water Street, the dockside lane the locals called "the landing" or "down front." At the bottom of the slight hill, past the big parking lot, the ferry dock poked out into the channel. To the right, a few dozen boats were tied up at the town's floating piers. The area normally bustled with activity from the ferry, the Town Hall, and the Rec Center, along with the little seasonal store, but not at this early hour. Only a couple of fishermen were at work down below, readying to push off in their skiffs and head out to their moored boats. He didn't give them more than a passing glance until one of the fishermen turned around to grab a lobster buoy.

Aiden stopped on a dime because that fisherman was Lily, now easily recognizable even though she'd scrunched her hair into some kind of knot behind her head and wore an orange oilskin jacket that came down well past her hips, protecting her from the morning chill off the water.

Lily didn't glance up, obviously too busy loading her skiff with supplies and replacement gear to notice him. Aiden considered leaving her alone, continuing his run. He knew from experience that most lobster fishermen liked to get out to their boats and start hauling traps at first light or even earlier. But she looked like she could use some help, what with a stacked pair of traps and more buoys, a big box, a plastic cooler, and a couple of spools of pot warp to load into her skiff.

His feet made the decision for him, pounding down the ramp and onto the floating pier, heading straight for the far end where Lily toiled.

Of course, she heard his thudding footsteps on the damp, composite planks long before he reached her. When she looked up, her lips parted in surprise.

"Hey, Lily," he called, "let me give you a hand with that stuff."

When she unleashed a welcoming grin, warmth spread through him that the swiftly rising sun couldn't possibly equal.

He slowed to a stop at the end of the dock and allowed himself a quick scan of her slender body. Underneath the open Grundéns jacket, she had on a white T-shirt and clean but faded jeans that clung lovingly to her curves. Except for the jacket, she wore essentially the same outfit he'd seen on her yesterday from the ferry, so he figured that was probably her standard lobstering attire in dry August weather. While some fishermen preferred to wear oilskin overalls and even jackets all year, Aiden knew from experience that the heavy gear was too hot for many in the summer, even the mild coastal summers of Maine.

Of course, Lily could even make oilskins sexy. But it was her eyes that pulled him in. Stunning emerald eyes that had always grabbed him low down and hard. Lily in lobstering gear, devoid of makeup and with her wild hair escaping from its twist, was as freshly beautiful as any woman he'd ever seen.

Unpretentious. Confident.

Real.

"Trying to work in some weightlifting along with your cardio?" Lily said, giving him the once-over. He was pretty sure he saw feminine appreciation in her gaze along with gentle mockery. "Well, be my guest, because I'm already later than I wanted to be. But I hope you haven't forgotten how heavy these suckers are."

She pointed to the pair of thirty-six-inch, green mesh traps—older ones that he suspected she'd had to repair.

"Hell, yeah, they're heavy. I can remember stacking them six high and five wide in the stern when I was a kid," Aiden retorted. It had been rugged work. The wire traps were heavy enough, but when you added the three bricks needed for ballast in each one and then stacked them higher than your head, things got really interesting.

"Sure, but look at you," Lily scoffed. "You're practically a giant. But think about little me out here, schlepping all this heavy gear around by myself."

Frowning, Aiden took a quick look around for her sternman. Usually, the sternman rode out to the lobster boat in the captain's skiff, but he could see no one around the dock other than old Forrest Coolidge and a young woman Aiden presumed to be his helper. "Are you going out without a sternman today? Lily, you know better than I do how dangerous it is to go out there alone."

He vividly remembered the stories about lobstermen getting tangled in pot warp and pulled overboard by sinking traps, sometimes to their deaths. Or getting a finger lopped off and passing out, bleeding half to death before help arrived. The idea of Lily taking those kinds of chances made every muscle in his body go cold and tense.

Lily's tanned complexion colored with a hint of pink under the bronze, and she looked at him with a rueful smile. "My latest guy disappeared awhile ago. Rumor has it he skipped bail and took off after he was hauled in for yet another DUI in Portland." She gave a little sigh. "I can't afford to miss much time fishing, Aiden. I've got boat payments to meet, and my savings account has less in it than my piggy bank."

"Sure, I get that, but—"

"—but hopefully this will be the last day," she interrupted.

That made him relax a bit. "You've got a guy in mind?"

"Well, I'm optimistic that I'll have at least a temporary solution in a couple of days. I won't be fishing tomorrow, anyway, because I'll be busy at the festival. And then it's race day on Sunday, and I should know by then. By Monday, I should have a sternman with me."

"Oh, so you'll be talking to somebody about it on race day?"

"That's the plan." She bent to pick up another buoy, painted neon orange with a lime green horizontal stripe around the middle. State law required every Maine lobsterman to have unique buoy colors, but she'd closely copied those of her father. Yet another indication, he figured, of how much her island heritage and tradition meant to her.

"Well, I hope he comes through for you," he said.

And he damn well meant it, because the idea of Lily slogging it out by herself day after day or suffering some horrible accident out on the water was something he couldn't bear thinking about.

Lily's stomach had clenched the moment Aiden, in all his sweaty, masculine glory, materialized out of the rapidly fading tendrils of morning mist. He was the last person she'd expected to see at dawn. Back in high school, he'd always been the last straggler to jump off his bike, barreling across the gangway onto the ferry with only moments to spare. She'd always made sure she sat almost directly across from the lower deck bench that Aiden had permanently claimed as his private territory. Half asleep and preoccupied by whatever was playing on his CD Walkman, he'd mostly ignored her for an achingly long time, but that had never stopped her from having adolescent fantasies about how wonderful life would be as Aiden Flynn's girlfriend.

But one sunny morning it had all changed. Aiden looked across to the opposite bench and actually *saw* her. At least that was how she remembered his charged stare and the slow smile that had spread across his lean face, already shadowed with a man's dark bristle.

The sudden notice had startled her. It wasn't like her reed-thin body had suddenly transformed itself into a *Playboy* model's body. Breasts and curves had been slow in coming, so slow that she'd sobbed her heart out to her mom on more than one occasion, terrified something was wrong with her. So she could hardly blame Aiden Flynn for not having noticed her. None of the other island boys had paid her the slightest attention either.

It hadn't helped that she spent a fair bit of her preteen and teenage years hanging out with Seashell Bay's prettiest girl. She loved Holly Tyler like a twin sister, but both Lily and Morgan had spent years suffering wounding comparisons—a good many of them self-inflicted—whenever the local boys came across the trio. The boys would circle Holly like dragonflies ready to mate, ignoring Lily and Morgan or, even worse, treating them like one of the guys.

That had changed during her sophomore year at Portland's Peninsula High. On an unseasonably hot day in October, she finally hit the radar screen of Seashell Bay's cutest boy—the boy Lily had crushed on for years, feud or no feud. And all these years later, she still believed Aiden's notice had been in large measure due to a particular red tank top she'd worn on that historic morning, a top that had become just a little too tight for her late blooming figure.

Back then, Aiden's surprised gaze had roamed hotly over her body, just as it was doing now. Only today, his look was so much darker and . . . deeper. Like he was both reliving a memory and seeing something in her for the first time. Something only a man could see.

Too bad he was also giving her shit about working without a sternman. That was making her already jumpy nerves bounce around like a pinball. She had to bite her lip to stop from blurting out a plea for help with her problem, knowing with dead certainty he'd say no. In high school, he'd told her bitterly and repeatedly how much he looked forward to the day when he'd never have to set foot on a lobster boat again.

And she would never forget the day Sean had shoved Aiden so hard that he'd staggered backward, windmilling his arms as he tumbled over the gunwale and into the sea. The jerk had made a wide, leisurely circle, leaving Aiden in the bone-chilling water for several long minutes before finally bringing the boat around for him to struggle up over the side. Lily's grandfather had seen most of that incident as he was coming in at the end of the day. He'd been too late to help Aiden, but he'd not spared Sean a blistering, profanity-filled lecture once they met at the dock. That had gone over about as well as one would expect. Sean had threatened to beat the crap out of Gramps while Aiden walked away, red-faced and humiliated.

After that episode made the rounds of the island, few people had wanted much to do with Sean Flynn, other than his drinking buddies and a few Doyle haters. Some had even wanted to report Sean to the Office of Child and Family Services in Portland, but the Flynns had closed ranks over that one—even Aiden. He was too proud to ask for help, and Lily knew he'd die before he ever inflicted that sort of shame on his mother.

But that was the day Lily had started to hate Aiden's father with every fiber of her being, and the hate still burned hot and steady.

So why was she challenging Aiden to the boat race, knowing what it would probably mean to him? Knowing what she would then demand of him once she won?

First and foremost because she so badly needed his help, of that there was no doubt. But she also couldn't help believing that it would be good for Aiden to get back out on the water. With *her* this time, not his asshole father. Maybe it was a naïve hope, but Lily truly felt that Aiden should try to come to terms with his island past, for everyone's sake as well as his own. His father's abuse had denied him the primal, loving connection most of the islanders felt toward Seashell Bay. Aiden had never been allowed to develop a true sense of affection and respect for the island way of life, because the man who should have taught him that was an abusive bastard.

If Aiden couldn't see that simple truth, if he couldn't understand that the island was worth saving—even if his father wasn't—then Lily was terrified he'd turn his back on Seashell Bay, on all of them, for good.

"I know you won't have any trouble lifting the traps, but I also know you've had a lot of trouble with your knees," she said, trying to sound normal and not like a guilt-ridden, manipulative jerk. "You had surgery over the winter, didn't you? I guess you're not playing because you're still recuperating."

Aiden gave her a grim-faced nod as he easily hoisted one of the traps and leaned over to set it down in the boat. "I had surgery, but I'm fine now. I just can't make sharp turns and pivots like I used to." He looked back toward Forrest Coolidge and Erica Easton, who were pushing off in their skiff, almost as if he was embarrassed. "But I'm not on the disabled list."

Lily didn't get it.

Aiden looked back at her and blew out a heavy breath. "The Phillies released me, Lily."

Clutching her buoy, she struggled to make sense of what he'd said. What did it mean for his future? A dozen questions swarmed from her brain to her lips. But she couldn't find the words to voice them so instead she grimaced in sympathy. "Aiden, I'm so sorry."

Darned if she didn't have to blink back tears as she finally put the buoy down in the skiff.

He shrugged, as if it didn't really matter. She knew it did.

"My agent's working on getting me hooked up with another team," he said.

Lily sincerely hoped that some other team would pick him up. Aiden had always said that baseball meant everything to him, and from an early age, he'd focused like a laser on making a career in pro ball. She'd known with absolute certainty—because he'd told her with absolute certainty—that he would never fish lobster, and he would never live anywhere near his father.

"I'm sure that'll happen soon," she said.

Of course, she had no idea if that were true, because she knew virtually nothing about the sport. Even when it came to Aiden's exploits, all she knew was only what the locals talked about. What was the point of following his career? From the moment he'd taken that final boat into Portland after graduating high school, she'd understood that dwelling on him would only bring her more heartache.

Aiden shrugged his broad shoulders. "I hope so. My options are starting to get pretty limited, though."

He bent his long, powerful legs and deposited another trap squarely on top of the one already in the skiff. Lily didn't even pretend to keep her eyes off his incredibly fit and gorgeous body as he worked with easy assurance. As an athlete, he might be losing a step, but as a man, he couldn't be more in his mouth-watering prime.

"Could that mean your stay might be..." Lily almost said *indefinite*, then winced at how needy that would sound. She regrouped. "Um, longer than I'd first thought?"

After lifting another trap, he straightened and gave

her a long, assessing look that raised the fine hairs on the back of her neck. "What exactly was your first thought, Lily?"

"Oh, you know, a few days," she babbled. "Don't forget I know better than anybody how you feel about Seashell Bay."

He gave her a slow grin that sent a few tendrils of heat licking down between her thighs.

"Lily, I'd say you know a lot of things about me better than anybody," he said in a voice that made her shiver. Then he took a step closer, crowding her a bit.

She eyed his broad, muscular chest, fighting the deranged urge to slip her arms around his neck and press against him. After all these years, that instinct was still so powerful it took her breath away. Everything about Aiden was familiar, from the burn scar on the inside of his forearm from a childhood accident to the lock of dark hair that dipped down onto his forehead. But he was different, too, excitingly so. He was a man, seasoned and experienced, with sexy laugh lines around his firm mouth and a knowing, sensual look in his dark gaze.

God, she'd loved him so much back in the day that it still made her chest ache to think about it.

Love. Lily gave her head a mental shake. As if a sixteen-year-old could truly understand what that meant.

When Aiden slid a big, warm hand onto her hip, she barely managed to stifle a gasp. "Aiden..." She raised her left hand and pressed against his shoulder, a halfhearted effort he saw through instantly.

"Have you forgotten how much you loved it when I touched you?" His voice was a low, thrilling combination of purr and growl that made her weak behind the knees.

Oh, hell no. Not again. Lily tried to force herself to step away from him, but her stupid body wouldn't obey the message her brain shrieked at her.

Until, that is, she glanced over his broad shoulder and saw what—who—was charging down the dock. Then she practically jumped, as if a five-pound lobster had just dug its claws into her butt.

Chapter 6

$\mathcal{L}$ily, what the hell's going on down there?" Her father's deep, raspy voice boomed down the pier from a throat ravaged by decades of cigarettes and whisky. Tommy Doyle had always been a bit of a drama queen, and he rushed down onto the floating pier as if she were being attacked by a band of pirates.

Lily took another step back as Aiden glanced over his shoulder. "Ah, your dad hasn't changed a bit," he said. "Apparently, he still wants to shoot every Flynn on sight. I can only hope he's not packing heat."

She gave him an exaggerated eye roll. But at least he was calm, and she prayed he'd keep his powder dry in the face of what was sure to be a rough encounter with her hot-tempered dad.

Her father charged down the pier as fast as his arthritic knees would carry him. Instinctively, Lily slid around Aiden to get between him and the man who hated every Flynn that had ever set foot on Seashell Bay Island.

"What's wrong, Dad?" she said, as he approached. "Why are you down front at this hour?"

His face almost as red as the hull of the town's fire rescue boat, her dad held a big clamp in his meaty fist. "Last night when you left, you didn't take the new hose clamp I got for you."

Sighing, Lily reached for it. She'd forgotten not only the clamp, but even that she'd asked her father to run into Portland to pick up the part in the first place. He didn't mind doing a few errands for her now and again, especially since there wasn't much else his rheumatoid arthritis would allow him to do anymore.

"Thanks, Dad. You're the best," she said gratefully, but she didn't like the expression on her father's face one bit.

"You're welcome, but what the hell's he doing here?" Her dad glared at Aiden as if the poor guy had just cut her lobster gear out of the water. "Why are you talking to this…this…damn Benedict Arnold?"

Yep, her father could drama-queen with the best of them. "Dad, come on. That is absolutely—"

"Morning, sir. Long time, no see," Aiden interrupted in a voice so calm and easygoing that it stunned her. His coffee-brown eyes betrayed only mild amusement.

The last time her dad had spoken to Aiden was to tell him how overjoyed he was to see him leaving the island and that the only thing that would make him happier was if Aiden never came back. It had taken her father five years to get around to admitting that awful fact to Lily. It still made her both ashamed of him and sick to death of the feud that a few silly old men wouldn't let die.

"Not near long enough, Flynn," her father growled. "I know why you're back. You don't give a shit about this island, but as soon as you get a sniff that you and your clan can make a pile of dough, you're all over it. Sell the island to the developers and to hell with the rest of us, right?" He stepped forward, invading Aiden's personal space as he stared up at the much younger and stronger man.

Stupid, stupid, stupid.

Though Aiden's shoulders hiked and his fingers started to curl into fists, Lily knew his reaction was pure male instinct. No way would he back away from anyone, but he'd never hurt her dad either.

Lily was almost as tall as her father, but she weighed barely more than half as much. Still, she clamped her hands onto his shoulders and stared directly into his face, now puffy with all the medicine he had to take for his arthritis.

"Listen, Dad, we are *not* having a shouting match on the pier while I'm trying to load gear. If you have something you need to get off your chest, please do it somewhere else and at some other time." She gave him a placating smile and lowered her voice. "Thanks for bringing the clamp, but why don't you head back home and have another cup of coffee, okay? I'm fine here. Aiden was out for a run and just stopped a moment to help me load up. That was pretty nice of him, don't you think?"

Tommy shifted his gaze to Aiden again, his glare still fierce. "We don't need any help from you, Flynn. Never did, never will. And the sooner you finish the dirty business you came for and get your ass off our island, the better we'll all be for it."

Lily wanted to shake her dad, hating the shuttered look that came over Aiden's face. God, as if he needed another old man from Seashell Bay giving him a hard time.

"I didn't come here to do any dirty business, Mr. Doyle," he said quietly. "And if you want to talk about the issues sometime, feel free to give me a call. I'm staying at Bram's." He gave a casual shrug. "You might be surprised to know what I think or don't think about what's going on."

Lily peered at him. What did he mean by that? Unfortunately, Aiden was wearing one of the best poker faces she'd ever seen.

"Yeah, well, don't hold your breath on that," her dad huffed, still not breaking away.

Once again, Lily had a close-up reminder of where she'd gotten her stubborn streak. "Please go home, Dad," she said, sighing.

He finally blew out an angry breath, gave Aiden one more dirty look, then turned and walked away. But a few feet down the pier he half-turned and gave her a funny little grimace. "We'll talk more tonight at dinner, Lily. You're coming over, right? Mother's making her blueberry cobbler."

Lily smiled at her father's roundabout way of telling her not to worry too much about what had just happened. He could be a blustering old warhorse at times, but he wasn't a cruel man and he'd never lifted a hand against anyone. "Sure, Dad. See you tonight."

In silence, she and Aiden watched her father's gimpy progress until he was up on Water Street. Then she turned to him with a rueful smile. "Dad doesn't mean half of what he said. He's just worried about the development, and you happened to be on hand to take the brunt."

Actually, her father almost certainly meant every word he'd said, but right now she needed to pour some oil on troubled waters.

Aiden shrugged as he reached for a spool of pot warp. "Blueberry cobbler, huh? Lucky you."

He sounded okay, but the heat between them had blown away on the crisp bay breeze.

Lily seemed to be in no hurry to push off in her skiff, prompting Aiden to cast a puzzled glance skyward. The sun climbed higher in a cloudless blue vault, which meant another sizzling hot day on the water. He'd worked many long days on a lobster boat in the full, blazing sun—anything else he'd done was a cakewalk by comparison, including covering center field during a heat wave.

The pier had returned to quiet, orderly calm. Lily's volatile father had been rude, but Aiden had expected no less, given how much Tommy hated the Flynns in general and his dad in particular.

Sometimes, Aiden thought it would be better for everyone if Doyle and his father locked themselves in a UFC cage and hammered it out once and for all with their aging, crippled fists. But he suspected that even a grudge match wouldn't do much to end the feud that had been passed down through the generations, nurtured with a bizarre kind of toxic affection. Thankfully, though, he figured the crap might finally peter out with Sean and Tommy. None of their children seemed to have much interest in perpetuating the bullshit that had started over a century ago. Bram was the only one of their generation to carry any lingering taint of the grudge, but Aiden didn't worry much about that. His brother's drinking and gambling problems were far more troubling than any perceived wrongs committed by the Doyles.

Unless, of course, the land development deal blew

everything up again. From what he'd learned since he stepped off the ferry, it definitely had that potential.

"Anything else I can help you with?" Aiden said.

Lily pulled her sunglasses down from the top of her head, covering her beautiful green eyes as she took her seat in the stern. "You seem strangely anxious to help out the competition, Aiden Flynn."

He sank into a crouch so they could talk without him towering over her. "I'm not exactly tuning your diesel for the race," he joked. "Just giving an old friend a hand."

Lily's lush mouth seemed to flatten at his choice of words. "Old friend" hardly described how he felt about her. But as enticing as she was, he was probably opening himself up to a world of hurt if he tapped into the chemistry so obviously still there. Especially given all the issues festering between their families. But, man, he wanted to take Lily with an urgency that just about knocked him off his feet.

"Well, I appreciate it." Her slender but capable hand gripped the throttle on the Mercury 7.5-horsepower engine, so ancient that it might have been a hand-me-down from her grandfather.

Lily was pretty and strong and full of energy, so at peace with her life that Aiden couldn't repress a flash of envy. Even when he was doing the thing he loved best, playing baseball, he'd always been aware of a restless need to keep moving, to keep looking for that next best thing.

Too bad he couldn't figure out what that thing was.

"I'm happy for you, Lily," he said abruptly. "You always wanted this, and here you are. Exactly where you wanted to be and where you belong."

Her lips curved into a wry grin. "Oh, sure. I always

wanted to be working my ass off in stink and slime to make less in a day than the cost of my fuel and bait."

Aiden knew she would never want to do anything else. "You know what I mean," he said. "You've told me more than once that you wanted nothing more than to fish lobster from your own boat and spend the rest of your life right here on the island."

Her smile eased away into thoughtfulness. "You're right, I did. And you told me you'd rather live anywhere else on Earth." She gave a little shrug. "So I guess we both got what we wanted, didn't we, Aiden?"

He'd always thought so, but wondered why he couldn't find the words to agree with her. Probably because everything had pretty much felt like crap since the Phillies cast him adrift. "Joking aside, you're happy now though, right?"

Lily's brave smile lit up her face and tugged at his heart. "It's been hard, but I'm content with my decisions. What else would I do if not this?" She tilted her head back to catch the sun on her face and spread her arms wide, as if to encompass everything around her, sea and land and air. He knew Lily had always loved the ocean, loved taking on its magical, dangerous ways.

Most of their high school friends hadn't had a clue what they wanted to do after graduation, but that had never been a problem for either Lily or Aiden. Maybe it had been their confidence in those dreams, the belief that nothing could knock them off their chosen courses, that had finally allowed them to come together on the night before he left the island for good.

But Aiden hadn't missed the fact that she'd used the word *content*, not *happy*, to describe her state of mind.

He couldn't help wondering if still being single at thirty might have something to do with her choice of words, because she loved kids and had always made it clear she wanted a small brood of her own someday. But according to Bram, Lily didn't have a boyfriend now and had apparently never been truly serious about anybody.

Other than you, whispered his traitorous mind.

He firmly squashed that thought. "You could do anything you wanted, but you were born to fish lobster. You always said it was in your genes, or like you had seawater running in your veins."

Lily gave a little snort. "Yeah, well, don't forget it's in yours too. Centuries worth of ridiculously optimistic genes that make us think we can actually make a living dragging bugs up from the ocean floor."

He had the DNA, for sure, but it was no match for the impact of a drunken pig of a father. Still, Aiden had to laugh at her apt description of the lobstering life.

"Those genes must have somehow skipped my sister, though," she added.

Aiden didn't recall much about Lily's little sister. Brianna Doyle was two or three years younger than Lily and a bit of a princess. "What's Brie doing these days, anyway? Still here on the island?"

"Not likely," Lily scoffed. "Not when the closest Neiman Marcus is over a hundred miles away. No, she's a junior at an architectural firm in Boston and happy as a clam. By the time she made it to high school, Brie was almost as set on kissing the island good-bye as you were."

Yet another reference to Aiden's decision to leave the island. After all these years, it clearly still grated on her. "Bram told me your pals Holly and Morgan left here early too," he said. "So I guess I'm not exactly unusual on that score, am I?"

Lily's gaze slid down to her boots. "Well, at least they come back home for regular visits. Morgan and Holly are here now, and Brie will be back later today. She always comes home for Blueberry Festival weekend."

Aiden sighed. "I can't say I do that, can I?" *But you know my reasons.*

He'd refused to come back to the island even when his mother was still alive. Instead, he'd arranged for his mom and Bram to visit him, sending them plane tickets to Philly or whatever city he was playing in that was within a reasonable distance of Portland. But that meant he'd missed a lot of holidays and other milestone events with his family. It was the price he paid to avoid his father.

She surprised him by standing up and extending a hand, silently asking to be helped out of the skiff. Aiden stood and grasped her by both the hand and the elbow, making sure she had her footing on the pier before reluctantly letting her go. Even in her masculine-looking lobster gear, she was still cute enough and sexy enough to get his temperature running hot.

"I understood why you left, Aiden," she said. "So I'm sorry if I sounded like I was judging you."

"Thanks." He wasn't sure where she intended to go with this. The fact that she'd hoisted herself out of the boat made it clear she had something she wanted to say.

Lily put her hands on her nicely curved hips, her feet planted apart like she was about to give him a lecture. Aiden remembered that stance so well. Lily Doyle had been feisty as a teenager, and time hadn't changed that.

But she surprised him with her soft tone, sweetly

colored by that gentle island lilt she would never shake. "You still hate it back here, don't you? You've been away almost half your life, but it feels to me like not much has changed since we were kids."

As far as Aiden could tell, she wasn't bitter or judgmental. If anything, she sounded sad for him. "*Hate*'s a strong word," he said cautiously.

Was she right that not much had changed? Sometimes it felt like everything had changed. He'd left Seashell Bay fourteen years ago with his dreams in full bloom, a pro contract in his pocket, and the promise of a major-league baseball career. Now, that career was in tatters and his future in the game murky at best. The golden boy had come home with a decidedly tarnished luster.

"I wish you could see the island the way I see it, Aiden," she said, her green eyes so earnestly intense. "See the people the way I see them. Seashell Bay is such a beautiful place, and the people are just so damn decent, despite their faults. I hate it that your father took that away from you."

Aiden pressed his lips together, his tangled emotions keeping him silent.

"There's so much good here," Lily went on in a gentle but relentless voice. "So much that's right for the soul. You just have to be able to see it."

He wanted to. He really did, but he could still see her father stomping down the pier, eyes full of suspicion and fury. And then there was his dad, whose contempt and anger toward him—an anger Aiden had never fully understood—had colored everything about the place. There was too much ugliness in his past, too much darkness to ever make the island right for him again.

But he couldn't say that. Not all of it, anyway.

"The only good thing I see in Seashell Bay is you, Lily, just like always," he said, briefly cupping her soft cheek. "But you're right, nothing's changed for me. Nothing fundamental, anyway."

When Lily's pretty mouth pursed in dismay, it was all Aiden could do not to grab her and kiss away the pain—his pain more than hers, he suspected. Instead, he turned away to gaze across the channel and think about the complicated mess his life had become.

"Well, I really should get going," she finally mumbled. "It's getting late."

"Yeah, you should." He turned to face her and smiled. Hell, there was no reason to take his crappy mood out on Lily, the one bright spot in his life right now. "But will I see you at the Pot tonight? Or are you going to be too busy plotting my downfall in the race?"

Lily's laughter was sweet music as it echoed over the still waters of the harbor. "No and no. I'm sure I'll be too exhausted to hang out at the Pot."

It sucked that he wouldn't see her, but he couldn't deny the pleasure in hearing that she obviously wasn't doing the bar scene. He guessed that made him a jealous asshole when he had no right to be, but he could live with it. "That's a shame. But if you change your mind, I'll buy you a drink. Or two."

"I won't," she said as she climbed back into her skiff. "But maybe I'll see you at the Blueberry Festival tomorrow." Then she suddenly cut him a teasing smile.

"What?" he asked, as she yanked the outboard's starter cord and the little engine came to life with a cough and a puff of acrid smoke.

"I still remember how darn cute you looked when you were selling those pies at the festival for your mom," she yelled over the motor noise. "You did that every year until high school, as I recall. What a good little boy you were back then."

Aiden gave her a mock scowl as he used his foot to ease the skiff away from the pier. He not only remembered the blueberry pies he'd sold to festivalgoers from a goofy booth, he could still practically smell them and taste their summer sweetness on his tongue. Nobody could bake a blueberry pie like his mother, God rest her sweet soul.

He stood and watched Lily's skiff putter out to the channel, feeling like he had a strange hole in the center of his chest. Then he turned and retreated back up the dock until he hit the road again at a flat-out run.

Chapter 7

As Aiden pulled into O'Hanlon's boatyard, he glanced out at the spectacular view of the sun setting over the bay. Sinking fast, it streamed muted shades of purple and orange from the horizon, outlining in sharp detail the other nearby islands. He took a long look, enjoying the sound of the waves slapping against the shoreline and the total absence of traffic noise. He'd forgotten the deep quiet of the island, his memory wiped by years of city living. Then he got out of the truck and headed straight past the shop to the marina, where Roy Mayo would be waiting for him on *Irish Lady*.

When Roy called Aiden's cell and cryptically suggested that he and Bram might want to mosey on down to O'Hanlon's for a "private" chat, Aiden had been torn between suspicion and relief. Suspicion because, well, a cryptic Roy was never a good thing, and relief because Aiden was sick of seeing his brother—three-quarters in the bag after polishing off a six-pack—sucked into yet another online poker game. Bram was so obsessed it made Aiden want to puke.

Tired of fighting with Bram about it, Aiden had spent most of the afternoon before Roy's call meandering across the family land, refamiliarizing himself with the near-wild beauty of Seashell Bay Island. His parcel, in the middle of the most rugged part of the property, featured the steepest bluffs and the best views of the ocean. At the bottom of those dark bluffs, narrow beaches strewn with seaweed and driftwood dotted the coastline, broken up by groupings of rocks of all sizes, some as big as a pickup truck. He'd loved climbing those rocks when he was a kid, one of the few good memories of his childhood.

His feet had then seemed to gravitate toward one particular spot where someone in his mother's family had long ago cut a zigzagging trail down a more gently sloping portion of the bluffs, a path now so overgrown by wild brush that he barely recognized it. When he finally reached the bottom and stood on the rocky beach, he'd had to give himself a thorough check for any deer ticks he might have picked up on his trek through the dense foliage. Getting Lyme disease was an ever-present worry on an island with a sizable deer population, and he sure as hell didn't need to add that to his list of woes.

He'd turned his back to the ocean to gaze back up to the top of the bluffs, remembering one summer afternoon— he was thirteen, he thought—when he and his mother had gone for one of their long walks, eventually wending their way down that same path to the sea. While he'd skimmed flat stones over the water, his mother had talked dreamily about how this piece of land would be a perfect place for him to someday build his home. It wasn't just because it had a world-class view, she'd said. It was because she wanted her grandchildren to be able to slip easily down the bluffs to the ocean and play on the rocks and in the sea, learning to appreciate the awe-inspiring gift they'd been given by their ancestors over the generations.

That was the land that Bram and his dad wanted to sell to developers. His mother would have hated the prospect, fighting tooth and nail and with every ounce of strength in her petite body to prevent it from happening.

Aiden still got a lump in his throat whenever he thought about his mom and how unfair it had been that she'd been stricken down by heart disease while relatively young. But being back here in Seashell Bay, especially on the land she'd gifted him, made him miss her in an even more profound way. Mom had cherished every rock, every tree, and every ounce of soil on this little outpost. In his mind, she was forever connected to it, even a part of it.

And in some weird way, the island itself seemed to mock him, making her absence that much more painful.

Aiden crossed the boat yard to where *Irish Lady* was moored and climbed over her gunwale. Roy was sitting in a canvas chair in front of the wheel, his feet up on a plastic crate and a beer in his right hand. A beat-up Boston Red Sox ball cap was pulled low on his head, almost covering his eyes. Damn near everybody in this part of the country was a Sox diehard. Not once could he recall seeing anyone with a Phillies cap or T-shirt, despite the fact that a local boy played for Philadelphia.

Had played for Philadelphia.

"Working hard, I see," Aiden said.

"Don't sass me, boy." Roy pointed to a minicooler in the stern. "Help yourself to a cold one."

"Don't mind if I do." Aiden picked his way around some greasy metal parts and popped open the lid of the cooler, then reached in to pull a Shipyard from the melted ice. He wiped the wet bottle on his jeans and opened it. "So, what's up with the old girl that called for this urgent pow-wow?"

Don't tell me the tub isn't even going to make it to the starting line. That thought froze him with horror.

Roy exhaled a rattling breath. "Well, Mike and Jessie did a good job getting her cleaned up and back in the water, and I've been doing some tinkering today on the diesel."

Aiden lifted a brow. "Tinkering, huh?" With engine parts strewn all over the deck, it looked more like a rebuild to him. Or a massacre.

"Nothing too dramatic, but when I took her out to the channel this afternoon and gave her full throttle..." He shot Aiden a little sheepish grin. "Well, let's just say there was a bit of smoke. Do you want the technical details?"

Aiden grimaced. "I know dick-all about diesel engines and don't want to. Just tell me you're going to be able to fix it. In time for the race, obviously."

Roy put his beer down on the deck and sat up straight, leaning over to rest his stringy forearms on his khaki-clad thighs. "There's a bit of a problem."

Crap. Realistically, Aiden knew he had a damn good chance of losing to Lily, but it would really stick in his craw if he had to pull out because this geezer had annihilated his father's boat. "Spit it out, Roy," he said as calmly as he could manage.

"The damn power chip in the engine control unit is blown."

" 'Is blown'? You mean *you* blew it on the test run, after your *modifications*, right?" Aiden said through gritted teeth.

Roy picked up his beer and leaned back again, the definition of old-school casual. "Shit happens, son. You wanted me to make this boat faster, so don't start whining on me now."

Aiden wasn't whining, but he was definitely second-guessing his father and brother for their confidence in Rocket Roy. "Can you get a replacement and somehow put all this back together in time? And preferably for at least one test run before the race?"

"Sure, but there are chips and then there are *chips*. I can get a run-of-the-mill unit in Portland tomorrow, but if you really want to win this thing, you need to upgrade. And it's going to cost."

"And of course you can't get that kind of gem locally, can you?"

"Nope. The only place I could find the one we need is in Washington."

"D.C.?" Aiden said hopefully.

Roy gave an evil chuckle. "Washington *State*. Seattle area."

"Of course," Aiden muttered, his mind trying to calculate how long it might take to get the part on a plane to Portland, then get it over to the island, install it and complete the reassembly of the diesel. He didn't like the number he came up with. "I don't care what that chip costs, but can they put it on a damn airplane and get it here on time?"

Roy glanced at his watch. "I asked the guy out there to stand by until I got word from you one way or the other.

There's a three-hour time difference, so he might be able to get it here by first thing in the morning. If we're lucky."

"Then do it," Aiden said. No freaking way was he settling for second best, at least not yet. "If you get the chip in the morning, will you be able to get all this ready?" He indicated the mess of parts scattered around the deck.

"Hope so," Roy said. "I'll tell you one thing, son. If that new chip is as good as they say it is, we could get 30 percent more horsepower and more torque too. I wasn't sure it would work in this baby, but after talking to the manufacturer, it looks like we're a go."

The elderly man's sudden, enthusiastic grin slightly eased Aiden's worries. He sounded like he knew what he was talking about, and Aiden had to admit it was pretty awe-inspiring to see a man so engaged and enthusiastic in the tenth decade of his life.

Aiden extended his hand, and Roy rose and shook it. "Then give it all you've got, Roy."

The old rascal gave him a wink. "One more thing before you go. As far as Miss Annie knows, I'm playing poker at your dad's place tonight. So you're with the program, right, son?"

Aiden grinned. "You bet your ass I am, sir."

At its last get-together, the little group that met tonight in Saint Anne's-by-the-Sea Catholic Church hall had decided to call itself the Seashell Bay Smart Development Coalition, or SDC for short. Lily had come up with the name, figuring who wouldn't be in favor of *smart* development for the island? In truth, though, for her and most others in the group, smart development was pretty much synonymous with *no* development. She liked the island the way it was, and if that made her something of a dinosaur, so be it.

She'd arrived a little late for the weekly meeting, because she'd spent extra time with Josh Bryson at the dock, chatting about *Miss Annie* and her new modifications, before heading to her parents' place to wolf down dinner. After hitching a ride with Morgan and her father, Lily had rushed in to take her seat at the head table beside the SDC chairman, Jack Gallant, who also headed up the Seashell Bay Fishermen's Association, and the secretary, the real Miss Annie. Somehow, in a moment of weakness, Lily had let Gallant and her grandmother cajole her into taking on the role of treasurer, even though she had about as much financial know-how as a barrel of bait.

Feeling tired and grungy after a long day on the boat, Lily prayed for a noncontentious meeting. But she knew it was a prayer of faint hope. Most residents had no reluctance to voice their opinions forcefully and at length. Lobstermen in particular marched to the beat of their private drummers, and that made reaching a consensus—especially a speedy one—rarely possible.

The fifty-something, grizzled Gallant rapped his gavel twice on the laminated wood table where Lily had eaten many a church supper. "There's only one item on the agenda tonight," he said gruffly. "Getting our message out at the Blueberry Festival. It's the perfect opportunity to not only hand out the leaflet but to buttonhole people too. So we're going to need as many volunteers as we can get." His thick brows pulled together into a unibrow as he frowned, shifting his gaze around the room. "I expect everybody here to sign up."

"But Jack, there are some folks here who are for the car

ferry," Dottie Buckle piped up. She shot a scathing glance at Town Selectman Albie Emory, one of the island's elected politicians.

"Dottie, I meant everybody who supports our position," Gallant said patiently.

"Then why the devil didn't you just say so, Jack?" lobsterman Rex Fudge said, after removing his unlit pipe from his mouth. "You got to be clear about things—otherwise a fellow can get confused."

Lily swallowed a laugh. Rex was a sweetie but not the sharpest hook in the water.

Gallant turned to Miss Annie, fidgeting with her usual bottled-up energy as she kept squaring the edges of the stacks of flyers in front of her. "You and Lily can hand out the flyer and that other thing," he said with a boat captain's authority. He turned to face the audience again. "You'll each get one copy now, but you have to pick up your share of the rest of the flyers on the way out."

Lily and Miss Annie got down from the platform and quickly distributed the flyer and that "other thing" Gallant had mentioned—a set of talking points aimed at helping the volunteers make their case in one-on-one conversations over the festival weekend. While Lily was largely responsible for the content of the documents, she'd asked the local schoolteacher, Tessa Nevin, to do the actual wordsmithing.

When she got back to her seat, Lily pretended to read the documents like everybody else, even though she had them down by heart.

"Okay, Lily," Gallant said after it was clear most people had finished reading. Only Rex still had his head down, tracing words with a nicotine-stained index finger. "Over to you."

Lily had no intention of making a speech. Hell, people could read, couldn't they? "I think everything you see is pretty straightforward. If you've got any questions, ask them now, because I'm sure lots of folks would rather be down at the Pot than sitting here on these awful chairs." She smiled at Father Mike, the town priest, sitting quietly at the back of the hall. "Sorry, Father. You know how much we appreciate the use of the hall."

But I'd rather be soaking in a tub of hot water and bubble bath, a glass of red wine in one hand and an Amelia Peabody mystery in the other.

"You got that right, Lil. The part about going to the Pot, that is," head EMT and town carpenter Brendan Porter said from the back row. Then he grimaced and looked behind him. "No offense, Father Mike."

Fellow EMT Boone Cleary snickered and gave Brendan a fist bump.

Cal Merrifield held up his hand. Morgan's father, who used to own the Pot, now ran the B&B. "I hate to bring this up, but I think the flyer is a little one-sided," Cal said in a slightly high-pitched, worried voice.

Miss Annie bounced in her chair. "Oh, for God's sake, Cal, of course it's one-sided. We're trying to win the damn vote, not hold a college debate!"

Cal ignored the laughter that rippled through the hall. "Everybody knows a car ferry would bring a lot more business to the island. That would benefit everybody. This group is supposed to be about smart development. To me, that means we should be trying to preserve our way of life, but moving forward too."

"Ah, Cal, my friend," Lily's grandfather, Preston, said quickly, leaning forward and patting Merrifield's shoulder, "it sounds to my old ears like you want to have your cake and eat it too. You want the car ferry because you think it'll bring more guests to your inn, but you don't want the big resort they're talking about building on the Flynn land. The way I see it, though, you're just not going to get one without the other."

"You got that right, Preston," Forrest Coolidge said to Gramps from the seat beside him. "And that's why we better make sure we get off our duffs and win this vote. Hell, some of our families have lived and worked on this island for the better part of two centuries, and I'll be damned if I'm going to let some greedy mainlanders wreck it." His craggy face was grim. "Not on my watch."

As the room broke into applause, Lily couldn't help smiling at her grandfather and Forrest, by far the two oldest men in the room and perhaps the most ardent in support of the cause. She thought she'd like nothing better than to be just like them, still working hard to preserve the beauty and serenity of the island way of life well into her seventies and eighties.

Suddenly, one of the women in the room made a squeaky gasp as she glanced at the doorway. When Lily looked over, her stomach did a couple of backflips.

Aiden leaned against the doorjamb, casually dressed in a tight, white T-shirt and old jeans that did wonders for his brawny physique, an easy smile on his oh-so-handsome face as he stared at the head table. Stared at *Lily*. Heat crawled up the back of her spine and neck.

"Aiden," Jack Gallant barked, "are you lost?"

Some people laughed, but it died as they caught Miss Annie's lethal glare.

Aiden's eyes shifted to Gallant. "I just heard about the

meeting a few minutes ago, and I figured maybe I could learn something by sitting in." He smiled as he let his eyes roam around the room. "That is, if you folks don't mind. I know some Flynn mug shots might be hanging on local dartboards these days, so if you don't want me here..."

"No, you should stay," Lily interrupted to forestall any more discussion. "Everyone is welcome here."

"I appreciate that," Aiden said.

He doffed his Phillies ball cap and sat down next to Tessa, who gave him a shy smile. Aiden towered over Tessa's slight form.

When Aiden smiled back, a stab of irritation jabbed Lily hard. Schoolmarm Tessa was young, cute, smart, and *unmarried*. Because she wasn't a native of Seashell Bay, she and Aiden wouldn't know each other.

Yet, her mind whispered. And the smoldering jealousy that made her gut burn told her everything she needed to know about how much she still wanted Aiden Flynn.

Aiden had driven to the church fully prepared to bust Lily's chops for lying to him about what she was doing tonight. Too tired for meeting him at the Pot, but not too tired to help run a meeting about the future of Seashell Bay. Or lack of a future, it seemed to Aiden, since most of the locals seemed hell-bent on keeping the island in some kind of retro time warp.

When Bram told him about the so-called Smart Development Coalition and their meeting at Saint Anne's tonight, Aiden's irritation had briefly flared, thinking that Lily had deliberately *not* told him about the meeting. Did she figure he was so closed-minded that he wouldn't even listen to what her group had to say?

But then he calmed down and realized that it probably wouldn't have crossed her mind that he might be interested in attending a meeting of a group that was trying its best to throw a monkey wrench into the Flynns' plans.

He'd listened to the discussion, and it hadn't taken him long to figure out where almost everybody stood. After that, he'd focused on the other reason why he'd subjected himself to the local gabfest in the first place—the auburn-haired beauty at the head table, still driving him crazy after so many years.

Well, if seeing Lily again meant staying to the very end, he'd suck it up and do it. Lily was worth it.

Besides, he wouldn't mind talking to the girl seated next to him—the blonde that somebody had called Tessa. If he didn't miss his guess, she was a mainlander, or at least had been for most of her life, and he'd always been curious about people who actually chose to move *to* the island. It might give him some useful insights into the development question.

Finally, Jack Gallant—one of his dad's old drinking buddies but now supposedly a teetotaler—banged his gavel down and adjourned the meeting after inviting everyone to head out into the foyer where the church ladies had set up refreshments. Lily quickly slid behind Gallant and started helping Miss Annie distribute small stacks of the flyers to people who lined up at the front of the room.

"I'm Tessa Nevin," the pretty blonde said with an inviting smile as she extended her hand. "I teach at the school."

Aiden returned her smile and shook her hand, even though part of his focus remained on Lily, intent on making sure she didn't slip away from him.

"Nice to meet you, Tessa. When I went to school here, my teachers sure never looked..." He bit off the politically incorrect comment midstream. "I mean they were all quite a bit older than you." And not nearly as attractive, that was for damn sure.

Tessa's blue eyes sparkled with humor and understanding. "I just love it here in Seashell Bay. Even after several years, some days I still feel like I'm living in a dream world."

That had Aiden mentally blinking. For anyone under the age of sixty, Seashell Bay had always struck him as a place to escape from, not actively seek out. "I guess the lifestyle suits you," he said, as they made their way out to the foyer. The church ladies had set up a table with coffee, tea, and trays of homemade chocolate chip cookies and blueberry muffins.

Tessa grabbed two paper cups. "I'm sure Lily will be along any moment, but in the meantime, can I get you some coffee?"

Aiden winced. "Sure, thanks. But was I that obvious?"

Tessa's laugh was gently mocking. "Uh, *yeah*. I think poor Lily might have a few scorch marks on her clothing from your X-ray vision." She filled one of the cups from the big aluminum urn. "How do you take it?"

"Black," he said, a little embarrassed. "So are you and Lily friends?"

She nodded. "Lily is friends with everyone on the island. Well, almost everyone."

"Everyone but the Flynns, you mean?" He sipped the coffee. It was lukewarm but hit the spot.

"Your words, not mine."

Aiden grimaced. "Stupid damn feud."

Tessa flicked a worried glance at the other folks in the room, all caught up in intense discussions. "Absolutely, but a lot of people think it's going to get worse before it gets better, given these development issues. What do you think, Aiden? Did you learn something this evening?"

"I'm sure Aiden doesn't want to be put on the spot like that, Tessa." From behind them, Lily's voice was rich and darkly sweet, like the local honey that came from the island. Aiden had always loved listening to her talk, even when she was giving him a hard time.

"After all, he's only been back a short time," Lily added as she sidled between him and Tessa.

"You're right, Lily," Tessa said with a nod. "I'm glad you came tonight, Aiden. Hope I see you around."

"Don't forget to pick up your flyers, Tessa," Lily said. "And if you could sign up for duty time at the festival, that would be great. The list is by the door."

Tessa gave her a cheeky salute. "Aye, aye, Captain. All hands on deck for the festival, right?"

"I wish." Lily sighed as Tessa hurried away.

"Coffee?" Aiden asked. "Or better yet, can I get you to change your mind about having a drink with me at the Pot?"

She shook her head. "I can see you're still like a bull-dog about some things, but I'm afraid not."

"Well, when I know what I want, I go for it," Aiden said.

Lily's brow creased in a slight frown, as if his response puzzled her.

As she reached for a cup, he stared at smooth shoulders and arms showcased by a dark pink tank top that seemed vaguely familiar. How she'd managed to fish for all those

years and still retain such...*femininity*, he supposed
might be the word...was a mystery. He'd seen evidence
of Lily's strength as they loaded her skiff, but the years of
demanding physical work hadn't diminished her beauty
one whit. If anything, they'd given her an air of quiet competence he found incredibly attractive.

"Thanks for getting me off the hook with the schoolteacher," he said.

Lily waved it off. "Everybody is curious about what
you think and what you might do. So you can't blame
Tessa for that. But if I were in your shoes, I wouldn't want
people bugging me about it everywhere I go."

Combined with what he'd heard at tonight's meeting,
her words stirred something inside Aiden, something
that had been brewing ever since he got to the island. "I
appreciate that, Lily, but can you really put yourself in
my shoes?" he said after a moment. "Because it feels
like you're absolutely convinced there's only one right
answer—your answer."

She jerked back slightly, but he wasn't backing down
now that he'd laid it out there. Sure, it might cause a
blowup, but this was too important to ignore any longer.

"Not everybody is buying into your vision," he continued. "I could see that here tonight, even at a meeting
of your own supporters. This stuff is complicated, not
black and white—not for anyone and certainly not for my
family."

Lily frowned as she searched his face for several long
seconds. "No, I just don't buy that, Aiden. Saying something is complicated is usually just a way of ducking
responsibility for taking a position."

Ouch. The girl could throw a solid counterpunch.

Still, what she said was crap. "Didn't I hear you just tell Tessa that I shouldn't be put on the spot? Or was that just bullshit?"

Lily took a step back, her eyes widening at the bite in his words. "No, it wasn't bullshit. I meant that you shouldn't be put on the spot tonight. But you're obviously going to have to make a decision soon enough. That's why you came back here anyway, right?"

"Nobody needs to remind me of that."

"Yeah, well, sitting on top of that fence must be pretty uncomfortable."

"I didn't ask for this mess, but I'll deal with it my own way, Lily. In my own time. You should be happy I didn't sign on to the damn deal already."

Lily shook her head slowly, as if exasperated. "Whatever, Aiden," she finally said, her gaze shifting toward the meeting room where only Gallant, Miss Annie, and a couple of others remained. "Excuse me. I should get back in there and pack up."

Lily was clearly itching to get away from him, which sucked, but he had only himself to blame. "I guess I'll see you at the festival tomorrow then," he said.

She'd started to turn away, but his comment brought her back around. "Really? And here I thought you might be tied up working on your boat." Her eyes narrowed to emerald slits. "You and Roy, that is."

He almost choked on a sip of coffee, unable to speak for a few moments. "There really are no secrets on this little rock, are there?"

"Not many, and not for long. You should know that."

This was not good. "Lily, Roy would like his involvement to stay on the down-low, for obvious reasons."

She gave him a grim nod. "I'm not a snitch, so it's not going to come from me. Miss Annie *will* find out though, and she'll be right pissed."

Aiden figured she was probably right. "I like the old guy, and I don't want him to get into too much hot water for helping Bram and me. Are you pissed at him too?"

She cocked her head, as if studying him. He hadn't a clue what she was thinking, but there now seemed to be a trace of amusement in her eyes.

"Me? Pissed at Roy because he's working on your engine? Oh, no, not at all, Aiden. Not at all."

As she turned and left him standing there, Aiden got the feeling he was in over his head when it came to both Lily Doyle and to understanding what the hell was going on in damn Seashell Bay.

Chapter 8

$\mathcal{H}$is bare feet up on the weather-beaten railing of Bram's deck, Aiden sipped coffee and gazed out at the placid, midmorning blue of the Atlantic. It promised to be a hot, steamy day, though hardly by Florida, Texas, or even Philadelphia standards. For coastal Maine, though, it would be a scorcher.

The Blueberry Festival organizers would be plenty happy with the weather. When Aiden lived in Seashell Bay, everybody—and especially the kids—had looked forward to festival weekend, and he doubted it was any different now. Who didn't love games, races, lemonade, candy floss, and enough sugary baked goods to guarantee a stomachache? He still remembered his mom's famous blueberry pies usually selling out by the time the dew was off the grass.

Even as a surly teenager, Aiden had loved the festival, welcoming the escape from the usual, hellish days on his dad's boat.

He was looking forward to the festival today too, for one obvious reason—seeing Lily again. Most of the

morning he'd been thinking about her and the little...
well, fight they'd had last night. He regretted that he'd
brought it on and that he'd snapped at her. It was no mystery why he'd done it though. The more he pondered the
choice between selling and holding on to his inherited
land, the more he realized that the consequences of his
decision would spread far beyond his own family. Though
he hadn't needed Lily to remind him of that, he shouldn't
have let her get to him either.

As easy as it would have been to sit on the deck all day,
it was time to head down to the festival. Besides, better
to keep busy than hang out here all day, waiting for his
agent to call with some news. Or spend another day fighting with Bram.

When he went back into the cottage, he rinsed out his
cup and then took a glance into Bram's bedroom. His
brother was still snoring, dead to the world after spending half the night drinking with a couple of buddies from
the mainland. Aiden shoved his feet in his sneakers and
headed out, striding quickly up the long lane to Island
Road. Ten minutes later, he turned up Bay Street, and at
the top of the gentle hill, he stopped for a moment and
gazed straight across the channel to the nearby islands
and the mainland shore far in the distance.

Aiden sucked in some deep, calming breaths, allowing
the serenity of the view to seep into him. He had to admit
that there was beauty here in Seashell Bay—serene and
close to timeless in its unchanging tranquility. While most
of the houses he'd passed on the way up the hill reflected
the island's bare-bones economy, they were almost all
maintained with close attention and loving care, the paint
kept fresh and the gardens flourishing. Just ahead on his

left, he could see the elementary school and library, which probably still housed the computers his mom had suggested he donate several years ago.

He chuckled as he passed Gracie Poole's property. The clapboard house hadn't changed much since he left. The heavily treed yard, on the other hand, was an even bigger mishmash of lobster fishing gear and any other paraphernalia that struck the fancy of Gracie and her husband, Seth. Dozens of buoys in every conceivable color pattern hung suspended from tree branches on fishing line or pot warp. Dories, oars, nets, wooden and mesh traps, and even a couple of old outboards had been set up in rough and ready displays. All kinds of weird items like matchbox cars, beach pails, and both rubber and wooden ducks were set up on stumps and stands, adding even more color to the wild and relentlessly cheery tableau. Aiden couldn't help thinking about how the neighbors in his Philly suburb would react to a yard like Gracie's.

As he approached the landing, he spotted Lily's red Jeep near the little seasonal store that sold a few basic groceries and a lot of beer. Aiden had already resolved that the first thing he would do when he saw her was apologize for his testy response last night. Nothing about the situation with the Flynn land was her fault, and she had every right to be concerned about his take on it. Yeah, she could have stifled that cutting remark about ducking responsibility, but Lily had never been one to pull her punches, not even as a teenager. That fiery, honest quality had drawn him to her back then, and damned if it didn't have just as powerful a pull on him now.

Oh, yeah, and her killer body too.

* * *

Finding a sliver of temporary shelter from the sun at the side of the Rec Center, Lily whipped off her sun visor and dabbed at her forehead with the handkerchief she'd borrowed from her dad. She thought briefly about heading back to the SDC's little tent to get out of the sun for a few minutes, but she could see it was still jammed. Jack Gallant and Miss Annie had been holding court there since early morning, and those two, along with close to a dozen volunteers, had been handing out the flyers and telling folks in stark terms what a car ferry would mean to Seashell Bay.

The younger volunteers, like Lily and Morgan, had taken the tougher assignments. Since eight o'clock, they'd been approaching people in the parking lot, at the food tents, and inside the Rec Center where artisans from both the island and mainland had set up booths to hawk their crafts and wares. She was pleased with the results so far, because the majority of people seemed to hold the car ferry proposal in about as much esteem as Congress. The battle, however, was far from won. The ferry's supporters might seem to be in the minority today, but that didn't mean there weren't lots of folks who would quietly vote in favor when the time came.

And predictably, the SDC wasn't the only organization hitting on the townsfolk today. Bay Island Properties had produced a glossy folded leaflet that Selectman Albie Emory, along with Boyd Spinney, a long-time crony of Sean Flynn's, were handing out under a professionally designed banner that read, A SEASHELL BAY CAR FERRY— IT'S TIME.

How creative.

Time for what, Lily wondered? Time for developers to make a ton of money by messing up her island home? *Not as long as I'm still breathing salt air.*

The crowd down front was swelling as each hour passed. At least a couple of hundred people were now crammed into the space between the ferry dock and the row of low buildings on the other side of the parking lot. The laughter and screams of kids jumping and rolling around in the bounce castle filled the air, punctuated by the occasional startled yell from the dunk tank as one of the festival volunteers splashed down into the cold water.

"Hey, you look like somebody who could use a drink. A peace offering too, after the way I bit your head off at the meeting last night."

Lily had been so focused on the busy scene in front of her that she hadn't noticed Aiden's approach from the side. With a crooked, charming smile that still had the power to make her heart flutter, he thrust an open bottle of water into her hand.

"I'm sorry about that," he said.

"Thank you for both the apology and the water, but a cold beer would go down even better right about now," Lily joked.

She took a long swig from the chilled bottle. Knowing that Aiden had just drunk from it too made the exchange seem strangely intimate. It had been a very long time since they'd shared a drink like that.

"A beer could definitely be arranged, but I'm guessing you have other plans for your afternoon." He nodded toward the flyers in her hand.

God, he looked good, casually dressed in a faded, close-fitting T-shirt that lovingly outlined his hard chest and baggy cargo shorts that couldn't hide his muscled legs. She felt a little light-headed just looking at him, and she knew it wasn't from being out in the heat.

She sighed, letting go of the enticing image of sharing a beer with Aiden on a secluded beach. "I'm afraid so." She had several more hours to spend preaching the cause, not to mention a turn in the damn dunk tank.

"I really like your shirt," Aiden said, his gaze sliding down to her chest. "It's pretty funny."

Given the heat in his eyes, she wasn't sure whether he was staring at the cartoon on her shirt or at what was underneath the thin fabric. Thank God she was wearing a slightly padded bra in preparation for the dunk tank, since she could already feel her body instinctively reacting to him.

She'd been getting laughs and compliments all morning on the shirt that she'd bought online to be a conversation starter at the festival. On a basic white background, the designer had overlaid a rough drawing of someone's hand pulling a smiling lobster out of a holding tank. The lobster was saying to his two buddies still crawling along the bottom, "Did you hear that, guys? I'm going to a party in a hot tub!"

"I thought it might make people laugh before I pummel them into voting down the car ferry," Lily said.

His gaze narrowed thoughtfully, telling Lily that something was weighing on him. She knew that expression from the years she'd spent mooning over his handsome face, and it was yet another way that Aiden Flynn hadn't changed.

She handed him back the bottle. "Okay, tell me what's on your mind."

"You always know when something's bothering me, don't you? Well, it's no big deal. I just hate sitting around waiting for my agent to call." He let out a ghost of a laugh. "Not much patience, huh?"

Lily's heart ached for him. Baseball had always been his dream, and he sure didn't sound ready for it to be over. "I'm really sorry, Aiden," she said, investing it with all the feeling she could. "I hope something works out for you soon."

But not too soon, she thought guiltily.

He shrugged. "Baseball can be a tough business. Kind of like lobster fishing in that way, right?"

Lily would never have made the comparison, but she saw his point. Still, as a fisherman, she worked only for herself and controlled her own destiny—or at least as much as the lobster stock and the elements would allow. Aiden, on the other hand, could be moved around by his bosses like a piece on a game board. A well-paid piece, to be sure, but could money truly compensate for the kind of freedom she felt on the deck of *Miss Annie*?

Taking in his brooding expression, Lily tried to lighten things up. "Maybe, but I bet you don't smell as bad as I do after a day at work."

"I'm not sure about that," Aiden said. "Between a post-game locker room and a lobster boat after a day at sea, I'd say it's a toss-up."

They both laughed, and just like that the tension between them broke.

"So, have you checked out the blueberry pies and the other baked goods?" She remembered how much he'd loved that part of the festival. As a tall, gangly teenager, he'd been able to inhale awesome amounts of food and never put on an ounce of fat. "If not, you'd better get over there before everything's gone."

Aiden ran a hand over his awesomely flat stomach. "I'd better steer clear. Nobody's going to want to pick up an old, fat ballplayer."

She had to stifle a laugh at his serious expression. Aiden Flynn was six feet four inches of lean, toned muscle, with about as much fat on his entire body as there was on one of her thighs.

When Aiden gave the water bottle back to her, their hands fleetingly touched, and her heartbeat picked up several notches.

Suddenly, applause broke out behind her, and almost as one, the crowd started to push in that direction. She turned and stood on her tiptoes to see above the heads blocking her view. Twenty feet away, Lily glimpsed Miss Annie and Gracie Poole in front of the car ferry supporters' tent. Her granny was stabbing her finger at a heavyset man wearing a white shirt and tie. "Aiden, I need to see what's going on over there."

"Right behind you," Aiden said.

Lily pushed her way between bodies until she was standing just beside her grandmother. Behind her, Aiden was using his elbows to clear some space for both of them.

"Why can't you just build your resort, Dunnagan?" Miss Annie said at close to full volume, her red face a startling contrast to her white hair. "We can live with that. We just don't need a big, stupid subdivision too, and we sure don't want your car ferry."

"You tell him, Miss Annie!" somebody behind Lily yelled.

"So that's Kevin Dunnagan," Aiden said in Lily's ear.

"Head honcho of Bay Island Properties," Lily said, though she'd never met him. "The jackass."

Dunnagan wiped his sweaty brow with a white handkerchief. "Look, ma'am, our plan for Seashell Bay can't just be broken up into pieces. It's a unified, well-planned whole."

"*Hole* is the right word for it," Gracie said to laughter.

"This is the only way development can happen," Dunnagan said, obviously frustrated. "All three pieces work together—the housing estates, the resort, and the car ferry, all very carefully planned to enhance the island. You folks will love it if you just give us a chance. Trust me, it'll be great."

Much of the crowd started to boo loudly.

"Great for *you*, you mean," Lily said over the din. "Sure as hell not for us."

Miss Annie looked at her and grinned. Behind her, Aiden squeezed her shoulder. She wasn't quite sure what that signified. Was he being protective, concerned for her in the crush of the crowd, or warning her to back down?

"You're wrong, miss," Dunnagan said, shaking his head. "The economic benefits to Seashell Bay will be huge. Think about all the construction jobs—not just the resort but hundreds of single-family homes. There are a lot of people here who could use the work, especially during the months when there's no fishing, right? We're talking upwards of a hundred jobs at the peak of construction, and plenty more when the resort opens. And when new businesses start up—and they will—that'll bring more jobs too."

"Sounds pretty damn good to me," someone shouted. Lily didn't recognize the voice.

When the crowd started to murmur, Lily's stomach tightened.

"Most of those are just temporary jobs," Miss Annie scoffed. "But the damage to the island will be permanent."

"What damage?" Dunnagan said calmly. "More jobs, more businesses, more stores—that doesn't sound much like damage to me."

"Spoken like a man who only cares about money," Miss Annie shot back.

"He's got a point though, Miss Annie," Carol Peabody said. "My boy can't work on a fishing boat, so work's hard to come by around here."

Lily had sympathy for her twenty-year-old son, Terence. Too scrawny to haul lobster traps, he'd been mostly unemployed since he graduated high school. But turning Seashell Bay upside down wasn't the answer.

"We're going to stop you from ruining this island, Dunnagan," Miss Annie vowed. "Just you watch us."

Dunnagan heaved a big sigh. "Then you'll have to win the car ferry vote. And if you do, the whole deal is off."

Miss Annie turned her back to him and pulled herself up onto her tiptoes, looking out at the crowd of at least fifty people behind her. "Why don't we tell Mr. Dunnagan what we think right now? If you don't want the car ferry, let's hear you say no!"

Loud shouts of "No!" resounded from the crowd. Lily figured maybe two-thirds of the people had joined in, but it was hard to tell. And many were shaking their heads.

Miss Annie swiveled to face Dunnagan again. "There's your answer."

"The only answer we care about is what happens on voting day," Dunnagan said. "We'll be working real hard to convince people right up to the moment they mark their ballots."

"So will we," Lily said in a loud voice.

"You tell him, granddaughter," Miss Annie said proudly. "All right, folks. I think we've made our point. Let's go have some fun."

The tension quickly bled away as the crowd around them thinned. Dunnagan started talking to Albie and a few of their supporters, and several shook his hand.

Lily turned around, straight into Aiden's muscular chest. "Let's get out of here, okay?" she said, feeling breathless.

"Sure." Again, Aiden used his size to good effect, guiding her through the crowd to a patch of shade.

"That was...interesting," he said.

Lily gave him a grim smile. "I suppose it was inevitable. We really shouldn't be politicking and fighting at the Blueberry Festival, but this is so important..." She ended with a shrug.

"I get it," Aiden said. "But let's talk about something else, okay?"

Lily nodded.

"That bounce castle looks like fun," he said with a grin. We never had that here when I was a kid. Maybe we should try it out."

He waggled his eyebrows at her in a comic leer, clearly intending to make her laugh. Unfortunately, she found the idea of rolling around with him on fluffy, bouncy cushions, getting all hot and bothered, an all too-enticing idea.

She nudged him into moving as she saw Morgan, soaking wet, climb out of the dunk tank. "The bounce castle? I guess you're still a kid at heart, aren't you?"

He fell into step beside her. "I play a game for a living, don't I? Some people say ballplayers never grow up."

Despite their differences and all the years apart, Aiden was still easy to talk to, and they were quickly falling back into old patterns, alternating between the serious and the light-hearted. "You seem pretty grown up to me, Aiden."

At that moment, Aiden clearly caught sight of Morgan coming toward them. His eyes had locked onto her drenched form. "Jesus," he breathed.

"Down, boy," Lily chided. She couldn't really blame Aiden for practically freezing at the sight of her friend. Morgan was beautiful all the time, but in a wet T-shirt—well, her form could only be called spectacular. No wonder so many young and not-so-young guys had surrounded the dunk tank for her turn on the plank.

"Sorry," Aiden said, his gaze swinging to Lily. "But I wasn't really thinking about Morgan."

Lily stopped and turned to him. "I find that hard to believe," she said wryly.

"Don't, because I was thinking how much I'd like to see Lily Doyle as soaked as Morgan is right now."

He looked like he meant every word, making Lily's breath catch in her throat. A bolt of delicious sensation shot through her body, curling a ribbon of heat around her insides. She fought it, arching her brows at him in mock disdain. She refused to let him see how badly she was still crushing on him.

"Good Lord, what I won't do for charity," Morgan sighed as she trudged up to them, pushing wet hanks of hair back from her face. A yellow towel was loosely draped over her shoulders. She wore a teal color T-shirt and tight khaki shorts that showed off her gorgeous legs.

"You're such a trouper," Lily said.

"Well, you are too," Morgan said. "And since it's your turn, you'd better get over there instead of jawing with Aiden Flynn."

Aiden clamped a big hand on Lily's shoulder. "Well, how about that for a wish coming true? Maybe I'll even take a throw or two, since it's for charity."

Lily hadn't seen that big a grin on his face for a long time.

"Forget it, buddy. No professionals allowed."

"Hey, I'm not even a pitcher," Aiden protested.

Lily wagged a finger at him as she backed away. "Throw one ball and you die," she threatened.

When Aiden made a sad face, she couldn't help laughing.

At the dunk tank, Jessie Jameson—the duty volunteer—helped her up the short flight of steps at the back, and Lily swung her body onto the white, vinyl-covered plank, gingerly taking her seat. Her toes barely touched the water, still cold despite the heat of the sun pounding down on it. Mesh in front and on the sides of the enclosure protected her from any badly aimed throws.

There were never any problems getting volunteers for the tank. At least a couple of dozen people every year signed up to take a turn getting soaked—some kids, more than a few men, but mostly the young women of the island. Yes, it was sexist, but it was all good fun too, and the women hooted as loudly at the guys as the men did at them.

The crowd around her was made up of mostly young guys in their twenties and thirties, along with a handful of small boys. Morgan had disappeared, no doubt to change back into the yellow sundress she'd worn earlier. Aiden stood alone, staring at Lily intently. She wagged her finger at him in warning again, even though she smiled.

"My turn," Dylan O'Hanlon said as he picked up one the yellow balls off the grass.

From about fifteen feet away, Mike O'Hanlon's seven-year-old son threw the ball hard at the yellow backstop, aiming for the small, round target in the middle—a mechanism that would release the seat and dump her into the water. Lily sucked in a deep breath, ready to be dunked, but Dylan's throw missed by a couple of feet and bounced back off the plastic tarp surrounding the target.

Aiden flashed Lily an evil grin and stepped forward. "That was a good try, kid, but I could help you with some tips if you like."

Lily rolled her eyes. She had to give Aiden credit. Maybe he wouldn't try to dunk her himself, but he had no scruples helping a kid do it.

"Uh, okay, mister," Dylan said tentatively. "I guess." He handed Aiden the ball.

"That's Aiden Flynn, dummy," his older brother, Rory, hissed loudly, giving him a punch on the arm. "He plays for the Phillies."

The kids might have missed Aiden's little flinch, but Lily didn't.

Forcing a smile, Aiden tossed the yellow ball between his hands like a juggler. "What's your name?"

"Dylan O'Hanlon."

"Your dad runs the boatyard?"

Dylan nodded.

"I know him." Aiden wrapped an arm around the boy's shoulder. "Okay, Dylan, it's important to lock your eyes on the spot you want to hit and keep them there until the ball has left your hand. But let's start by lining up your left shoulder with the target."

Aiden gently rotated Dylan into the correct position. "Now, watch me, okay?"

He took up the same position, standing right beside Dylan. As he reared back, Lily flinched, wondering if he was going to throw the ball after all.

Aiden took a forward stride and followed through with his arm but didn't release the ball.

"See, Dylan?" he said, handing it back to the boy. "You lead with your elbow, and you make sure you're throwing over the top, not sidearm or anything like that. You were kind of slinging it just now."

Dylan looked up at Aiden. "Will you help me more if I miss again? I really want to dunk Lily."

Aiden patted his back. "Sure, but don't worry. You're going to nail it this time."

Lily watched their easy interaction with both amusement and fascination. Aiden was good with kids, but then again, that shouldn't have surprised her. He'd been great with Bram growing up and had always gotten along with kids in the lower grades too. Unlike some of the jerks she'd gone to school with, Aiden had never teased the little ones and had always been happy to toss a ball with them.

Dylan squeezed the ball hard and squinted at the target, tight-lipped.

"Relax, buddy," Aiden said. "Don't strangle the ball."

Dylan nodded, easing his grip. The boy sucked in a deep breath, wound up like Aiden had instructed, and let fly. The ball thudded into the target, and with a shriek, Lily slid off the seat and splashed into the water as the crowd let out a loud cheer.

She'd pinched her eyes closed as she submerged but opened them again after her head dipped below the surface. A bunch of kids were rushing to stare at her through the clear plastic window in the front of the tank. Aiden, naturally, was right behind them.

Lily got her feet under her and thrust up out of the water.

"Thanks, Mr. Flynn," Dylan enthused. "That was awesome!"

"No problem, kid," Aiden said in a smug voice.

Lily laughed as she swiped water from her face. She scrambled out of the tank and waited until Jessie reset the seat. Aiden moved quickly to her side as she dripped water all over the already soaking grass.

"Way to rock the wet T-shirt, babe," he said in a low voice, dramatically patting his chest as if his heart was thudding. Then he gently brushed back her wet hair and let his fingers drift down over her throat, coming to rest on her banging pulse. She shivered, and it wasn't from the dunking.

"I gotta say you just made my week—maybe the whole damn month," Aiden said. His gaze slid downward as his mouth curled up in a sexy, openly appreciative grin.

Instinctively, Lily crossed her arms over her chest as her nipples responded enthusiastically to his hot gaze. Now she knew for sure that she was in way more trouble than she'd thought.

Chapter 9

$\mathcal{B}$ram, put the life jacket on," Aiden barked. "You know the rules. They're mandatory in the race." Reversing, he guided *Irish Lady* away from O'Hanlon's dock as his brother carelessly coiled the nylon mooring lines.

"It's too hot and bulky," Bram complained. "I'll put it on later."

Christ. His brother never encountered a rule he didn't want to challenge. "Fine, but if you get us disqualified, I'll feed you to the lobsters. I'm not losing this race because you're acting terminally stupid." Aiden swung the boat around so the bow pointed past the town landing to Paradise Point, where the races would start. Ahead, a large cluster of boats of varying sizes cruised slowly or idled alongside the course.

Bram joined him in the pilothouse. "My life jacket isn't the problem, bro, it's me. You should have asked one of the little dudes in town to be your second man in the boat instead. You could have saved a lot of useless weight."

Aiden had insisted Bram race with him, because he knew how much his brother wanted to be there, despite his protests. It was Aiden's chance to partly make up for their father never letting them race.

"And deny you the opportunity to gloat at Lily as we smoke past her?" Aiden replied.

"I bet Lily's going to have Morgan with her. Those two combined probably don't weigh much more than one of us."

Aiden pushed the throttle forward. Their boat class was scheduled to race in ten minutes, and he should have been in a waiting position before now. "If Roy's magic works, we'll kick their asses anyway."

Bram reached forward to unlock one of the windows and push it open. "Remember Dad telling us stories about the old days before they came up with all these rules? Guys used to knock out all the windshield glass to reduce drag, or even rip up deck boards to cut weight. Then they'd have fights on the dock because one guy ran too close to another at some point in the race."

"Ah, the good old days," Aiden replied sarcastically. As a young, rough-and-ready lobsterman, Sean Flynn must have been in his element.

But there were no good old days in Aiden's memories of *Irish Lady*. He still knew every square inch of the boat, especially the stern where he'd busted his ass day after day. In the summers, Sean had often let the sternman go and made Aiden work for pocket change, saving the 20 percent he would otherwise have paid the helper. Lots of times he'd make Aiden miss school to fill in, even on days when he should have been studying for exams. Aiden didn't mind when he knew it was hard to find a substitute, but usually it was clear that his father didn't even bother to try finding someone else.

Though Aiden had made sure that nobody had seen it today—not Bram, not Roy, not Mike O'Hanlon—just taking that first step onto the gunwale of *Irish Lady* had been hard. And it still felt lousy. She was a good old boat and had provided food for his family for a very long time, but if it were up to Aiden, he'd probably sink her.

"Dad loved it, didn't he?" Bram said. "And speaking of the old man, the bastard is all over me, Aiden. He's acting like it's my fault that you're not coming around on the land deal, and I'm fucking sick of the pressure. I just want you to make up your mind soon, okay?"

Aiden corrected his course by a few degrees to steer well away from the rocky coastline north of the town landing. He hated that Bram had to bear the brunt of their father's impatience, but he wasn't about to be pressured into anything. "Sorry, man, but you've got to deal with it. Dad is what he is."

"Easy for you to say, dude. You can get out of here anytime you want. Me, I've got to live with the old man and put up with all his crap."

"Really?" Aiden shot back, his patience with that attitude fraying. "I don't see anybody holding a gun to your head, bro. You could move out tomorrow. What's stopping you?" *Unless you've already frittered away every last dime you inherited from Mom.*

Bram glared silently for a moment before turning away. He reached down and flipped open the small cooler he'd stashed under the bulkhead. "How about a beer?"

"No thanks. I need to have 100 percent concentration if we're going to have a hope of winning."

Besides, it had taken Aiden all morning to shake off the hangover he'd inflicted on himself last night. The

Blueberry Festival had been fun for a while, and he'd enjoyed seeing Lily again, even though she'd pulled a Houdini after he came on to her a bit at the dunk tank. So after chatting with a few of the locals and downing a blueberry muffin he'd picked up at the baked goods table—and the muffins were as good as he remembered—he decided he needed a break from the island. Needed a break from his father, from Bram, from everything in Seashell Bay. Since the best way to accomplish all that was to head into Portland, he'd called one of his high school teammates—a guy he'd kept sporadically in touch with over the years— and arranged to have a beer after dinner.

After a stroll around the Portland Harbor area and a leisurely meal at DeMillo's floating restaurant, he'd met up with Adam Wicker at Bull Feeney's pub on Fore Street. Wicker had been a star pitcher for Peninsula High when Aiden was a sophomore outfielder. After playing college ball at Florida State, he'd been drafted and signed by the Indians. But not long after he finally made it to the majors, he blew out his arm, had surgery, and never regained his velocity. By twenty-six, he'd retired and returned to Portland to coach baseball at Peninsula.

Aiden had long felt sorry for his old friend, but as one beer turned to three or four, he started to revise that opinion, because it was clear that Adam was totally content with his life. Married with a three-year-old son, he'd recently been hired as head coach of the University of Southern Maine baseball team. That was a very big step up from high school coaching.

Adam had listened sympathetically when Aiden filled him in on his lack of success in finding a new team. When Adam suggested he consider coaching at a university when he was ready to retire as a player, Aiden had quickly moved on to another subject. He'd thought that coaching might someday be in his future, but in college? That possibility had never once crossed his mind, maybe because he hadn't gone to college. But Adam certainly seemed happy with where he'd ended up.

After midnight, the well-lubricated ex-teammates promised to keep in better touch and headed off in their different directions—Adam in a cab to his home in South Portland and Aiden on foot to the water taxi dock.

"The boat sure ran great on the test run this morning," Bram said, uncapping his beer.

Aiden, Bram, and Roy had headed out far enough to avoid getting tangled up in heavily buoyed areas and opened *Irish Lady*'s throttle to full speed for almost two minutes, covering about the same distance as the three-quarter-mile racecourse. The old girl had really torn it up.

"Roy was happy," Aiden said. The old guy had practically danced a jig.

"Man takes pride in his work," Bram said.

Aiden caught sight of *Miss Annie* idling beside another boat. Morgan was talking to Boone Cleary in *Foolish Pride* while Lily stared forward as four boats in another class tore past on their way to the finish line.

It was all serious business for his girl.

Aiden got a little mental jolt at the way *his girl* had slipped so easily into his head, but he forced himself to shake it off and concentrate on the upcoming race.

The lobster boat races were more of a party than a fierce competition, from what he remembered. A dozen guys had rafted their boats on the side of the channel, lining them up with the buoys that marked the finish line. Most had food tables set up in the stern so the spectators could eat, drink, and watch the races, moving from boat to boat in a continual party. Onshore, islanders watched from flimsy cabanas or, slathered in sunblock, from beach chairs and loungers. Kids and dogs were everywhere, on boats, on the shore, and swimming in the channel. Farther away, about half a dozen of the older kids amused themselves by jumping off the public dock, cannonballing down into the chilly water with gleeful abandon.

When they were young, Aiden and Bram had watched the races with their mom from Paradise Point Beach, cheering their asses off for their father when he raced. Not because they'd wanted him to win, but out of mortal fear of what the old bastard would do when he got home after a loss. Aiden could still remember how his mother had plastered a cheerful look on her face to mask her frustration with her husband's lousy moods, pretending to friends and neighbors that nothing was wrong.

As if everybody on the island hadn't already formed a good idea of how Sean Flynn treated his wife and kids.

Blocking out the miserable memories, Aiden guided *Irish Lady* alongside Lily's boat. "Let's say hello," he said to his brother.

"Let's try to psych her out," said Bram.

Aiden shot him a hard look. "Forget it. As if that would work with Lily anyway."

Bram shook his head. "Shit, man, you can't think straight when it comes to that woman. What are you trying to do, give the old man a coronary? You gotta steer clear of Lily. Even if you somehow got in her pants, it wouldn't be worth the grief."

"What I do is none of his business," Aiden growled. "Or yours, for that matter."

Bram grimaced. "Look, if you need to get laid, you can do it with just about any other babe on this island and Dad wouldn't give a damn. Anybody but Lily Doyle. Hell, why don't you check out Morgan? She's hot, she's unattached, and she's not out of bounds."

"Out of bounds?" Aiden said, incredulous. He suddenly felt like he and Bram were fifteen again, still under their father's tyrannical thumb. "What the hell is wrong with you?"

"I gotta live with the guy. You don't."

"Unbelievable," Aiden said. He turned to wave at Lily and Morgan.

Lily looked gorgeous and confident in a nautical blue-and-white-striped tank top, tiny white shorts, and white sneakers. Her hair was pulled back into a high, bouncy ponytail. She was in her natural element—in her lobster boat with the wind in her face as she gazed over the gunwale.

And the look on that lovely, determined face was as clear as the blue sky over their heads. *Get ready for a beat-down, Aiden Flynn.*

As *Irish Lady* approached and the other boat, *Foolish Pride*, moved away, Morgan leaned closer to Lily and whispered in her ear. "Aiden looks a little worried."

Lily studied the object of Morgan's analysis. Even though Aiden handled the boat with competence, his rather grim expression told her he was anything but relaxed. "Well, he should be. The guy's never raced a boat in his life. It still amazes me that he agreed to do this."

Morgan tucked a few loose strands of hair behind her ear. "You really think he'll honor the bet once you tell him what you want? He could just up and leave. There's nothing holding him here."

Lily's instincts denied that. "Aiden will make good on the bet."

He was that kind of guy when she fell in love with him all those years ago, and she refused to think he was anything less now. Still, she supposed it could just be wishful thinking on her part. What did she truly know about him now and about the life he'd led since leaving the island?

"What if we lose?" Morgan said. "Roy might have worked some magic with that old beater. We've all seen what he can do with golf carts and outboards."

Lily scoffed. "Sure, he's a genius with the little stuff, but when it comes to big diesels, his record is sketchier. And I'm not sure poor old *Irish Lady* is going to be quite up to Roy's brand of creative fixes."

Morgan's eyes started to dance with laughter. "Maybe not."

"In my memory, Aiden only knows one way to play," Lily said. "Flat out. Pedal to the metal. It might be more than *Irish Lady*'s engine can take."

Morgan nodded. "Go big or go home."

"Exactly, and this time, let's hope it's go big *and* go home," Lily said, "because I don't want to have to find out what Aiden has in store for me if I lose this wager." Especially if what she suspected he wanted turned out to be true. Lily's defenses against him were already on very sandy soil, and a full-out seductive assault on his part might well bring them tumbling down.

With a bright smile fixed in place, Lily turned to wave

to Aiden as he maneuvered his boat to a rocking stand-still a few feet from hers. Bram tossed a trio of white boat fenders over the gunwale for protection in case the boats drifted too close and bumped.

"Hi, guys," Morgan called over the idling motors. "Ready to race?"

"Totally, and you'd better get ready to bounce around in our wake," Aiden replied with a teasing grin. Lily was relieved to see a genuine smile on his face. As high as the stakes were, she did want him to get some pleasure out of the beautiful day.

"Hold real tight onto something, Morgan," he added, "because you're going to be rocking and rolling."

Lily laughed. "Actually, she'll need a free hand to wave at you two as you fade into the distance behind us."

Aiden glanced up at her mast and let out a surprised laugh. "Is that flag supposed to intimidate people?"

For the race, Lily had hoisted a skull-and-crossbones pirate flag on her mast instead of her usual Stars and Stripes. "Aye, matey, because my *Miss Annie* always takes the booty and never takes prisoners."

Aiden grinned. "Booty, huh?"

As Lily rolled her eyes, the starter boat tooted its horn twice to let the entrants in the next race know it was time to line up at the start buoy.

"Good luck, guys," she said, pushing her throttle forward. "We'll see you after the race—if you're not too depressed to stick around."

"Can't wait," Aiden shouted over the rumble of the big engines.

Four boats had entered their diesel class, one less than last year when Lily won. Besides *Miss Annie* and *Irish*

Lady, there was *Foolish Pride* with Boone Cleary at the helm of his father's boat, as well as a boat from the mainland that Lily had never seen before—*Miss Fortune*. It was a cheeky name that Lily, always borderline superstitious, thought might be tempting fate a little too much.

She lined up her boat more or less in the center of the course, parallel to the thirty-foot starter craft. Aiden brought *Irish Lady* next to her on her starboard side, and Cleary slid *Foolish Pride* in between Aiden and the starter boat. Finally, the mainland boat, freshly painted in brilliant white and fire engine red, motored behind Lily and took up its position on her port side. Lily just prayed the newcomer didn't blast past her to the front. She had every expectation that with Roy's tuned engine, Aiden would be plenty fast off the line, and she sure didn't want to get caught in two strong wakes.

Moving slowly, the four boats formed a line, and the skippers watched for the go signal. When a race crewmember on the starter boat judged that no boat was pushing itself ahead of the pack, he dropped his flag with a dramatic flourish.

When Lily pushed her throttle forward, *Miss Annie*'s diesel rumbled up to a roar.

"Woo-hoo!" Morgan yelled at Aiden and Bram. "See you dudes later!"

Her bow rising as she quickly built speed, *Miss Annie* poked ahead of *Miss Fortune* and *Irish Lady*. Lily gripped the wheel hard and kept her eyes focused on a point on the horizon so she'd run a true course, not veering into either of the neighboring boat's paths. She'd rely on Morgan to tell her what the other racers were doing.

"We've got a length on *Miss Fortune* already, and we're

half a length up on Aiden," Morgan called out over the din of four straining diesels. "I think Boone might be out of it already."

Lily fought the urge to glance back over her shoulder to catch a glimpse of Aiden. *Stick to business, Lily. Win this thing.*

There wasn't too much chop in the channel, but even still, their flat-out speed made for a jarring ride. Lily was glad she didn't have to contend with another boat's wake too. Not yet, anyway. Aiden, on the other hand, had to deal with hers.

They'd already passed the halfway marker. In the lead, *Miss Annie*'s diesel hummed, and her hull cut easily through the waves like the champ she was. But out of the corner of her left eye, Lily saw *Miss Fortune* cutting into her lead.

"Aiden's nearly even with us!" Morgan yelled.

Lily took a quick look to her right. Morgan hadn't exaggerated. *Irish Lady* was right beside *Miss Annie*, and there was nothing she could do about it—her boat was already at full throttle.

This cannot happen.

Lily started sweating, all her muscles tensing up. All she could do was watch as Aiden, looking totally commanding and in control, powered his boat past hers and into the lead. *Miss Fortune* was hanging in there too, if not closing the gap a little.

"Look at that asshat Bram," Morgan yelled in a frustrated tone.

Lily cut a glance to see Bram wave at them as he did some stupid, little dance steps. "Just ignore him. This isn't over yet."

Irish Lady's stern cleared Lily's bow and took a lead of more than a length. But it only lasted seconds before Lily heard something loud—some sort of horrible choking sound—ahead of her, and *Irish Lady* slowed like she was trying to cut through sand. In little more than a heartbeat, *Miss Annie* had shot past Aiden's boat, obviously now powered only by momentum.

Though Lily had half-expected something like that to happen, it was still a shock. She'd tried to catch Aiden's eye as she passed but his head was down, fixed on his controls.

"His engine's shut down," Morgan shouted, stating the obvious. "But forget Aiden, Lily. *Miss Fortune*'s right with us now."

Had the mainland boat been keeping something in reserve for the final few hundred yards? The finish buoy was so close, but it seemed to Lily like it was a mile away. There was nothing more she could do but hope. *Miss Annie* was topping thirty miles an hour, a touch faster than she'd ever run in a race. The sweet girl didn't want to be beaten any more than Lily did, and Josh Bryson had obviously done a great job of getting her ready.

But *Miss Fortune* took matters into her own hands within seconds of the finish line buoy, powering smoothly past to win by a boat length.

"Ah, hell," Morgan moaned as Lily powered down. She put her hand on Lily's shoulder and gave it a little squeeze.

"Don't worry about it," Lily said. "It's no big deal. The better boat won today."

Right now, she didn't give a hoot about the trophy or the bragging rights that went along with winning the race class. All she could think about was *Irish Lady* and her captain and the humiliation Aiden had to be suffering right now. She swung *Miss Annie* around in a tight circle, her heart aching for him. Yes, she'd wanted to beat him, but not like this.

"What are you doing?" Morgan asked as Lily steered back down the course.

"I'm going to give Aiden a tow."

Her friend gave her a puzzled look. "I thought the race officials have a boat on standby to do that."

Lily shook her head. "In the big race venues they do. But not here. In Seashell Bay, neighbors help each other out. Remember?"

Morgan had been on the mainland for such a long time that she occasionally forgot some of the island ways. Her pal wrinkled her nose in acknowledgment. "Right. Of course, I feel bad for Aiden, but at least you won the bet."

At the moment, Lily wasn't quite sure how she felt about that. Now that it had become real, she suddenly had a horrible attack of nerves. On top of his ignominious defeat, she would now be asking him to do something she knew he would loathe. Her stomach did a few somersaults at the idea that he might think her a total bitch to even ask.

She made another 180-degree turn as she approached *Irish Lady*, lining up in front of Aiden and then reversing until her stern was a few feet from the other boat's bobbing bow. Aiden had obviously figured out what she was going to do since both he and Bram clambered around to the bow, ready to receive the tow ropes.

Since Lily hadn't towed anybody for years, her nerves jittered a bit at the thought of damaging either *Miss Annie* or *Irish Lady*, or both. Towing was a dangerous business. Lobster boat hulls weren't designed for it, and the engines didn't produce the kind of torque ideal for pulling something of equal weight. But she'd be damned if she was going to let somebody else with a bigger boat step into the breach instead. She was fully responsible for this situation. If she hadn't concocted the bet, *Irish Lady* wouldn't be stranded in the channel, and Aiden and his father wouldn't be facing a potentially huge repair bill.

Maybe she should forget all about the bet. Hadn't she done enough damage already?

"Hey, thanks for the help, ladies," Aiden said as Lily pulled two coils of rope from a compartment in the stern.

Lily peered anxiously at him as she hurled one rope across the narrow gap between the boats. "I'm really sorry, Aiden."

He caught the rope in his big, capable hand. "Thanks. For about a minute there, I really thought we had you beat."

"You almost did," Lily said as she tossed the second rope at Bram, who was glowering and muttering under his breath. "Your old girl showed some real spunk, and you handled her beautifully."

Aiden cut her a rueful grin as he started to secure his line to one of the forward cleats. "Thanks, but it wasn't exactly a great feat of seamanship. Anyway, did you beat the other guy?"

"Sadly, no." Lily could hardly believe how unfazed Aiden was by the calamity that had struck his boat or by his loss in the bet. Where she'd feared possible anger and recriminations, he was giving her nothing but smiles and concern for whether she'd won or lost.

She started to tie off her ends of the ropes to cleats on *Miss Annie*'s stern rail.

Aiden came up from his crouch, bracing himself against the gentle swells rocking their boats. "So, are you going to tell me what I have to do for you now or do you want to keep me in suspense?"

His smile was easy and assured, but Lily thought his dark eyes reflected some concern too.

While she didn't want to play coy with Aiden, there was no way she was going to have this discussion by exchanging shouts between boats, nor did she intend to have it in front of Morgan and Bram or anyone else.

"Could we talk about that tonight at the festival social?" Lily said in voice she hoped would reflect more confidence than she felt. "I presume you're going to be there?"

Aiden's eyes widened, as if the thought hadn't crossed his mind. Maybe he didn't even know about the big party and dance at the VFW Hall that had marked the end of the Blueberry Festival every year for the past decade. She suspected Bram might not have mentioned it, because she couldn't remember the last time Aiden's brother or father had shown up at the social.

Aiden didn't respond for a few moments, simply staring at her with a slightly puzzled look. But then he shot her a crooked grin. "I guess I am now, Lily. In fact, I wouldn't miss it for the world."

Chapter 10

$\mathscr{T}$he evening peace was shattered by a squeal of brakes and then a crunch of loose gravel. Aiden knew who had just pulled up and didn't bother getting up from his seat on the porch.

"Hi, Dad," he said when Sean Flynn stomped around from the driveway.

"I want to talk to you, but I need a drink first," his father grumbled by way of greeting.

Because the old man could never have a conversation without being well lubricated, it seemed. "I'm not going anywhere," Aiden replied, as his dad headed inside.

He shifted in the uncomfortable deck chair, regretting that he hadn't left for the Blueberry Festival social before his father rolled up. Hell, maybe he should just split now. He couldn't wait to see Lily, and not just because he'd finally learn what prize she would claim for beating him in the race.

Still, leaving now would just piss off the old man even more, and that made no sense. The guy hadn't just dropped by to shoot the breeze. Not unless he'd had a personality transplant.

"Your sack-of-shit brother is asleep," Sean growled as he kneed the door open, a glass in one hand and a lit cigarette in the other. "Tell me how I managed to get such slapped asses for sons." He set his glass on the flat, narrow railing and sucked hard on the cigarette before flopping down onto the other chair.

"Maybe we picked it up from you," Aiden said. "You know, Dad, for a guy who wants my support on his precious land deal, you've got a funny way of showing it."

"Don't give me that crap. You're a Flynn, just like me, so you'll do whatever the hell you want whether I kiss your ass or not. Don't expect me to get warm and fuzzy with you all of a sudden. I'm not a hypocrite, and I'm not your sainted mother."

Aiden snorted. "That's for damn sure. But you are wrong about one thing—I'm nothing like you." At least he hoped to God he wasn't.

His father waved a hand, sending even more smoke wafting in Aiden's direction. He'd always hated the acrid sting of cigarette smoke, even as a little kid.

"At least you boys didn't turn out to be weak little pussies," the old man replied in a smug tone. "You can thank me for that, not Rebecca."

That brought Aiden to his feet in a rush. "Don't ever talk about Mom like that, you hear me?" he snapped, looming over his father.

He hated the way the old man had treated his mother, always so sharp-tongued and critical. Why Rebecca Flynn had stayed loyal to her husband was one of the mysteries of the universe, as far as Aiden was concerned. "Just say whatever it is you came over to say. I'm heading down to the dance in about two minutes."

His father peered up at him, looking oddly disconcerted. Then he seemed to shrug it off. "What the hell happened out there today, anyway? Roy said that engine was purring like a damn kitten this morning."

Aiden struggled to dial back his anger. "It was. And in the race, everything was going fine until it blew. Maybe *Irish Lady* just wasn't up to it. Roy probably tried to get more out of that old diesel than he should. Our fault, right?"

"Can't blame Roy for giving it a shot." Sean slugged back a drink. "Shit happens. It's just too bad you had to lose to a damn Doyle."

"It's not a problem, Dad."

His father waved his cigarette. "We've got a hell of a lot bigger things to worry about."

Aiden moved away from him, staring out at the calm sea, dreading what was coming next.

"Look, Aiden," Sean said, "you need to get serious about the future of this family." His face was already going red, his eyes bloodshot and full of anger.

"Go on, I'm listening," Aiden said.

His father swigged his glass dry and then slammed it down on the rail. "I just don't get why you're screwing around instead of getting on with making a decision. It doesn't make any damn sense. Bram says he's explained everything to you six ways from Sunday, and you've seen the plans. What the hell else do you need to get your ass in gear?"

Aiden had already heard enough. He leaned against the rail, crossing his arms over his chest. "You think the only thing I've got on my mind right now is your land deal? Well, my baseball career might be about to circle the drain, so excuse me if I'm not 100 percent focused on your dreams and your timetable."

Sean lumbered to his feet too, visibly wincing. It was another indication that the heavy smoking and drinking, combined with a hard working life, had aged his father beyond his years.

"My dreams? Dammit, this isn't about dreams. It's about our future—your brother's and mine. We've only got one asset left, and we've got to take advantage of it—right now, while we've got a good deal on the table."

"You think I don't know all that?" Aiden said. It was bad enough having to be responsible for Bram, but as much as he hated the idea, he knew the old man needed him too.

"Then what's the problem? Just do your duty to the family. And it's not like there's nothing in it for you. Hell, you'll make a real nice chunk of change from the sale. I figure since the Phillies cut you loose, you might need it." He finished with a trace of a sneer.

"Good old Dad," Aiden said bitterly. "Always so supportive."

Sean snorted. "Oh, suck it up. You had a pretty good run—hell, when you get right down to it, you did better than I thought you ever would."

"That doesn't say a hell of a lot, since you never thought I'd make it in the majors. But hey, you didn't know shit back then, and you still don't know shit now."

Sean tossed his cigarette butt all the way to the rocky slope below, then poked his finger into Aiden's chest. "What I know is that Bram and me are screwed unless you get your head out of your ass and sign onto this deal."

Aiden turned away again, throttling back the impulse to give his dad a hard shove. "This discussion is over for now. I'm going down to the dance."

"Yeah, sure, so you can sniff around Lily Doyle some more?" his father called out, as Aiden headed off. "I'd be real careful if I were you. Sure, she's a nice piece of ass, but don't you ever forget she's a Doyle and you're a Flynn."

Aiden spun around in the drive so hard he kicked up gravel. "Like I said before, I am a Flynn, but I've never been like you and I never will be. So deal with it. Let me tell you something else, Dad—I can't wait to get the hell off this island and never hear another word about your sick, dumbass feud." He stabbed a finger in his father's direction. "And if you ever slag Lily that way again, you might be on the receiving end of a fist for once."

When he was a kid, anything close to what he'd just said would have earned him a smack in the face or a punch to the back of the head. Now he just heard a few mumbled curses that rolled off his back as he walked away, but it was still hard work keeping his father out of his head. Because despite their nasty little argument, Aiden still worried about him, especially because there was a very good chance that Sean would finish the half bottle of scotch on the kitchen counter. His dad could never say no to a drink.

Or a whole bottle.

He turned back to the house with a sigh. "Dad, you're already half drunk or worse. Stick around here and have some coffee, okay? Don't try to drive home like this."

Sean waved Aiden off. "What I do is none of your goddamn business."

Aiden shrugged, knowing how useless it was. "Okay, well, see you later."

But he only made it to the edge of the deck before the

door creaked open and Bram clumped out. "Jesus, man, your agent's on the phone. Damn thing woke me up, but I'm going back to sleep so switch it to vibrate, okay?" Not exactly a pretty picture in his soiled T-shirt and sweat shorts, his brother shoved the phone into Aiden's outstretched hand and went right back inside.

Aiden's heart rate doubled in a nanosecond. "Dude," he said into the phone, trying not to sound too excited.

"Aiden, did I get you at a bad time?" Paul Johnson's words came out low and flat.

Shit. After almost ten years of working together, he knew every tone and nuance in his agent's voice. Paul definitely wasn't calling with happy news.

"I'm not going to like this, am I?" He forced himself to take a deep breath.

"No, I'm afraid the Orioles and Royals both passed. They're going to promote some guys to fill their gaps. I'm sorry, man. I really pushed hard for you."

Bringing up a youngster from the minor leagues was a cheap move that teams often used to cope with injuries to their regulars. Aiden didn't like it, but it didn't surprise him either.

"I know you did," he said, grateful as always for Paul's dedication. "But somebody's eventually got to need a veteran for the stretch run. There's still time, right?"

His career couldn't be over. Not yet—not when it seemed like yesterday that he'd played his first game in pro ball. How could he be done already when he still had fire in his gut and a lot of baseball left in him?

Paul's sigh echoed over the line. "Buddy, I hate like hell to have to say this again, but remember what I told you about having a backup plan?"

Aiden shook his head, as if his agent could see him. "Come on, Paul, are you really telling me that absolutely nobody's going to sign me?"

"Aw, hell, Aiden, I didn't say that. But you don't want me to start stringing you along, do you?"

"No," Aiden said gloomily.

"Look, man, this sucks big time. But we can say that until I lose what's left of my hair and it won't change squat. I can't get anybody interested right now, and the odds on that changing aren't great. Not next week, not next month, and probably not even next season. Your numbers have been going down, and the GMs are just too leery of your health to take a risk."

Paul always laid it out straight, which was one of the reasons Aiden had stayed with him over the years. But that didn't mean he didn't feel like puking at his agent's assessment. And unfortunately, Paul Johnson—one of the best in the business—was rarely wrong.

He found it impossible to hold back his bitterness and frustration. "You think I need a backup plan? Well, I guess my plan is to see if there's a little junior college or high school in the Ozarks or some other place in the boonies that could use a baseball coach. What the hell else can I do?"

Paul didn't answer immediately. Maybe he thought Aiden needed a moment to get his head on straight. He was probably right.

"There are still some options," his agent finally said. "Not at the major-league level, but maybe I could get some team to add you to the roster for minor-league depth. Or if worse comes to worst, I could try to hook you up with one of the independent-league teams."

Aiden's gut twisted tighter. Every word felt like a rusty knife slicing through him.

"Or there's always Japan," Paul added.

Aiden sank back down into his deck chair, staring at the ocean and the rugged beach below. The serene view in the fading twilight seemed to mock him.

"Japan? Really?" he asked, incredulous.

"Look, I'm just saying it's an option. Their Pacific League uses the DH position. It'd be an adjustment, sure, but if you had some success over there, it would probably make it easier to get the teams here interested again."

Maybe, but it was a long shot. It was uncommon for an American player to return to the majors once he'd been relegated to playing in Japan. If he were on the way out, Aiden figured he'd rather get on with life instead of trying to prolong his career in humiliating fashion.

"Look, Aiden, you need some time to think. So kick back and try to enjoy your time up there, okay? When you're ready, I'll be here for you. Just like always."

"Yeah, I know. Call me if anything changes." Aiden stabbed the End Call button. His dad just looked at him, for once having the brains to keep his mouth shut.

Great. Just great. Stuck on this godforsaken island with no job and no prospects.

And a big-ass decision to make that would profoundly affect the life of every person on Seashell Bay Island.

Including his.

The band—four local guys and a young female vocalist from the mainland—were blasting out a steady beat of soft-rock classics that even the old-timers seemed to enjoy. But Lily couldn't focus on either the music or the conversation at her table. She was too busy watching the front door of the crowded VFW Hall, her nerves crawling with a weird combination of anticipation and dread as she waited for Aiden to show up.

Lily and Morgan had arrived two hours ago and Holly a few minutes later. Morgan had claimed a table in a corner at the rear of the room, and soon Brett and Laura, along with their old friend Ryan Butler, home for a brief vacation, had joined them. Lily's sister, Brie, had arrived soon after that, sitting with Lily instead of at a table with their parents, Miss Annie, Roy Mayo, and a few other oldsters. After the evening kicked off with speeches by members of the festival organizing committee, the boat race chairman had presented the trophies and prizes to the winners. Then the dancing and serious drinking had begun.

Lily had watched with regret as the skipper of *Miss Fortune*, a fisherman from Boothbay Harbor, collected the hardware she had won the previous two years. Along with the winner's trophy came a hundred gallons of diesel fuel donated by the East Bay Lobster Company. While Lily didn't much care about the trophy, her dwindling checking account would have seriously thanked her for the savings on fuel.

Her gaze once more drifted to the front of the hall. Had Aiden decided to skip the social after all? It was getting late, but she found it hard to believe he wouldn't show up after his promise to meet her. Then again, he could have returned home to a truly nasty blowup with his father, since Sean must have been spitting nails at both the loss of the race and the damage to *Irish Lady*'s engine. As she conjured up the worst-case scenario, she could even imagine that a disgusted Aiden might have jumped on a late ferry and left the island for good.

"Maybe he decided to give the social a miss after all," Morgan whispered, clearly reading her thoughts. "He might be too embarrassed by what happened this afternoon."

Lily wasn't buying that theory. "He sure didn't look embarrassed when we towed *Irish Lady* to O'Hanlon's. But I'm a little worried that he might have gone home to some awful fight with his father."

"Hey, what are you two whispering about over there?" Brett Clayton boomed out from the other side of the table in a slightly slurred voice. He gave Laura a little nudge with his elbow. "Lily's been practically jumping out of her skin waiting for the baseball hero to show up."

"Shut up, Brett," Laura said, loud enough for the people at the neighboring tables to glance at her. "I hardly ever get a night away from the Pot, and I'm not going to have you go spoiling it. So watch your motoring mouth or I'll be cutting you off." She invested that warning with a meaningful glare. Brett gave Laura a sheepish look and retreated into sullen silence.

"I'm looking forward to seeing Aiden again," Ryan Butler said from beside Brett. "It's been a hell of a long time." Ryan, a Seashell Bay local who'd joined the military right out of high school, had arrived on the same boat as Brie yesterday for his annual visit to his folks.

"Me too," Brie piped up. "He's awesome cute, isn't he, Lil?" Her annoying sister flashed her a mischievous grin.

Lily had told Brie absolutely nothing about Aiden, other than that he'd be racing against her today. Brie, though, had clearly wormed a lot more information out of one or more of Lily's girlfriends.

Her beautiful baby sister, decked out as usual in her gorgeous designer clothes, almost always made Lily feel like the proverbial ugly duckling. Still, she figured she'd cleaned up pretty nicely for the social, and she actually felt halfway attractive. Her pale green polka-dot dress with its tight bodice and short, flirty skirt—bought at a discount store in Portland—had won her a few admiring glances from the men in the hall as she took to the floor for dances with several different guys. Without doubt, though, her sister Brianna had once again stolen the show, with her Boston salon haircut and her designer outfit. The cost of the sleek linen dress and Kate Spade sandals would have probably kept Lily in fuel and bait for two weeks.

Lily loved Brie to death, but she often wondered how they could have possibly come from the same gene pool. Finishing the remains of her beer, she stood, smoothing her skirt. "Time to powder my nose," she joked to Morgan.

"Want me to come?" Her friend had obviously read her troubled look.

She managed a weak smile. "Thanks, but I actually just want a few minutes alone, okay? Maybe I'll grab a little air." She really had no need to use the rest room.

Morgan nodded and gave Lily's hand a quick squeeze.

Avoiding the tables crowded around the room, Lily hugged the wall as she slid toward the double doors that opened into a foyer at the front of the building. The dance floor was rocking, and all the tables were full. If there were two things islanders loved, it was drinking and dancing, and the festival social was a grand occasion for both.

The committee had decked out the hall with the usual blue-and-white streamers and balloons, and it had hung advertising posters from East Bay Lobster and a half-dozen other festival sponsors. The blueberry basket centerpieces on the table were a tradition too, but except for those rather meager decorations, the hall retained its usual no-frills atmosphere.

Just as Lily reached the doorway, Aiden strode into the foyer. They both stopped as if they'd run into glass walls. Aiden's mouth had been set in a grim, hard line, but then it started to curve into something like a smile. Lily's tense muscles started to relax when she saw his expression soften.

"Hey, you're not leaving yet, are you?" he said, coming close. He towered over her, and his commanding height always gave her a bit of a pleasant shock.

And, boy howdy, did he ever look good in close-up.

Aiden wore a light blue cotton shirt. The sleeves were rolled up to his elbows, exposing his tanned, powerful forearms. The top two buttons were open to reveal just a glimpse of hard, male chest, lightly dusted with black hair. His chinos showcased a lean waist and long athletic legs. The shirt and pants were clearly expensively tailored, but he also wore beat-up old Sperry Top-Siders, which saved him from looking just a little too perfect and a little too removed from island life.

He was totally, completely, hot.

Lily's mouth went a little dry as she answered him. "Uh, no. I just needed a little break from all the noise."

He glanced over her shoulder into the hall. "Or is it just a little too dull in there for a wild woman like you?" he teased.

"Actually, it's fun," she said after a brief hesitation. Though she'd been waiting for him all night, a sudden attack of nerves left her tongue-tied. But if she tried to put off telling him what she wanted from him any longer, she would probably go into full meltdown. "I guess the first thing you'll want is to find out about our bet."

He shook his head. "No, the first thing I want is a drink. It's been a day, as they say around here."

Ouch. Not just his words but his expression had her worried. Maybe she'd been right to fear that a battle had erupted with his drunken jerk of a father. The fact that she would have caused it made her feel slightly sick to her stomach.

He pressed his hand against her lower back to shift her around. "We can talk about the bet later. Right now I just want to have a beer and hang out with you."

Short of digging in her heels and dragging him into a discussion he didn't want and, truth be told, neither did she, there seemed to be no choice but to go with the flow. Lily had never liked ducking a problem, but this was so clearly not the time to hit Aiden with something he would probably hate as much as a root canal.

No, make that half a dozen root canals.

"Sure," she said, sounding a little breathless. Not that she blamed herself for her squeaky tone, not with his big, warm hand resting just above the swell of her bum. "We'll squeeze in another chair at my table. People are really looking forward to seeing you."

Aiden's sceptical expression suggested he didn't think that was truly the case.

As they moved through the noisy hall, Lily leaned into him to make herself heard above the band. "Holly and

Laura and Brie are there, and so are Brett Clayton and Ryan Butler. Remember Ryan?"

Aiden scanned the room looking for the table in question. "Hell, yeah. When did he get here? To the island, I mean."

"Last night, on the same boat as my sister, unfortunately." Lily let out an exasperated laugh when Aiden lifted his eyebrows in a silent question. "Brie talks about him constantly. She thinks he's such a hunk, and her, uh...enthusiasm is getting a little tiring."

"Ryan's a solid guy. He broke my home run record at Peninsula."

Aiden's hand moved to Lily's bare upper arm and wrapped around it in a grip that felt gentle but possessive. She had to resist the urge to melt into his big body.

"Is he still in the army?" Aiden added. "Last I heard he was finishing up another tour in Afghanistan."

That would have been over two years ago, when Aiden came home for his mother's funeral. "I never ask him what he's doing anymore, because he ducks those sorts of questions. Our Mr. Mystery Man, Morgan calls him."

When they reached the table, Lily hung her purse over the back of her chair as Aiden shook hands with the men and hugged the four other women. When he got to Ryan, they gripped each other in a bear hug. Getting the drift, Brett and Laura shifted over to make space for Aiden to sit between Ryan and Lily. For the next few minutes, the two men leaned close, hunching over in animated conversation while Morgan and Holly fetched a round of drinks for the table.

Lily had to admit they were quite the sight—two big, ridiculously gorgeous guys, both full of a self-confident masculinity that would have most women mooning after them like idiots.

Aiden and Ryan spent several minutes deep in a conversation that seemed all about sports. Lily was just starting to get irritated at being ignored—irrationally, she told herself—when Aiden suddenly turned to her. "Dance with me, Lily," he said in a deep, smoky voice as his gaze raked over her.

Blunt. Decisive. Hot.

Because it was getting later in the evening, the band had started to do a few down-tempo numbers from their playlist. Lily recognized the opening lines of the song—Aerosmith's "I Don't Want to Miss a Thing"—and knew exactly why Aiden had suddenly asked her to dance. Though the tune was a slow-dance staple, what were the odds that the band would play the one song she'd come to associate with him? Although they'd never officially dated, they'd danced a lot at some of the Portland high school dances the spring he graduated and, for some reason, especially to this particular tune. To her, it had always been their song, and he'd obviously remembered too.

When Aiden got up, holding out his hand, she felt everything inside her go soft and shivery. She snapped a quick glance at Morgan, who nodded her support with a wry smile.

Sucking in a deep breath for courage, Lily stood on rubbery legs and let Aiden guide her into the middle of the suddenly jammed dance floor. Everybody liked the slow dances, young and old. Even Miss Annie and Roy hustled onto the floor—evidently Granny hadn't murdered Roy yet—as did Lily's mom and dad.

When Aiden's arms came around her, she let out a

sigh, only then realizing she'd been holding her breath. Sliding into his embrace was so easy, so natural, that it happened without any conscious thought or movement on her part. She remembered the feel of him as if it was yesterday, and she couldn't help glancing up at him with a rueful smile.

This time, though, there was a difference. He was no longer a teenager but a man, with a hard, muscled body and a maturity about him that made him even more appealing. Heat flared in his dark gaze, and his right arm went firmly around her back, pulling her against him with a controlled, irresistible power. Lily rested her cheek on his broad shoulder and closed her eyes, breathing in his clean, familiar scent and letting the years melt away as she remembered how wonderful it had felt to be in his arms.

The scary part, of course, was how good it *still* felt. It was even better, actually, because now she knew what she'd been missing. Their bodies meshed perfectly together, her curves fitting just right against his tough, masculine frame. Everything inside her went deliciously weak, and she leaned into him, instinctively seeking support.

"You remember, don't you?" he whispered, his warm breath caressing her ear. He dipped a bit, rubbing his bristled cheek against hers.

She would have laughed at the idea of ever forgetting if her throat hadn't gone tight with emotion. She remembered everything about their time together. No matter how brief those episodes had been, it had changed her forever. Aiden had rocked her world.

"Of course I do," she murmured back. "I'll never forget it."

He pulled her even closer as they circled the floor. Her breasts rubbed against his hard chest, making her entire body tingle.

"I feel the same way," Aiden said in a husky tone that rumbled right through her. "Even after all this time."

His words robbed her of what little breath she'd managed to hold on to. What did he mean? Was this simply a walk down memory lane or something more meaningful? She leaned back against his arm, searching his face—now gone all serious and intent—for the answer.

"Oh, Jesus, will you look at that." Her father's gruff voice, right next to Lily, had her practically jumping out of her shoes. She jerked her gaze over to see her parents dancing right next to them.

"Oh, no," Lily's mother groaned, craning around. "Tommy, the old so-and-so's got that look in his eye."

Suddenly, Aiden stiffened. He let out a low curse, loosening his grip on Lily. She whirled around to face the problem, already guessing who had "that look" in his eye.

Sean freaking Flynn, his white shirt half-untucked and stained with what looked like mustard, standing at the edge of the dance floor and stabbing an accusing finger in their direction. Instantly, Aiden stepped in front of Lily and planted his big frame as a protective block against his father. She rested a comforting hand against his back and leaned around him to get a better view.

When Aiden took a step forward, so did her father.

Panic spiking, Lily grabbed at her dad's hand, but he shook her off. "Stay out of it, Dad," she warned.

"No, you stay out of it, girl," her father barked. "This isn't a woman's fight."

Her mother slid over and wrapped her arm around

Lily's shoulder. "Your father can handle himself, sweetheart. You know this isn't the first time he and Sean have gone at it."

Lily gritted her teeth. "I am so sick of this bullshit."

But part of her acknowledged that maybe her mother was right. Maybe her father and Sean Flynn needed to have it out, once and for all. But this time Aiden was caught squarely in the middle. And "once and for all" never seemed to happen, not when it came to their hardheaded fathers.

Sean staggered closer, his meaty fists clenched at his sides. His bloodshot gaze flicked back and forth between Aiden and her dad, his red, contorted features gleaming with sweat. The man looked like an absolute wreck.

"I had to see it with my own eyes," he slurred at Aiden. "My son with...with...*her*." He pointed around Aiden at Lily. "My son chasing a damn little Doyle skirt."

When Lily's dad plunged forward, Aiden restrained him with a blocking arm. "Don't, Mr. Doyle. It's me he's after, not you or Lily."

He stepped between the two older men who were both snorting like mad bulls. When his father took another menacing step forward, Aiden shot out a warning hand. "You need to go home now, Dad. Right now." His tone was glacial.

"He can't come in here like that and insult my daughter!" Lily's dad fumed. "Damn no-good drunk. He's been getting away with this crap for too damn long."

Aiden cut her dad a lethal warning glance over his shoulder. "That's probably true, but I hear that particular door swings both ways, sir."

Though his voice remained calm, Lily could tell Aiden

was probably itching to slug one or both of the potential combatants. She knew he never would—not unless absolutely necessary. Some abused kids grew up to be abusers themselves. Not Aiden. He had such a good, generous heart, and he understood the effects of violence all too well. He'd always made it clear how much he hated it.

"Mr. Doyle, I want you to let me take care of this," Aiden said before turning back to confront his father.

"Doyle, you and that crazy daughter of yours are going to ruin me!" Sean shouted around his son. "You can't stand it that I'm gonna be worth more than you. That's why you want to screw me out of selling my land. All that yapping about saving the island is just a pile of horseshit. If it was about anybody but me and mine, you wouldn't give a sweet damn about the development."

By now, the band had stopped playing, and everyone in the hall was watching the battle in stunned silence. Out of the corner of her eye, Lily could see Ryan gently move Miss Annie—who'd probably marched up to subdue Lily's father—out of harm's way. Most of the townsfolk looked tense, disgusted, or just plain furious the evening had been so rudely disrupted by yet another episode of the Doyle-Flynn feud.

Suddenly, Lily was so sick of it all she couldn't take it another minute. "That's not true and you know it," she snapped at Sean. "Not everything in Seashell Bay is about your family or your land, Mr. Flynn. Why don't you just grow the hell up and get over it?"

Aiden turned and shot her a glare. "Jesus, Lily, are you trying to make things worse?"

She swallowed, her stomach hollowing out at the expression of bitter frustration in his gaze. For Aiden, this type of confrontation would be an all-too-familiar reminder of everything he hated about Seashell Bay, since Sean had often pulled these sorts of scenes when his sons were kids. It was awful and humiliating for all of them, but especially for Aiden.

Lily scanned the faces in the crowd. Sean had a smattering of cronies in the room, and she wished those men would step forward and drag him away. She wished, too, that Micah was there, but he was on duty, and by the time someone called him to the scene, the confrontation would already be over.

Aiden wrapped his arm tight around his father's shoulders and whispered something to him. Though Sean tensed and tried to pull away, his son had him pinned solidly against his body. The older man jerked and cursed, but soon enough Aiden had walked him—dragged him, might be more accurate—out into the foyer.

When her father tried to follow, Lily stopped him dead in his tracks with a furious glare. Then she rushed out after Aiden. She couldn't bear the thought that father and son might wind up in a fight. Aiden would prevail, of course, but what would a public brawl with his drunken father accomplish but to sear more horrible memories into his brain?

Aiden turned his head when he heard the sound of her heels clicking on the foyer floor behind him, but he kept an iron grip on Sean. "Go back inside, Lily, and stay there."

Startled, she had to force the words out of her tight throat. "Are you taking him home?"

"Damn right I am. Unless he doesn't shut up and I decide to throw him off the pier instead."

"Screw you," Sean snarled.

"Will you come back?" She hated how she sounded so forlorn and needy. As if Aiden didn't have enough to deal with right now.

"You're damn right I am," he growled. "I've already let this old man ruin too much of my life. He's not going to screw up tonight if I can help it."

Chapter 11

Aiden pushed his father into the passenger seat of the rusty old Explorer, putting his hand over the old man's head to prevent him clunking it in the process. Most of the rage seemed to have leached out of his dad in short order, something Aiden had learned to anticipate over many years of dealing with these episodes.

It had been that way for as long as he could remember— explosive rage followed by glum silence and, occasionally, by a degree of remorse. Part of Aiden wasn't surprised that his dad had followed him to the social and pulled his sad sack act. Not after their bitter argument tonight and what he'd said about Lily.

God, he'd only been back a few days but he was already sick of the whole thing. Sick of the pressure, sick of the arguments, sick of *everything* on this island outpost except Lily Doyle.

"I can drive myself home, boy," his dad slurred after Aiden got him buckled in. He seemed to have finally become aware that Aiden had stuffed him into the passenger seat. "Just leave me be."

Aiden had already reached into his father's pocket and confiscated his car keys. "I'll be more than happy to do just that—after I get you home."

He slammed the door shut and, as he rounded the front of the car, saw Lily still standing in the foyer of the VFW, her palms plastered on the glass of the door as she stared anxiously out. He was going to flick a hand in good-bye to her when a police cruiser—the only police cruiser on the island—pulled up right behind the Explorer, blocking it in.

Had Lily called the deputy? He didn't think she had her phone when she'd followed him to the foyer. Anyway, she must have seen that he had the situation under control. Somebody had called, though, and that sucked because he didn't need or want Micah Lancaster butting in.

Micah slid out of the cruiser, adjusting both his gun belt and hat before pulling out a big flashlight and aiming it at the Explorer. "I got a report of a disturbance at the social," he said to Aiden over the hood of his cruiser. "I presume that's your father in there?"

"Everything's under control, Micah. Dad's in no shape to drive, so I'm taking him home as soon as you move out of the way."

"Hey, not so fast. Your father drove here, didn't he?" Deputy Pain-in-the-Ass strode around to the passenger side and shone his flashlight in at Sean.

For about a second, Aiden thought about claiming that he'd driven his father to the social. But that lie would fall apart if Micah talked to anyone inside. "Yeah."

"Okay, then how much did he have to drink inside?"

When Aiden hesitated, Micah shook his head with disgust. "He didn't drink inside, did he? He was already drunk when he got here."

Aiden shrugged. There was no point lying. All Micah had to do was go inside and talk to one person—any person—to discover the truth.

"Well then, I'll just have him blow in my little machine right now," Micah said. "If he's over the limit, he can spend the night behind bars. Probably do him some good, don't you think?" The deputy opened the door. "Please get out, Mr. Flynn."

Ever polite to his elders, our Micah, Aiden thought grimly. Though his father deserved what he was about to get, some latent and stupidly protective Flynn instinct prodded him into reluctant action. "Come on, Micah, why don't we just let him go home and sleep it off? He didn't hurt anyone, and this isn't the big city."

When Aiden was growing up, it had been standard practice on the part of the deputy on duty to give slightly buzzed islanders a stern warning and then escort them home in the cruiser. Except in egregious cases of drunk driving, of course, but those were infrequent enough.

But maybe Aiden had gotten so used to seeing his father half in the bag at all hours of the day and night that he hardly thought of him as being drunk anymore. Not even tonight, when he'd barged into the social in his fit of rage—it had just seemed par for the course. But he had been slurring his words, hadn't he? Not to mention unsteady on his feet. Christ, now that he thought about it, it was lucky the old man hadn't driven off the road on the way to the VFW. Or worse, hit some poor person walking along the verge.

"You don't know shit about Seashell Bay anymore, Aiden," Micah said, sounding weary more than anything else. He looked back down into the car. "Like I said, Mr. Flynn, get out. I won't say it again."

Why am I trying to save the old man from one night in the slammer? Aiden couldn't come up with a single good answer.

"Whatever," he said. "Maybe you're right that he could use a night in jail." He glanced back up toward the hall. Lily still stood there, huddling as if she were cold. Suddenly, he wanted nothing more than to fold her into his arms and warm her with all the fire he felt for her.

And maybe that heat would chase away the sick chill he felt deep inside his chest, a coldness that never seemed to completely fade away.

The deputy helped Sean out of the car. After steadying him and then leaning him against the side of the cruiser, Micah took out his breath tester and shoved a little plastic tube in it. Sean bitched for about five seconds, questioning Micah's parentage, but then reluctantly blew into the mouthpiece. Micah glanced at the reading on the cellphone-sized device, then pushed a button. A second later, he nodded to Aiden. "Okay, he's coming with me."

After stowing Sean into the back of the cruiser, Micah straightened up and cut Aiden a not-unfriendly glance. "Go back to the party, Aiden. I'll take care of your dad. Just forget about him for a while and try to enjoy yourself."

Lily hadn't been able to turn away from the horrid little drama playing out in the parking lot, terrified about what might happen. And terrified that Aiden might be so sick of his screwed-up father that he'd sprint for the first boat leaving the island. She couldn't bear the thought of him leaving, and not just because she needed a temporary sternman. All it had taken was a couple of minutes in Aiden's arms for her to be swamped with a longing she couldn't even describe. The tangled mix of emotions had her all twisted up inside. Physical passion, a yearning for simpler times, regret for what might have been...it was all that.

But there was something else, something that frightened the hell out of her—a sense that Aiden was somehow a last chance for her.

But a last chance for what? It seemed crazy to think that some part of her might be expecting a future with Aiden. Still, she couldn't deny that his return to Seashell Bay had stirred up some very powerful and dangerous emotions, given that he would never stay on the island.

She glanced over her shoulder back into the hall. Morgan and Holly were hovering not far away, watching her with concern. They'd followed her out, wanting to stay with her in the foyer, but Lily had shooed them back inside. Right now she needed to be alone with her thoughts. And she needed to be with Aiden, even if only from a distance.

She peered again through the glass door, her heart aching for him as he watched the police cruiser pull out of the parking lot. What must he be thinking? That nothing had changed, even after all his years away from home? Lily had to admit that, if she were in his shoes, she'd want to get the hell off the island as soon as she could too.

As Micah's cruiser disappeared, she saw Aiden stick his hands in his pockets and stare out into the starlit darkness of the bay. Lily's heart told her to run to him, but she held back. He needed a few minutes to choke down the shame and anger of dealing with his drunken, abusive father, like he'd had to do so many times in the past. For that, he wouldn't want a witness, or even comfort.

After what felt like forever, he turned and started back to her.

Lily pushed the door open and rushed down the steps of the hall to meet him. He towered over her, his gaze narrowed as he studied her face. The parking lot lights cast an eerie fluorescent glow, bleaching them to the shades of a faded black-and-white photograph. Aiden's eyes were cast in shadow, obscuring his expression, but there was no mistaking the taut line of his jaw or the grim set of his mouth.

She swallowed hard, her gaze dropping to her silly, gold-sparkled flats. "I'm so sorry that had to happen," she said, sick with shame about her outburst at Sean in the hall. "Micah's taking him home?"

He raked his hair back with an impatient hand and then wiped his brow with his forearm. Between the warm evening and the stress of the situation, it was no wonder he was sweating. He was clearly furious but also clearly doing his level best to bottle up his anger. She'd always known Aiden hated the idea that he might be like his father, so he did everything he could to keep his temper locked down.

"No, to jail for the night. Micah's obviously fed up with him too." He sucked in a deep breath. "And I'm the one who should be saying I'm sorry, not you."

She shook her head. "You can't change your father. Everybody knows that. And it wasn't entirely his fault either. My dad didn't exactly help matters." She sighed. "And neither did I."

Aiden studied her for a few moments, as if weighing what to do next. Then he reached out and took her hand, sliding his fingers through hers. "Let's just go for a walk, okay? I don't think I can face going back in there right now."

Her heart started to thud at the idea of being alone with him, even under such crappy circumstances. "Sure, but nobody thinks badly of you, Aiden. The opposite, actually, especially after how well you handled things. It could have been a lot worse."

He didn't answer, simply tugging her gently through the parking lot and down a flight of wooden steps toward the VFW's small dock. As they passed the pier, hand in hand, Lily gazed at the lights of the town landing on the other side of the shallow cove. The only noise was the faint echo of music coming from the hall, and she could hear the steady slap of small waves against the pilings beneath the pier. They seemed to echo the beat of her heart, because she knew exactly where he was taking her.

The graveled path continued through scrubby bush to Sunset Beach, the smallest of the island's five beaches. Despite having the best sand—meaning more sand than pebbles—Sunset was less popular because of the nearby dock and volume of boat traffic passing close by.

Now though, late at night, it couldn't have been more tranquil and perfect. The sliver of a moon threw only the faintest of lights, but it didn't matter. Lily could have navigated this area blind and so, obviously, could Aiden. Even though they'd slowed to a stroll, he led her confidently down to the beach.

Lily took off her shoes and left them at the path. Aiden did the same, then took her hand again as they wandered along the edge of the water. Although he seemed comfortable with the silence—and with holding her hand in his warm clasp—Lily's anxieties finally got the better of her.

"You know this isn't your fault, Aiden. Don't you? None of this is your fault."

He gave an absent nod, almost as if he wasn't really listening. "A big part of me just wants to sell my land and head back home. That way Bram will get the money he needs, and I'll never have to lay eyes on the old man again."

She tugged on his hand, exerting just enough pressure to let him know she wanted him to turn and face her. Some instinct whispered that he wasn't yet ready to give up on Seashell Bay and that he needed her to help him work it through.

"But what about the other part of you?" she asked softly.

Though Aiden didn't say anything, he did turn to look at her.

Lily rested her other hand on his chest, just for a moment, before dropping it to her side. "I hope you don't go. I really, really hope you don't."

There, I've said it.

Aiden's gaze roamed over her face. Even though it was so dark, her vision had adjusted, and she thought she saw yearning in his expression and a hunger that hadn't diminished over the years.

Then he gently released her hand. "But you know I have to," he said in a low voice.

That short, brutal exchange summed up everything. Impulsively, she'd taken the risk and put her feelings out there, but his answer hadn't changed.

Clearly she was an idiot because instead of stepping away from him, instead of taking her cue from the gentle rejection, she moved closer and slipped her arms around his waist. It was the dumbest thing she could imagine doing, but she did it anyway.

Because it was Aiden, and it was a beautiful, summer night in Seashell Bay. It was their past and their present all coming together in a tangled web of starlight, pushing her to claim the moment they'd been too afraid to grasp that long-ago night.

"Stay for a little while anyway," she whispered.

For several agonizing seconds, it seemed that fate held them in the balance. Then Aiden let out a huge breath and folded his arms around her, holding her tight. "For a while," he murmured, brushing his lips across her temple. His masculine stubble softly chafed her skin, making her shiver.

Torn between heartache and relief, Lily turned her face up. Aiden captured her lips in a kiss that went from tentative and sweet to hot and passionate in the space of a few heartbeats, as she'd known it would. The feel of his mouth on hers, his tongue sliding inside to claim her with a fierce, almost desperate possession, transported her back to that night when they'd finally said yes to each other. It felt wild and new and yet so familiar in the best possible way. The years between them dropped away, almost as if he'd never left.

Just like riding a bike.

That crazy thought made her giggle.

Aiden nuzzled her lips, sweeping his tongue across them with a hot lick before he eased back a bit. "What's so funny, Lily-girl?" he asked with a mock growl as he let his big hands drift down to cup her butt.

She smiled at his old nickname for her, even as she shivered at the feel of his hands stroking her. He nudged her hips tight against his oh-so-muscular body. That did delicious things to her insides, making her grow soft and damp.

"Nothing," she whispered. "Well, maybe I'm just a little nervous."

"There's nothing to be nervous about, babe," he said in a husky voice. He gently squeezed her ass. "It's just me."

Easy for him to say.

But she knew it wasn't easy. The dark, almost brooding expression on his handsome features seemed to war with the hot desire she saw there too. The last thing she wanted him to do was start thinking again, to second-guess himself. If Aiden pulled back this time, Lily was sure she would die from a combination of frustrated lust and heartfelt disappointment.

She slid her hands around his neck and pulled him back down to her mouth, desperate to taste him. Energy sparked between them, hot and wanton, as his tongue surged into her. In a nanosecond, the kiss turned raw, openmouthed, and delicious. Lily sucked his tongue into her mouth, greedily making up for the years apart. She'd had a thousand dreams like this—she and Aiden in each other's arms, finally leaping over all the stupid fences they'd let their families and Seashell Bay put up between them.

Aiden's hands slid to her waist and lifted her onto the tips of her toes, pulling her even closer. The feel of his erection nudging her, right in that perfect spot, felt like a long, cold drink of water after a punishing drought. Lily whimpered into his mouth and plastered her body to his, loving the wet slide of their tongues, the heat rising between them. She wound her arms tightly around him and slid one leg up to curl along his muscled thigh. Her skirt slid up, and the crisp cotton of his pants brushing against her bare inner thigh pulsed a hard shiver of sensation through her body.

He growled deep in his throat then clamped a hand on the back of her thigh, his long fingers tangled in the flimsy fabric of her skirt. Every touch sparked a delicious fire. Lily wanted to rip her clothes off and rub every part of herself against his wicked-hard body. She squirmed just thinking about it and went from damp to wet in an instant. God, she needed him to touch her there—and soon—or she'd probably lose what little control she had left.

As if sensing her need, he clamped his hands on her ass and lifted her another inch to bring the rock-hard bulge in his pants into direct contact with her sex. A sweet little contraction pulsed deep inside her, a delicious harbinger of things to come. Wanting more—so much more—she angled her body into him, pleasure and need pulling a soft moan from between her lips.

The next thing she knew, the world seemed to tilt on its axis. Her eyes popped open—she didn't even know she'd closed them—to see Aiden bringing her down to the sand, one strong arm behind her back, the other sweeping under her thighs in a powerful move that had her flat on her back a second later. She lay sprawled on the sand with Aiden straddling her hips as he tugged a few buttons loose on his shirt before he impatiently yanked it over his head.

One of his big hands wrapped around her shoulder. "Lift up, babe," he ordered in a darkly sensual voice.

He helped her lift as he shoved his shirt underneath

her upper body and head. She couldn't help smiling. Lily didn't mind getting a little sandy—okay, a lot sandy—as long as she did it with him. Still, the unconsciously thoughtful gesture made her melt. It was just so typically Aiden.

With a happy sigh, Lily greedily ran her hands over his broad chest, tracing the outline of his pecs and then trailing her fingers over his six-pack and down to his belt. Her hands shook as she went for his buckle, fumbling to get it open.

"None of that," he rasped, gently pushing her hands away.

Lily's heart stuttered, afraid he was having second thoughts. But he simply came down onto the sand, stretching alongside her. A cool breeze blew in from the cove but she felt only warmth—from the heat of his body and from his hands as they started to move over her.

"I want to see you, Lily-girl," he whispered as he slowly pulled her flimsy skirt up over her hips. He took in her tiny, black lace panties and once more growled low and deliciously deep in his throat. "Man, that's the prettiest damn thing I've seen in a long time."

When he dragged his fingers right over her happy spot, a bolt of sensation zinged deep in her core. Gasping, she arched up, stunned how close she was to the edge.

He let out a husky, teasing laugh as he cupped her sex. "Not yet, babe. I'm not anywhere close to being finished with you."

Lily could only let out a whimper, her heart already racing like an engine at full throttle. She clutched his shoulders and stared up at him, trying to imprint both his face and the moment in her memory. It was as good as she'd ever imagined, as good as all those long years ago. Better, because they were no longer a pair of dumb, hormonally addled teenagers, half drunk on beer and each other, rushing toward the finish line.

And because tonight they would truly finish it, not holding anything back from each other. Now they knew exactly what they were doing, and the slow, sexy movement of Aiden's hand on her body suggested he had no intention of rushing anything.

With his big hand possessively spanning the width of her belly, he leaned down and took her mouth in a raw, hot kiss that stunned her with its intensity. It was openmouthed, wet, and hot, and he kissed her like a man who'd been holding himself back for a long time. Lily moaned into his mouth, her body starting to shake with a barely controlled sexual need that had her dragging him down on top of her, his übermasculine body crushing her into the sand.

It still wasn't enough.

With a trembling hand, she fumbled for the side zipper on the bodice of her dress. She needed to be out of it, needed to feel his hands on her breasts.

With a soothing murmur, Aiden pulled back slightly from the kiss. His fingers brushed hers away and eased the zipper down. When he rolled off her, Lily immediately missed the heat and weight of his body, but then he slipped the dress straps from her shoulders and worked down the top low enough to expose her breasts. With the fitted bodice, she hadn't bothered to wear a bra.

She clutched his biceps and stared up at him. His gaze roamed over her, drinking her in. Suddenly, she wished it wasn't so damn dark. Did Aiden like what he saw?

With his face obscured by shadows, she couldn't tell. Lily wasn't exactly a lingerie model, especially when it came to her boobs. Since Aiden had actually dated lingerie models—and, yes, she'd read about them in the gossip rags—she couldn't help but wonder if he might be disappointed with her less-than-ample assets.

"God, Lily," he rasped. "You are so fucking beautiful."

Her heart twisted. "Really?" she whispered.

He jerked a bit, as if startled. "Of course you are." Then he laughed—low, soft, and sexy. "But maybe I should just show you."

One hand slid up to cup her breast. Her nipple instantly pulled into a tight point. He gently squeezed, pushing her up that much more, and then he leaned over and sucked her into his mouth.

She gasped as a deep, sexual hunger rolled through her body in response to the play of his lips. Within seconds she felt ready—so ready that she wriggled desperately against him, trying to ease the growing ache between her thighs. But Aiden, damn him, took his sweet time. He licked, sucked, and nibbled at his leisure, while his hand played with her other breast.

Moaning, Lily gave herself up to it. She wrapped her shaking hands around his head, holding him tight against her. He wound her up as tight as a spring, making her so wet and oh-so-ready for him to be inside her. She'd been waiting forever for this moment. She needed it, needed him, right now.

"Aiden," she moaned. She clutched his shoulders, pushing against them. It was like trying to push a rock wall. "I need more," she gasped in desperation. "Please."

After a last nuzzle, he finally pulled back, almost

reluctantly, she thought. He braced himself, leaning over her, his dark hair mussed from her wandering hands.

When he didn't move, staying there gazing down at her, Lily's heart sank and every muscle in her body went tight with frustration.

Please, God, don't let him be having second thoughts.

Not again, not like their last time together, the night before he'd left for good. That time they'd both called a halt to the proceedings just before they reached the point of no return, too worried about what would happen if they crossed that final barrier. But that was then and this was now. She was so ready—more than ready to be with him in every way, regardless of the consequences.

But if he wasn't, if he pulled back, she just might kill him.

"Aiden, please," she whispered again, her voice raw with yearning. She should hate that she sounded so needy, but right now she didn't care. All she cared about was Aiden. "What—"

He swooped down and planted another hot lick of a kiss across her lips. "Hush, Lily," he murmured. "I'll take care of you."

When his hand slid down across her belly and slipped between her thighs, she whimpered out her relief. His fingers nudged under the lace of her panties to move skilfully over her wet flesh.

"Oh, oh," she panted. "That's so good."

"Open your legs for me, babe," he said, his voice so deep it seemed to vibrate through her. "I want to feel all of you."

God, she could practically come from that hot, sexy voice alone.

She did what he wanted, letting her legs fall wide open. He slid his hand into her panties and pressed two fingers into her while his palm nudged up against her sweet spot.

As she started to rock against him, he leaned down to her again, capturing her mouth in a kiss so bone-meltingly raw that she could feel tears start to prickle her eyes. In this moment, nothing stood between them—not family, not the island, not the opposing choices that had pulled them away from each other. There was only the sea and the beach and a sky full of stars overhead.

Lily started to shake, her body pulling tight, right on the brink. His fingers slid through her moisture with the perfect rhythm, then he pushed his fingers back inside. Arching up, she moaned against his lips.

"That's it, Lily-girl," he murmured against her mouth. "Come for me now. Come hard."

Her eyes flew open, and she stared up into his gorgeous face. Then he twisted his hand, just a little, just right, and she crested the wave. It flowed over her, tumbling her to the edge of pleasure. She grabbed his arms and dug in, curling her body up to him as she choked out a cry.

"Jesus, Lily, you're so beautiful."

His voice vibrated with emotion—with need, she thought, maybe even sadness. It brought the tears stinging back to her eyes, and she had to blink them away even as she struggled to bring her trembling body under control.

Tentatively, she brought her hands to his chest then slipped them down to his belt. When she started to undo it, he covered her hand with his.

"Don't," he said.

Lily froze. They stared at each other, and she read his

decision in the grim set to his mouth. She had no doubt that he wanted her. She could feel the evidence of that desire pressing huge and hot against her thigh, and she sensed his frustration in the way he rigidly held himself above her.

It wasn't much consolation.

She should feel stunned by his decision. But somehow, she didn't. She should have known he'd pull away, because that was what Aiden did.

It was what he always did. He did it to protect himself, and she'd always understood and accepted that. But not now, because this time he'd stripped all her protection away, leaving her open and vulnerable.

And alone. Again.

With a heavy sigh, he lowered himself to the sand and rolled onto his back. They were only inches apart but it might as well have been miles.

Burning with embarrassment, Lily sat up and flipped her skirt down over her thighs. Then she started to pull up her bodice. When he reached over to help her, she flicked his hand away.

"Don't," she said, echoing him.

"Lily, I'm sorry," he said.

The regret in his voice made her want to cringe, cry, or bash him over the head. None of those options were particularly appealing—well, except possibly for the head bashing—so she decided that the almost-silent treatment was probably best. That way she wouldn't be tempted to blurt out something she might regret later.

"Forget it," she said in a brisk tone as she zipped up. She thought it was a miracle that she could force the words past her tight vocal cords.

Once she got her dress sorted out, she pushed herself to her feet and started brushing the sand off the back of her skirt. Aiden silently rose and picked up his crumpled shirt. He gave it a quick shake then pulled it on without bothering to do up the rest of the buttons, leaving his muscular chest and abs exposed. In the dim light of the moon, he looked frustrated, sorry, and so totally hot and sexy that she wanted to scream at the unfairness of it all.

She turned away to head back to the parking lot. Aiden stopped her with a gentle hand on her shoulder. "Hold up a minute, Lily. Isn't it about time you told me what you want for winning the bet?"

She whipped around and stared at him. "Un-freaking-believable. Really? That's what you want to talk about right now?"

He shoved his hands into his pockets and gave a fair attempt at a casual shrug. But the tense line of his mouth—a mouth still damp from her kisses—told her another story.

"For the moment, yeah," he said. "Besides, it's probably not a good time to talk about what just happened. There's already been too much drama for one night."

Okay, now she was really getting pissed. It amazed her how stupid guys could be, even smart ones like Aiden. "Drama? That's what you call what just happened between us?"

He winced. "Well, maybe that wasn't the best way to describe it—"

"Ya think?" she said, propping her hands on her hips. She was probably coming off as a first-class bitch, but right now that was her only defense.

Aiden sighed. "Lily—"

She waved a dismissive hand. "Never mind. And don't worry about the bet. You've got enough on your plate, what with your father and all the *drama*." Somehow, the bet didn't seem as important now. In fact, it struck her as downright insane, which she probably should have realized from the start. Holly and Morgan had certainly tried to warn her. "Let's just call it square."

Her dismissal brought his eyebrows snapping together in a heavy scowl. He crossed his arms over his chest. She couldn't help but notice the way his biceps bulged and remember how hard and awesome his body had felt when she'd come apart.

Stop thinking like a horny teenager, you idiot.

"No way," he said in a voice she recognized. Aiden Flynn had decided to dig his heels in. "A bet is a bet, and I'm honoring mine. So spit it out. What do you want me to do?"

She almost said, *Okay, pal, you asked for it.*

But as she glared up at him, taking in how tightly wound he was, she couldn't help thinking about how difficult his life was right now. Yes, she was mad at him—furious—but she was a big girl and she needed to suck it up. Ultimately, Aiden was always going to reject her. She knew that, and she'd still walked right into that emotional propeller, eyes wide open. So if she got shredded, that was on her not him.

She also knew how difficult it would be for him to do what she wanted him to do. What right did she have to ask him to take on something that would bring back every rotten memory from his rotten childhood?

"Let it go, Aiden. I can manage fine on my own."

He froze.

Oops. Lily swallowed past her dry throat as she realized she'd said too much.

Aiden gave her a brief puzzled look, but then his eyes lit with understanding. "Oh, man, I get it." He shook his head. "Jesus, how could I have been so stupid? You need a sternman. That's what the bet was about."

"Look, I'll be okay," she blurted out, her body hot with humiliation. How had she ever thought she could pull this idea off? She was a horrible person who would no doubt burn in hell for even coming up with it. "You don't have to do anything."

Surprisingly, he pulled off a rueful smile. "I see why you were dancing around the topic all night. Of all the harebrained ideas, Lily."

Well, at least it didn't sound like he hated her or wanted to toss her into the water. That was progress, she supposed.

"I know," she sighed. "It was a truly stupid idea that got out of hand."

Aiden gave a little snort that she didn't even try to read. She just waited silently for what he would say next.

"Doesn't matter," he said. "I've never gone back on a bet, and I don't plan on starting now. I'll meet you tomorrow at sunrise, unless you want to head out even earlier."

Wow.

Lily felt like she'd just been hit by a rogue wave. Given what had happened between them a few moments ago, she wasn't even sure if she still wanted Aiden on her boat, spending long fishing days together—alone. Wouldn't the tension between them be unbearable?

But she badly needed a sternman. There was no doubt about that. Could they really find a way to manage this?

"Lily, this isn't up for debate," Aiden said in a hard voice, taking the matter out of her hands. "Like I said, I always honor my wagers."

She sighed. *What a freaking mess.* "Sunrise will do just fine."

Chapter 12

*A*iden could almost imagine the poker up Lily's butt. At the pier, in the skiff, and now aboard *Miss Annie*, she'd barely spoken a word. Not that he particularly felt like talking. His head ached like somebody had cranked it into a vise, the result of too much tension and too little sleep. Between his jackass father's antics and that heart-stopping episode with Lily on the beach, he'd spent all night tossing and turning and reliving every moment—especially the one where Lily came apart in his arms.

As he watched her guide *Miss Annie* out to the channel, he didn't know whether to congratulate himself for doing the honorable thing or to kick himself for being a moron. He was leaning toward the latter, because Lily still looked incredibly hot in her no-nonsense, tight yellow T-shirt and trim-fitting jeans. Hell, she looked hot in anything, and how he was going to keep his hands to himself when they were stuck together on a freaking boat was a question for the ages.

But he had no choice. As much as he wanted her, Aiden had jammed on the brakes before it was too late. It had been a gut instinct more than anything else, a decision made in a heartbeat. One of the hardest of his life, given what he was rejecting—Lily, half naked on the beach, soft and slick from the orgasm he'd just given her, and all his for the taking.

Still, he'd walked away and then spent most of the night trying to figure out why.

He didn't much like the answer he'd come up with, but there it was—he was worried about getting too close and then having to walk away again. Not only for what it might do to her, but for what it would do to him. He had an unshakable sense that once he and Lily finally had each other, he'd never be able to let her go. And that would never work, because she would never leave the island and he would never stay. It was a setup for a life of heartache and frustrated promises.

"We need to take on bait," she said curtly, not looking back at him as he stood at the stern rail. She nodded to the northeast channel where, through the dissipating mist, Aiden spotted the bait smack moored at a floating platform. *Miss Annie*'s diesel hummed contentedly as she cut through the light chop. The weather had turned overcast, and a stiffening breeze from the east blew Lily's hair around her face. She looked focused and in complete control.

"I can hardly wait," Aiden muttered in response to her comment.

He knew all about refilling bait bags from years on his dad's boat, and it sucked. All bait smelled bad, but unless it was perfectly fresh it could stink to high heaven. That was why he'd worn Bram's old oil gear this morning— orange Grundéns pants held up by suspenders, the bib halfway up his chest. They'd be hot later in the day, but they'd keep the slime off and could be easily washed with the deck hose at the end of the day.

"Are people here still using fresh herring?" he asked.

"We mostly use pogies these days."

"How much does a barrel go for now?" he asked, trying to get her talking. As pissed as she was at him, surely she couldn't give him the cold shoulder forever. Hell, he was the one who should be mad, given how she'd snookered him into this job.

"About 130 bucks, give or take."

"Wow," Aiden said, surprised at how much prices had gone up from his lobstering days. "How many traps will that cover?"

"Depends. Maybe a couple of hundred. We'll get two barrels."

"You're planning on hauling four hundred traps?" That was a crapload for one day.

She finally turned a bit to look at him. "You don't think you can handle that, Mr. Big Shot?"

Oh, yeah. Still pissed.

Aiden could handle four hundred, all right. He'd done it before. But at 120 pounds soaking wet, would Lily be up to that many? The captain worked as hard as the sternman, unless that captain happened to be Sean Flynn on his bad days. But questioning either Lily's commitment or her physical stamina was a fast road to trouble.

Still, he hated that she pushed so hard. "How many have you been hauling on your own?"

She gave a little shrug and turned away from him. "Two hundred on a really good day. I need to catch up or I'll drown in all the red ink."

Given the grim tone to her voice, he decided to let it go.

Lily eased the boat alongside the platform, close to the blue-and-white smack. A big, muscular guy with long, black hair and tattoo-covered arms waved at Lily as one of his crew grabbed the mooring ropes and tied them to platform cleats. Took a moment, but Aiden finally recognized the tattooed guy. Billy Paine. Or, as Aiden and his pals had called him, Billy-Pain-in-the-Ass.

"Morning, Lil," Billy said. "You're looking sexy as ever today."

Aiden rolled his eyes. It was clear that Billy's I'm-God's-gift-to-women attitude was still intact.

"Two barrels this morning," she said.

Billy hooked a thumb in Aiden's direction. "So, *this* is your new sternman? Trading in your Phillies uniform for Grundéns, are you, Mr. Famous Athlete? That must be quite some comedown."

"Stow that shit, Billy," Lily snapped before Aiden could react. She climbed over the gunwale and onto the platform. "I'm really not in the mood for your act this morning. Just get your guys moving with the bait, okay?"

Billy frowned but held up two fingers to one of his crewmembers. The guys got busy hooking a bait barrel onto a hoist that would swing it onboard *Miss Annie*.

"I've got to express my appreciation, Flynn," Billy said as he strolled over. "I'm fifty bucks up today, thanks to you."

Aiden gave him a stony stare, refusing to bite.

"I bet Lily would beat you in the race," Billy said with a smirk. "Had to give three-to-one odds to get any takers."

"Glad I could make your day," Aiden replied. "But I'm curious. Do you always shoot your mouth off like this? If so, I'd be buying my bait somewhere else if I were Lily. Must get pretty boring to listen to your tired, old routine every day."

Billy's grin vanished. "You know, Flynn, you're not one of us anymore. You should watch your fucking mouth before it lands you in trouble."

Aiden snorted. "Really? From you?"

Now old Billy just looked mean. "I guess I shouldn't be surprised you've taken a job with Lil since you don't have one in baseball anymore. We knew that would happen soon enough. Heard your old man say so plenty of times."

Aiden stepped up onto the gunwale and launched himself onto the platform toward the asshole. He managed one stride before Lily jumped forward and yanked hard on his arm. He stopped, but only because he didn't want to pull her off her feet.

"Jesus, will you two ratchet down the bullshit?" She stepped between the two of them. "Billy, just shut up about Aiden. He's doing me a big favor while he's on the island, and I'm very grateful for it. Anyway, you're the one who kept nagging me about how dangerous it was to fish alone."

With a sly grin, Billy planted a meaty paw on Lily's shoulder. Aiden wanted to rip his head off.

"Fair enough, but how about having a drink with me tonight at the Pot, Lil?" Billy said. "You and me always have a real good time, don't we?"

"Only in your dreams," Lily gritted out.

Billy laughed. "That's my sweet Lil."

Aiden resisted the urge to toss the idiot into the channel, since Lily could obviously handle him.

She stomped off to the far end of the platform and stood there with her hands on her hips. Billy picked up a clipboard and wrote out the transaction details. Finally, after a minute or two of blessed silence, the bait was onboard, the hoist was removed, and Lily was untying the mooring ropes while Aiden secured the barrels on the deck.

"See you later, Lil," Paine said with a suggestive smile, as Lily eased *Miss Annie* away.

After Lily cleared the platform, she turned to Aiden with an apologetic grimace. "He can be such a jackass. But he's worse today because of you. Sorry about that."

"No worries," he said.

After all, Lily had raced to his defense and put Paine in his place. Not a bad start to the day, after all.

Lily could not afford to worry about the screwed-up state of affairs with Aiden. Hauling traps was a dangerous business, even in good weather and seas. It was too easy to get sloppy, doing the same thing day after day. One mental slip, and the next thing you knew, your hand was caught in a pot hauler or in tangled ropes, and a few bloody fingers would end up flopping onto the deck.

Or you could space out thinking about anything from the price of fuel to the origin of the universe, blissfully unaware that pot warp was coiling around your foot as traps hurtled over the side of the boat. A moment later you'd be overboard and in a life-and-death struggle to cut yourself free as the weighted traps dragged you down to the ocean floor.

Lily cast a nervous glance back at Aiden. The guy hadn't fished in fifteen years, and he was wearing Grundéns. Nothing could kill a man faster than getting yanked into the water dressed in oil gear. Most lobstermen said that once those pants filled with water you were done for. That was why she fished in jeans, preferring slime and fish guts to drowning. But a lot of fishermen wore oil gear, so she couldn't really criticize Aiden for doing it, especially since he'd clearly rather be anywhere than on a lobster boat.

With her.

She slowed the boat as she approached her first trap line, set about a hundred feet off Wreckhouse Point, the northwestern tip of the island. From her screened-in porch on a low cliff near the point, Dottie Buckle waved as she'd done a thousand times, and Lily returned the greeting as she motored up to her orange-and-green buoy. It bobbed beside the boat while its partner buoy—on the other end of the trap line—was visible in the distance, around three hundred feet away.

She cut the engine and turned to Aiden, who'd taken up his position to her right. His expression was partly hidden by the shadows cast by his red Phillies ball cap.

"Ready?"

"As ready I'll ever be," he said grimly.

Repressing a distracting spasm of guilt, Lily reached down with her gaff hook and hauled the buoy aboard. Dropping the gaff, she lifted the nylon pot warp over the hauling block and tossed the buoy down on the gunwale. With moves born of years of lobstering, she ran the line through the pot hauler and twisted the control until the plates started to spin, pinching the rope in between them and pulling it up from the water. While the wet, slimy rope coiled on the deck, Lily watched for the lead trap to break the surface, ignoring the loud whine, squeals, and pops from the hauler. She glimpsed Aiden out of the corner of her eye, his gaze glued to the point where the trap would surface. He unconsciously bounced on the balls of his rubber boot-clad feet.

She couldn't hold back a smile. Now that they were actually hauling, satisfaction and excitement surged through her, giving her a boost. Whatever her qualms about working with Aiden, he was so fit and powerful that she had to believe she could make some serious money, at least for as long as he helped her. Even when she'd had a sternman in the past, especially that weasel Johnny Leblanc, she'd rarely felt as ready to fish as she did now.

"Here it comes," Aiden said.

The big mesh trap broke the surface. Lily stopped the hauler and then yanked the trap up onto the gunwale. She could see four lobsters inside, and her growing optimism pumped even higher. She slid the trap along the rail to Aiden so he could clear it, then restarted the pot hauler to bring up the next of her six-trap trawl.

Her new sternman didn't hesitate. Aiden threw open the trapdoor and scooped out the crabs and small fish, chucking them over the side. Then he picked out the first lobster. It was an obvious short, so he tossed it into the water too. The next lobster looked like keeper size, so he flipped it over to sex it, then reached back to drop it in the holding tank. After they finished cleaning out all six traps in this trawl, he'd have the job of measuring each lobster in the tank, throwing out all those with bodies smaller than the three-and-a-quarter-inch legal minimum. Then he'd band the keepers with a tool for that purpose.

Aiden worked smoothly and efficiently. Despite his long absence from the fishery, his muscle memory was serving him—and her—well. Being a highly trained, fit athlete obviously didn't hurt either.

She stopped the hauler and pulled the next trap onto the rail. This one was her responsibility to deal with while Aiden finished cleaning out the lead trap and changing its bait bag. She whipped the trapdoor open, cleaned out the junk, and tossed two keepers into the tank. The last lobster was a big female. Lily knew from the "V" that a previous fisherman had notched into her tail that she was an egg-bearing female and thus protected by law forever. Lily silently wished the girl well as she dropped her back into the sea. Hell, she'd need some luck, because the life of a female lobster wasn't exactly a picnic. Male lobsters—aggressive bastards all—mated by taking the females into their dens and waiting for them to shed their shells, thus rendering the ladies completely vulnerable. At that point, the male made a personal choice—either eat the female or mate with her.

Lily had always tried not to think of that as a metaphor for her sometimes disastrous dating life.

Aiden toted the lead trap to the stern rail and then returned to grab Lily's so he could switch out that bait bag too. "You're doing great," she said. "After you get a few more trawls under your belt, your speed will be up to scratch."

Aiden gave a little snort. "You sweet talker, you."

Lily gave him a little poke to his bicep—which was like poking a rock—as he finished with the trailer trap and took it away to the stern, lining it up beside the lead trap.

She switched on the pot hauler and brought another pair of traps up. They continued to work side by side, saying little, until the trawl was done and all six traps were emptied and lined up on the stern, ready to be dropped back into the water. Aiden finished checking the lobsters with the brass gauge, throwing out another three shorts in the process, while Lily inspected the rope coiled beneath the traps in the stern. From the looks of the lobsters in the tank, she estimated they had already caught about ten pounds.

Returning to the wheel, Lily turned the boat around and sailed back to where they'd started.

"Can we take a five-minute break?" Aiden asked as she slowed the boat almost to an idle.

Lily gave him a teasing smile. "Okay, but surely you're not tapped out already? We've barely started."

He shook his head and popped open the cooler he'd brought with him this morning. "I'll be good for a long day, but I didn't get much sleep last night."

From the sarcastic look on his face, she guessed he was holding her responsible for that state of affairs. "Join the club," she said drily.

What were you thinking about all night, Aiden Flynn? About how you sawed off the tree limb I finally climbed out on?

If she'd had any guts, she'd confront the issue right now. She'd ask him why, after he'd been coming on to her since he got to the island, he'd pulled back just when he was about to hit a home run.

But she didn't even know what she wanted Aiden to say or do. She'd spent hours last night trying to convince herself that her behavior on Sunset Beach had been a colossal, stupid, hormone-driven mistake. Still, it made her stomach hollow out every time she thought about his rejection.

And about how good she'd felt with his arms wrapped around her when he'd sent her flying to the stars.

Aiden pulled a bottle of Gatorade out of the ice. "Want some?"

"Good grief, no. That stuff is kind of gross at the best of times. I'll stick with good old caffeine, thanks."

She reached for her thermos of coffee perched on the bulkhead next to the GPS and depth recorder.

Aiden sat on the rail and took a swig of the bright green drink. "I must have swallowed about five thousand gallons of this stuff in the last twenty years. I think my stomach's probably neon green by now. I probably glow in the dark."

Lily couldn't help a little laugh, even though she was still struggling to get past the wreck of last night's humiliation. After filling her mug with coffee, she leaned back against the wheel and studied him.

Though Aiden had looked solid working the traps, she warned herself not to be fooled. He obviously had a lot going on inside. She couldn't bear the idea that he might hurt himself because he was tired or distracted.

"How are you feeling so far?" Lily took a nervous sip, kind of dreading what he might say. He probably wouldn't be honest about his feelings anyway. Men rarely were, in her experience.

Could a solid and productive day of work—helping out a grateful friend—start him on a path that would allow him to release some of his long-standing resentment toward life on Seashell Bay Island? She decided it probably wouldn't. That would be too much to hope for, at least for as long as Sean Flynn was alive.

Aiden gave her a quick, questioning glance and then shrugged. "Ask me at the end of the day. I'm trying not to think too much. The faster we haul traps the better, as far as I'm concerned."

"Oh, okay." She wanted to believe it was the memories he wanted to escape, not her.

"I just want to get into a zone where it's just a day of mindless physical work, doing exactly the same mechanical things four hundred times, like on autopilot." He tipped the bottle and took another big swallow. "I'll think about lying on a white, sandy beach in Barbados instead of mucking around in Casco Bay."

Lily's temper stirred at the casual dismissal of her work, her life, and her home. She turned away to stare straight ahead through the windshield at the rocky shoreline. "Welcome to my life," she muttered.

"What?" Aiden said.

"Nothing."

He got up and came to her, his jaw set in a grim line. "Don't give me that. You're the one who asked me how I felt, remember?"

She turned to face him. "Aiden, how do you think that made me feel? You just called my work mindless and mechanical, and you act like the bay is a...a sewer." Anger suddenly boiled up inside her. "This from a guy who spends his life swatting the air with a bat."

His head jerked dismissively to the side. "Don't go twisting my words. That's not what I meant," he said sharply.

Aiden started to turn away, but stopped himself. He gave her a long, hard look and then finally let out a sigh as he pushed up the brim of his ball cap. "Look, I'm sorry, Lily. I was just talking about a way to help shut out some rotten memories. I didn't mean to insult you. You do good, hard work that's far from mindless. I totally respect you for that."

Lily slowly blew out the breath she'd been holding. *Talk about overreacting.* "Sorry, I'm a little wound up today. Billy really got me going."

Aiden's raised eyebrows told her he didn't buy that excuse, but all he said was, "I get it."

"Okay. Ready to set some traps?" she asked, screwing the top back on the thermos.

"Aye, aye." He put the Gatorade back in the cooler and started to do a final check of the traps and ropes.

When Aiden gave her the go-ahead, Lily pushed the throttle forward, and soon the lead trap and buoy slid over the side, sixty feet of pot warp spooling out behind them. Tightening ropes yanked each of the remaining traps off the boat in succession until the tail trap and marker buoy went over the side. Lily breathed a sigh of relief. The first set had gone off without a hitch. But with sixty or so to go, it was going to be another very long day in the boat— a boat that pretty much felt like an emotional tinderbox about to blow up any moment.

Aiden had almost forgotten how much crap lobster traps dragged with them on their journey up to the surface. Muck, slime, seaweed, and every type of creature that slithered along or swam near the bottom, edible and inedible, hitched a ride. At the end of the day, it made for a hell of a stinking mess. He'd just finished hosing down the deck of *Miss Annie* after giving it a quick scrub with a mop and liquid detergent. Now it was time to hose down his Grundéns, although he knew the smell would linger in his nostrils for hours afterward.

Lily had skillfully brought the boat back to the mooring and finished tying her off as Aiden completed the last of his assigned chores. Her clothes were dirty, her hair had whipped itself into a tangled-looking mess, and her lips had started to chap from the wind and salt air. Still, he couldn't take his eyes off her. She looked strong and earthy but still feminine, with her damp T-shirt plastered to her sweet curves and her pretty face flushed and glowing.

There was something incredibly appealing and sexy about her when she was in her element, so skilled and competent and confident in every facet of her work, from boat handling to navigation, to cleaning and setting traps and making sure both captain and sternman stayed safe. Her love for what she did shone through so crystal clear he'd have to have been blind to miss it.

And that made it even harder to stay away from her. All day long, he'd fought an almost primal urge to yank her into his arms and kiss the little sun freckles sprinkled on her nose and cheeks, moving on to her lush mouth and getting an even longer taste of her sweetness than he'd had last night.

He didn't do it, and not just because Lily probably would have kneed him in his junk and then kicked his ass back to work. No, he couldn't take the chance of repeating the mistake of fourteen years ago. He'd hurt Lily back then by leaving the island and not even coming back to Seashell Bay for a visit. He hadn't called her or written a letter. He'd lived his new life, and he'd tried to forget everything about the island, even sweet Lily Doyle.

Though Lily and he had never formally dated, that didn't mean they hadn't bonded. On all those ferry rides back and forth to high school every day, at town dances, and just hanging out with their friends on long summer evenings, Aiden had been more open with her than with any living soul except his mother.

But then he'd let Lily down.

So he just couldn't do that again, no matter how much he ached to be with her. No matter how much he burned for her touch.

"A great day's work," Lily said as she came up behind him. "Well over three hundred traps, and more than six hundred pounds of lobsters."

Aiden knew how badly she needed the cash and felt a surge of satisfaction that he'd helped her. She'd make over fourteen hundred dollars for the day before expenses.

"Then I think a good day's work deserves a reward," he said. "How about we get cleaned up and I'll buy you a beer and a burger at the Pot? Eight o'clock sound good?"

It was already seven, and the sun was dropping steadily toward the horizon.

Lily shook her head, looking regretful. "Sorry, I'm afraid not. I've got choir practice at Saint Anne's tonight. Can't miss that or Father Michael would have my head."

"Choir practice?" Aiden echoed. Church choirs had always struck him as a refuge for the blue-rinse set, but apparently not. Just as apparent was how deeply Lily was involved in island life.

"Uh-huh. I'll probably have a hard time staying awake, though. But even if I didn't have the choir, I wouldn't be heading to the Pot in any case. Not when we need to get a good rest so we can haul even more traps tomorrow." Her gaze cut nervously down to the deck. "That is, if you want to do this again. You know you don't have to, Aiden.

Really, you've already done more than enough to make good on a silly bet."

Aiden took off his gloves and tipped Lily's chin up so that she was looking at him instead of her boots. Her cheeks flushed an even brighter red, but her gaze held steady.

"But you still need me, Lily," he said. "And if you still want me, I'll be back tomorrow. You deserve the help, you know."

With a wistful smile, Lily moved his hand away. But then, in a gesture so quick and fleeting that Aiden barely registered her lithe movement, she went up on her tiptoes and brushed the lightest of kisses across his cheek.

"Thank you, Aiden," she whispered. "For everything." Then she turned and picked up her gaff hook from under the rail.

And suddenly she was all business again, gaffing the skiff and pulling it alongside the lobster boat, leaving Aiden more confused than ever.

Chapter 13

 $\mathcal{T}$ he wind ruffled Aiden's thick, black hair as he started a wide turn around Wreckhouse Point. He looked thoroughly comfortable at the helm. Perched on the starboard rail, Lily watched his every move, not because he might do something stupid, like run over another fisherman's trap lines, but because she just couldn't help looking at him. Really, what sane woman wouldn't want to look at him?

This morning he wore a tight-fitting black T-shirt, tan cargo shorts, and sports sandals. After their first day on the water, Lily had suggested he stow his Grundéns gear on the boat and change when they reached their first trap line. Aiden had been totally down with that idea. So now as he piloted the boat, she got to take a good, long look at his very fine ass. Well, why shouldn't she? He'd been zeroing in on her butt every day, hadn't he? He maintained his hands-off policy, but that didn't stop him from looking— a lot.

Despite the off-the-charts sexual tension, Lily and Aiden had established an efficient fishing routine. They'd hauled every one of Lily's eight hundred traps in their first three days together and were starting all over again this morning. To her relief and joy, they'd been—as Gramps liked to say—ass deep in lobsters. If they could keep up the current rate for a while longer, Lily had visions of not only making her boat payment this month, but possibly even putting aside some cash toward her dream of some-day owning a house that wasn't at the back of her father's lot. As much as she loved her family, there were days when she could use a little more privacy.

But she'd still had no luck finding a permanent stern-man and likely wouldn't during the prime fishing months of August and September. So as soon as Aiden either got good news from his agent or just decided he'd had enough of Seashell Bay, she'd be back to fishing on her own and struggling to make a profit.

That was a very depressing thought, for many reasons.

Still, Aiden was growing more comfortable on the boat every day. There were times when his expression would go grim and he might even stop work for a few moments. When that happened, she was pretty sure he was reliving some bitter memory from his father's boat. But he always came around quickly. Lily had done everything she could to encourage him, praising his work—with good reason—and letting him take over the boat's controls, something he clearly enjoyed. He was just like any man in that respect—he always wanted to drive.

Aiden eased back on the throttle and slowed *Miss Annie* as they neared the buoy that marked one end of her trap line. To starboard, Sea Glass Beach was deserted as usual at this early hour. Sometimes though, Dottie Buckle and her best friend, Nancy Peck, would take an early morning stroll to check out whether any interesting glass had washed ashore with the overnight tide. Their little canvas bags in one hand and sticks in the other, they would poke at clumps of seaweed, looking for hidden treasure.

Seeing those ladies strolling and chatting happily in the distance often made Lily's heart ache a little, wondering if she'd ever have a friend to walk the beach when she was older and done with hard labor on the sea. Though she was really close to Morgan and tight with Holly, too, her best pals weren't likely to come back to Seashell Bay to live. Maybe someday they'd change their minds, if she was lucky, but not as long as they were pursuing careers off-island.

Just like Aiden.

She shook off the moment of melancholy. "I'll take over now," she said as she stood up.

Aiden cut the engine and let go of the wheel as Lily grabbed it. He reached down into a locker below and pulled out his oil pants and rubber boots, slipping on the gear in seconds and then stowing his sandals in the locker.

"You're looking a little, uh...blue all of a sudden," he said.

Lily shrugged. She wasn't about to talk to him about loneliness or her fears about growing old alone. They'd been doing fine, talking only intermittently and mostly about the weather, movies, and music, with a little politics slipping into the conversation too. She hadn't been surprised to discover they still shared similar tastes in music—country and some pop rock—but absolutely none in movies. Lily enjoyed serious drama and romantic comedy, while Aiden went for guy movies like *The Fast and the Furious*. As for politics, she liked that they shared a healthy cynicism in most everything and everyone political. When he'd asked with a raised eyebrow how she squared that orientation with her leading role in the Smart Development Coalition, she'd retorted that she viewed the island development issues as ones of survival, not politics.

That had ended that brief discussion on a slightly uncomfortable note.

"It's nothing," Lily said, as they took their positions along the rail. She reached for her gaff hook. "Just a stray, fleeting thought. Doesn't that sometimes happen to you too? You think about something innocuous and get a little sad for a moment?"

He nodded as he pulled on his gloves. "Sure, especially when I think about baseball these days."

Lily didn't reach for the buoy. Not yet. Something felt different, like he wanted to talk.

"Did your agent call again?"

"No. And when he does—*if* he does—it'll likely be with some crappy offer to play in the minors or an independent league."

Wow. No wonder he avoided talking about his future.

Lily didn't know what words of comfort she could offer, because she knew so little about the inner workings of pro baseball. But she had to say something. "If you decide it would be better to quit, will you be okay financially?" It hadn't occurred to her before this moment that he might actually need the money from the sale of Flynn lands.

Just then, the boat rocked in the swell of another lobster boat heading farther offshore. Distracted by the conversation, Lily hadn't been prepared for it and had to grasp Aiden's shoulder for balance. Instantly, he wrapped an arm around her waist to make sure she was steady. She felt the zing of his touch clear down to her toes.

After a couple of tense moments, he slowly let her go.

"Yeah, I guess so," he said, as if nothing had just happened. Too bad she could barely catch her breath.

"I'll get some pension money eventually, in about thirty years," he added with a cynical laugh. "I still have some investments, but I got hammered by the real estate crash, like a lot of people."

Lily winced in sympathy.

"Anyway, it's not like I have enough to be able to sit on my ass and do nothing for the rest of my life," he continued. "Not even if I wanted to, which I don't. So, one way or the other, in baseball or in something else, I'm going to need a job."

She decided she might as well confront the elephant lumbering around the deck since Aiden was, for once, in a mood to discuss his life. "The money from selling your land would come in handy then, I guess."

Aiden gave her a puzzled glance. "Sure, but I don't think of it in those terms. Regardless of how much I get from the land, if I wind up selling, I'm still going to work. I *need* to work. I'd go crazy if I didn't."

"People are saying that the sale will net you guys a bundle," she said, pushing it. "Though everything in that regard seems to be a state secret."

He stared at her, his expression carefully bland.

Nothing to see here, lady. Keep on moving.

"You might be able to live off the proceeds of the sale," she prodded.

A wry smile touched the corners of his mouth. "You don't give up, do you? Well, I suppose I could do that, if I lived in a place like Seashell Bay. But not in Philly. Or in San Francisco, which is where I'd really like to end up someday."

Lily didn't miss the faint note of contempt in his voice when he said *Seashell Bay*. She had never been to either Philadelphia or San Francisco, but she supposed they were nice. The latter had always sounded so exotic to her, with its hills and cable cars and foreign lifestyle—foreign to her, anyway. She still found it hard to think of Aiden Flynn as a big-city kind of guy.

"If you stop playing, you'd like to get some kind of job in baseball?"

"What else? It's what I love, and it's all I know." He shot her a glance full of meaning. "Lily, you know what it's like to do something you love. You can't imagine doing anything else."

Oh, yeah, Lily knew, all right. She knew how awful she'd feel if she could never fish again.

Aiden smiled. "Besides, I'm a little old to retrain as a plumber."

She matched his smile. "People are always going to need plumbers, Aiden. But you're hardly old. You turned thirty-two at the beginning of June, right?"

"You remembered," he said.

"June fifth."

"Wow. Really good memory."

The date had remained engraved on her brain. Or on her heart. "Do you remember what I bought you for your eighteenth?" she asked softly.

There was a moment of silence with only the gentle

slap of water against *Miss Annie*'s hull. The sound was rhythmic and peaceful. "How could I forget? You gave me a Stetson and a road map of Texas."

She remembered his rich laugh when he'd opened the big hatbox, but now he seemed a little... sad, maybe, at the memory. "And I said I thought they'd be useful since you'd been drafted by the Texas Rangers."

"They would have been really useful if I'd actually spent any time in Dallas instead of bouncing around in their minor-league system until they traded me."

They were both silent again for a minute, clearly remembering. Lily's heart had been a lead ball in her chest when she shopped for his birthday. What do you buy a boy who's about to leave you, probably forever? Every one of her early ideas had felt maudlin, coldly calculated to make him remember her, and she'd rejected them as making her seem needy and petty. Instead, she'd chosen light-hearted gifts that she hoped would make him laugh. After all, it wasn't like he actually owed her anything or had made any commitment beyond friendship.

A friendship that had meant the world to her at the time.

"What happened to the Stetson, Aiden?"

Again a faint smile curled up the corners of his mouth, one that made her want to wrap herself around his awesome body and kiss him. "I've still got it at my house in Philly. On top of a bookcase."

Stupidly, a glow lit her up at the idea that he'd kept her silly present. That had to mean something, right?

Before she did something truly idiotic—like carry through on that urge to lock lips with him—she straightened and grabbed her gaff. "Well, I guess we'd better stop jawing and haul some traps, huh?" She leaned out to reach for the buoy.

"I still remember your birthday too, you know," Aiden said.

Lily almost dropped the gaff into the water. She turned to stare at him. He leaned against the rail, arms crossed over his chest, gazing at her with that sexy smile and a light in his eyes that made her stomach feel squirmy and girly.

"You do?" she whispered.

His lips parted in a slow grin. "Yep. In fact, I'm pretty sure it's this Saturday."

Actually, Aiden was positive that Saturday would be Lily's thirty-first birthday. It wasn't that hard to remember, since it fell two days after his mother's. Maybe Lily didn't remember that connection. That made it a special week in two ways, especially since he was destined to spend it in Seashell Bay.

"Any particular plans for the big day?" He would have loved to do something special for her, but that probably wasn't a good idea. He tried like hell to remember why.

Lily shrugged. "Just the usual dinner with my folks. At their insistence, I might add, not mine." She made a little scoffing noise. "Hey, once you get past thirty, you'd just as soon forget birthdays, right?"

"Tell me about it." Aiden had never worried about his age until lately. "Thirty is the top of the hill for most ballplayers, and after that it's a steep slope down until you're done. At thirty-two, most players are already thinking about the end of the line."

"True, but at least pro athletes make good money.

Lobster fishermen, not so much, and we don't exactly have a secure life either. So many burn out, get an injury, or develop a chronic condition that trashes their ability to work." She grimaced. "Our dads are perfect examples."

"Bram too," Aiden said. His brother's life had been flipped upside down in a few horrible seconds.

"It's not an easy life, that's for sure."

Lily was right. Compared to the hardship and insecurity fishermen faced—and, in their dads' cases, while raising young families—Aiden's troubles didn't match up. He'd been blessed by good fortune, all things considered.

"We're really cheering each other up, aren't we? I should just shut up and count my blessings," he said.

Lily's gorgeous green eyes widened. "Aiden, I didn't mean it as a criticism. You're right to be thinking about your future. Everybody should. I'm just saying that we *all* need to remember that things could always be worse."

He nodded. "Agreed."

Her little lecture gave him a perfect opening to make the point that she should cut him some slack on the land deal. "So, given what you just said, can you get where I'm coming from on the sale of my land, under the circumstances?"

She'd picked up the gaff again but didn't dip it in the water to hook the buoy. Instead, she leaned against it with one hip thrust out in an unintentionally sexy way that certainly drew Aiden's attention.

Down, boy.

"Maybe you should spell it out for me," she said. "It sounds like you want to."

"Fine." *Let's get it out on the table.* "To me, the deal is all about Bram, period. I want you to understand that,

Lily. It's not that I don't care about my old man in some totally screwed-up way, but after all those years of hard drinking and smoking, well..."

"It'll be a miracle if he sees seventy," Lily said.

"Probably. But Bram—hell, he really needs help. He's got almost no money left as far as I can tell. I don't even know how he keeps gambling. He told me he makes enough on the games to break even, but I have a hard time believing that."

"I worry about him too. Maybe your father lends him money?"

"I doubt it, because Dad says he's in bad shape too. Always seems to have money for booze and smokes, though."

"People always manage to find money for those things," Lily said.

Aiden couldn't miss the bitterness in her voice. He knew she was thinking about her dad. Tommy Doyle wasn't nearly as big an asshole as Aiden's father, but he had his own struggles with the bottle. "Dad gets Social Security, that's all, and Bram has absolutely no income. He's been living off some money Mom left him when she died, money she'd inherited and kept separate from Dad. But that must be nearly gone by now after all his gambling."

"I'm so sorry, Aiden," Lily said, her gaze soft with sympathy and concern.

That was one of the things he'd always loved about her—she wore her heart on her sleeve. And God, it felt good to talk to her about the worries that were keeping him awake night after night. He'd confided in her when they were teenagers, and now he realized how much he'd missed that. Lily Doyle was one of the few people he could trust with the secrets of his soul.

He decided to lay it all out for her. "I can't help worrying that Bram might be in debt to . . ."

"A loan shark?" Lily guessed when he paused.

"Something like that. Maybe I'm just being paranoid."

She grimaced. "No, you're right to worry. Look, I know Bram can't fish anymore, but has he even tried to find a job? The word on the island is that he doesn't want to work, especially now that he thinks he's going to make a pile of money selling his land."

There was some truth to that, but there was another side to the story too. "Maybe, but you can probably put yourself in Bram's shoes, because all you ever wanted to do is fish, right? Well, it was exactly the same for my brother. All he ever wanted was to be a lobster fisherman, just like his dad. He always loved boats, loved the sea. When he was old enough, he worked his ass off as a sternman and then waited for years until a commercial license finally came available. He saved every dime so he'd be in a position to buy *Irish Lady* when Dad was ready to retire." He stared at her, willing her to understand what he was trying to say. "I was proud of him."

Lily braced her legs against the swell of a passing ferry, totally focused on him.

Aiden's throat went tight, like it did every time he thought about Bram's accident. "But then it all came crashing down. One little distraction was all it took. It could have happened to anybody." He shook his head. "It could have happened to you."

She nodded. "It still could. I think about that all the time, because there's always danger waiting on the water."

Then she gave a funny little shrug. "Then again, you city folks can step off the curb and get run over by a bus, right?"

"Sure, but my point is that the accident changed Bram forever. It sucked the life out of him. You can understand why."

She nodded, her lips pressed tight with reluctant agreement.

Aiden turned half away from her, leaning on the railing and gazing at the beach past Wreckhouse Point. Two little boys, maybe seven or eight, were racing along the thin strip of sand, followed by a lumbering old black Lab. There was no adult in sight, and that was just fine. Short of drowning—and every kid on the island learned to respect the water at an early age—there wasn't much to worry about. Life didn't come much safer than it did on Seashell Bay Island.

At least until you took to sea on a small fishing boat.

"Bram and I spent a fair bit of time together after that," he continued. "In Philly, or somewhere on the road where I was playing. I wanted to get him away from the island and the bad memories for a while." Aiden shrugged. "He was okay as long as we didn't talk about his future. Every time I said a word about that he threatened to split if I didn't get off his case."

"Hardheaded," she said quietly. "Like a true islander."

"Anyway, even if he wanted to get a job now, who would hire him? His head's messed up, he barely graduated high school, and he drinks way too much." Aiden clenched his fists against the anger he had bottled up over Bram's rotten luck. "One way or the other, Lily, I have to make sure he's going to be okay. I love my brother, and

I'm not going to let him sink into some kind of pathetic drunken poverty if I can help it. I will not let him turn into my dad."

Lily leaned over and gave Aiden's shoulder a sympathetic squeeze. He liked the feel of her slender but strong hand on him too much. "Of course you won't. But Bram has to be able to help himself too, right?"

"Yeah," Aiden said. Actually, he would have liked nothing better than to scoop Bram up and whisk him to Philadelphia or wherever else he ended up, but he'd already floated that idea to Bram and had been met with wounded disbelief.

Aiden, I'm your brother, not your charity case.

Bram, like most Flynns, intended to live out his days in Seashell Bay and be buried in the family plot at Saint Anne's-by-the-Sea. The island held his brother in its relentless grip, and nothing Aiden did or said would change that.

"I think he needs help," Lily said in a careful voice. "Professional help and a support group for his gambling." She gazed up at him, searching for his understanding and, possibly, approval.

"You're talking about a shrink?" Aiden tried not to sound too defensive. Lily wasn't trying to manipulate him to her advantage. He knew she cared for Bram.

"Some kind of therapy." She shifted from one sneakered foot to the other, clearly uncomfortable but not backing down.

"Well, you might be right, but you've known Bram all your life, Lily. Seriously, can you see my brother on a shrink's couch? Hell, maybe we could talk Dad into going too. Get a two-for-one discount."

Lily turned away and shoved the gaff into the water, hooking it under the buoy. "It's easy to be cynical, Aiden, but I don't hear you coming up with better answers."

When she fed the pot warp into the hauler and started it up, it effectively ended the conversation, since Aiden wasn't about to shout over the loud whine of the machine. Sighing, he widened his stance and got ready to receive the lead trap.

There wasn't much more he could say, anyway. Lily was right that he didn't have any better answers. And Bram's bad habits were obviously becoming more deeply ingrained.

Every day Aiden spent in Seashell Bay pounded home the fact that his family was deep in an epic shithole. And he sure as hell didn't have the faintest idea how to make it right.

Chapter 14

Lily parted the curtains and scowled out her front window at the fog that refused to quit. It was already late morning, and yet the murk had only slightly dissipated since dawn. Now, though, she could at least glimpse the outline of her parents' house on the other side of the trap lot. Still, she didn't dare take her boat out. When it was this bad a couple of hundred feet inshore, on the water it would be heavy enough to make fishing dangerous even with radar and GPS. *Miss Annie* would remain at her mooring.

One thing she could easily see out her window was her mother bustling down the pea gravel track that connected Lily's place to her parents' house. Her mom carried a square Tupperware container cradled against her stomach as she strode purposefully past Lily's Jeep.

Muffins? Coffee cake? Banana bread?

Lily was glad she'd made a fresh pot of coffee. When her mom showed up midmorning with baked goods, it meant she intended to stay for a chat. She'd no doubt correctly guessed that Lily would be in a blue funk over the weather that had prevented a day's fishing.

Lily had called Aiden at five forty-five to catch him before he headed down to the dock. She'd expected him to be relieved, but to her surprise, he'd sounded a little disappointed when she told him he was off the hook for fishing today. He'd even told her—with apparent sincerity—to call him right away if the fog broke enough later to let them head out.

His unexpected response had left her standing in the kitchen, staring at the disconnected phone as she tried to figure him out.

Lily smiled as her mother pushed open the door. "Hi, Mom."

"Good morning, honey. Goodness, that fog was as thick as terry cloth out there first thing this morning, wasn't it?" Edith Doyle shook herself as if the fog had been clinging to her slight form. She wore a gray cardigan over a white blouse and black mom jeans, and her graying hair was pulled back into a ponytail and secured by a neon-pink scrunchy.

Her never-ending supply of brightly colored scrunchies never failed to crack Lily up.

Her mother kicked off her shoes at the door. "I thought you could use some blueberry muffins to cheer you up on such a foggy morning."

"You're the best, Mom. Thanks," Lily said as she headed into the kitchen.

Her mother padded behind in her stocking feet. When she pried off the Tupperware lid, the amazing smell of freshly baked muffins filled the room. Lily's mouth started to water. Her mom's baking was better than chocolate and almost as good as sex, and she could feel her mood starting to lift.

Soon after they sat down and took their first sips of coffee, her mother cocked an eyebrow. "You look quite out of sorts this morning, sweetie. Is it more than just the fog?"

When she paused significantly, Lily knew she was in for it.

"Are things not going so well with Aiden after all?" Mom asked.

Lily had told her parents—after some prodding—that Aiden was adapting to work on the boat much better than she'd anticipated, but she'd refused to go into detail. Trust her mother, though, to not let sleeping dogs lie.

"Aiden's doing well enough," Lily answered, "given all the stuff he has to deal with. I don't think he realized just how awful the situation was with Bram until he came home."

Her mother nodded. "I'm sure he didn't fully understand—not when he'd all but disappeared from his family's life." She held up a hand when Lily started to protest. "I know he'd fly Rebecca and Bram out for visits, but that barely scratched the surface. Rebecca always worried about Aiden. She thought he was running away from his family and his past."

"Well, heck, what else could he do? With a father like Sean, who could blame him?"

Her mother sighed. "He can't do anything about his father, but it's not too late for Bram. At least I hope not."

Lily pushed her half-eaten muffin aside. "That's the only reason Aiden would ever agree to sell his land. He only cares about the money because of what it could mean for Bram."

"That's all well and good, but I'm sure Sean could have come up with a smaller project that would have made the family plenty of money without ruining the island. No, this particular deal is all about Sean's greed and ego. The man thinks people have been persecuting him for years, so he's darn well going to show everybody who's really in charge in Seashell Bay."

Lily resisted the urge to rub her temples. "We've gone over this so many times, Mom. That's all water under the bridge. There's only one deal on the table, and it's going to be up to Aiden to decide whether it goes ahead or not. I'm going to do all I can to push him in the right direction, but I get where he's coming from. Aiden's not like his father. He just wants to do the right thing."

"Well, I have to say the man handled himself well at the social the other night, unlike his father. And yours, I might add. I gave your father quite a talking to when we got home. Sean was an idiot—no surprise there, of course—but Tommy would have played right into his hands if Aiden hadn't stepped in. I told your father that this feud nonsense has to end. It's the twenty-first century, for goodness' sake."

It had been quite an evening, followed by that steamy encounter on the beach with Aiden. Not that her mom would ever hear about that little incident. "Aiden was great. And I was glad Micah stuck Sean behind bars for the night, the old goat."

Her mother grimaced. "The town should name a jail cell in his honor. He's been in it enough."

Lily waggled her hand. "A little exaggeration there, Mom."

"Okay, maybe a little."

"Actually, I wouldn't mind if the next time Micah throws him in jail, he sends the key to the bottom of the channel. Sean Flynn is a horrible man. The way he treated his wife and then what he did to Aiden..." Lily had to stop when her throat grew too tight.

"So true," her mother said in a quiet voice.

The old mahogany grandfather clock chimed the hour, as it had been doing in Lily's living room for a year now. It had been in the Doyle family for well over a century, but Gramps had gifted it to her on her last birthday, saying it was about time a girl took charge of the "damn noisy thing."

"Why did Mrs. Flynn put up with it?" Lily asked. "I know it was a different time, but she deserved so much better. I realize he never hit her—he saved that crap for his sons—but he made her life a misery. She was such a nice woman too."

"Yes, she was, and yes, she did deserve a better fate." Her mom sounded more thoughtful than sad. "But it wasn't always that way between them, you know."

Lily's mug had been halfway to her mouth, but she set it back down. "What are you talking about?"

"Well, to really understand about Sean and Rebecca, you need to know that he wasn't always the sad, broken creature you see now."

Lily snorted. "I'd call him an unrepentant asshole, myself."

"Language, dear. Anyway, I'm several years younger, but even as a child I knew all about him. And I can tell you firsthand that Sean Flynn was always a wild and impulsive young man. For a girl like me, he was also larger than life too. He was boisterous, fun-loving, handsome, and so very full of himself." She gave a slight, rueful shake of the head. "A true bad boy, if people still use that term."

Lily blinked. It was bizarre enough to think of Sean Flynn as the classic, sexy bad boy and even more bizarre to hear her mother referring to him that way. "Okay, this is making me feel slightly queasy."

Her mother waved that away. "He was the best kind of bad boy, one with a good heart underneath all the bluster. Everyone liked him, even your father—though it was grudging, of course. God knows they fought often enough, in the way high-spirited young men sometimes do, feud or no feud."

When Lily choked out a disbelieving laugh, her mother shrugged. "It's true. Rebecca wasn't the only girl who fell in love with Sean, but she was the one who got him to the altar. I think they were nineteen, maybe twenty, and Sean was working as sternman on his father's boat. But soon enough—it can't have been more than a year later— Sean was drafted and sent to Vietnam. I can't remember many of the details, but I believe he had more than one tour there."

Lily froze. Now that was truly a surprise.

"All I know for sure," her mom went on, "is that when he finally came home, he wasn't the same man. In fact, he was a shadow of that man—a ghost, really. Everything bad that's happened since started at that point."

Every muscle in Lily's body seemed to lock into some kind of weird spasm. Nor was her brain functioning that well, unable to process an image of Sean Flynn that was completely at odds with what she knew about him. Aiden had never breathed a word to her about his father having been in the military, much less slogging through the Vietnam meat grinder she'd learned about in school.

"God, Mom, what happened to him over there?"

"No one knows for sure. Not even Miss Annie, and you know how close she and Rebecca became over the years. Sean wouldn't even talk about it to his family. But Rebecca once told your granny that his nightmares never stopped. He would talk and shout in his dreams about awful, ugly things he must have seen over there."

Jesus.

"It sounds like PTSD." Lily knew it had afflicted thousands—probably tens of thousands—of Vietnam veterans. "But did people try to talk to him about it? Get him some help?"

Her mom shook her head. "People went out of their way to try to help, believe me. But Sean hated that, and he lashed out at anyone—and I mean anyone—who even raised the subject. So it didn't take long before people stopped trying. I guess we all thought it best to pretend that part of his life had never happened. It seemed easier that way."

Lily rubbed her jaw because she'd been clenching it hard enough to crack a lobster shell. "It's difficult to believe that people managed to keep their mouths shut about Sean's military service all this time."

"Well, Rebecca and Sean had other problems, and they eventually came to seem more important."

"What could be more important than PTSD?"

"For many years Rebecca couldn't get pregnant, and it tore them both up something fierce."

Okay, that Lily could understand. Popping out babies had always been really important on the island, especially to the older generation. Hell, it was still important, since so many of the younger residents left for college or mainland jobs and never came back.

Her mom carried on with the grim saga. "At one point, they went to a fertility clinic in Boston. Sean desperately wanted sons to follow in his footsteps, and Rebecca just badly wanted children." She gave Lily a grimace that held a world of sadness. "She hoped that having children would change Sean. Give him something to focus on besides the problems with his fishing business, which were getting worse all the time because of his anger and his drinking."

"Well, he focused on his children, all right," Lily said cynically. "Like a boxer focuses on a punching bag."

Her mother began to look irritated. "We all know that story, dear. All I'm trying to do is give you some idea why Rebecca stayed with Sean until she died. That's what you wondered about."

"Okay, I get that it must have been complicated. But I still don't see how she could stand by while her husband abused her sons. If she wanted to take it herself, that was her decision. But she should have protected the boys better, Mom."

"By leaving? Where would she have gone?" Her mom shook her head. "I know it was tragic, but Aiden seems to have turned out to be a fine young man, and Bram was on the right track until that accident. Rebecca did a darn good job with them under terrible circumstances. Yes, she suffered and kept quiet, but she was hardly the only woman in her situation to do that. Even here in Seashell Bay."

Lily couldn't argue about how Aiden had turned out, but at what price? No one could know the long-term effects of that kind of abuse.

Her mother reached over and briefly pressed her hand. "I know it's hard not to hate Sean for what he did and for what he's doing now. But your father and I talk about how it's hard not to feel pity for the man at the same time. Sean's been caught in a vicious pattern of shame and self-hatred for over forty years, Lily, and he's probably going to die a lonely and bitter old man."

Lily wasn't nearly as sympathetic as her mother. "Caught because he would never even think about getting help—professional help."

"Not many lobster fishermen would," her mother said.

Lily sighed. The men here were hard, proud, and stoic. Would they talk about their feelings to anyone, much less a stranger? Not much chance.

She put down her cup, rubbing her eyes. A few minutes ago, she'd been so eager to get on her boat that she'd been climbing the walls. Now she just wanted to crawl back in bed and hide under the covers.

Her mother pushed away her empty plate, as if to signal the end of the discussion about Sean Flynn. "But let's get back to you, sweetheart. You've been moping the last few days, and you know it. You haven't been the same since Aiden came home."

Haven't been the same was mom-speak for "fixated on Aiden." Her mother had an excellent nose when it came to this sort of thing. Of course, Lily and Aiden had probably been emitting enough pheromones to choke a horse. You'd have to have been in a coma to miss it.

Lily gave a little shrug. "I don't know quite what to make of it either."

Her mother's eyebrows lifted in gentle disbelief. "Oh, I think you do."

"Do we really have to do this now?" Lily said.

Her mother simply gave her a polite smile and settled

back in her chair. Clearly, she wasn't budging until Lily gave her some answers.

Grumbling, Lily got up and grabbed the coffee carafe from the warmer, quickly refilling their cups. "I need more fuel if we're going to have another of our fabulous mother-daughter talks." Then she adopted what she hoped was a martyred expression. "Okay, I'm ready. Lay it on me."

Her mother laughed. "Oh, stop being so dramatic. I was simply going to say that I think you're having a little bout of the what-ifs. It's completely natural when the first boy you fell in love with suddenly shows up again."

"Uh-huh," Lily murmured. Best to remain polite and noncommittal when Supermom was on the job.

"Don't forget that I saw how your world revolved around that boy for years. And I certainly noticed how you were looking at him Sunday night at the dance. I know you're now a mature woman and not a love-struck teenager, but the expression in your eyes when you're with Aiden hasn't changed a bit. You need to be careful, Lily."

Well, that was stating the obvious. "You don't have to worry, Mom. Aiden will leave as soon as he makes a decision about selling his land. And he won't be coming back. There's absolutely no need to talk about us as if we were a couple or something."

Her mother's gaze narrowed. "Nonsense. You've been comparing every man to Aiden ever since he left the island. You know it, and so do I. And nobody can ever match up, can they?"

When Lily started to protest, her mother waved a hand. "Don't even try to deny it. I know as sure as I'm sitting here that what you two are doing now is only going to make it worse."

"What we're doing is lobster fishing. Hauling and setting heavy, stinking traps. It's hardly the setting for torrid romance, Mom."

"You're just dodging the question."

Lily wanted to pull her hair out with frustration. "Look, Aiden won't stay, and I won't go. That's the bottom line for us, same as it was fourteen years ago."

Obviously reacting to her tone, her mom pushed back in her chair. "If you say so, Lily. I should get going now."

Crap.

She didn't move as her mother went to the door and crouched to tie her sneakers.

"I just want you to be happy," her mother said, straightening.

And there it was, the final mom arrow to the heart.

Sighing, Lily got up. "I know you do. And I know you think I've been…wasting opportunities to meet someone."

"It's just that—"

"I get it, Mom, I do. But do you really think I want to keep living alone in a little cottage at the back of my father's trap lot? Spending more time with my parents than with friends, much less a boyfriend? Of course I want to get married and have a family. But I can't just snap my fingers and have a genie pop out of her bottle and make it happen. I'm not going to settle just because my biological clock is ticking. You don't want me to either, and you know it."

Her mother wrinkled her nose, looking rueful. "All I was trying to say was that you need to be careful. You and Aiden are worlds apart and always have been. Don't expose yourself to that heartache again."

"Aye, aye, Mom. Message received," Lily said in a firm voice, escorting her onto the little porch.

This time it was her mother rolling her eyes before she gave Lily a quick peck on the cheek and headed up the drive, eventually disappearing into the mist.

Her mom, bless her heart, was just being her protective self. But Lily was all too aware of the danger, despite her denials. That night on the beach after the dance, she would have gone anywhere with Aiden and done anything with him, regardless of the consequences.

And, scarily enough, she knew she still might.

Chapter 15

$\mathcal{S}$aint Anne's-by-the-Sea hadn't changed much since Aiden's mom had been buried in its small, oak-shaded cemetery, although he'd been too wrung out on that shitty day to take much notice of the white clapboard church where Flynns had been ushered through the various milestones of life since the 1880s. He'd spent a hell of a lot time here as a kid, when his mother had dragged him and Bram to Mass every Sunday and religious holiday without fail. The gray shingle roof tiles had been swapped out for red, but other than that everything looked the same—the steeple topped by a plain bronze cross that rose over the church, the stained-glass windows of biblical figures that graced the sides, the one-story church hall that parishioners had built themselves several decades ago.

Aiden had spent hours in Saint Anne's when he was young, desperately praying for his dad to change and for his mom to be happy. Now he had to shake his head at how naïve he'd been.

As he skirted the church on the flagstone path overgrown with grass, heading to his mother's grave, he could see that the church cemetery had greatly expanded. The island's live population might not be growing, but the dead contingent sure was.

Leaving the path, he strolled between the headstones. The fog had long ago dispersed, and the early evening gave Aiden a perfect view of the vibrant sunset over the bay, blurred bands of red and orange fading into a dusky pink swath that cut across the sky. He stopped for a moment and gazed back over Island Road toward the channel, glimpsing a couple of Lily's neon-bright orange buoys. They'd hauled and reset that particular trap line twice this week, with damn good results too.

But they'd stayed off the water today, which didn't mean Aiden hadn't been obsessing about Lily pretty much all day. Instead of feeling relieved that he could head back to bed after she'd called him, he'd tossed and turned for nearly an hour before going for a punishing run through the fog. When he'd passed Tommy Doyle's property, just barely able to glimpse Lily's red Jeep behind stacks of old traps and other lobstering gear, it had taken a considerable amount of willpower not to knock on her cottage door and . . . well, who knew what might have happened if he had?

But fantasies of early morning sex with a naked, sleep-mussed Lily aside, Aiden still couldn't figure out what to do about her. With every hour they spent together, he wanted her more and more. Hell, his body literally ached for her—certain parts of it, anyway. But he still couldn't get his head around what would happen if they gave in to what they clearly both mutually desired. He'd had sex for the sake of sex, and he knew exactly how that felt before and after. And also he knew that sex with Lily could never just be that kind of emotionless physical gratification. It would leave a mark on him, one he wasn't likely to forget.

Knowing Lily, he seriously doubted she'd be able to treat it as just a quick hop in the sack to scratch an itch either.

Damned if he didn't go to bed every night looking forward to morning, just so he could be with her again—even though that meant long, punishing hours on a lobster boat, his least favorite place in the world.

Which simply reinforced the idea that Lily was driving him batshit crazy.

Aiden gave his head a shake and turned back to the cemetery, focusing on why he was here in the first place—to pay his respects to his mother. Tomorrow would have been her sixty-seventh birthday, had her heart not failed her. He'd taken the ferry into Portland this afternoon and gone to the best florist to track down long-stemmed white roses. His mom had loved white roses, and he now carried eighteen of them, his age when he left to pursue his baseball career with his mother's full blessing.

He knew exactly how much he owed her—everything, really, because she'd always encouraged him to follow his dream and had done all she could to support it. If not for her, Aiden would probably still be stuck in Seashell Bay, following in his father's footsteps in more ways than one.

Treading carefully around the old gravestones, he made his way to the family plot, a slightly sloped area of about a hundred square feet enclosed with a low fence of misshapen rocks and mortar. His mother was buried in the southwest corner, with places both on the granite headstone and in the grass-covered earth for his father to join her. Sean Flynn's reserved space was the last unused piece of ground inside the low walls. Aiden presumed that would be it for the long line of Flynns of Seashell Bay, unless Bram were to suddenly get his act together and start a family.

His mom's grave looked surprisingly well tended, with the grass around the stone carefully trimmed. Such was not the case with the other graves in the plot, where long grass and weeds crept up the sides of the markers. The church took care of cutting the grass in the whole cemetery, but clipping around the headstones was left up to family members.

Frowning, he stopped abruptly just outside the three-foot gap in the wall. Someone had left a spray of wildflowers in front of his mother's marker—the kind that grew in the fields at the south end of the island. And on top of the headstone itself were a couple of small items glinting in the waning light.

Pieces of sea glass?

Slipping through the gap, Aiden crouched down and carefully set the roses beside the wildflowers and read the inscription on the polished gray and black memorial he was seeing for the first time.

REBECCA C. FLYNN
BELOVED WIFE AND MOTHER
Born 1948 *Died* 2013

Rebecca Flynn had certainly been a beloved mother, but a beloved wife? The inscription was probably standard, but if that sentiment reflected his father's true feelings, he'd certainly managed to keep them under wraps.

From Aiden's perspective, he'd seen very little affection and regard between his parents, at least from his dad's end.

He reached out to pluck the two smooth pieces of sea glass from the top of the headstone. One was almost circular and in a green so sea-washed it was almost colorless. The other piece, sort of rectangular, was a translucent white. His mother had loved sea glass, and she used to spend hours on the beach with him and Bram looking for prime specimens. Gazing down at the small, delicate pieces, he wondered who could have left such a tribute.

His brother? He doubted it, especially when Bram had made it plain he didn't much like visiting the cemetery. It was probably Miss Annie. She and Mom had been thick as thieves, despite the difference in their ages. Then again, the old gal was friendly with every soul on the island other than Sean Flynn.

"Hullo, Aiden," said a familiar voice. "It's good to see you, son."

Aiden stood and turned. "Hello, Father."

Father Michael Malone was making his way through the grass to the Flynn plot, stopping just outside the low wall. He wore his Roman collar and a black long-sleeved priest's shirt with a pair of faded blue jeans. His hair was mostly white now, and he'd developed a bit of a gut, but he still looked healthy and surprisingly young for a man who'd been ministering to Seashell Bay folks for years.

"Your mother would be so happy you came here for her birthday," Father Michael said.

"I'm early. It's tomorrow, actually." Aiden stepped out of the enclosure and extended his hand.

The priest smiled as he returned Aiden's handshake. "Yes, I know. God bless her soul."

Aiden wasn't surprised. His mother had always relied on Father Michael for advice and solace. She faithfully attended Mass every Sunday morning and Wednesday evening, and she volunteered for everything from arranging food for weddings and funerals to repainting and redecorating the rectory.

"You were a good friend," Aiden said. "I know how much that meant to her."

"It was easy to be her friend." Father Michael pointed to the roses. "I assume those are yours, Aiden. They're lovely. Rebecca's favorite, as you obviously remembered."

Aiden nodded. "I see someone brought wildflowers. And the sea glass. I'm guessing Miss Annie left them. I know she and Mom both collected and exchanged good pieces."

The priest smiled. "That's a very good guess because Miss Annie does visit here quite often. But no, she didn't leave those flowers. Nor the glass."

Aiden frowned. It couldn't be Bram, and who else on the island besides Miss Annie would make a special trip to visit her grave? "Huh, I wonder who it is."

"The same person who comes here every week, without fail—even in the worst weather—to make sure there's not a stray blade of grass or a weed marring your mother's grave. Your father, Aiden."

What the hell? His father had treated his mom like crap, so that didn't make any sense. "Really? That's hard to believe."

"This isn't a once-a-year thing, Aiden. Sean brings wildflowers every week when they're in bloom, and on occasion he brings a bouquet from Portland too. He couldn't be more faithful and devoted."

Aiden could practically feel his eyes bugging out in disbelief.

The priest gave a rueful chuckle. "Well, at least in that regard. We certainly don't see him in the pews as often as we'd like."

"Yeah, or ever," Aiden scoffed.

Father Michael's eyebrows pulled up. "And are you a regular at Mass then in one of those lovely Philadelphia churches?"

Aiden had to repress a wince at the innocent reminder that his life in Philly was essentially over. "I'm on the road a lot, and we play every Sunday during the season," he said.

I used to play every Sunday, that is.

"Well, perhaps you will join us here this Sunday? I'm sure you'll be staying on the island at least that long, won't you?"

A beat-up old minivan motored noisily by on Island Road, the driver honking as a woman in the passenger seat waved at them. Father Michael waved back and, automatically, so did Aiden. Everybody in Seashell Bay waved to each other when they passed by, whether in a car or a golf cart, on a bike or on foot. If you didn't wave back, you were definitely a Come-From-Away or, as everyone abbreviated it, a CFA.

"I don't know how long I'll be here," Aiden hedged. "I'd originally thought only a few days, but then I got roped into helping out Lily, so..." He shrugged. In truth, he had no idea anymore.

"Yes, I heard about the consequences of losing the bet you two made on Darts Night," the priest said with a glint of mischief in his eye.

"No secrets on this island," Aiden said dryly.

"Well, I believe it's still a secret what you intend to do about selling your land to Bay Island Properties. When do you think you might reveal your plans in that regard, Aiden?" Father Michael adopted a beatific, innocent smile, but Aiden wasn't fooled.

"Yes, my son, I know," Father Michael added, taking in Aiden's expression. "But you know priests—we can get away with sticking our noses into just about anything, can't we?"

More than once since he'd come back to the island, Aiden had contemplated hanging a sign around his neck saying, I DON'T KNOW, SO DON'T BOTHER ASKING.

Then again, he guessed he should count himself lucky that people weren't beating down his door to lobby him. If he'd been most anywhere other than Seashell Bay, that was probably what would have happened. The locals might be nosy, but they also had an old-fashioned sense of courtesy. Funny how he'd forgotten that.

"I know people are anxious to hear, Father, but the honest answer is I don't know. I've got a lot on my mind these days." He shifted restlessly, starting to feel the old urge to escape.

"I'm sure. You feel a great obligation to your brother." He paused a moment. "And perhaps to your father, as well."

Aiden glanced down at his mother's headstone. "Mom would have wanted me to do whatever I can to help them."

"She would be distressed about Bram, of course. Rebecca was a wonderful, loving mother. But I'm not at all sure she would have approved of what Sean is trying to do. She decided to split her inherited land the way she did for a reason, you know."

Aiden shot him a puzzled look. "She wanted Bram and me to have our own parcels, ones with plenty of space and great views. She'd always hoped we'd both build homes there and raise families."

"But that wasn't the only reason, Aiden."

Great. Now good old Father Michael was wading into the toxic family stew. "Just spell it out, Father," Aiden said with a sigh.

The priest gave him a patient smile. "Shall we take a little stroll?"

As they walked back together to the flagstone path, Father Michael took up the discussion. "Your mother was a very private person, as you know, but she did need someone she could trust. Someone who would respect that privacy and not gossip." He cut Aiden an assessing glance. "But I truly think she'd want me to tell you this now, given the urgency of the situation."

Aiden repressed his impatience—both with the topic and Father Michael's meandering pace. "I know you think the car ferry and Dad's land sale are going to spell the end of life as we all know it on Seashell Bay Island," he said, exaggerating for effect. "Maybe that's not a bad thing."

"Aiden, you know your mother was never a proponent of that type of development here," Father said earnestly. "But I'm telling you that her aversion to her land being used that way ran far deeper than people know. When she told me what she intended to do in her will, I understood for the first time how strongly she felt."

Now Aiden was listening hard.

"Your father was livid about her intentions," the priest went on. "He simply wouldn't let up on her. She was quite desperate to talk to an objective third party."

"I can understand why she'd choose you, Father," Aiden said.

"Your mother regarded the land she'd inherited from her family as a sacred trust that had been handed down through many generations. Rebecca saw herself as a steward of that land, one charged with loving and protecting it for future generations. Your father, of course, believed that to be the height of foolishness. And a betrayal of him and his sons." He grimaced, glancing at Aiden. "Your parents' marriage had been troubled for a long time, but that was rock bottom for Rebecca. At one point, she even thought about cutting Sean out of the will completely. But she simply couldn't bring herself to do it. Despite everything, she still carried a good measure of love for the man, and she understood all that he'd gone through."

All that he'd gone through? What the hell did that mean?

Before Aiden could ask, Father Michael continued, "Rebecca decided to split the land up between the three of you, not just because she wanted her boys to live there, but because she wanted there to be only one way the land could be used for any kind of large-scale development. That was with the full agreement of her husband and both sons. It was the best way she could think of to protect her legacy."

Okay, that made sense. That was just the sort of thing Aiden's proud, canny mother would do. Force the three of them to reach some sort of consensus if they wanted to develop the land.

But she also would have known that Bram would always back their father—which would place the burden of the decision on Aiden. Had she deliberately planned it that way? Probably, which made him want to let loose with a long string of curses.

He mentally dialed back his anger and frustration. "You're saying, Father, that she anticipated exactly what's happening now?"

The priest gave a little shrug as they circled behind the last row of gravesites. "You'll draw your own conclusions about that, Aiden."

Now he did mutter a choice curse, not caring if Father Michael heard him. "Yeah, I'm drawing the conclusion that she was leaving it up to me to stop my father from doing something she'd think was stupid and wrong."

"I suspect that's why she left you the block of land in the middle. Not the biggest parcel, certainly, but the prime one, is it not?"

Aiden swallowed that bitter pill. He'd always thought she'd bequeathed him that piece because the two of them had talked about how perfect it would be for his house, perched out on the bluffs. But he'd been only ten or eleven at the time of that discussion. When his mom made her final will, she'd pretty much resigned herself to the likelihood that he'd never return to Seashell Bay.

"Yes," he said. Unlike his father's scrubby acreage, Aiden's land was on the bluffs, and that made it pretty much perfect for a resort.

They came to a halt at the edge of the cemetery, Father Michael regarding him with eyes warm with sympathy. "I know you're greatly troubled by your brother's situation, Aiden. It has pained me too, seeing Bram change for the worse."

"I'm sure you've tried with him, but my stubborn-ass brother won't listen to anyone."

"My point, Aiden, is this. Coming into a significant amount of money will not necessarily help Bram. I fear the opposite might be the case, in fact, unless he agrees to get some help."

Aiden grimaced. "I hear you."

"As his big brother, you're in the best position to convince Bram to get the help he needs. Otherwise, experience has taught me that a person in his situation is almost certain to fritter any amount of money away and end up in an even worse position. That's the way it is with any addiction."

Father Michael fell silent, waiting for Aiden to come to the inevitable conclusion.

And dammit, how could he disagree? "I get it, Father."

"A windfall of money won't fix Bram, Aiden. He needs a purpose, and he needs some kind of work to help him recapture his self-esteem."

Aiden inhaled deeply, catching the faint scent of the pine trees in the grove behind the church. "But I'm afraid it may already be too late for Bram. Money might be the only answer we've got left to keep him from sliding further down the rabbit hole."

Dusk was coming on quickly now, with the last rays of the setting sun casting long shadows across the headstones. But it was still light enough to see the frown on the priest's face.

"I refuse to believe that, and neither should you," Father Michael said. "Look, son, you may think I'm just trying to lobby you, and I won't deny that I hope you'll reject the developer's plan for your lands. But I truly felt an obligation to honor your mother's intent as faithfully as I could. If you think I've crossed a line, I sincerely apologize. I promise you I won't raise the issue again."

As frustrated as he was, Aiden had no doubt his mother would have agreed with Father Mike's decision to speak with him. "No worries, Father," he said in a quiet voice.

"Thank you, Aiden. I hope to see you on Sunday." The priest sketched a quick blessing before turning and heading back to the church.

In the quiet of the darkening cemetery, Aiden stood as still as one of the gravestones. His mind churned with a thousand memories of his family and eighteen years of life on the island. Despite his Catholic upbringing, Aiden had never been especially spiritual or believed in a lot of woo-woo crap. But weirdly, coming home this summer was beginning to feel like some sort of destiny. He could almost laugh at the irony of it all—the guy who'd turned his back on Seashell Bay now held the key to its future.

Chapter 16

*H*ey, Lily?"

Lily glanced back to see Aiden get up from his seat on the starboard rail and make his way toward her in the wheelhouse.

She flipped up her sunglasses to peer at him as the sun suddenly disappeared behind a lone but massive cloud. "Something wrong?"

"Nope, but I was wondering if you could rearrange that birthday dinner with your parents tomorrow night." He braced himself against the back of her chair. "That is, if you were to get a more...uh, unusual opportunity to celebrate," he added, sounding almost sheepish.

Lily canted sideways to look at him while keeping one hand on the wheel. When this close to him, her body instinctively responded with a little shiver that skated over her skin. She forced her eyes to remain on his face, resisting the temptation to inspect a brawny frame showcased by the usual tight T-shirt and low-riding, snug-fitting jeans.

Not that looking at his face was any hardship. With his

dark stubble and rugged features, he reminded her of one of those male models or actors showcased in glossy celebrity magazines.

Except better, because Aiden was the real deal.

A real deal who'd been carefully keeping his distance all week, but now was suddenly invading her space in a big way. And honestly, she liked the way he loomed over her, all big and hard and masculine without being in the least bit threatening. At least not to anything other than her heart, that is. But why was he asking her about her birthday plans?

With a shock, she registered the slow build of heat in his dark eyes, and then she knew. He was going to ask her out on a date.

Her throat went tight. Not trusting her voice, she answered by tilting her head and giving him a silent, questioning look. She couldn't fail to miss the wry cast to his smile, which told her that he knew his behavior was more than a little contradictory.

"I know this is a surprise and it's pretty late to be asking, but I'd really like to do something special for your birthday." His hand drifted to her shoulder. He gave it a light stroke, almost like he was petting her. "After all, I've got fourteen years to make up for," he finished in a deep, sexy voice that made her stomach do a funny little flip.

Fumbling a bit, Lily grabbed the throttle lever and cut the engine. She was not going to have this discussion while the boat was still in motion.

"This is kind of out of the blue, isn't it?" Predictably, her voice wasn't much more than a squeak. She pulled in a couple of deep breaths to steady herself.

He shrugged. "I've had a lot of time to think out here

this week. My mind hasn't been a hundred percent focused on lobsters and bait."

Lily tried to recapture some control over the conversation. "No? Then you've been falling down on the job, mister."

He laughed, and the sound lit her up like a falling star. Aiden so rarely laughed that when he did, it was like a bright burst of light.

"Really?" he said. "After we've been hauling in close to record catches? I don't think so."

"Don't get cocky on me, Sternman," she said in her best captain's voice. But he was right. He'd been doing a magnificent job. They had formed a hell of a lobstering team, and her bank account was growing happier with each passing day. "But I'm all ears, so let's get on with it so we can pull some traps while we talk."

"Aye, aye, ma'am." His dark gaze turned serious. "Lily, you've been working your tail off, and I think you could use a break. In fact, we both could. And before you tell me I'm crazy, I'm not suggesting we lose any fishing time. I'm talking about doing something late tomorrow and Sunday."

She'd already made it clear to him that despite it being her birthday, they'd be hauling until four o'clock, the legal limit on Saturday during the summer. There was no chance she'd miss a day of fishing when the traps were filling up every day.

"I'm listening," she said. *I'm listening so hard my brain might pour out of my ears.*

Aiden nodded, and now she thought he looked a little awkward, which was definitely intriguing.

"Like I said, I want to do something special for you.

Something fun. I talked to a buddy of mine by the name of Cole Rogers. He was a senior on the Peninsula baseball team when I was a sophomore. You wouldn't know him, because he graduated before you were in high school."

"I remember hearing the name."

"Cole flew helicopters in the navy for years, and now he's got his own charter operation in Portland. Flies corporate types mostly, but does some tourist excursions too. Anyway, he's all set to fly us up the coast late tomorrow afternoon."

Lily stared at him, mystified. "You want him to take us on a helicopter tour of the bay for my birthday?"

"No, not a tour. He'll fly us up to a resort—a place he recommended on Penobscot Bay, not too far from Castine. We'll spend the night there, and then he'll come and take us back to Portland late Sunday afternoon. So I was hoping you could postpone dinner with your parents to Sunday."

She felt her eyes go wide. "You're saying we would spend the night up there?" This time her voice came out in the Minnie Mouse register.

Lily had indulged in more than one fantasy since Aiden arrived, ones that involved the two of them naked and between the sheets. Well, naked other places too. Could he possibly be proposing what she thought he was proposing?

His smile was both tender and amused. "I guess I could have phrased that better. I'm talking about separate rooms, of course. I've already booked them, hoping you'd say yes. And the whole trip is on me, start to finish. All it'll cost you is around twenty-four hours of your time. Nonfishing time."

Separate rooms, of course.

Well, that certainly squared with the way he'd broken off their steamy session on the beach. But it hardly fit with his body language right now. Despite his casual grin, he loomed possessively over her, and she thought his hot, dark eyes were sending an entirely different signal.

Lily decided to stall for time until she could figure it out. "What resort is your friend talking about?"

She'd visited the quaint little coastal town of Castine two or three times. Home of the Maine Maritime Academy, it was nearly three hours away from Portland by road but no doubt less than an hour by helicopter.

"It's called Coastal Harmony Resort. I gather it's only been around a year or so." He gave another one of those shrugs that did such fabulous things to his shoulders. "I know it's kind of a weird name, but Cole says it's one of those green places—you know, focusing on harmony with the local environment and all that stuff."

"Maybe he's talking about ecotourism," Lily said. It did sound interesting, and she vaguely remembered hearing something about an ecoresort being developed up the coast. But she rarely took vacations, and lobster fishermen didn't go anywhere in the good weather months except out in their boats.

"I guess. Anyway, Cole said it's one of the hottest resorts on the coast. High-end facilities, but with a casual atmosphere and a great restaurant. And I figured you'd probably like the green thing too."

The way Aiden said *the green thing*, Lily couldn't help a soft laugh. An ecofocused resort was hardly his cup of tea, she suspected. But it touched her that he'd come up with the idea for her sake, because he was right.

Environmental issues had always been important to Lily, even all those years ago when she and Aiden had been teenagers. Now, as a lobster fisherman and an islander, her way of life depended on the environment—the plentiful marine stock, the pristine coastal waters, and the natural beauty of the Maine coast. "You thought right," she said softly.

Aiden's big hand came up to cradle her chin, his rough fingers oh-so-gentle on her skin. He dipped his head a bit to meet her eyes. "Live a little, Lily. All you ever do is work your lovely little ass off. It's time you did something nice for yourself, even if it's just for a day. Let me take care of you, okay?"

While Lily's brain insisted on recalling her mother's warnings, her heart knew what it wanted. And her body was clearly on board too. Yes, their relationship was totally up in the air. Yes, she had no idea what would happen between them. But all that was just background noise that didn't seem to matter, not when he was gazing at her with those dark, smoldering eyes, silently urging her to say yes.

"Well, I'm sure Mom and Dad wouldn't mind rescheduling, but I've got an SDC meeting Sunday afternoon at three o'clock, and I can't duck out of it. With the car ferry vote next week, we'll be mapping out a last-minute blitz strategy. People would kill me if I blew that off."

Aiden's eyes narrowed for a brief moment, and her heart stuttered, but then he gave her a smile. "We can get you back in time. Easy."

"You're sure?"

"Absolutely. So are we a go? Cole wants me to call this morning to confirm."

A twenty-four-hour minivacation at a luxury resort, alone with Aiden Flynn. Honestly, what could possibly go wrong?

Plenty, but who the hell cares, at least right now?

Aiden was right. She deserved some fun. They both deserved some fun, and this sounded like a good way to get it. She'd deal with the consequences later. "We're a go."

Aiden parked behind a long line of junker cars about a hundred yards down from the Pot. He'd asked Bram to come with him, but his brother had elected to stay home playing online poker—again. When Aiden had given him mild shit about it, Bram had flared up, telling Aiden to fuck off before he ruined his winning streak. Aiden had responded by stalking out, resisting the temptation to rip the computer from its connections and toss it over the bluff.

The shitty scene had come at the end of an otherwise perfect day, although it blew him away that the word *perfect* could describe long hours spent on a lobster boat. Somehow the heavy traps had seemed almost weightless, and he'd barely noticed the ever-present muck and slime. And when a feisty lobster, flailing his claws like he was on speed as Aiden tried to band him, had sunk his damn pincher into his forearm just above the glove, he'd done nothing more than grumble a mild curse. That little injury—one that made Lily wave a finger at him—had been his fault, anyway. He'd been daydreaming about helicopters and resort bedrooms and Lily Doyle dressed in nothing but a red, lacy thong. He'd richly deserved the painful wake-up call from the desperate bug.

Did Lily actually wear thongs? Not likely, but whatever she wore next to her skin in those warm, soft places, he couldn't deny how badly he wanted to get his hands inside it.

Yeah, he was going crazier every day with wanting Lily. And he couldn't stand keeping his distance from her anymore.

In fact, staying away from her was beginning to feel... wrong. With every moment that passed, he felt an irresistible pull in her direction and the same weird sensation he'd had in the cemetery—that in some way he couldn't explain, everything that was happening on the island this summer was meant to be.

So thank God Lily had said yes to his last-minute idea for a trip up the coast. He'd booked two rooms because he didn't want to pressure her, but unless his radar had gone completely rusty, Lily was still feeling as much heat for him as he was for her. With any luck, the second of those booked rooms would remain empty.

He strolled down the road to the neon-lit Lobster Pot, taking his time and letting the small aches and pains of the day work themselves out. He and Lily had hauled well over two hundred traps, and she'd been almost delirious with joy when Billy-Pain-in-the-Ass weighed the catch. It made Aiden feel damn good that he was helping to get her financially back on her feet.

After they'd finished up, Aiden had tried to cajole her yet again into having a drink with him at the Pot, but she had other plans. A night out with Morgan, Holly, and maybe one or two other friends was a birthday tradition for her, just like dinner with her folks. So Aiden would have to enjoy her from a distance—and likely put up with lobbying from one or two half-drunk locals about the damn car ferry—but it was still a hell of a lot better than staying at home with Bram. If Aiden had to spend one more night watching his brother on the fast track to nowhere, he'd go nuts.

Aiden stepped inside to see the place jammed to the rafters with what looked like half the town's population. Behind the bar, Laura pulled on draft levers with practiced ease while her assistant bartender poured shots for a gang of paramedics, including Brett Clayton, huddled at the far end. Maybe a dozen islanders stood around talking or playing darts or shuffleboard.

He finally caught sight of Lily across the room, one of six women at a table near the dartboards. When Holly Tyler noticed him, she said something that caused Lily to twist around and give him a smile before returning her attention to her friends. Though it was girls' night out, a couple of guys he didn't recognize were standing around Lily's table, beer bottles in hand. Reading their body language, he guessed the boys were making lame jokes and trotting out stale pickup lines, hoping to score with the best-looking women in the room.

From what Aiden could see, the guys were batting zero.

He spotted a free stool at the bar and sat down. Dooley, the assistant bartender, slid over, leaning into the bar on hands the size of catchers' mitts. "What's your pleasure?" he said in a voice that sounded dragged out over broken beer bottles.

"Beer," Aiden replied. "Please."

"We've got six on draft and twenty in bottles." Dooley pointed at a row of longnecks lined up in front of the mirror behind the bar. "I can give you some time to work through all the possibilities if you need it," he added sarcastically.

"You're a riot, but I'm too tired tonight to think. Just surprise me, okay?"

Dooley reached below the bar and plunked a bottle of Moosehead Lager down in front of Aiden, uncapping it. "This Canadian beer is about the best you're gonna find around here, in my humble opinion."

Aiden took a long swallow. "I think I agree with your humble opinion." The lager was definitely what the doctor ordered.

"Damn hard work hauling lobster traps, eh? Guess you've had a tough week." Despite the heavy crowds, Dooley seemed in no hurry to rush away. He started stacking glasses in a rack on the counter below.

"Jesus, a guy can't fart on this island without everybody in town hearing about it," Aiden sighed. No doubt every person on Seashell Bay Island knew about the bet with Lily—not that it truly mattered anymore. "So how long have you been on this godforsaken rock, Dooley?"

The bartender grabbed a wet cloth and wiped down the bar after the guy sitting next to Aiden got up and left. "Must be going on a year now."

"Planning on sticking around for a while?" Aiden was always interested in why Come-From-Away types remained on the island. It always seemed nuts to him.

The barkeep shrugged. "Maybe. Laura's a good lady to work for. What about you?" He reached down again and came up with a Budweiser, sliding it down the bar to the hollow leg that was Boone Cleary.

"Probably just a few more days. A week, tops." The words came out fast and easy, like they were programmed.

Leaving soon was still Aiden's plan, but he couldn't help thinking about how he would feel getting back on the boat and leaving Seashell Bay—and Lily. Until a few days ago, he'd figured he'd feel nothing but blessed relief.

Not anymore.

"Well, I'm sure Lily is real grateful for the help," said Dooley before moving away. It felt kind of like a dismissal, but Aiden decided he liked Dooley anyway. He seemed to fit into the crazy patchwork of people that made up life in Seashell Bay.

He took a quick glance at the big mirror over the bar, catching another glimpse of Lily's table in the reflection. It was all he could do not to barge over there and try to drag her away. But only a selfish jerk would act that way. This was her night with her friends—which didn't mean he wasn't damned tempted to try and lure her to the dark side with him.

A heavy arm landed on Aiden's shoulders, and a blast of garlic breath hit him in the face. "How are you, son?" Albie Emory asked jovially as he slid onto the empty stool next to Aiden.

Crap.

"I'm good, Mr. Emory. You?" Aiden answered, resigning himself to what would surely come next.

The older man ordered by making some sort of mysterious hand signal to Dooley. "Tired, and my throat's about as dry as my wife's corn bread," he said with a hearty laugh. "Spinney and me are making the rounds tonight to see who we can count on for the car ferry and who we can't."

"Uh-huh," Aiden said, trying for polite and noncommittal as Dooley poured the selectman a Jack and Coke.

"We've got lots of support," Emory said. "But some of the diehards talk about this place like it was the frigging Galapagos Islands—stuck in time." He glanced meaningfully at Lily's table. "If people like them get their way, this island's going to suffocate and die. Hell, it's already happening."

Emory looked gloomy for a few moments, but perked up when his drink arrived. Aiden hoped that if he just kept his mouth shut, the old guy would soon talk himself out.

"People like you and me and your dad, we've got to make sure that never happens, right?" Emory asked, peering hopefully at Aiden. "We need to win the vote and get the new dock built."

"Well, you're certainly doing your part, Mr. Emory," Aiden said.

Emory shifted a little to his right and plunked his arm on Aiden's shoulders again, as if they were coconspirators. "Aiden, you could make a real difference. If you were to speak out in support of the ferry, I think it would definitely pull some votes for us."

Oh, the hell with that. "I doubt it, sir. In fact, if I did what you're suggesting, it might do more harm than good. You know folks here don't like outsiders coming in and telling them what to do."

The selectman's forehead wrinkled up like a Basset Hound's. "True, but you're hardly an outsider, Aiden. You're a Flynn, and the Flynns built this island as much as any family."

"Yeah, but I'm a CFA now."

"Oh, don't go talking rubbish. I can tell you most islanders are pretty darn proud of the local boy who made good in big-league baseball."

"If so, they're keeping it pretty well hidden," Aiden said drily.

Emory leaned right in. "Listen to me, son. You've got generations of islander blood inside you. You could go away for fifty years, and you'd still be a Seashell Bay man. And maybe someday you'll come back to stay too. Eventually, everyone does."

Aiden could feel his eyebrows crawling up his forehead in disbelief. "Maybe they used to, but times have changed. Now people go where the jobs are."

"That's what I'm saying," said the old guy, changing tack. "A car ferry could change all that and bring in the jobs. Think about what I said, Aiden. You can make a difference, and you'd surely make your dad proud."

Emory finished the rest of his drink and clapped Aiden on the back before sauntering back to his table of cronies. Mentally sighing, Aiden finished his beer.

He shoved a ten at Dooley and told him to keep the change. Emory's little pitch had pretty much sucked the energy out of him. It was time to get some sleep, especially because his plans for Lily over the next few days didn't include much shut-eye. Besides, if he stayed much longer, someone else would probably start to lobby him and he'd already heard enough. Everything was going to come to a head next week with the big vote, but at least he had the weekend with Lily to look forward to before all hell broke loose.

A commotion stopped Aiden in his tracks before he reached the door, the entire bar clapping and cheering. Turning, he saw Laura pushing backward through swinging doors from the kitchen, following by two grinning cooks and a busboy. She was holding a big chocolate birthday cake topped with sparklers. People started singing the birthday song.

For Lily.

Smiling sheepishly and looking sweeter than any cake, Lily swept her gaze around the crowd, as if thanking all of them. Laura set the cake down in front of her and kissed her on the forehead. Lily's girlfriends all gathered around her in a fiercely loyal and loving group.

Aiden sang too. He sang, and he thought about all the love that surrounded Lily, and the invisible bonds that stretched like webbing through the Pot, connecting everyone in it to each other and to the island.

Including him.

Chapter 17

$\mathcal{L}$ily hadn't known what to expect when she and Aiden arrived at the Portland Harbor heliport. As excited as she was for her birthday trip, she'd never flown in a helicopter, and visions of being trapped in one of those tiny tourist bubbles that often hovered over Casco Bay brought out the claustrophobic in her.

But Cole Rogers's four-passenger helicopter was no miniature chopper. It was a freaking sky limousine.

She and Aiden sat in a pair of sinfully luxurious leather seats separated by a wide console with polished teak cup holders, spaces for books and magazines, and a built-in minibar. A small door connected the cockpit to the cabin, but Cole had closed it before liftoff, giving Aiden and Lily some privacy.

For a lobster fisherman who'd never flown on anything but a packed, cheap charter jet to the Caribbean, it seemed surreal to be flying over Portland Harbor in a helicopter obviously built for corporate big shots. When Aiden said that he wanted to do something special for her, he sure hadn't been kidding. It was only a short trip up the coast, but she was getting a glimpse into the life of the rich and famous, squired in ultrafast luxury to her destination by a private pilot. And she fully intended to enjoy it.

"Want some coffee?" Aiden said, as they banked over Peaks Island. "Cole said there's a carafe and mugs in the cabinet opposite us."

Lily tore her gaze away from the big island below. Aiden had insisted she take the left-hand seat so she would have the best views as they flew up the coast, and she had to admit that it was incredible to see everything from the air. Her whole life, she'd seen Peaks and the other surrounding islands only from the ground or on the sea. From a few hundred feet up, Casco Bay seemed like an entirely different and almost magical world.

"Not right now, thanks," she said, smiling at him. "I don't want to take my eyes off this. It's so beautiful from up here, Aiden."

Aiden's gaze drifted over her, heating with a clear appreciation he didn't even try to hide. "Not as beautiful as you are, Lily. You look totally amazing in that dress."

Lily felt herself blushing. She'd picked a short, yellow wraparound sundress, casual and cute but definitely dressier than what she usually wore. Of course she'd done a quick Internet check on Coastal Harmony, and from what she could tell, it was decidedly upscale—no jeans or ratty T-shirts, at least in the publicity photos on their website. The fact that Aiden looked so amazing in a navy sport coat, cream polo shirt, and tan chinos was another reason she was happy she'd chosen a nice outfit.

"You're not too shabby yourself," she teased. "But then again, you're used to this sort of thing. I'm assuming you've flown in a helicopter before?"

"Lots of times. Mostly for corporate product shoots, but a friend of mine in Philly—an old-money guy—would sometimes fly players to his McMansion on the Jersey Shore in one like this."

"Pretty sweet," Lily said, snuggling her shoulders back into the plush seat. "But why are we flying straight east over the bay? I thought Cole would just hug the coastline."

Aiden leaned over, his arm brushing against her bare shoulder as he glanced out her window. It made her shiver in a good way. A very good way.

"I asked him to go right over Seashell Bay before turning onto his straight line route," he said. "I thought you'd like to see the island from the air."

She'd been hoping for that but hadn't asked, not wanting to come off as pushy. Clearly, Aiden had read her thoughts. It was another example of how thoughtful and how tuned to her state of mind he was.

The southern tip of Seashell Bay lay just ahead. On their present course, they would pass right over the center of town and the ferry dock. "Thank you, Aiden. This is really special. I still can't believe it."

Aiden reached out and squeezed her hand. "Like I said, babe, you deserve something special on your birthday. You work so damn hard—harder than anyone I know."

Her heart did a little flip, especially at his use of the casual endearment. "You must be forgetting that I get to goof off all winter," she managed in a wry tone.

Most people she knew worked very hard, especially her fellow fishermen, but she didn't doubt the sincerity of Aiden's compliment for a moment. His respect for her had become more apparent with every day they fished together on *Miss Annie*.

The sound of the rotor seemed to deepen as Cole slowed and lowered the craft to skim over the lobster boats in the bay. When they crossed over Foley Point, Lily gave an excited cry. "Look, Aiden—there's my boat!"

At her mooring, *Miss Annie* rocked gently in the swell of a passing ferry on its way to Cliff Island. Her lobster boat looked tiny from the air, insignificant to anyone who didn't know what it meant to her.

But Aiden knew.

"Yep, there's the old gal," he said, craning to look. "She sure looks different from up here, doesn't she?"

"So small. Almost like a toy." A toy that had given Lily independence and the means to do exactly what she wanted with her life.

"Yeah, but she's the sweetest little boat in these islands as far as I'm concerned."

Astonished, Lily gazed into Aiden's dark, serious gaze. "I never thought I'd hear you call a lobster boat sweet."

Aiden gave her a shrug and a wry smile as the helicopter climbed away from the island.

Lily went back to staring out the window as she tried to sort out her jumbled emotions about the incredible, generous man sitting beside her. He'd done all this for her, trying to come up with something that would be truly memorable. And he'd nailed it. As much as she loved fishing, she spent six days a week on a smelly boat, working what most considered a man's job, until she was so tired she could barely get herself home. A luxury vacation to a high-class resort—complete with a swanky helicopter ride—was the stuff of dreams or fairy tales. For once in her life, Lily felt like an honest-to-God princess, pampered and cherished and without a care in the world.

And it was all because of Aiden Flynn, a man who seemed to know her better than she knew herself.

Lily craned her head to look up at Coastal Harmony Resort, perched a hundred feet above the dock where two tour boats were moored. Initially, she'd thought the name was kind of weird and off-putting, since luxury resorts rarely existed in harmony with the natural setting. Most times, they chewed it up. Still, she had to admit that Coastal Harmony did a pretty good job of minimizing damage to the local coastline.

After their spectacular flight up the Maine coast today, she'd spent almost an hour drinking chai tea and talking with one of the co-owners while Aiden worked out in the fitness center. The resort had been built to the highest ecofriendly standards, and the owners were committed to offering only programs that respected and supported the local community. It was a formula that seemed to be paying off by making a name for the resort as a go-to destination for the environmentally conscious crowd—a crowd that seemed to have a fair amount of bucks.

Aiden had been right. Lily liked the place a lot, and it had been a very relaxing way to spend the afternoon.

Until they'd sat down for dinner in the sheltered patio overlooking the bluffs. Big candles in hurricane lanterns on the tables, huge pots of roses scattered over the flagstones, and the sound of the water lapping on the rocks below had made for an ultraromantic setting in the deepening dusk. Aiden was smoking hot too, in a beige linen jacket over a black silk shirt and black pants. He looked casual and sophisticated and like he totally belonged at an expensive resort like Coastal Harmony.

One look at him and Lily's nerves had started dancing the freaking tango.

She'd dressed up as well, wearing a fifties-style white poplin dress she'd gotten on sale last year, cut narrow through the bodice and waist but with a flared, pleated skirt. She wore her only pair of dressy sandals along with the diamond-stud earrings her parents had given her for her thirtieth birthday. The dress was her favorite, since she thought it made the most of her assets and showcased her trim waist.

But next to the gorgeous hunk of expensively dressed masculinity walking beside her, she felt awfully...plain. She'd noticed several people glancing at them during dinner and figured they might be wondering what a guy like Aiden was doing there with *her*.

Oh, get over yourself, girl.

That was just the nerves talking, nerves she'd tried to calm with perhaps one too many glasses of wine. Aiden had ordered a second bottle as the fish entrée was being plated, making her think he was determined to loosen her up—and maybe himself too. Still, despite the lubrication the alcohol provided, there had been some long and rather awkward silences. Maybe Aiden was as wired as she was over what might happen later tonight.

She knew one thing for sure though—if there was going to be a move in that direction, it would be up to Aiden to make it.

"Thank you again for this incredible birthday present," Lily said to Aiden, as they meandered along the waterside path below the bluff. She'd already thanked him three times, including at dinner, but she felt compelled to keep blurting out her gratitude. "It's the biggest surprise and best present I've had since Gramps bought me a nine-millimeter when I moved out of my father's house," she said.

Aiden let out a choked laugh. "He gave you a gun? For what, fending off pirates?"

Lily grinned. "Gramps maintains that women should always be ready to defend themselves. He hounded me until I took some shooting lessons too."

"I'd better keep that in mind the next time I think about crossing you."

Lily stopped to face him. "Seriously, though, what I really need to thank you for is helping me bring in the best catch I've ever had in a single week. It's meant a lot to me."

Aiden grimaced a bit, as if embarrassed by the depth of her gratitude. "It hasn't been much more than a start, right? I hate to think of you having to go back to fishing without a sternman. And not just because you'll make less money either."

She forced a smile. "I'll be careful. Don't worry about me."

"But I do worry about you." He reached for her hand. "Look, Lily, I have to give Dad an answer about the land sale next week. If I don't, I might have to borrow that gun of yours to defend myself."

"I know. It's all right. Really, it is."

Of course, it was far from all right. She still desperately needed help to have a few more good weeks of fishing. But most of all, it wasn't all right because she could hardly bear the thought of watching Aiden ship off on the ferry again, leaving her just like he did fourteen years ago. She'd let down her defenses and opened herself up to a hurt she knew was going to be so much worse this time around.

"No, it's not," he said. "There's no reason why I need to leave right away. Not anymore, since my agent's come up empty. I'm still thinking I should be able to land something short-term when teams expand their rosters in September, but I figure I can handle some more time on *Miss Annie* until then."

"Seriously?" Lily had to blink back a sudden rush of hot tears, shocked by the depth of her relief.

Aiden reached out to gently stroke her cheek. "I wanted to make that the *real* surprise of this trip."

Struggling to rein in the surge of emotion, Lily went up on tiptoe and brushed her lips quickly across the angled slash of his jaw. "Okay, this definitely tops Gramps's gun as my best gift ever."

Aiden laughed, then took her hand again and led her down the last twenty yards of the paved path until they reached the dock. "It's so peaceful here," he said, after they sat on one of the wooden benches facing the water. "It reminds me of Seashell Bay at night. That's one thing I'd forgotten about the island after being away for so long. It's so quiet it's almost eerie."

Lily absorbed the peace of the evening and the presence of the man beside her. Though the hotel was just a short distance away, they seemed cocooned in a bubble with only the birds and the gentle lapping of water against concrete pilings to keep them company. "And here I thought you'd become a confirmed city boy after all these years."

Aiden gazed thoughtfully out at the water. "I thought so too. But since I've been back here, Philly seems kind of intense to me now. The traffic, the crowds, the noise—it's been nice to get away from all that for a little while."

For a little while. The phrase had her mentally cringing. "But I guess you must miss your social life, right? For a celebrity athlete, it must be pretty cool."

When his eyebrows arched in surprise, she gave him a weak smile. It was nervy of her to probe for personal details, but she needed to know how he felt about his old life. Why she needed to know was another question—one she intended to ignore for the moment.

He lifted his broad shoulders again in a casual shrug. "I like hitting the bars and restaurants around Rittenhouse Square as much as the next guy, I guess. And it's not hard to get used to being treated like you're special." Then he laughed. "But hey, I have to admit that the Pot has its charms too."

Lily gave him a cautious smile. "And exactly what charms would those be?"

When Aiden slid an arm around her shoulders, she knew the spike in her body heat had nothing to do with the warm evening breeze.

"Oh, charms like Darts Night, where sexy but devious locals can sucker newcomers into reckless bets they're sure to lose," he said with a grin.

"Ouch. That shot didn't exactly tickle, big guy. Anything else?"

"Well, it's got a couple of real nice bartenders," he said after a moment.

Since he was clearly playing with her, she pretended to pout. "And? I'm sure you must be forgetting something."

"Let me think." He thoughtfully rubbed his chin with the hand not stroking her bare shoulder. "Okay, I could say that the Pot was where I got reintroduced to the nicest, most decent, and hardest-working woman I've ever known." He paused for a couple of beats. "Not to mention the hottest babe in the entire state of Maine."

Lily had expected him to say something flirtatious, but she hadn't expected him to use words like *nice* and *decent*. That certainly wasn't the average guy's approach to getting into a girl's pants. But Aiden's response sounded completely genuine. And that meant the world, because it confirmed for her what she'd always hoped to be true— that at his core, he believed in the same things she did.

She closed her eyes against the sting of tears.

"Hey, Lily-girl, what's wrong?" Aiden whispered as he tightened his embrace.

"Nothing. I'm...I'm just feeling a little overwhelmed all of a sudden," she managed to choke out.

"By what I just said?"

Lily nodded, finally opening her eyes and shifting to meet his now-serious gaze. "That and everything else that's happened this week. I still can't believe any of it, or that we're here together." She let out a tiny laugh. "It's kind of like a dream. A really good dream."

Aiden moved to brush his lips across her cheek. "You should believe it, because this is exactly where I want to be at this moment. Right here with you, Lily."

Without any conscious thought, she turned into his embrace. Their lips slid together in a soft, almost chaste kiss that ended too soon. But then Aiden moved his hand from her shoulder to the back of her head, urging her into a hot, fierce kiss. He surged into her mouth, his fingers tunneling into her hair as he held her, silently urging her closer. The feel of his tongue, boldly sweeping in and demanding a response, soon had every bit of blood pulsing madly through her veins.

Lily clutched at his broad shoulders, digging her fingers into the smooth fabric of his blazer as she returned his kiss with a rising desire that felt almost desperate. When his other hand moved to her knee, she registered a slight shock at the feel of his callused palm on her skin as he pushed up under her skirt.

Between his hand tracing lazy circles on her thigh and his mouth devouring hers, it didn't take long for Aiden to reduce Lily to a state that resembled the chocolate lava cake they'd had for dessert, all hot and liquid inside. In her boneless condition, she had to wonder if she'd be able to make it back up the hill without Aiden having to hoist her over his shoulder in a fireman's carry.

"Oh, my God," she gasped, pulling back a bit. "If you don't stop, I'm going to be in big trouble."

"I like your kind of trouble," Aiden murmured. In the soft glow of the lamppost at the end of the dock, he looked utterly wicked and utterly hot.

Then he rose to his feet, pulling her up with him. "Besides, we're just getting started."

Lily couldn't fail to miss the burn in Aiden's dark gaze or his need to get her back to his hotel room. In fact, he'd towed her along behind him so fast that she'd laughingly implored him to slow down. And when another guest had stopped them in the lobby and asked Aiden for his autograph, Lily had expected the top of his head to blow off. But he'd mustered up a smile and signed the guy's ball cap before hauling her off to the staircase.

Aiden unlocked the door to his room and shoved it

open, ushering her in. "Jesus, I thought we'd never get back."

"Well, big-deal celebrities get attention," Lily teased.

Aiden threw the safety latch on the door. "The only attention I want right now is yours."

Then he began stalking her across the room, whipping off his jacket and dropping it on the floor. When the backs of her knees hit the mattress, Lily collapsed, leaning back on her elbows. That brought her to perfect eye level with the very impressive bulge in Aiden's pants.

"Ah, so I see," she said.

Out on the dock, she'd been wild for him. But now that it was actually going to happen, her emotions were wound so tight she hardly knew what to say, much less how to act.

Aiden had his shirt half off. He paused after glancing at her, then leaned down and braced his hands on either side of her shoulders. "Nervous?"

She scrunched her face at him. "A little. Dumb, isn't it?"

He kissed the tip of her nose. "You seemed pretty eager out there on the dock, remember?"

She jabbed him in the chest. "That's not what I meant, you big jerk."

He let out a soft laugh. "Believe me, I know." His expression grew serious. "It's been a long time coming, hasn't it?"

Her throat muscles went tight so she simply nodded.

"If this isn't what you want, you need to tell me now. I promise I won't push you." He gave her a lopsided smile. "As much as it will kill me not to."

She stared up into his face, taking in the honesty in his expression. That Aiden wanted her as much as she wanted him wasn't in doubt. If he also had the strength to step back out of consideration for her unsettled emotions, then she could find the strength to step up and be with him—no matter what happened later.

Lily flattened a hand and pushed against his chest. "What I want is for you to get out of those clothes. Now."

He shook his head. "You're a bossy little thing, you know that?"

She rose to unzip her dress. "Well, I *am* the captain, after all."

"And I'm ready for your orders, Captain." Aiden spun her around and finished unzipping her. As she shimmied out of the dress, his hands went to her butt, tracing a finger up the back of her panties.

"You have a seriously great ass, babe," he murmured as he cupped her. Then he reached up and unhooked her bra.

He started to pull her against him, but Lily wriggled loose and climbed onto the bed. On her hands and knees, she glanced back over her shoulder and gave him a taunting smile before she slowly crawled up to the pile of fluffy pillows.

"You're asking for it," Aiden growled as he practically ripped his shirt off.

"You bet I am," she replied, lazily stretching her arms over her head.

She enjoyed teasing him, and from the look in his eyes and the way he was yanking off his clothes, it seemed to be working. But Aiden was used to dating supermodels and actresses, for God's sake. Lily knew she was slim and strong, but she didn't have all that much going on in the curves department.

The little voice of doubt in her head disappeared when

Aiden finally shed his pants, leaving him in nothing but a pair of black-knit boxers. The guy was magnificent—well over six feet of brawny, sculpted male, with a nice dusting of dark hair on his chest that narrowed down over his six-pack to the huge bulge in his briefs.

She got an eyeful of just how huge when he shucked off the boxers.

"Wow," she said, sounding like an idiot. "You're freaking gorgeous."

That surprised a laugh out of him. "I think that's my line." Then he turned serious, and his eyes narrowed in a smoldering inspection. "In fact, gorgeous doesn't even begin to cover it. You're incredibly sexy, Lily."

She blushed, feeling shy again. When she started to pull the plush duvet down to wriggle under it, he clamped a hand on her ankle.

"No way, babe," he said. "I want to get a good look at you. I've been waiting a long time for this."

"And whose fault is that?"

"Mine." Aiden ran his big hand up her leg to settle on her thigh as he climbed onto the bed. Gently, he nudged her wide and tugged on the little pink bow at the top of her lacy panties. "If I'd known you were wearing underwear like that while on the boat, I would have had to do something about it."

"I'll remember that for future reference." Her voice came out on a squeaky note because his hand had slipped under her waistband. When he slipped two fingers inside her and gently scissored her open, Lily fell back on the pillows with a moan.

Then he pulled out. "Let's get rid of these," he said, his voice rough and urgent as he drew her panties off.

A moment later, she was completely exposed, and he moved down between her legs, using his broad shoulders to push her wide open. Every muscle in her body went weak as she took in the possessive, hungry expression in his eyes.

"God, you're so pretty down there, Lily," he murmured in a husky voice. "And so wet."

When he rubbed a finger over her, she almost climaxed. She arched her back and clamped her fists into the duvet, trying to hold back the beautiful spasms. It was too soon. When she came, she wanted Aiden to be deep inside her.

He flashed a wicked grin. "I take it that felt good. Want me to do it again?"

She did her best to glare at him. "What do you think?"

His head came down, and he flicked his tongue across her sensitized flesh. If his hands hadn't been planted on the inside of her thighs, holding her down, Lily would have shot right off the bed.

For the next few minutes, he subjected her to delicious torture, spreading her wide while he licked her, teasing her over and over. She tried to hold something back—retain some semblance of control—but it was too hot, too good, and she finally surrendered to his expert attentions, moaning out her need.

"That's it, babe," he murmured, pulling back a bit. "Just let go. Let me take care of you."

"Then why the hell are you stopping?" she gasped.

"Just a slight adjustment." He slipped two fingers back inside her. Then he moved down on her again, slowly dragging his tongue over her aching sex, sending her right to the edge.

Lily reached down and clamped her hands on his

shoulders. It felt wonderful—God, it felt like heaven—but she wanted more.

"Aiden." Her voice caught. "I want you inside me. Please."

He turned his face, and she felt his smile against her inner thigh. Then he glanced up, his eyes warm with laughter and tenderness. "Whatever you want, Lily."

He took his time about it, making a slow tour up her body. She shivered at the feel of his mouth on her belly, and his rough palms sliding up her sides. When he reached her breasts he obviously decided to take a little detour.

"So sweet," he said as he thumbed her nipples to tight points. "I bet they taste good too."

Lily was tempted to whack him for such a corny line, but then he leaned down and drew one nipple into his mouth with a hard suck. She felt the pull all the way to her core. She squirmed beneath him but he didn't let up, massaging both her breasts as he moved back and forth between the rigid, aching tips. Growing almost desperate, she arched against him, rubbing herself along his thick erection.

"You're driving me crazy," she finally gasped.

"You and me both," he muttered. He rolled slightly to the side and reached a long arm over to the bedside table. Lily hadn't noticed before, but there was a box of condoms there, ready and waiting.

"You were obviously confident about the way things would go tonight," she said.

"Let's just say I was hopeful." Aiden shook a condom free and went up on his knees.

Lily stared at him, dumbstruck by how absolutely gorgeous he was and by the fact that they were finally going to make love.

He glanced up as he rolled the condom over his erection. "Ready?" he asked in a gravelly voice she felt through her entire body.

Throttling back on the urge to burst into tears, she held her arms out to him. "You have no idea."

He let out a husky laugh. The tip of his erection nudged her entrance as he slid an arm under her shoulders. Bracing himself on one forearm, he slowly pushed into her as he held her gaze.

Lily felt her eyes grow wide as he stretched her to an impossibly, beautifully tight fit. She dug her fingers into his biceps as she instinctively pulled her legs up to cradle his lean hips.

Oh. My. God. Lily was overwhelmed, both emotionally and physically, and the tears that had been threatening now dampened her eyes.

Sucking in a ragged breath, Aiden's eyelids closed for a few seconds, his features pulled taut with pleasure. Then he opened his eyes, and Lily's heart jolted at the tenderness she saw in his gaze.

"I know," he whispered, leaning down to kiss away the tear that had trickled down one cheek. "I feel the same way, Lily-girl."

She blinked, not entirely sure what he meant. And how could she possibly respond, since she didn't really know the true state of his emotions?

But then he began to move, sparing her the need to answer. Her body curled up to him, seeking pressure along every point of connection. Aiden took her lips in an openmouthed kiss, tasting her with a sweet urgency that had her trembling in his arms.

He reached a big hand down to her thigh, silently

urging her to wrap her legs around his waist. When she did, it brought her up to the perfect angle. His thick length rubbed against her, building the pleasure and the heat between them.

Then, just as she hovered on the edge of orgasm, Aiden came up on his forearms. Arching his back, he pushed into her with a heavy, fast stroke.

Lily felt the luxurious spasms begin inside her. When he buried himself deep, grinding into her, the release swept over her in a beautiful, welcome tide. She cried out, clutching at his broad shoulders while he stroked into her again and again. When his body finally went rigid, she wrapped her arms around him, holding him tight as he came. And when he slowly collapsed on top of her, pushing her into the mattress, she eagerly welcomed his weight.

Swamped with emotion, Lily hid her face against his shoulder. Even as every muscle relaxed in the aftermath of the best and most meaningful orgasm she'd ever had, her heart—and what little was left of her brain—acknowledged the enormity of what had just happened.

She was truly, deeply, and stupidly in love with Aiden Flynn.

"That puts an amazing cap on an amazing day," Aiden said, trying to catch his breath. Actually, amazing didn't really describe it. Life-changing felt more like it, although he wasn't close to admitting that to her—or to himself, for that matter.

He gently eased out of her and rolled onto his back, tucking her sweet body under his arm. He craned a bit to look at the bedside clock as he tried to corral his emotions into some semblance of order.

Exactly midnight.

"Happy birthday one last time, Lil."

She stretched, then draped her right leg over his thigh. "Thank you, but does that mean you're kicking me out of your room? Because I'm thinking that while the day might be over, there's a lot of night still to come."

Aiden stroked the velvet-soft skin of her inner thigh, letting his fingers slide up to tease her sweet, damp curls. "What do you think?"

He had every intention of making love to Lily for most of the night, and for breakfast too, if she was game. Cole Rogers wasn't picking them up for the return flight until after lunch.

She didn't answer right away, which was okay with Aiden. After that mind-blowing orgasm, his brain was pretty much mush. He stared vaguely at the ceiling in a halfhearted attempt to focus his eyes.

"What I think is that I *shouldn't* be thinking so much," Lily finally answered.

Aiden's gaze—and his mind—snapped back into focus. For a couple of moments, he debated whether to answer her with words or with kisses—ones in places that would make her forget everything that troubled her. Things that obviously had to do with him and with... whatever it was that was happening between them.

He came down on the side of words because he didn't want her agonizing over anything. "What is it that you don't want to be thinking about?"

Lily rolled over onto her stomach and snuggled closer, resting her folded arms on his chest. "It's stupid. Here I am, getting so much more than I asked for or ever would have expected, and then I turn around and want even more. It makes me feel like I'm being ungrateful and... kind of petty." She gazed earnestly at him, all big green eyes and lush red lips.

Aiden responded only by tracing his fingers down her cheek and neck, grazing the tops of her shoulders.

With a sigh, she scrunched up her nose. "It's just that every time I think about you leaving again..."

He didn't miss the *again* or the slight quaver in her voice. That aching tone seemed to bang straight through his rib cage to his heart.

"And I'm afraid that this trip and...everything...is just going to make it that much worse when you do," she said. "How's that for ungrateful, huh?"

"I'm sticking around for a while, remember?" Aiden replied, trying to reassure her.

But really, what was he supposed to say? What did she want him to say? That he was ready to give up on baseball, move back to Seashell Bay, and spend the rest of his life hosing down the slimy deck of a lobster boat?

A moment later, he gave himself a mental beatdown for that dickhead thought. Lily didn't expect any such thing. She was simply voicing regret that fate would keep them apart, just as it had all those years ago.

"And I'm totally grateful that you'll be here," she said. She stretched up to give him a quick kiss. When her pretty nipples rubbed against his chest, his dick twitched back to life. "Just ignore me. I'm being an idiot. The combination of alcohol and fabulous sex will do that, I suppose."

Aiden drew his fingers through her silky, tousled hair. "Baby, none of this is easy for me either. I didn't intend for it to happen, but I'm not sorry it did."

Lily's eyelids fluttered down, as if she were hiding

from him. Then she rolled over onto her back and put a few inches between them. "I'm not sorry either," she said softly.

The lack of conviction in her voice didn't completely surprise him, but it sure made him feel like crap.

"You don't look at Seashell Bay the same way as you did before, do you?" Lily said after few moments of uncomfortable silence. "I've seen the change, and some part of me wanted to—"

"—believe that I might decide to return to my roots?" he finished for her.

She turned onto her side to face him, propping her head on her hand. "Something like that."

Okay, maybe he did look at the island in a different way now, and Lily was responsible for that. Not just for what had happened between the two of them, but for forcing him to start grappling with his past. But he had no desire to go any deeper into that past. Not tonight, anyway.

"Honestly, when I was young, I could never get what people saw in the place," he said. "Leaving aside the crap I took from my dad, the only time I wasn't bored was when I was in Portland. But even the city was no great shakes back then."

"Portland's changed a lot since we were in school. It's a great city with a lot going on now."

"Unlike on the island," Aiden said drily.

She rolled her eyes. "And that's exactly the way we like it. But if the car ferry and all that new development go ahead, then I guarantee you'll see plenty of changes."

"And you hate that idea. I get it. You're afraid it will turn out to be the worst-case scenario." Almost unconsciously, he began playing with her hair again. "And I have to say that the more I hear about the plans, the more I understand why you're worried."

Lily skimmed her palm down his chest to settle on his abdomen. Aiden wished she'd keep heading south, since then they could switch to more interesting topics.

"You're right," she said. "We don't like change, but we're not blind or stupid either. We know we have to adapt. Still, we don't want a huge sea change like Bay Island's proposal would bring. There's got to be another solution. A different kind of development."

"Like what kind?" he asked as he trailed his fingers down her spine.

Lily shivered under his touch. But he didn't think she was done talking, despite his attempts at distraction. "I was fantasizing a little this afternoon about a place like this in Seashell Bay. An ecoresort—one big enough to create some jobs, but not huge and disruptive like the proposal we're fighting."

Aiden's hand froze on her back. It was the last thing he expected to hear, especially coming from Lily. "Okay, but what are the chances somebody would be interested in developing something like that on the island? Especially with Coastal Harmony already here on the Maine coast?"

When Lily's hand moved again, gliding in soft circles from his belly to his groin, his concentration started to slip. "Ecotourism is really popular, and it's only going to get bigger," she said. "Kind of like this." She flashed him a wicked grin as her hand slid home.

Aiden sucked in a sharp breath as Lily grasped his now-erect shaft and slid her thumb across the bulging head. "I'm listening, but talk fast."

"I spent an hour talking to one of the owners while you

were working out. He told me that there was a lot of potential for similar types of resorts up and down the coast."

Aiden tried to concentrate—not too easy with her slender fingers working his dick. But it didn't take much brain power to understand why Lily would like the idea. Coastal Harmony must have brought dozens—probably hundreds—of jobs to the local community just to run and maintain the place. And then there were the staff that planned and operated the excursions—whale watching, birding, nature walks, hiking and cycling trips...jobs that matched the locals' skills.

"Must be a lot of jobs involved in a place like this," he said.

She gave him a dazzling smile. "I'm sure there are. And an ecoresort wouldn't need a car ferry to succeed either. Tourists looking for an eco experience wouldn't want to be driving their cars all over the island, if they even had cars. They'd much rather cycle or walk, or use golf carts."

It sounded right, but what were the chances of turning Seashell Bay into an ecotourism destination? Aiden didn't have a clue, and switching gears at this point would be a monumental undertaking for his family.

What he did know for sure, though, was that his dad would either laugh his ass off or try to clock Aiden with a whisky bottle if he even raised the possibility.

"But it's obviously just a dream," Lily sighed. "Your father would never let his land go for something like that."

"Yeah, you just read my thoughts."

She grimaced. "I'd never say this out loud, but it's obvious to me that your father isn't going to give up even if the ferry proposal fails. Bay Island might back away, but there'll be some other outfit willing to step up, sooner or later." She let go of his aching erection and flopped onto her back. "I'm afraid we're going to have to keep fighting for a very long time."

He grunted an acknowledgment, surprised at how much the idea of ongoing warfare in Seashell Bay stuck in his craw. But his stubborn, rage-filled father would never give up as long as he could draw breath, ruining as many lives on the island as he could. Something would have to be done with the Flynn family land no matter what happened with the car ferry, something that could support Sean and Bram and yet, if possible, not trash the quality of life for everyone else on the island.

And figuring out what that something could be was squarely on his shoulders.

But right now all that would have to wait.

Lily let out a surprised little squeal when he suddenly climbed on top of her. "Ms. Doyle, I'd say it's time for a little distraction from our worries."

Much to his satisfaction, she seemed to agree.

Chapter 18

$\mathcal{B}$ram's bloodshot eyes practically glowed with fury. "You have got to be fucking kidding, man!"

"It's just an idea at this stage," Aiden replied calmly, "but I want you to start thinking about it."

As soon as he got back from his weekend escape with Lily, Aiden had dragged Bram out for a walk along the bluffs. Lily's idea about an ecoresort had taken root in his head. Maybe all the spectacular sex had rotted his brain, but it was actually starting to morph from a wild idea to a halfway realistic possibility. Now Aiden needed Bram to at least consider the idea, and he needed it right away.

Bram windmilled his arms, forcing Aiden back a step. "It's a heinous idea. Anyway, it's too late. Dad gave Dunnagan his word that we'd go ahead with the deal. And a verbal commitment is as good as a contract."

Aiden sighed. He loved his brother, but Bram had always been gullible. "That's bullshit. Not in this situation. You told me yourself that they're only going ahead with the project if they get all three of us to sell *and* if the car ferry vote passes, *and* they get their new dock built."

With his disheveled hair and unkempt beard, Bram looked even worse than usual. Aiden reached out a hand to grasp his brother's shoulder, trying to forge some kind of connection.

Bram jerked away. "Don't fuck this up, Aiden. Dad will kill you." He stomped off toward his cottage, angrily slapping at a couple of low-hanging tree branches.

Aiden caught up with him in half a dozen strides. "Look, I'll never do anything right as far as the old man is concerned, but if I'm going to push Dad in a different direction, you need to support me." He grabbed Bram's arm and pulled him back to the path that meandered along the shoreline, a rocky track they'd followed a million times as kids.

"Okay, I know you're smarter than me," Bram said, "but I can't see how some kind of fruitcake resort for environmental wackos could ever work here. And anyway, I can't see us getting even close to the price Bay Island's agreed to pay from anybody else. They need to build both the resort and the housing development to make the numbers work."

Aiden had been struggling with those economics himself, both in bed last night and late the next morning when he and Lily had coffee with the co-owner of Coastal Harmony, Colton Booth. Booth was a Phillies fan and had religiously followed Aiden's career, and he seemed more than predisposed to be helpful.

Aiden had floated the idea that Coastal Harmony might be interested in developing a sister property on Seashell Bay Island. But while Booth had clearly been interested in the concept, he'd said that his partners weren't able to assume the level of debt necessary to develop a new resort. Still, Aiden and Lily had come away with the clear

message that if other investors could be found—investors
willing to pony up most of the money—the Coastal Harmony group could be interested in a management contract
and, possibly, a minority financial stake in the project.

It was still a total Hail Mary pass, but Aiden was determined to try to put the ball in the air. "You're right," he
said to his brother. "But money's not everything."

"Easy for you to say," Bram said.

Aiden blew out an exasperated breath. "You know I've
always been there for you, so stow that crap. Besides, you
need to start getting realistic about this situation. If you
and Dad keep pushing this deal to the bitter end, you two
could end up getting nothing. If the dock proposal doesn't
pass, Bay Island will dump the whole idea."

"That's a hell of a big if," Bram said with pigheaded
stubbornness, "because the vote's going to pass. There
aren't enough dinosaurs left on the island to stop it."

Dinosaurs? Lily and Morgan were hardly dinosaurs,
and from what Aiden had seen and heard, opposition to
the car ferry and the development was hardly restricted
to the island's old fogies. Still, even Lily acknowledged
that the vote was going to be close. "You'd better hope so,
if you keep pinning all your hopes on this deal," he said
sharply.

Bram kicked at the dirt, sending a spray over the bluff.
"Hell, you know where they'd want to build the kind of
resort you're talking about." He swept his right arm
around in a circle. "Right here. On *your* land and probably some of mine, because of the cliffs and the view. Dad
got the worst land out of Mom's will, so nobody would
want to use his for a resort. He'd be screwed, Aiden. We
couldn't do that to the old man."

Aiden couldn't argue that point. At best, based on what he'd seen at Coastal Harmony, he figured an ecoresort might take a quarter or so of the combined acreage of the Flynn lands, relatively little of which would be on Sean's property. "We'd have to see what we could do about that," he acknowledged.

He'd been thinking about an idea since he left Castine, but he wasn't ready to voice it yet.

Bram eyed him morosely. "So when are you going to hit Dad with this shit? You better give me plenty of warning so I can get off the island until the lava cools down."

"Soon. I wanted to know that you're okay with it first."

"It doesn't even matter what I think, because Dad's committed to Bay Island, period." Bram snorted. "So bro, you're finally going to have to choose between your girlfriend and your family. Or are you going to keep pretending that nothing is happening between you two?"

Though every muscle in his body tightened, Aiden forced himself not to react visibly. All he'd told his brother about the trip—and he hadn't said a word to his father—was that he was giving Lily a birthday present. Those two would obviously draw their own conclusions, but he didn't give a damn.

"All the pressure I'm getting is coming from the old man and you," Aiden said, "not from Lily and her people."

"Bullshit."

Aiden was determined not to throw fuel on the flames. "No matter what, I'm going to do everything I can to help you. Don't ever forget that." He blew out a heavy breath. "But brother, you're sure not making it easy."

Bram studied him and then slowly shook his head. "That's the problem, isn't it, Aiden? This whole thing should have been dead easy for you. Sign on to the Bay Island deal and get on with your life. But no, you got yourself mixed up with the Doyles, and it all went for shit. No, bro, you're the one who's making it hard, not Dad and me."

When Lily gave a tap on her horn, Morgan pushed open the screen door and dashed across the porch of the old Victorian her father now ran as the Golden Sunset B&B. She quickly climbed into the Jeep.

"Oh, man, you *so* didn't get any sleep last night," Morgan said, as Lily made a three-point turn out of the gravel driveway to get back onto the road. "I want every last detail, and I want it right now."

Lily hadn't looked in a mirror since she'd left Coastal Harmony a few hours ago, but no doubt the bags under her eyes were appalling. She was running on coffee, adrenaline, and sizzling memories of the best night of her entire life. She hoped that combination could power her through the rest of the day.

"My room was a bit noisy," she said. "Those ecotourists are total party animals."

Morgan laughed. "You're such a liar. I'm betting the maid didn't have to lift a finger this morning in one of those rooms. Or did you cavort back and forth between the two? Come on, give me some color, girlfriend."

"You're not going to leave me alone unless I reveal every salacious detail, are you?"

Morgan tucked her flying blond locks back behind her ears. "Oh, you know how I crave salacious detail. It's because I don't generate nearly enough of it myself."

Lily could never quite get Morgan's near-celibate lifestyle. Her friend was so gorgeous and smart and hip. But she always claimed that her teaching duties kept her far too preoccupied to do any serious dating, and even when she came back to Seashell Bay for the summer, she almost never went out with a guy. Like Lily, she looked at island men like brothers, and vacationers were almost always married.

"All right then," Lily said, "but you'll have to settle for the synopsis right now because we'll be at Saint Anne's in a few minutes. And I am not going to be talking about what I did last night within sight of my church."

Morgan rubbed her hands gleefully. "Unless you're in the confessional, of course."

After some of the things Lily and Aiden had done, a confession might just have been in order. Who knew that sex could be that…explosive. In Aiden's arms, she'd come apart again and again. It was as if they both had been determined to make up for fourteen lost years in one spectacular night.

Especially when that night might wind up being all she and Aiden ever had.

Lily stuffed that awful thought as far back as it would go in her mind. She took the sweeping turn past the town trash transfer station onto Bay Street. As they descended the hill toward the landing, she took a couple of minutes to fill Morgan in on her dinner with Aiden, their walk to the dock, and their hurried trip back to his room. That was all she was going to say about sex with Aiden Flynn—for her own sake. Thinking about him made her want him more than ever, and wanting him would end up badly for her.

"God, it sounds dreamy," Morgan said. "But are you sure you're going to be okay after all that?"

Her pal, bless her, hadn't tried to talk Lily out of the

trip up the coast, even though Morgan regarded Aiden as far from trustworthy when it came to her BFF's heart. Her protective instincts on Lily's behalf were fierce.

Lily pushed her eternally sliding sunglasses back up the bridge of her nose. "I sure hope so." She wouldn't sugarcoat the situation, because Morgan wouldn't buy it, anyway. "I'm not under any illusions that Aiden's going to stick around, though he did tell me he'd stay awhile longer to help out on the boat."

Morgan raised a skeptical eyebrow. "Awhile longer?"

Lily attempted a smile. "I'll be grateful for anymore help I get from him. Aiden saved my ass this summer."

"I do have to give him credit for that, if nothing else." Morgan's acknowledgment was grudging.

Lily swerved out to stay clear of Peggy Fogg. Evidently on her way to the Pot, Peggy was resplendent in her old-fashioned waitress uniform. She was riding her bike up the wrong side of the road, as usual.

"You shouldn't be too hard on Aiden," Lily said after waving to Peggy. "He's changing. I feel it more every time we're together. He doesn't hate the island anymore. Not like he used to, anyway."

Morgan rested her hand on Lily's arm. "Honey, is that your analytical brain doing the talking or something farther south? I mean, it's hard to think straight after a night like you just had, right? You probably need a little time to put things in perspective."

Lily slowed to make the turn into the church driveway. "What I know for sure is that Aiden's comfortable on my boat now. Actually, I'd say he's even happy there— and happy to be fishing with me." She braked to a grinding stop on the gravel, parking in between Jack Gallant's ancient F-150 truck and Miss Annie's golf cart, its rear cargo carrier loaded with three banana boxes strapped down by bungee cords. Lily shifted to face Morgan. "Do you understand how big a deal that is? This was a guy who could barely even look at a lobster boat when he moved away, and yet he sucked it up and honored his bet. To be able to put those horrible memories behind him and start to enjoy himself on the boat—with me—well, I don't know how much more you can ask a man to change than that."

Morgan didn't look convinced.

"I'll be all right," Lily said, patting her hand. "No matter what, I'll be all right. I promise."

Despite her brave words, she struggled to take in a full breath as she envisioned Aiden standing on the deck of the ferry, waving good-bye to her. She hated that image to the very depths of her soul.

As they got out of the Jeep, Morgan said, "Did Aiden give you any hints about selling his land or not? People are dying to know."

"Not really," she hedged.

Morgan slipped an arm around Lily's waist as they started to walk toward the church. "No skating allowed. Come on, give."

Lily came to a halt. "Okay, maybe it's just wishful thinking on my part, but I think Aiden might not mind if the car ferry vote went down in flames. That way the Bay Island deal would fall apart of its own accord."

"Holy Jesus." Morgan cast a sheepish glance up at the cross on top of the steeple. "Sorry, Lord." Then she grinned at Lily. "But that would be pretty amazing if it was true."

Lily thought so too.

"Still," Morgan went on, "we both know that the old man will never stop trying to get his way. Not even if we win the vote."

Lily didn't know if she should reveal anything about the possible ecotourism resort idea. It seemed like such a total long shot, and Aiden had been pretty closed-mouthed about it on the trip back home. But Morgan had been her best friend since they were little kids, and Lily knew she could trust her completely.

"You're right," Lily said, "but Aiden seems interested in pursuing some other kind of development. Something I think almost everybody on the island could live with."

"Are you kidding me? What?"

Even though they were already late for the meeting, Lily quickly told her friend the basics and swore her to secrecy.

"That would be absolutely awesome," Morgan said, "if it ever came to pass. My only worry at this point would be whether Aiden's father would blast him with his shotgun for even proposing such a thing."

Lily winced. Though Morgan was obviously exaggerating for effect, she couldn't help but worry how violently Sean might react.

Morgan shook her head. "I'm afraid it sounds like a pipe dream to me."

Her friend was likely right, but Lily refused to give up all hope. "Maybe, but the first thing we have to do is get every last person out to vote against the car ferry. Otherwise, it may be too late even to dream."

Chapter 19

$\mathscr{A}$iden didn't feel much like drinking, but he didn't feel much like being alone either—not after his fight with Bram. So he was sitting at the bar in the Lobster Pot, despite the fact that it was a beautiful, sunny day, nursing a beer and making sporadic conversation with bartender Kellen Dooley.

The muted TVs carried the Red Sox and Rays game from Fenway Park in Boston. Aiden tried not to watch, but every once in a while he glanced up, falling into his bred-in-the-bone habit of analyzing every pitch and the batter's reaction to it. To him, doing that was like breathing. Unconscious. Natural. Essential.

Essential? He sure hoped it wasn't essential or else he was good and screwed. It was looking as if the only time he would set foot on a major-league field again would be if he took a stadium tour.

Stop watching the damn game.

There was no point in wasting mental energy on that frustrating exercise when he should be focusing on how he could possibly make Lily's ecotourism resort idea work.

The first order of business was to make some phone calls, but that couldn't happen until later tonight. Every guy he knew was playing that afternoon, like they did every Sunday afternoon from the beginning of April until at least the end of September.

When his cell phone vibrated in his pocket, Aiden grabbed it and glanced at the call display. His pulse rate zoomed when his agent's name popped up. After their last disappointing conversation, Aiden hadn't been expecting a call anytime soon, and his expectations were pretty much rock bottom.

"I guess you're calling to tell me I can hit cleanup for a beer league team in Moose Jaw, Saskatchewan, right?" Aiden said, trying to make a joke out of the crappy situation.

Paul chuckled. "Glad to see you've got some of your sense of humor back, buddy. But actually I can do a little better than that."

Aiden surged to his feet. He knew his agent's code for breaking news. *A little better* was Paul-speak for something he was probably going to like. "Well, be still, my heart," he said, heading for the door. "Hold on a sec, okay?"

Though there were only a half-dozen people in the bar, he didn't want to be overheard. "Go ahead, Paul. I'm outside." He cut around to the side of the building. It was quiet there, with a spectacular view over the bay.

"It's Oakland, Aiden. The A's are interested in signing you to a minor-league deal. They'll assign you to their Triple-A club for now, but that'll probably change. Sacramento's regular left fielder went down for the season, and they see you as taking over there. Their assistant GM told me you'd likely be the first guy called up if one of their corner outfielders gets hurt."

Aiden's mind slowed to a crawl as he tried to process the news. Despite anything positive he'd said to Lily or anybody else, he'd been pretty much convinced he'd never get an offer again, and this one had caught him off guard.

"The money's not bad—standard stuff for the situation." Paul named a figure. When Aiden remained silent, he asked, "You still there, man?"

"Yeah, I'm here," Aiden said. "Just thinking." Wondering what the hell to do. The offer was a long way from what he'd hoped for, but it wasn't a nightmare either. So why wasn't he more excited about it? He'd been telling himself for weeks that this was what he wanted—what he needed.

"Look, Aiden, I know it's not a major-league deal, but it's a pretty good opportunity. A chance to show you can still be a productive player." Again Paul waited for Aiden's reaction. When none came, he added, "I have to tell you I think this is the best we're going to get, my friend."

"I hear you," Aiden said.

A minor-league contract was bordering on humiliation for a major-league veteran with Aiden's years of service. Paul was right, though—it was an opportunity to prove he could still play and get back to the Show. Aiden liked the idea of playing in Oakland too, or even Sacramento if he got stuck there for a while. He'd given some thought about retiring to the Bay Area, and this might prove to be a good chance to give that part of the country a test run.

But what were the chances that a longer-term opportunity with the major-league club would come to him, no matter how well he hit in the minors? He knew the A's already had productive veteran outfielders, as well as a solid young prospect on a fast track to the Oakland Coliseum. Then again, if Aiden played well for the A's, they might trade one of their current starters, or even the prospect, and hand a regular job to him.

Was that enough of an incentive for him to take the offer?

Christ. His emotions and thoughts pinwheeled all over the place, and yet he'd have to make a rational decision that would affect the entire course of his life.

And then there's Lily. When had she become such a big factor in his decision?

"When do they need an answer?" he asked, breaking the fraught silence.

Paul groaned. "They expect a call back by tomorrow. But what's the holdup?"

I need more time to think—about everything. "I'm in the middle of a family emergency, Paul." That actually wasn't far from the truth. "Look, just say whatever the hell you need to, okay? Try to buy me at least a day or two."

His agent cursed under his breath. "They're interested, but I'm not sure they're that interested."

Aiden was operating purely on gut instinct. He didn't want to blow the opportunity with the A's, but damned if he was ready to jump at it instantly. "You won't know unless you give it a shot."

"I don't get it, Aiden. I really thought you'd go for this."

"And I might," he shot back. "I'm just not in a position right now to snap my fingers and say yes. I've got a hell of a lot on my plate, Paul."

Paul heaved a sigh. "I thought all you had on your

plate these days was a big, fat, juicy lobster tail. What the hell is going on down there on that godforsaken island, anyway?"

"You wouldn't believe me if I told you. Just let me know what the A's say, and we'll take it from there, okay?"

"Fine, Aiden, but it would be a mistake to let this one go. Time's not on your side."

The second she heard a crunch of gravel in her driveway, Lily set down her cup of coffee and bolted up from the kitchen table where she'd been balancing her checkbook. After Aiden told her he'd drop by this evening, she'd barely been able to think of anything else. Every time she passed by the bedroom, her addled mind envisioned the two of them sprawled all over each other in her antique, four-poster bed. If tonight went as she hoped it would, it would be the first time she'd shared that bed with a man. Lily was glad she'd saved that particular milestone for a night with Aiden.

But when she opened the door, Aiden flashed her only the briefest of smiles. "Hi," he said.

Lily frowned as she ushered him in. Something had clearly happened in the last six hours to flatten his mood—something that now set her alarm bells clanging. "How about a beer?"

Aiden wandered into the living room and flopped down onto the sofa. "No, thanks. I'm good." He patted the sofa cushion. "Just come sit down so we can talk."

Uh-oh. Lily's stomach took a sickening nosedive. In her experience, when a guy said he wanted to talk, it was a signal she was about to hear something she wouldn't like.

"How did your meeting go?" he asked, after she cautiously sat and crossed her legs underneath her.

Lily was certain that it wasn't the car ferry vote that was on his mind, but she played along. For now. "We're all set to make sure we get the vote out tomorrow. We have to be, because it looks like it's going to be a pretty tight margin one way or the other."

Aiden smiled, but his dark eyes looked strained and weary. "For you to miss a day of fishing so you can pull the vote, I'd say it must be damn close."

"The Jenkins sisters and Holly took sort of a poll down at the store over the weekend," Lily said. "They set up a mock polling station so people could record their intentions anonymously. Holly told us today at the meeting that the vote was split almost right down the middle—about 40 percent in favor of the ferry and 40 percent against, with the rest undecided."

"How many people voted?"

"Over a hundred."

He nodded. "A good sample, since most people shop at the general store."

Her impatience finally got the better of her. "I can tell something's bothering you. What's going on, Aiden?"

He rubbed his jaw, as if it ached. "Let me give you some good news first."

Good news first, then bad news. Lily's mouth went totally dry. "One second." She got up and fetched her coffee, then sat back down and took a sip. It was barely lukewarm but she didn't care.

Aiden shifted to face her directly. "I told you I was going to sound out a few players who might have some interest in investing in an ecoresort, right? Well, I got hold of four of them, and three were generally positive. One guy, Kirby Weston of the Red Sox, sounded really excited." He snorted. "I guess Kirby's got to find something to do with the 168 million bucks he's getting over the next eight years. He's a big-time environmental guy, so this would be right up his alley."

"Wow," Lily said, genuinely impressed with Aiden's quick work. "That really is good news."

"One of my teammates—former teammates, that is— wants to hear more too," Aiden said. "So I'm going to call Booth in the morning and see if I can set up a meeting with him and Weston and anybody else who wants to come. The Phillies will be in Boston this week, so the timing's right. If I can get Booth down there to meet those guys, you should go too, Lily."

Despite the impending bad news, Lily couldn't help feeling excited that her off-the-wall idea might actually have some kind of real-world chance. "I hate to miss another day of fishing, but sure, I guess we could do that."

Aiden's intent gaze bored into her. "No, I meant *you* should go, not us. I don't think I'll be able to make it."

She peered at him, confused. "You don't think you'll be able to make it? What exactly does that mean?"

When he reached out and grasped her hand, squeezing it, Lily knew the bad news was about to blow in. Then it hit her with blinding force. "Oh, my God, you got a call, didn't you? Some team wants to give you a job." The words practically choked her.

Aiden gave a tight nod as he let go of her hand.

Lily struggled to recover, determined not to get weepy. She should hardly be surprised, should she? She'd known all along this moment would come, despite her stupid, girlish hopes that it never would.

"Where?" she managed.

"Oakland. Well, Sacramento, for now. But my agent says I would be the first outfielder to get called up from the minor-league team."

For a guy who'd just received the call he'd been desperately waiting for, Aiden looked more grim than happy.

As for her, Sacramento might as well be the moon. "A minor-league team," she said numbly. "Isn't that a... comedown?"

When he flinched a bit, she felt awful.

"Sure, but it's an opportunity. A chance to play a few more years if I do well. It's probably the only chance I'll get."

She nodded, hoping she didn't look like her world was ending. "I understand." She forced a smile. "Well, that's good."

What else could she say? Beg him not to grab at the opportunity he'd been holding his breath to get? She'd never stand in the way of Aiden and his dream. Besides, even if he said no to this offer because of her—not that he would—he'd inevitably end up resenting her, and that would poison any chance they had to be together.

"If I go, it looks like I'll have to be out of here by the day after tomorrow at the latest, and that makes me..." Aiden grimaced. "It makes me feel like I'm letting you down. I'm sorry, Lily."

It almost felt like he was asking her permission to go. He had to know that she'd have a hard time on the boat without him, but did he also know that she'd have a hard time living without him?

Of course not, because she'd been in full denial mode herself.

She could never tell him how much she dreaded losing

him again. Aiden had done so much for her, and even now he was working hard to find a way to rescue Seashell Bay. He was doing that for her as much as for any newfound reconciliation with the island and his past. How could she ladle more guilt onto him for doing the only thing he'd ever wanted to do?

"I'll go to Boston," she said decisively. "I'll do whatever it takes to move our idea forward."

He blinked once and then gave her a relieved smile. "Thanks, babe."

She knew he was thanking her for a whole lot more than attending a meeting.

"But this time I hope you won't wait fourteen years to come back and visit," she said, forcing a smile. "Even if the ecoresort idea goes nowhere."

"I won't. Everything's different now, Lily."

She searched his dark eyes, thinking about what *everything's different* actually signified. What he'd just said felt right. A lot had changed since Aiden came back. *She'd* changed since Aiden came back.

No, he wasn't going to stay in Seashell Bay, but what about her? Did she really have to spend every moment of her life on the island, chained to her boat and her family? Especially if that meant losing Aiden again?

"Well, maybe I could come visit you in Oakland," she blurted out. "When fishing season is over, I mean. I'd love to see the West Coast."

Okay, that sounded stupid, like she wanted a vacation out there. But she didn't just want a damn vacation with Aiden. She wanted more—a lot more.

His tense mouth relaxed into a slow, pleased smile. "That would be great. I'd like that a lot."

Lily could breathe again. "Okay, then," she said, which sounded totally lame. *Now what the hell do I say?*

He reached over and tugged gently on a lock of her hair. "Look, though, we're getting ahead of ourselves. I haven't even said yes to Oakland's offer yet."

Maybe not, but you clearly want to go. "I understand," she said mechanically, trying to get her whipsawing emotions under control.

Aiden stole a glance at the grandfather clock. "As much as I'd like to stay, I've got to go talk to Dad now. Fill him in on what we want to do with the ecoresort." His grim expression indicated he'd rather swim through a snake-infested swamp.

She grimaced in sympathy. "Well, good luck with that."

"Bram went nuts when I told him this afternoon, but I swore him to silence so I could break it to Dad myself, in my own way. Otherwise, the old man would be waiting for me on the porch with his shotgun."

Lily jabbed him in the shoulder. "Don't even joke about that. Look at how crazy he got at the festival social. I'm sorry, Aiden, but your dad's been unstable for as long as I've known him." She bit her lip, realizing how mean that sounded. "But I guess it goes all the way back to Vietnam, doesn't it? It must have really messed him up."

Aiden was just about to get up, but he froze. "Vietnam? What are you talking about?"

She stared at his blank expression, mystified by his reaction. "Um, well, how he changed after he came back. I assumed it was because of what he'd experienced over there in the war."

Aiden slowly rose to his feet and stared down at her. "Why the hell would you think he fought in Vietnam?"

She felt her mouth gape open. *Oh, sweet Mother of God, he really doesn't know.*

Even as she tried to absorb that stunning realization, she scrambled for an answer that wouldn't rat out her mother. "Oh, I heard it somewhere. You know how people on the island talk."

Actually, it appeared that in this case, people in Seashell Bay had kept silent for an entire generation, no doubt out of respect for Rebecca Flynn. Lily's mom had made it clear that Rebecca had asked people not to talk about it, especially in front of Sean, but who could believe that Aiden and Bram would have been kept in the dark all those years? It was a horrible thing to have done to them.

"No fucking way," Aiden snapped. "My folks never said a word to Bram and me about him serving in Vietnam or anywhere else. That has to be a bullshit rumor started by one of Dad's enemies."

Lily could barely stand to look at the expression of growing disbelief and betrayal in his eyes.

Back away fast, girl.

"Well, it certainly wouldn't be the first time that sort of thing happened," she said.

He glared at her for a few more seconds, then strode to the door and grasped the knob. "That's one more thing for tonight's agenda then. I guess it's not surprising I hadn't heard that rumor, but Bram and Dad sure as hell must have."

Lily scrambled to follow him. "Maybe it would be better not to complicate things even more tonight. You're going to hit your dad with something pretty big, after all."

The anger in his gaze as it swept over her made her heartsick.

"Screw that. I'm sick of all the stupid secrets and gossip on this island. I'm sick of being guilt-tripped and manipulated, and it's going to end now." Aiden jerked the door open and was gone.

Bram was rocking in the porch swing of the family house, beer in hand, when Aiden pulled up. How many times had the two of them sat on that swing with their mother in the middle, reading to them from a book or a magazine like *National Geographic*? Now though, like most things in the house—a gracious old Victorian that had nurtured three generations of his mother's family—the swing was deteriorating, its boards so weather-beaten that Aiden was surprised it could still hold Bram's weight.

He took the scuffed wooden steps two at a time and stood in front of Bram, barely managing to keep his emotions under control. Telling Lily about the Oakland offer had been tough enough without her throwing that bullshit about Vietnam at him. That had felt like a punch to the head. Why the hell would someone even tell her something that stupid?

"You didn't say anything to the old man, did you?" he asked.

"Hell, no. You asked me not to."

Aiden gave him a grateful nod before heading into the house, Bram following right behind. From the foyer, the place looked even worse than from the outside. Dust coated every surface, and a couple of posts were missing from the oak staircase to his left. Half the bulbs in the chandelier were dead, and the remaining ones cast crazy patterns of light over the dingy walls of the entry-way. His mother would have been appalled—though not necessarily surprised—to see the current state of the family home she had inherited and lovingly preserved.

"Dad?" he called out.

"Kitchen," his father growled from the back of the house.

Aiden strode down the hall and into the farm-style kitchen. His father sat at the big, rectangular table, the sports section of the Portland paper spread open in front of him.

"Don't tell me you've made a decision?" Sean said sarcastically without looking up.

Aiden throttled back his anger. "Okay if we sit down?"

His father waved a careless hand.

"I'll grab you a beer," Bram said nervously.

Aiden nodded, even though he didn't need a drink to steady his nerves. He didn't look forward to this conversation but he didn't dread it either. He was doing the right thing, and no amount of threats or abuse from his father could change that.

After taking the beer Bram held out, Aiden got down to business. "I have made a decision, as a matter of fact. I've thought about it nonstop since I got here, trying to consider all the implications. And I've finally decided that the kind of development you and Bay Island Properties want isn't right for Seashell Bay."

His father's head jerked up, his eyes bugging out of his skull. "Son of a bitch!" He slammed his first down on the newspaper. "What the fuck is the matter with you, anyway?"

Sitting between them, Bram flinched and looked away.

"Just let me finish, okay?" Aiden said. "Then you can call me all the names you can think of and throw me out of your house."

Sean glowered at him across the nine feet of battered oak that separated them. "I'll do worse than that, boy, if you keep up this bullshit."

"Guys," he said, ignoring the threat as he glanced back and forth between his father and brother, "I'm really sorry that I can't go along with what you want. I wish I could. What Bay Island wants to do is just too destructive. We're a small island town, not suburbia, and that kind of tract housing doesn't fit here. And it's also not right because it'll split our community for a long time, if not totally trash it. It's already caused huge problems."

"*Our* community," his father sneered. "That's pretty rich coming from a guy who only bothered to show up when his mother was buried."

Aiden clenched his fists under the table. He would not lose control tonight. Besides, his dad had a point. Aiden had evaded his responsibility to his family and the people he loved for far too long.

The old man leaned forward, his skin mottling an ugly red. "Well, I guess we now know that you care more about those losers like the goddamn Doyles than you do about your own family."

Aiden ignored the bitter taunt. "It doesn't have to be Bay Island or nothing. There are better alternatives to their plan. In fact, I've already started working on one." He mentally prepared himself for another explosion. "A proposal to build an ecotourism resort on our land."

His father looked confused for a second. "A what?"

Bram rolled his eyes.

"Hold your fire." Aiden said. Rapidly, he explained the basics of his idea—Lily's idea, truth be told. But there was no point trying to elaborate when the old man was giving the impression he was about to stroke out.

"That's about the dumbest damn idea I've ever heard," his father spat out. "How much would your fancy-ass resort pay for our acreage, huh? Nobody in his right mind would fork out even half of what Dunnagan's giving us. Not unless they could build the housing too."

"They wouldn't want Dad's land either," Bram finally piped up. "Aiden, you know any kind of resort would only want to build on yours and mine."

"Damn right," Sean said, nodding at his younger son.

Aiden had his answer ready—the one he'd been thinking about all day, and the only chance he could see for getting his father's agreement.

"That's an issue we can deal with ourselves," he said. "I'm prepared to do a land swap with you, Dad. You can have my acreage, and I'll take a piece on this end of your property." He stared at his father, willing him to get what he was saying. "You'd get a nice chunk of cash that way—selling my current land and maybe even a small adjacent section of yours. An ecodeveloper would probably need Bram's and mine and a little of yours."

His father hooted with derision. "Why would I go for that? I've got a great deal in the palm of my hand. The only thing holding it up is you."

"You're not hearing me," Aiden said sharply. "There's no way I'm selling my land to a developer that's going to ruin the island. It's not what I want, and it's not what Mom would have wanted either. So the Bay Island plan is dead in the water."

Sean shot to his feet, jolting the table hard in the process. "Like hell it is. Screw you, Aiden, because we'll find a way to do it without you. You can keep your little piece of useless land in the middle and take it straight to hell with you!" He stormed to the fridge and pulled out another beer.

That heated declaration had Aiden frowning. Since he'd come home, everybody had been saying that his land was the key to the Bay Island development, and the plan couldn't go forward without it.

"I seriously doubt that Dunnagan will go ahead without my property," he said, keeping his voice deliberately calm. "But in any case, he's made it clear that he won't want to go ahead with anything once the car ferry is defeated tomorrow."

"Dream on, boy. We're winning the vote."

"We'll see. All I know for sure is that I'm going to vote against it, and I'm going to ask the 'No' team to make sure everybody knows my position. One of your buddies told me it would help your cause if I spoke out in favor of the ferry, so I figure that should work both ways."

His father's glare was as ice-cold as the Atlantic in January. "Fill your boots then, and see how far it gets you. You're nothing on this island. Never were and never will be."

Bram had been picking nervously at the label of his beer bottle. He finally looked up, his tight features reflecting his distress. "Dad?"

"What?" Sean thundered.

Bram winced but forged on. "I think I get where Aiden is coming from—about how the plan will change everything on the island. And he's right that Mom wouldn't have liked it, so maybe we need to rethink this."

"Oh, Christ. Go on, then." Sean's voice was brutally cold. "Say your piece."

"Maybe it's not such a bad idea to look at what Aiden's trying to put together. Maybe it could even turn out to be some kind of win-win situation." Bram's eyes had been fixed on the opposite wall, but now he met his father's angry glare. "I've always supported you, Dad, you know that. But it's not like I've been totally comfortable with the Bay Island deal. Sure, the money would bail us out, but it's not going to be much fun to live someplace where at least half the people blame us for wrecking the town. And hate our guts. I love it here, and I don't want to be forced to move."

Though Aiden wanted to stand his brother up and wrap him in a big bear hug, he held still.

Their father stared at his younger son, his puffy face filled with incredulity. "Jesus, Bram, not you too?" He didn't shout, but the pain and sense of betrayal came through loud and clear.

Aiden seized the moment. "We can do this together, Dad. I promise I'll work with you to make this plan happen and see that you and Bram get what you need. The islanders will love it because it'll bring jobs and tourists, but without all the cars and the rest of the downside. Lily's on board, and you know how much clout she has in Seashell Bay. It's doable. It really is."

Sean clutched at his forehead and closed his eyes. "Get out." His voice was low and weary. "Get out right now, both of you. You're nothing but a pair of damn traitors."

Bram bolted up, his face a mask of unhappiness. But Aiden took his time because he still had something that needed saying. His father might try to lie, but his old, half-drunk eyes would tell the truth.

When his father finally opened his eyes again to give

him a malevolent stare, Aiden forced his voice to stay calm and level. "So Dad, before we go, I have to ask you about Vietnam. What happened over there, anyway?"

And the old man's eyes did reveal everything. Horror and utter disbelief were written there in bold, unmistakable strokes. What Lily had said was true.

"What the fuck are you talking about?" his father managed in a strangled voice.

Bram grabbed at Aiden's arm. "Bro, what's going on?"

Aiden could barely speak past the constriction in his throat. So many lies, and so much wasted time and emotion. It made him ill just to think about it.

"I'll tell you when we're out of here," he said to Bram. Then he looked at his father. "I think I understand—I really do. And maybe it explains some things about what happened in this family. I just wish you and Mom could have been honest with us, instead of hiding the truth. It would have made a difference."

His father simply stood there, his face sagging and blank, swaying on his feet like a small earthquake was rattling the kitchen.

"Someday I hope you'll be able to talk to us about it," Aiden said. "Someday I hope you can tell us the truth."

Chapter 20

$\mathcal{L}$ily's downward dog collapsed into a facedown-plant on her yoga mat, with her forehead pressed against her crossed arms. She liked yoga about as much as she liked fog, but it did seem to relax her. And this morning she surely needed to relax—the result of being both wired and tired after a restless night and only a few hours of sleep.

Since the polling station at the Town Hall didn't open until eight o'clock, she'd hoped to sleep in until six thirty or even seven. Instead, she'd given up on sleep much earlier. A combination of coffee, the Internet, and now yoga had helped get her going. She knew, however, that it would be a long, tense day pulling the vote.

Damn you, Aiden Flynn.

Lily had hoped against hope that he'd come back last night after confronting his father, but it hadn't happened. She'd upset him by spilling the beans about Vietnam— that much had been obvious. But it might have been their last opportunity to be together before he left for the West Coast. So as each hour passed, the knot of disappointment in her gut had tightened more painfully. She'd wanted him in her arms at least one last time, and the thought of having to settle for just one night with Aiden—as spectacular as their lovemaking at Coastal Harmony had been—was crushing her.

Lily worried about him too. What had happened last night at his father's house? Had it been so horrible that Aiden didn't even want to talk to her? She'd poised her finger to dial the phone half a dozen times as the night wore on but had pulled back each time. She couldn't stand the idea that he would think her needy or clingy.

She rolled onto her back and stared up at the ceiling fan slowly rotating above her, silently lecturing herself to get over it and stop acting like a heartbroken teenager. Today was too important, and she needed to concentrate on the vote.

As she pushed herself up from the floor, she heard footsteps crunching on the gravel out front, followed by two sharp raps on the door. "Lily, it's Aiden."

She flew across the living room and yanked the door open, drinking in the sight of the gorgeous but weary-looking man on her doorstep.

He dredged up a smile. "I know it's early, but I wanted to catch you before you headed out." His gaze lingered on her body, inspecting her scoop neckline racerback and skin-tight yoga pants. He definitely began to look interested.

"Sure, come on in. Did you walk?" Dumb question. She'd have heard a car or truck pull up to her cottage.

"Yeah, I wanted the exercise."

She held the door, and he slipped past her. He wore jeans, Nikes with no socks, and a green Seashell Bay T-shirt. "Nice shirt," she said wryly.

He tossed her a grin as he headed for the sofa in her

small living room. "They had a two-for-one on them at the general store. Got a blue one too."

"Wow, what a steal." Aiden Flynn proudly wearing a Seashell Bay shirt? It didn't compute, but she loved it.

Lily ducked into the kitchen and poured two coffees. She set one down in front of Aiden and pulled her rocking chair around so she could face him. "How did it go last night? With your dad, I mean."

He took a careful sip of the hot coffee and then set it down. "He thinks the ecoresort idea is a crock. The only surprise was his claim that he and Bay Island could go ahead without my land if they had to."

That caught her unprepared. "Are you serious? Everybody thought your land was the key to the deal."

He grimaced. "It means we can't rule out an alternative proposal, even though I'm not sure how seriously we should take Dad's threat. He looked pretty shaken when I told him I wouldn't sell to Dunnagan's company under any circumstances."

Lily jerked up straight, almost spilling her coffee. "You won't sell to them under *any* circumstances? Not even if our ecoresort idea doesn't get off the ground?"

He gave her a slow smile. "Not even then. And get this. In the end, Bram backed me up. He didn't say he wouldn't sell, but he told Dad he thought they should seriously look at our idea. Jesus, I thought the old man was going to stroke out on the spot."

Lily struggled to find words. "That's…that's…incredible." And how about Bram? Because of Aiden's determination and strength, it appeared that his brother had finally found it within himself to stand up to their dad.

"I just can't agree to Dad's plan, Lily," Aiden said.

"Being back here...talking to you and Morgan and Miss Annie and all the others...I know it's not right for Seashell Bay. And Mom would have hated it. I understand now why she left that middle parcel of land to me, and I just can't ignore her wishes. It meant too much to her."

Lily had to blink back hot tears. "I'm so grateful, Aiden. I don't even know what to say."

"You don't have to be grateful, Lily. I was an idiot. I never thought I'd say this, but Seashell Bay is unique, and most people love the island as it is. It's just too good in its own weird, time-warp way to let some big developer screw it over just to make a profit." He grimaced. "I almost messed up, and I just hope it's not too late."

"It isn't, Aiden. I believed in you. I might not have shown it as much as I could have, but deep down I knew you'd do the right thing for everybody, including your family. You always do."

He looked embarrassed and tried to cover it up by taking a long drink of coffee. "Thanks, but the fight's not over. Dad and Dunnagan might cook up something else that would still be bad. So the only way to kill more threats is to win the vote today. I can't see any way a major housing development could go ahead without a guarantee of car ferry service to the island."

"Dunnagan said Bay Island's wouldn't, if we can believe him," Lily said, feeling a new surge of determination. "And we're going to work our butts off today to make sure we sink that ferry."

"On that note, the other thing I told Dad and Bram was that I was going to vote against the ferry myself, and that I was going to ask you and your people to spread the word. If I can sway even one vote, I'll be happy."

She didn't know whether to laugh, cry, or jump his bones. "We'll tell everybody. We're going to knock on the door of every supporter and every undecided, offering them a ride to the polling station." She had to stop and get her voice under control. "I don't know how to thank you, Aiden. You don't know how much this means to us."

Aiden's eyes were full of emotion too. But then he gave a quick nod, as if to shake off the moment. "You're welcome, babe." He drained the rest of his coffee and stood up. "Refill?"

Lily rose too. "Not for me, but I'll pour you one."

"No, I'll get it."

She followed him and watched as he filled his cup. She drank in the broad shoulders that stretched the cheap, silly T-shirt and allowed her gaze to linger on his über-masculine body. For the rest of her life, no matter what happened, she'd never forget the feel of Aiden wrapped around her as they made love, making her feel so safe and cherished.

And as she watched him move about her little kitchen, looking as if he'd spent every morning of his life fixing his coffee right there by the sink, the problem she'd been stewing over finally resolved itself with the answer slipping easily into her mind. She'd been reducing the issue to one stark question—what was more important, Seashell Bay or Aiden? And when it came right down to it, the answer was so obvious. Because as much as she loved Seashell Bay—a wonderful, special place that deserved to be protected—without Aiden it would be empty of so much that mattered to her. The thought of giving up the life she'd worked so hard to build scared the hell out of her, but Lily knew now that she could do it to be with him.

If he could change—and he'd already changed so much—then she could too. She could start over and have a great life anywhere as long as he was there. It might not include fishing or her boat, but it could bring lots of other challenges and opportunities, ones she would gladly meet with the man she loved.

If, that is, he wanted the same thing with her.

Aiden took a drink of coffee and then let his gaze drift over her, his expression morphing from lazy appreciation to outright hunger. "Do you always look this hot when you get up?" Then he grinned. "Well, you did up in Castine, obviously, but I'm talking about when you've got clothes on."

The heat in his eyes had her knees going weak. "I guess that means I'll have to buy a few more of these Lululemon outfits, because the rest of me must look like crap."

"Not even close." His voice was a low rumble. He put his cup down on the counter and reached for her. "Come here."

She fell into his arms in a rush. He held her tight while gently stroking her back.

"I missed you so much last night, you big jerk," she managed.

"I'm sorry, Lily. I missed you like crazy too." Aiden pulled back a bit to look at her. "And you were right about my dad. About Vietnam. Hell, you were right about everything all along."

Overcome by a desperate urgency, Lily grabbed at his shirt, yanking it up so she could get her hands on his body. "Nothing matters except that you're here now."

Aiden swooped down and took her mouth, and she gladly surrendered. His fingers reached for the hem of her tank top as he deepened the kiss, his right hand moving up to find the curve of her breast. The searing contrast between her sensitive skin and his callused hand—even more roughened now from all the work on her boat— made her tremble all over with unbearable anticipation.

Anticipation but also a slice of anxiety because, despite her newfound understanding that she would do whatever it took to be with him, would Aiden want that from her? Even as his hands moved over her body, Lily knew this could very well be their last time together.

Aiden's hands actually shook as he helped Lily out of her cute, little yoga outfit. God, she was so freaking sexy, and he berated himself as ten times an idiot for staying away from her last night. But he'd been royally pissed off at his dad, and he hadn't wanted to dump all that anger on Lily. Besides, since Bram had been pretty devastated by the revelation that the old man was a war vet, Aiden hadn't wanted to leave him alone. They'd talked for a long time while his brother downed several more beers and then stumbled off to bed.

But Aiden was here now, and he was going to make the best of their time together. He didn't even want to contemplate the thought that he'd soon be leaving her, and God only knew when he'd see her again.

As Lily peeled off her yoga pants, she banged her elbow against one of the kitchen cabinets.

"Hey, slow down, babe," he said, rubbing her arms. "Don't hurt yourself."

"The hell with that," she said in a funny, tight voice as she pulled his T-shirt over his head. "I want you inside me—now."

Yeah, he could get down with that idea. The sight of her

lithe body, strong and tanned from long days on her boat, had him rock hard. And when he looked at her beautiful face, her eyes shining with so much emotion—so much love for him—he knew this moment would be forever burned into his memory. When he left, he would carry the image of Lily as she was right now as something he would always cherish.

She stood before him naked but for a tiny pair of briefs. When he pulled her into his arms, she wrapped herself around him and eagerly accepted his kiss. As the kisses grew deeper and hotter, Lily yanked down the zipper of his jeans and slid a hand into his boxers. Aiden hissed at the feel of her cool, slim fingers along his hot length.

"Let's take this into the other room, babe," he whispered as he lifted her off her feet.

She wrapped her legs around his waist and kissed him again with bone-melting determination. Aiden carried her to the living room. When he set her on the edge of the couch, she leaned back and whipped off her panties, exposing her sweet nest of curls.

"Christ, you're so gorgeous." With what little mind he had left that hadn't been melted away by the vision of Lily naked, he jerked the drapes shut across her big picture window. He extracted a condom from his pocket, and then he skimmed off his jeans and boxers before getting himself sheathed in record time. He felt a bit like a horny teenager, but Lily was right there with him.

As Aiden went down on his knees before her, she wrapped her legs around his hips and her arms around his neck. He had to clench his teeth against the urge to push into her. No finesse, just burning need.

"Don't hold back, Aiden," she murmured against his

cheek. She leaned up and nipped his earlobe as she rocked against him. When the tip of his cock slipped inside one beautiful inch, he lost all semblance of self-control.

"Not with you. Never with you." His voice was a rasp he hardly recognized. He slipped a hand under her ass, tilting her, and then drove home. When she let out a moan and arched her back, pushing her pretty breasts against him, Aiden almost came on the spot.

Holding her still in his arms, he struggled for a few moments to catch his breath. Then he began rocking into her. Lily clutched his biceps, her emerald-flecked eyes wide as she stared into his face. Her lips were parted, and her gaze was alive with sensual heat, but he also saw a sweet, sad vulnerability that slammed his heart.

But the uncertainty he saw in that gaze soon burned away as Aiden began stroking into her. He held her steady with one hand while the other roamed over her smooth skin. There was nothing gentle between them—nothing like the lazy, seductive lovemaking they'd enjoyed on Saturday night. This was all about need and, he feared, about good-bye—at least good-bye for a very long time.

They took each other with a desperation that leveled his emotions to smoking ash. All too soon he felt her muscles contracting around him, pushing Aiden toward his own orgasm.

"Aiden," Lily gasped out. She seemed to fall into him, pulling him even more closely into her embrace as she climaxed.

With her warm, welcoming arms tight around him, her sweet body milking his cock, Aiden went over the edge. He pressed his face into her shoulder, muffling a groan as his orgasm hit him like a freight train.

As he shook in the aftermath, Aiden held Lily tight and wondered how the hell he was going to ever let her go.

When Aiden strolled into one of the downtown Portland Starbucks, he spotted Adam Wicker sitting at a window table reading a copy of *Baseball America* while he sipped his venti-sized something or other. Adam had called Aiden first thing in the morning, asking for a meet-up later in the day.

Since he and Lily had bagged fishing because of the vote, Aiden had little to do but cast his ballot and make some phone calls to nail down the Boston meeting with potential investors. He'd managed to connect right away with Colton Booth from Coastal Harmony. Booth had been impressed with the efficiency and speed of Aiden's plans, and he had agreed to come to Boston for the proposed investors' meeting. Colton's enthusiastic response had sure helped Aiden's state of mind, and he'd caught an afternoon ferry to Portland in a pretty good mood.

Adam shook Aiden's hand. For a few minutes, they shot the breeze about some of the high picks in baseball's annual amateur draft held back in June. But from the get-go, Aiden sensed that his old teammate had something on his mind besides simply checking in with a friend. About ten minutes into the conversation, Adam got around to it.

"Aiden, I've been thinking a lot about our conversation at Bull Feeney's the other day. When we talked about what you might want to do after you hang 'em up."

More free advice? Not something Aiden needed anymore. "Actually, I got an offer yesterday, believe it or not. From Oakland."

Adam looked a bit taken aback, but finally smiled. "Wow, that's excellent news, man." He didn't seem all that enthusiastic.

"Yeah, they want me in Triple-A for now, though, so it's not exactly a wet dream. But my agent said there's a good chance I'd be called up soon enough."

Adam raised his cup in salute. "I'm happy for you, Aiden. I really am."

"Thanks," Aiden said automatically. He paused and then finally said the words he'd been testing out in his head for the last few hours. "It's a decent offer, but I've decided I'm not going to take it."

That surprising conclusion had pretty much come together during the ferry ride into town. He'd stayed at the rail, watching for a long time as the pretty, multihued houses of the town and the rocky shoreline receded in the distance. He'd forced himself to imagine that it was a final good-bye—that last one he would ever make. And realized that it was a good-bye he no longer wanted to say.

Especially to Lily.

Now that he'd actually said the words, Aiden couldn't believe the sense of relief welling inside, confirming the rightness of the decision. The only thing left to do was call Paul Johnson, who would, of course, think he was insane. But if this was insanity, he could live with it—especially if he had Lily.

"Wow. That's kind of surprising," Adam said. "You think you'll get something better if you hang on longer?"

Aiden snorted. "Hell, no."

"So?" Adam probed.

Aiden shrugged. He liked Adam, but he didn't know him well enough to start baring his soul to him. "I guess coming home is looking more attractive than bouncing around between the minors and majors for the few years I have left. I didn't realize how much I'd left behind here in Maine...until I came back to the island."

Other than the fact that he wouldn't be leaving Seashell Bay anytime soon, Aiden didn't have much of a clue about his future—though he had no intention of working as Lily's sternman any longer than he had to. But he certainly wasn't strapped for cash, and trying to get the ecoresort idea off the ground could keep him busy for months. Then there was Bram. His brother needed him, and Aiden could no longer risk the consequences of ignoring that fact. His father probably needed him too, although Aiden wasn't quite ready to go there.

"I definitely understand that feeling," Adam replied. "Pretty much the same thing happened to me. It was a little tough to leave the majors, but I've never looked back since I came home."

"Never?" Aiden said skeptically.

Adam laughed. "Well, maybe a little."

Aiden couldn't see how anybody who had played in the major leagues wouldn't miss it at a gut level, especially when they were forced to give it up rather than retire when they were good and ready. How could you not still long for the incredible rush of jogging out onto the playing field with the music blaring and tens of thousands of rabid fans cheering their lungs out, doing what you loved best in the world? Hell, yeah, he was going to miss it. Still, he'd had a good run, and his end in baseball was hopefully a great beginning to a life with Lily in Seashell Bay.

She was totally worth the sacrifice. It had taken fourteen years and some hard time on a lobster boat to figure it out, but Aiden had finally realized what mattered most in his life—the woman he loved, his family, and the place that he now could truly call home.

Adam pushed his coffee cup aside and gave Aiden a level stare. "Okay, Aiden, it's time for me to admit that I'm not sorry to hear you're turning Oakland down. In fact, I came here this afternoon hoping to make you an offer myself."

Well, this was a day of surprises, wasn't it? "Yeah? What kind of offer do you have in mind?"

"One of my assistant coaches just landed the head coaching job at a small university in Maryland, and that's created an opening that I think you'd be perfect for. We've got five assistant coaches, and we specialize. So my plan would be to have you work primarily with the outfielders, since it's obviously right up your alley. I know you'd be good with young players. You were a great leader when we played at Peninsula."

Aiden didn't say anything as he absorbed the startling proposal, but he nodded for Adam to continue.

"I can offer you a two-year contract, but the job could go on pretty much indefinitely if it works out. The salary's not much, obviously, not compared to what you're used to. But the university atmosphere is great and there's not much travel. I love being home almost every night with my wife." He gave Aiden a knowing wink.

Aiden had to admit that coming home to Lily every night would be a powerful incentive.

"It's a Division III program, right?" he asked, trying to focus on baseball and what the job would mean.

"Yeah, we're not in with the big schools in Division I, but the coaches here before me built a fantastic program with a history of winning. It's great baseball."

And it was here, in Portland, near Lily.

He spent the next half hour grilling Adam with a dozen or more questions. But he didn't hear a single thing that bothered him. Living on the island and commuting to Portland wasn't going to be a problem—he'd get his own boat for the good weather and take the ferry during the rough winter months.

When he couldn't think of anything more to ask, Aiden stuck out his hand. "I think we've got a deal, buddy. But can I ask one thing?"

"Shoot."

"I'd like to have at least a couple of weeks before I start. To get things in order in Philly and so on." What he really needed was time to work on the resort proposal, especially pulling the Boston meeting together and going down there with Lily. He almost laughed out loud at all the things that were now on his plate, when only a few days ago his life had seemed completely stalled.

Adam shook his hand. "Deal. We can live without you for a couple more weeks," he said in a joking tone. "Good thing it's the off-season, though."

"Thanks, Adam. I think this is going to be good."

When Aiden said good-bye and strode down Exchange Street on his way to the ferry—on his way back to the island and the woman he loved—he began to realize just how good it was.

Chapter 21

$\mathcal{D}$ragging her tired ass, Lily pushed through the door of the Rec Center and headed outside to the jammed parking lot. The crowd had been building steadily since seven, though she hadn't joined the throng until the polling station at the Town Hall next door closed at eight, forty minutes ago. Right up to closing time, she'd been busy scouring the island for the unaccounted antiferry voters and undecideds. When she called it quits, she was satisfied that there wasn't a single thing more she could have done to torpedo the car ferry proposal.

The vote count would be well underway by now, with Morgan, Miss Annie, and Gracie Poole scrutinizing the results for their side. Morgan had wanted Lily to do it instead, but she'd begged off. The result was going to be so close that it would have been torture for her to endure that nail-biting process. Better to head over to the Rec Center and hang out with the rest of the island's residents until the results were announced.

The opposing forces had separated into opposite sides of the spacious main room. The smaller group—the pro side—had congregated around a pro-ferry banner and a table of refreshments provided by Bay Island Properties. Kevin Dunnagan was resplendent there in a natty blue suit, holding court in gregarious fashion with his main man, Boyd Spinney, but Lily thought he looked far from confident. Sean Flynn was nowhere in sight, which didn't surprise her. The man was practically a recluse these days. Though Bram had popped his head in the door, he'd immediately retreated outside to talk to a small group of friends.

Needing a little time alone, Lily reversed her steps and headed down to the ferry dock. The next boat wasn't due for nearly an hour, so it was deserted but for a couple of teenagers who were making out enthusiastically inside the little shelter where travelers waited in bad weather. Lily gave the kids plenty of space, moving to the end of the dock and staring out across the quiet bay. She breathed in the peace of the gently lapping water and watched the glittering pinpricks of light from neighboring islands.

The teenage kissing and groping took her mind back to Aiden, of course—not that he'd left her thoughts for more than a few minutes all day. When they made love this morning, it had been the sweetest, most heart-wrenching moment of her life. The sex had been glorious—she suspected that sex with Aiden Flynn couldn't be anything but glorious—but she'd cried like a baby as soon as he walked out the door. Because who knew how Aiden would react when she told him she wanted to move to California with him? There was a hell of lot undecided between them, and Lily still wasn't certain he'd want her to go.

Fortunately, her mini nervous breakdown had lasted only as long as it took her to shower, slurp down another cup of coffee, and throw on a little makeup to hide any lingering evidence of her meltdown. After that, she'd jumped in her Jeep and gone out to do her job, like she did every day of her life. Only today the stakes were so much higher than on any other morning of her life.

A deep male voice called her name. She turned to see Aiden striding toward her down the dock, and her heart did a crazy little flip as he moved into the soft glow cast by the light standards. Abandoning any pretence of being cool and in control, she hurried to meet him.

"It feels like you've been gone forever," she said, as he pulled her into his arms. "Is that stupid, or what?"

"Well, we have been spending at least twelve hours together on that boat every single day."

She pulled back a little, holding onto him by his leather belt. "I wasn't thinking about us in the boat, big guy," she said.

"I know. I missed you too." Smiling, Aiden stroked his fingers through her hair and pressed a kiss against her forehead, holding her for a long moment. Finally, he let her go.

"No results yet?" he asked, taking her hand to lead her back toward the Rec Center.

Lily bumped her shoulder against him as they walked, loving the feel of him. "Should be any time now."

Walking hand in hand down the dock with Aiden on a warm summer night had been one of her fantasies for years. And if she hadn't been such a nervous wreck about everything, Lily would have called this moment unbearably romantic.

"Bram said Dad told him to call the second he hears the result," Aiden said, "so I'm hoping that means he won't show up. He's probably blind drunk by now."

Lily prayed that Sean would stay away. Nobody needed a replay of the ugly scene at the Blueberry Festival social. Or worse. "I hope you can steer clear of him tonight, Aiden."

"I'll go home with Bram for a while in case Dad goes raging over to his place. Just so he doesn't have to face the old man alone."

Lily hated the idea of Aiden having to deal with Sean but understood why. And she loved him even more for being such a thoroughly good guy.

"A few undecideds I drove today told me that they'd decided to vote no. So that was great news," she said, trying to lighten the mood. "I have a pretty good feeling about the result."

Aiden stopped and swung around to face her. "Then this sounds like a good time to give you some more good news."

Puzzled, she smiled up at him. "I'm listening."

"I spent a lot of time on the phone today getting things arranged. It's all set for us to meet Booth and the potential investors in Boston on Thursday. That is, if you're still willing to take another day off fishing."

Thursday was fine with Lily. But then, with a mental jolt, she registered what he'd just said. "Are you saying that you're going, after all?" she asked in a hesitant voice.

Aiden hooked his thumbs in the pockets of his jeans, acting like Mr. Cool. But Lily didn't miss that he was trying to hold back a smile. "Well, since you won't be needing me for fishing, I don't have anything else on my agenda on Thursday. We'll go down for the day and be back on *Miss Annie* at dawn on Friday."

She grabbed the front of his T-shirt, fisting the material

in a convulsive grip. "My God, Aiden. Are you trying to tell me you're not going to Oakland? Or are you just trying to torture me?"

His face went dead serious. "I'd never joke about something that important. I called my agent and told him to respectfully decline the offer. I also told him he could stop making calls because I'm officially retired from major-league baseball as of tomorrow."

If Lily hadn't been standing upright, the concrete dock solid beneath her feet, she would have thought someone had just knocked her flat. Her heart wanted to soar out over the water, flying in cartwheels of joy, but her brain could barely grasp what he'd just said. Aiden's entire life had been about baseball. Could he really give it up, just like that? And why was he doing it now?

"Why, Aiden? Why retire when Oakland wants you?" She could barely force the words past her tight vocal cords.

Aiden took her hands, interlacing his fingers with hers. "Because sometimes you can't have everything you want, Lily. Sometimes you have to make choices."

That sounded almost...ominous, but before Lily could respond, an enormous whoop went up from the direction of the Town Hall, loud enough to make her practically jump out of her skin. She peered around Aiden to see Morgan fly out of the door and race toward them, her blond hair streaming behind her.

"Lily! We won! We won!" her friend yelled down the dock from fifty feet away. "We did it!"

Lily didn't know whether to jump for joy or collapse in a heap from relief. Her body decided for her. Instinctively, she yanked Aiden's head down to plant a hard kiss on his mouth, then started jumping and whooping like a crazy person.

Morgan rushed up and launched herself into Lily's arms. For a few ridiculous, wonderful minutes, they hugged and yelled and spun around in circles, just like they'd done when they were kids. Finally, when they stopped to catch their breath, her best friend planted her hands on Lily's shoulders.

"More than anybody, tonight belongs to you, sweetie," Morgan exclaimed. "This is your victory more than anybody's."

Tears were already streaming down Lily's cheeks, but her friend's words reduced her to a puddle of mush. They'd all worked so hard, but Lily had put everything she'd had into the campaign. And to have Aiden here with her, knowing that he supported her, made the victory that much sweeter.

Morgan let her go and swung around to face Aiden, wagging a finger at him. "And as for you, Aiden Flynn..."

He took a step backward, holding up his hands in mock alarm.

Morgan laughed. "Aiden, you need to know that what you told Lily this morning made a difference. We really spread the word that you'd come out against the ferry." She threw her arms around him in a fierce embrace. "You came through when it counted, dude. Thank you so much."

Lily smothered a big grin. Morgan didn't even know the half of it.

"What was the actual vote count?" Aiden asked after Morgan let him go.

"We got almost fifty-three percent. The margin was forty-six votes."

"Whew," Lily said. "A little too close for comfort. I'm afraid we might see Bay Island take another run at it sometime."

"Don't worry," Aiden said, reaching for her hand. "I'm not going to let that happen. *We're* not going to let that happen."

Morgan looked at Lily and pointedly raised her eyebrows, but Lily wasn't sure how to respond. After all, it was Aiden's plan, not hers, and he should be the one to formally break the news.

"Come on, you two. Let's get moving," Aiden said. "There's going to be a victory party at the Pot, right?"

Lily glanced at the parking lot where dozens of ancient cars and golf carts were trying to maneuver their way out in typically disorganized Seashell Bay fashion. She went up on tiptoe and whispered in his ear. "Yes, but we're not done talking about the other stuff, are we? We'll continue that later?"

"Absolutely," Aiden whispered back, pulling her tight against him. "But right now you're going to celebrate, Lily Doyle. You and Morgan both. It's not every night you can say you've saved an island."

The Lobster Pot was jammed. Laura had cranked the music up to ear-splitting levels, and people were dancing on the tiny dance floor and in the gaps between the tables. It reminded Aiden of crazy celebrations for the World Series or the Super Bowl. That made perfect sense, because tonight's vote was more important to the islanders than any Super Bowl could ever be. Miss Annie had told him a few minutes ago that more than a few of the ferry's supporters had shown up too, which he took as a good omen that the town's residents would be able to put any bad feelings behind them.

He'd lost Lily in the crowd awhile ago. She'd been mobbed the moment they walked in, and Aiden hadn't had a minute's peace either. Everyone wanted to thank him for his role in the victory. As soon as he finished one bottle of beer—or even just put it down—somebody shoved another into his hand. When he looked around the boisterous crowd and saw Lily and Miss Annie, the rest of the Doyle clan and their old friends, and especially Bram, he realized that he'd never had this feeling—the feeling that he'd finally come home.

Still, there was one problem left to deal with. He made his way to the bar where Bram sat on a stool talking to an animated Jessie Jameson. He didn't like to drag his brother away from a conversation with a pretty girl, but he tapped him on the shoulder and beckoned him outside.

Aiden headed away from the noisy rear patio toward a quieter spot at the front of the building. "I can't stop thinking about the old man," he said. "You think he'll be okay?"

Bram shrugged. "Like I told you, he hung up on me without a word when I gave him the vote result. But hey, he'll be fine. He's got plenty of scotch in the house, so he'll just drink until he passes out."

Aiden wasn't so confident. "Let's just hope he doesn't take a notion to jump in the car and head down here."

Bram frowned and then looked kind of sick.

"At least we know part of the reason he's been such a nutjob all these years," Aiden said.

"You mean that fucked-up Vietnam stuff?"

Despite their father's reaction last night, which had

made it obvious to Aiden that the rumors were true, his brother had remained pretty skeptical.

"When I was in high school," Aiden said, "I remember asking him once whether he'd been drafted during the Vietnam War. He looked me straight in the eye and said no."

"So maybe it is all bullshit then."

"It's not, man. I spent an hour today in the public library in the city. One of the librarians told me that getting a copy of his service record would take a Freedom of Information request, but she suggested I try looking for Vietnam medal recipients, since there are lists of everybody awarded a Silver Star or higher. I figured the odds weren't great that I'd find his name there, but it didn't take very long to check it out." He shook his head, remembering the shock of seeing Sean Flynn's name in the records. "I hit pay dirt."

Bram's mouth gaped open. "Really?"

Aiden gave a little snort. "Our beloved father was awarded a Silver Star in 1969."

Bram let out a low whistle. "He not only served in Vietnam, he got a medal?"

"The third highest medal in the service."

"Jesus. Then Vietnam's what fucked him up?"

"Makes sense, doesn't it?" Aiden said. He stared at the full beer bottle in his hand and then set it down on a window ledge. "Look, maybe we should go talk to him. Somehow, it doesn't feel right to be partying here as if he doesn't even exist. He might throw us out on our asses again, but at least we'll have tried to extend a hand. Make sure he's okay too."

Bram screwed up his face. "I don't know, man. It could get ugly."

"What are you two gentlemen conspiring about out

here?" Lily said as she peeked around the corner. She looked relieved at seeing him, as if she'd feared he'd taken off on her.

"We were just talking about Dad," Aiden said. "I'm a little worried about him."

Lily's smile vanished. "Oh. Of course."

He turned to Bram. "I'm going. Come or not—it's up to you."

Bram shrugged. "Yeah, I'm in."

Aiden stepped up to Lily, resting his hand on her smooth shoulder. "I'll see you later, after we talk to Dad."

"Are you sure that's the smart thing to do right now?" she whispered.

"Don't worry. I'll meet you back here, or at your place."

Lily stretched up and pressed a kiss on his cheek. "Please, please be safe."

"Always, babe."

As he and Bram turned toward the parking lot, a rusted-out Voyager minivan screeched to a stop right in front of them. Kevin Butler—Ryan's father and a veteran lobsterman—jumped out, leaving his engine running.

"I'm glad I found you boys," Butler said in a grim voice. "I went to Bram's first, but then I figured you might both be down here."

"What's going on, Mr. Butler?" Bram asked.

"I'm worried about your dad. I was heading to O'Hanlon's to get some gear off my boat when I saw Sean casting off in *Irish Lady*. He didn't look real steady on his feet so I yelled to ask him where he was going at this time of night."

Fuck. "What did he say?" Aiden said. "How long ago was this?"

"Ten minutes. Fifteen, tops. He yelled back that he was going straight to hell," Butler said. "At first I thought he was just being Sean—you know how he likes to yank your chain—so I told him he should be extra careful out there, but I'm not sure he even heard me." Then Butler grimaced. "And it took me a few minutes to register it, but I saw a trap perched on his stern rail. Just the one. That's when I figured I'd best go find Bram quick."

"Christ!" Bram cried. "Didn't you think to go out after him instead? You of all people know that a drunk shouldn't be out in a boat, especially at night."

Butler looked stricken. "You'd better believe I'd have gone after him, son, but my boat's at O'Hanlon's for repairs. It can't go anywhere right now."

Bram started to apologize, but Aiden cut him off. "We need to get to O'Hanlon's."

"That trap on the rail...just one trap...and nobody's used *Irish Lady* for fishing for a long time, so..." Butler didn't have to finish his sentence. Everyone there was surely thinking the same horrifying thought.

Aiden barely heard him as he glanced at Lily, who'd moved quietly up beside him. "I'll call you." He turned to follow Bram, who had already started for his truck.

Lily grabbed his wrist. "And do what when you get to the boatyard? He's already in his boat, Aiden. On the water."

She was right. He wasn't thinking straight. He needed a boat, and he needed it now.

Lily read his thoughts. "We can go out in my skiff. If he's not in the channel, then we can head to *Miss Annie* and start to search farther out."

Aiden knew they had no time to debate options.

"Let's go," he said. "Thanks, Mr. Butler. We owe you." He grabbed for Lily's hand but she was already racing to her Jeep. He took off after her and yelled at Bram to meet them at the dock.

"I'll go inside and get some of the boys to get their boats out," Butler shouted from behind them. "You'll need the lights."

Aiden stopped and turned. "And call out the fire rescue boat. We might need it."

"Aiden, there's a floating lantern in the storage box under Bram's seat," Lily shouted over the roar of her outboard. She had the throttle twisted to full power now that they'd cleared the boats in the harbor. "And some rope."

Lily prayed they wouldn't need the rope.

Aiden reached down and pulled out the gear, turning on the lantern and shining it across the still waters of the channel ahead of them. He handed it to Bram and then rummaged around, digging out the six-inch sheathed knife from Lily's emergency kit.

"We might need this too," Aiden said as he shoved the knife into his belt.

"I bet he's gone to Wreckhouse Point," Bram said, his voice wavering a little. "He used to say he wanted his ashes scattered there off the point. Back in the day, he loved to watch the sun rise behind the lighthouse."

Aiden frowned as he grabbed the lantern back. "Scatter his ashes? What about the cemetery plot beside Mom?"

Bram squeezed his eyes shut for a moment or two. "He told me once he didn't deserve to be buried at her side. I thought that was just the booze talking, but..." He trailed off.

Lily made a straight course for the point, paralleling the shoreline. Sean had at least a fifteen-minute head start on them, probably more, so if he was hell-bent on doing something stupid, they might already be too late. But was Sean really desperate enough to kill himself over a development deal? She felt sick just thinking about it and the effect it would have on Aiden. As much as he'd fought with his father, Aiden might see that horrible outcome as blood on his hands, and maybe on hers too.

She prayed to every saint she knew that Bram was right about Wreckhouse Point. Otherwise, they were going to be searching for the proverbial needle in a haystack, with a whole lot of water to cover inshore, much less farther out in the ocean.

"There!" Aiden said, beaming the lantern at an area about eighty feet off the tip of the point.

Lily saw it too—the outline of a boat that looked like *Irish Lady*. Her heart rate kicked up a notch as she quickly closed the gap between them. The other boat wasn't moving.

"Dad!" Aiden shouted over the gap between the boats.

"It's us, Dad!" his brother yelled.

No answer.

Aiden crouched, his shoulders hiked and tight with tension. He gripped the lantern in one hand and the side of the skiff in the other. "Dad!" he shouted again. "Jesus, no!"

Lily saw it a split second after Aiden. The lantern beam washed over the side of *Irish Lady* to reveal Sean sitting on the starboard rail, his feet in the water and the lobster trap perched on his thighs. One hand clutched the trap while the other tilted a bottle toward his mouth. She could just make out a rope looped through the trap's becket and dangling down his leg to disappear beneath the water. She had little doubt that the other end of the rope was tied to Sean's ankle. If he went into the water, the fifty- or sixty-pound trap would drag him to the bottom in seconds.

Mother of God, he's really going to do it.

Lily had the throttle wide open, coaxing every ounce of power out of the straining outboard. If she could cut power on her approach as late as possible, there was a chance the skiff could block Sean from jumping. Better yet, Aiden or Bram might be able to push their father backward into the boat as they passed.

But Sean wasn't waiting. A couple of seconds later, he cocked his arm and threw the bottle at them. The missile fell well short of the skiff.

"Stay still, Dad! We're coming to you!" Bram yelled as Lily throttled back.

She thought she saw an eerie smile on Sean's face. Clutching the trap to his chest, he slid off the rail and into the black water.

Aiden's instincts took over. His shoes already off, he yanked the knife from his belt as he dove over the side of the skiff. The sudden shock of the cold water robbed him of breath, but he ignored it, stroking down hard in a vertical line.

He knew the water was fairly shallow off the point, and he thanked God his father hadn't gone farther offshore. Still, the water seemed endlessly deep as he kicked with every ounce of strength in his legs through the murky depths. He'd seen exactly where Sean went under and knew the weighted trap would have pulled him straight to the bottom. Aiden was pretty sure he'd be coming down almost right on top of his father, but would he be able to hack through the line and haul the old man back to the surface before he drowned?

Light from Lily's lantern on the surface penetrated the deep just enough for Aiden to catch a glimpse of his father below him. He wasn't exactly sure what he'd expected to see, but it wasn't the desperate scene that was unfolding. His father wasn't floating downward peacefully, submitting to the cold, unforgiving Atlantic waters. No, Aiden could see him jerking around, apparently fighting a desperate battle to get loose from the trap.

Aiden powered down to the bottom and switched the knife to his right hand before grabbing hold of the becket with his left. Sean made a half-hearted grab at him but, a heartbeat later, his arm fell away and his body seemed to collapse in on itself. Aiden's chest squeezed tight, his lungs starting to burn from lack of oxygen.

A moment later, he was shocked to see Bram knife down through the water and grab their father by the shoulders. A shot of adrenaline coursed through him, and Aiden pulled the rope taut against the becket and started sawing away with desperate strokes.

But the fucking pot warp was tough as old boots. Aiden hacked at the line with everything he had, but it took precious seconds for the strands to finally break and separate the rope from the trap. Finally, the line broke free, and Aiden let the knife fall away. Bram was already kicking upward, lugging their father in his grip. Aiden kicked up hard too, and easily caught up to them, since Bram was holding all the old man's weight. He grabbed Sean's belt and clawed upward, pulling desperately toward the surface.

When they broke through, Aiden sucked in great, painful breaths and tossed his head to clear the saltwater from his eyes. They'd surfaced only about ten feet from *Irish Lady*. Lily had boarded her and now stood at the starboard rail with the boat's powerful lantern in one hand and a ring buoy in the other. Another brilliant light from a boat closing at high speed bathed them in its white wash.

"Help him aboard," Aiden choked out to Lily, as they dragged Sean between them.

He and Bram pushed up on their father's legs and waist, managing to lift his torso from the water. Lily dropped the lantern and buoy and hooked her hands under Sean's armpits, heaving him into the boat with a strength born of endless hours of hauling lobster traps.

By the time Aiden clambered over the rail, Lily had her fingers on Sean's neck, checking for a pulse. "You know CPR?" he gasped.

She gave a quick nod, already starting compressions on Sean's chest. Her face tight, she pushed down again and again and then tilted his father's head back and blew into his mouth twice before resuming the compressions. A minute or two later—though it seemed like an hour to Aiden—the fire rescue boat pulled alongside and a pair of EMTs climbed aboard—Brett Clayton and Jessie Jameson. Jessie elbowed him out of the way while Brett knelt and moved Lily aside.

"We got this now, Lil," Brett said.

Only when Aiden pulled himself to his feet did he register that his heart was beating so fast it felt like it was going to hammer its way through his rib cage. As he watched the paramedics work, he sucked in slow, deep breaths, trying to calm down.

Breathe, Dad. Please just fucking start breathing.

After what seemed an eternity, Sean finally choked and spewed water as Jessie turned his head to the side.

Bram had been leaning against the wheel, looking scared to death, but let out a relieved string of curses when Sean started to moan. Aiden forced a smile and bumped fists with his brother before pulling him into a fierce embrace.

"That was too damn close," his brother said, clutching at him like he used to do when he was scared as a little kid.

Aiden patted his back. "I hear you, bro. And we're going to make sure it never happens again."

Chapter 22

*A*iden finally emerged from the ER's treatment area into the waiting room, haggard looking but calm. Lily rushed to meet him. Hugging him fiercely, she silently vowed to be with him wherever he went, no matter how far away it might be.

"He's going to be fine, right?" she said against his shoulder. "That's what Bram said."

Bram had come out earlier and told Lily that Aiden wanted some time alone with their father. Since Bram was practically dead on his feet, Lily had put him in a taxi and sent him to the ferry terminal to catch a boat back to the island. She'd already decided to wait for Aiden and take him back to Seashell Bay on *Miss Annie*. After rescuing Sean, Lily had dropped Aiden and Bram at the dock so they could go home and quickly change into dry clothes while she retrieved the boat from its mooring for the trip into Portland.

Aiden relaxed his grip. "They want to keep him a few days to assess his mental state, but the doctor said there's no cause to worry about his physical health."

"That's good, especially since he's already scared us all half to death," she said, holding back the crazy urge to burst into tears. Lily had spent most of her life loathing Sean Flynn, but now she knew how much she wanted him to make it—for Aiden's and Bram's sakes, as well as his own.

Lily slipped her hand into Aiden's as they left the ER. She started to head for a taxi parked just past the entrance.

"I'd rather walk back to the boat if that's okay with you," Aiden said.

It was about a mile to the wharf where she'd docked *Miss Annie*, but Lily wasn't about to argue. If he wanted to walk, they would walk.

When she shivered a bit at the cool night air, Aiden took off his fleece jacket and slipped it around her shoulders. They made their way to Congress Street and headed east. It was late, and the streets were mostly empty. A peaceful hush settled around them. After the trauma and the challenges of the day, it felt like a blessing to be strolling quietly with Aiden by her side.

"When Bram and I finally got to see Dad, he broke down," Aiden said after a few minutes of silence. "I mean completely broke down. I never thought I'd see something like that in my life. The old man's always been as tough as a cheap steak, like anger was his only emotion."

Lily squeezed his hand but remained silent.

"Bram and I just stood there staring at each other. No clue what to say or do. Finally, after he calmed down, he told us he knew the second he hit the water that he'd made a mistake and that he didn't want to die. That's why he was struggling so hard when I found him."

Lily could barely imagine it. Getting dragged to the

bottom by a lobster trap was every fisherman's worst nightmare. "I gather that's a pretty common reaction with people who try suicide," she said.

"It's so weird, but he said he'd always thought dying would free him. That it was the only thing that could free him. He'd just never had the guts to do it until today."

"I'm so sorry, Aiden," Lily said. "But what he did isn't your fault."

"I get it, but you can imagine how Bram and I felt," Aiden said in a somber voice. "And here's the kicker— Dad couldn't believe the three of us came out to save him. He said he was sure we'd be happy to be rid of him. Then he said he couldn't blame us." He shook his head. "Hearing that was almost worse than anything."

Oh, man, Sean Flynn so needed help. Lily hoped that tonight would prove to be some kind of tipping point, making him finally do something to change his life.

"What did you say to that?" she asked softly.

"I told him that he'd been a complete asshole over the years, but I'd been wrong to give up on him. And to give up on my home. It made sense when I was younger and didn't understand, but when I was old enough to try and figure it out..." He tightened his grip on her hand and glanced down at her. "Because you should never give up on family or the people you love, no matter what, right?"

Lily almost choked on a rush of emotion. "No, never," she said, squeezing his hand back.

"I told him that I was going to do everything I could to help him. That I'd make sure he got a good price for his land, and that I'd be here to help him with anything he'd need from now on."

Her pace faltered. "You'll be here? In Seashell Bay?"

He'd told her he was retiring, and she'd hoped that meant he might come back here for good. Maybe that's what he'd been trying to tell her while they were waiting for the vote count. But now that the moment of truth was here, she was almost afraid to ask.

Aiden stopped under a street lamp on a quiet corner, took her by the shoulders, and turned her toward him. He leaned in to plant a swift, soft kiss on her mouth. "I'll be in Seashell Bay for as long as you are, Lily."

She gaped up at him as her brain went sort of fuzzy. A guy like Aiden wouldn't give up on a career—and vow to stay on the island—unless he loved her, right? That's what it had to mean.

Only one way to find out.

Saying a quick prayer for courage, she let out the words she'd held behind a self-imposed wall for fourteen long years. "I love you, Aiden. And just to be clear, that means I'm *in love* with you. Totally and completely."

Aiden pulled her close, resting his chin on the top of her head. "I hear you loud and clear, Lily-girl. And I love you that much too. I'll never leave you again, not for anything. I promise."

When he tipped her face up to claim her mouth in a deep and passionate kiss, Lily's legs went wobbly. But the joyful energy that surged through her at that moment blasted away her fatigue and worry, leaving in their wake a profound sense of wonder and gratitude that she and Aiden had finally found their way to each other. It had to count as a miracle, as far as she was concerned.

All too soon, he broke away and held her at arm's length. "You know, I think we can make the ecoresort work, and I've even got a plan for getting Bram involved so he doesn't spend his life just sitting around drinking and gambling."

"Bram was amazing tonight," Lily said, resting her palms on his chest. "I thought I was going to have a heart attack when you dived in, but you both were heroes."

Aiden shook his head, as if he still couldn't believe it. "When he came down and grabbed Dad, I felt like I... like I truly had my brother back."

"So what have you got in mind for him to do?"

"Well, if we get the resort off the ground, I'm hoping he might be willing to take over the tour operations. Do the excursion planning and act as guide on some trips. Bram knows these islands better than anybody, and nobody's more comfortable on the water than he is. Colton Booth told me he could help train him on the organizational stuff."

"I think that's a fantastic idea," Lily said. If Sean could somehow get himself together, and if Bram discovered a new purpose in his life, the chances of Aiden finding lasting happiness in Seashell Bay would be so much better.

She snuggled against him, sinking into his heat and strength.

Aiden's arms locked around her. "I've been saving one last piece of good news till the end."

She looked up and gave him a puzzled smile. "Holding out on me again, are you?"

"I'm retiring, and I'm not leaving Seashell Bay, so let's be clear on both those things." He moved a hand up to rest on the back of her neck. "But I'm not leaving baseball either."

That gave her a bit of a jolt. "You're not?"

"No. I'm not going to be playing, but baseball is still

going to be my job. I've been offered an assistant coaching position here at USM, Lily, and I'm taking it."

Lily stared at him, her mouth dropping open. She didn't know much about college baseball, but she did know that Aiden could easily commute to the Portland campus every day. "Holy crap. I mean, that's...wonderful, but... but are you sure that's what you want?" She swallowed, nervous all over again, but she had to say it. "Are you sure you won't regret passing on the opportunity in Oakland?"

Aiden frowned. "What do you mean?"

"I would follow you, you know," she blurted out. "I know you thought I'd never leave the island, but I would if I had to, Aiden. For you. I know I should have told you that before. I'm so sorry I chickened out this morning, but the day just seemed to get away from me."

"Now you tell me." But then he grinned, and Lily knew everything was going to be all right.

"I'm glad you told me that, but it doesn't matter," he added. "I'm sure this is the right decision for me. For us. You'd be miserable if you left Seashell Bay, and I'd be miserable if I left without you. So let's not get into any second-guessing or regrets. It's all good. In fact, it's perfect. I love you, and we're going to be happy together, right on our goofy, little island." He shook his head. "God help me, I never thought I'd say that." Then he laughed again.

Grinning like an idiot, Lily gave him a poke in the ribs. "For that cheap shot, Aiden Flynn, I'm going to make you haul a hundred extra traps tomorrow."

Aiden leaned down and kissed her. "Aye, aye, Captain."

Epilogue

Lily hadn't set foot inside the Flynns' old wraparound Victorian for many years—not since Sean had stopped lobster fishing. Before that, Miss Annie would sometimes take her along when they surreptitiously visited Rebecca Flynn while Sean was out on his boat. It had been a gorgeous house back then, and its bones were still good, but on a November afternoon it looked pretty gloomy.

"The place needs a lot of work," Aiden said.

They surveyed the spacious living room with its bow window and soot-crusted original hearth. Chunks of plaster had flaked off the walls and ceiling, the chandelier tilted from its loose base, and one of the windows had a crack running diagonally across it. But at least the place was spotless. Aiden had hired Peggy Fogg's daughter to do a deep cleaning during the two months his father had spent in a rehab program in Portland, and now Mary stopped in every week to keep it tidy. That wasn't a big deal, given that Sean had been staying with Miss Annie and Roy since his recent return to Seashell Bay.

"Brendan Porter will help out," Lily said. "He's a great

carpenter, and he can fill in when you don't have time to work on the house yourself. And I've got some time on my hands now too."

Lily had just pulled her lobstering gear for the season. She'd had a very good three months on the water and had made enough money to put herself on a much sounder footing. Aiden had continued to work sternman for her until he started at the university. After that, Lily had stopped fishing for a week. But then she had been able to hire Erica Easton after her captain, Forrest Coolidge, was hospitalized with a stroke. It looked as if Erica would be available next season too, since the stroke had left poor Forrest facing a very long rehabilitation.

Aiden took her gently by the lapels of her barn coat and tugged her up for a quick kiss. "Yes, but we agreed that you'd focus on the resort during the initial planning stages, since you're the one with all the good ideas. You and Bram. I'm better off spending my spare time with a hammer and a paintbrush."

She smiled at him, still not quite believing how everything had come together so quickly. Aiden had already lined up much of the project financing and ensured that the long process of legal and regulatory approvals was underway.

Bram's role in the project so far had been a revelation. Like his dad, he'd also completed an alcohol rehab program. He and Sean were now seeing the same Portland psychologist—insisted on and paid for by Aiden—and he'd given up online gambling. In fact, he'd gone so far as to turn over his computer to Aiden to lock away. The difference Lily had seen in Bram since August was more than encouraging.

She batted her eyes in mock flirtation. "Oh, I can think of better ways to spend your spare time, big guy."

Aiden laughed. "You're insatiable, woman. It's shocking."

"Yes, but I know how much you love it."

He grabbed her by the waist and pulled her against him. "We've still got a long way to go to make up for fourteen lost years."

She pushed open his leather jacket and nuzzled into the solid warmth of his chest. "Then we'll just have to work even harder."

He hugged her for a few moments and then pulled her to sit beside him on the ratty, old couch in the bay window. "I haven't told you yet what Dad said last night."

Aiden had spent the evening with his father, Miss Annie, and Roy Mayo while Lily met Morgan in the city for dinner and a concert. But Aiden had been waiting for her at the ferry dock when she got off the boat, and they'd focused on other, more interesting things than talking as soon as he got her back to her cottage.

"He told me he wants to stay with Miss Annie and Roy a little longer," Aiden said. "You know they've invited him to stay with them as long as he wants, and he says he's happy there. Says those two old coots—his words, not mine—are good at keeping an eye on him so he doesn't drink."

Miss Annie had stepped up to the plate when Sean got out of rehab, insisting that Aiden remain with Lily at her cottage instead of babysitting his father, as she called it.

"God bless Granny and Roy," Lily said, "but that setup obviously can't last forever."

"Dad realizes that. He just wants to stay there for a few more months—basically until he's sure he can live alone again without falling off the wagon." Aiden gave her a wry smile. "I actually believe him, Lily. You've seen how much he's changed."

Lily hadn't had a civil conversation with Sean Flynn for ten years before the night he ended up at Maine Medical Center. Now he'd started to treat her like a human being and not a scum-of-the-earth Doyle. They still had a ways to go, but the progress was undeniable. Sean had even managed to talk to her father for a few minutes last week without getting into a fight.

Maybe, just maybe, the decades-old family feud was finally coming to an overdue end.

"That's good." She nodded. "So we've got a few months to fix up the place and get it ready for him."

"Not exactly," Aiden said. "Dad and I talked about doing another swap."

"Swap?"

"I've agreed to build him a house a quarter mile down the road—he wants something small and easy to deal with—and in exchange, he's going to give me the family home."

Lily stared at him. They hadn't talked much about the future, but she'd assumed—hoped, anyway—that he'd keep living with her until they could someday build their own house on the land he'd already swapped with his father. "Uh, it's a wonderful old house, but I thought it might have too many . . . bad memories for you."

Aiden gave his head a little shake. "I can get past that. This was my mom's house too, and I like remembering her here. Besides, we'll create our own memories. Great ones."

Lily's throat got tight so she just gave him a big smile.

He rose and pulled her up from the couch. "Come on, I want to show you something."

She followed him up the staircase to a small, second-floor room in back that offered a panoramic view of the ocean. "I remember this. It's the room your mom used for reading and sewing."

The pale yellow room looked almost exactly the same now as in her memory. A cushioned rocking chair in one corner, a love seat opposite, bookshelves on two walls, and a braided area rug that covered much of the floor. A pair of lopsided clay vases that Aiden and Bram had made one summer at the Rec Center stood on a small table, the colorful dried flowers inside them perpetually cheery. Lily had taken the same workshop, and her mother still had her tragic effort at a vase on display too.

"Mom called this room her hideaway. We'd spend hours in here—she'd be sewing or knitting while I had my nose in a book." Aiden gave a little chuckle. "She would make me read a chapter and then tell her what happened in it before I was allowed to go outside and hit baseballs or play catch with Bram or my friends."

Lily smiled. "Smart lady. I'm going to keep that strategy in mind for the future."

Our future and our children.

"I know Mom would be happy to see us take over her family home and restore it," Aiden said. "And I think she'd love to have her favorite room get a different kind of use."

"Like?" Her breath had caught, but she tried to sound casual.

Aiden's lips curved into a broad smile. "I was thinking along the lines of a nursery."

Lily flashed him an answering smile, feeling a little too choked up to answer.

Aiden reached into his jacket and pulled out a small blue box—the kind you got at a good jewelry store—and her heart rate went into triple digits. He eased it open to reveal a stunning emerald ring.

"I love you, Lily Doyle," he said in a serious voice. "Marry me and we'll renovate a house, build a resort, raise some kids, take care of our parents, and catch a million lobsters, right here in Seashell Bay. Oh, and maybe we'll win a few conference baseball championships too."

She held out a trembling hand to let Aiden slip the ring onto her finger. Then she threw her arms around his neck and pulled herself up on tiptoe to kiss him. "That sounds like a plan, Aiden Flynn. The best plan ever."

With his arms wrapped tightly around her, Lily knew the man she'd always loved had finally come home for good.

Ryan Butler returns to Seashell Bay
a decorated Marine. His military
career may be over, but his life
with bed-and-breakfast owner
Morgan Merrifield may be
just beginning.

A preview of

Summer at the Shore

follows.

Chapter 1

$\mathcal{R}$yan Butler dumped his army-issue duffel bag onto the deck and grabbed a bench seat beside the ferry's port rail. As usual, he'd kept his gear to a minimum for a visit home. And it struck him as weird that he still thought of Seashell Bay Island as home, despite his determined escape years ago. Most summers, he'd spend only three or four days with his folks, but this vacation could last a lot longer. He had plans, of course, but his years in the army had taught him the necessity of keeping them flexible. If the island started to close in on him, he'd jump on a ferry and head somewhere else. He had some money, some time, and no responsibilities, so he could pretty much do whatever he wanted, whenever he wanted. Ryan called that freedom, and he needed a good dose of it right now.

After his latest grueling contract with Double Shield Corporation, Ryan had made clear to his controller that he needed a serious break. For ten months, he'd been babysitting diplomats in Baghdad. For six more after that, his job had been protecting a Fortune 500 CEO and his team as they bounced their way across a string of countries that varied from half-assed safe to outright deadly. Those jobs paid great but left him with an even bigger dose of uncertainty about his future than when he'd left the military. A little of the hired gunslinger's life went a long way, and he sure as hell couldn't see doing it in the long term.

As for the alternatives? At this point he hadn't a clue.

A year and a half ago, simmering frustration with his army career and the lure of good money had prompted him to leave Special Operations and hook up with Double Shield, a private military contractor. But it hadn't taken long to realize that money wasn't enough. In fact, his restlessness had only increased after he'd taken the corporate gig. At least in the army, Ryan had felt as if he had roots that kept him grounded. Now he was drifting. His bank account was getting fatter, but that was about the only good thing he had to show for his life over the last eighteen months.

He twisted in his seat to take another look over Casco Bay, breathing in the tangy scents of the sea air and the fishing boats. He must have taken one of these ferries between Portland and the island hundreds if not thousands of times, including every day of his four years at Peninsula High. The ride could be a boring pain in the ass, but it was relaxing. Forty minutes to an hour of pure peace. Put the earbuds in and zone out.

Except for the occasional mad morning rush to finish up homework before the boat docked in Portland. Okay, maybe more than occasional.

A cheerful serenity cloaked the harbor scene even though tourists and locals alike rushed to make boats to the various islands, towing children and dogs, as well as groceries in carts and battered canvas bags. Coming home had never particularly thrilled him, and yet Ryan had spent enough time eating dust and dodging bullets and IEDs to regard the good old USA, and coastal Maine in particular, as probably the closest thing to peace he'd ever find. Yeah, it was caught in a retro time warp that certainly wasn't for an adrenaline junkie like him, but he did appreciate the laid-back beauty of the place that remained unchanged from one year to the next.

The ferry horn sounded one blast to signal the boat's imminent departure. A couple of tanned and fit young deckhands—probably college students—finished securing the cargo while two others pulled the metal gangway onto the boat. Like them, Ryan had spent the summer after his high school graduation crewing on the island ferries. It had been hard, hot work, but something about that final summer, working and partying with his high school friends, had been almost idyllic.

And then he'd left for the military and soon enough to Afghanistan, Iraq, and then Afghanistan again. In the process, he'd lost too many army buddies and seen enough ugliness to last several lifetimes.

"Hold up!" a voice cried from down the pier. "Please, guys, I really need to make this boat."

Ryan recognized that feminine voice even before he saw Morgan Merrifield running full tilt boogie down the concrete platform of the ferry terminal. Her pretty face flushed and her blond hair flopping forward into her eyes, she lugged an overstuffed L.L.Bean bag in her right hand and pulled a wheeled cart with her left. Instinct made him jump up and rush down to the boat's lower deck to help her.

Though one of the deckhands was rolling his eyes at

her, the other one grinned and started to push the gangway back across the gap between the platform and the
boat. With the sweetest smile God ever put on a woman's
face, Morgan thanked them as she set her bag down and
fumbled for her ticket. Ryan waited a moment for the guys
to secure the gangway, and then strode across to help the
girl he'd known since she'd barely started to walk.

"Yo, Morgan, it looks like you could use a hand with
that. If taking my help wouldn't offend your girl-power
pride, that is," he teased.

Morgan and her best friend, Lily Doyle, had always
been hardheaded when it came to proving they were as
capable as anybody on Seashell Bay. In Lily's case, that
determination had translated into fighting the sea as captain of her lobster boat. In Morgan's, it was all about organization. Morgan Merrifield could organize the living hell
out of anything, whether it was a referendum campaign
or the kids' events at the Blueberry Festival. She'd been
born to be a teacher, and Ryan figured she probably ran
her elementary school classroom as efficiently as an Army
Ranger instructor ran his drills.

"Ryan," she gasped, her gaze widening in surprise. She
stared for a few seconds then flashed him a glorious smile
that sunk deep into his bones. "Oh, heck, offend away. Be
warned though. That bag is heavy."

Though he easily hoisted the canvas tote, she wasn't
kidding about the weight. Lugging the heavy load would
have done in a lesser woman. But Morgan kept herself in
shape, and today she looked as lithe and toned as ever.

Incredibly feminine, too, he didn't mind noting—
slender but with truly nice curves in all the right places.

"What's in this sucker, anyway?" he asked.

"Beer, among other necessities." She cast him a mocking glance as she maneuvered the cart across the narrow gangway onto the boat. "By the way, it's real nice to see you again too, old pal."

Ryan followed her on board, laughing at her good-natured dig. "Likewise, Morgan. But why do you need to lug beer all the way from the mainland? The stores on the island stock all kinds of it."

"I've got a regular guest who insists on having his beloved Moosehead, and damned if I didn't forget to ask the Jenkins sisters to order it in. I was shopping in town today anyway, so I thought I'd pick some up." She brushed a hand back through the silky, shoulder-length hair that kept blowing across her face, and her rosebud mouth curved into a sly smile. "We make a little money running an honor bar. It helps the bottom line a bit."

Ryan switched the bag to his other hand and helped her steer the cart around a pile of suitcases left on the deck. "Well, aren't you just the considerate host? Or is it hostess? I don't want to be politically incorrect."

"You, politically incorrect? Perish the thought. But yeah, I'll do special stuff for guests to keep them coming back. God knows we can't afford to lose any more business." For a moment, her cheery expression dimmed.

The deckhands yanked the gangway on board again and closed the gate. Morgan wheeled her cart across the cabin to the port side and found an empty bench.

Ryan plopped the bag down beside her. "Okay if I sit with you? Or would you rather be alone?"

She looked at him like he'd just lost his mind. "What, you think I'd rather be alone than sit with the hottest dude to ever walk the halls of Peninsula High School? Every female on this boat is thinking I've hit the jackpot, you idiot."

Though she was clearly kidding, Ryan had a sudden flash of Morgan clinging to him like a second skin at the festival dance last summer. Neither of them had been joking then.

"Oh, come on," he said, his brain momentarily seizing up as his gaze drifted to the truly nice cleavage exposed by her blue tank top.

Lame, man. Really lame.

Ryan dropped onto the bench next to her. The urge to pull her into his arms to comfort her surprised him with its intensity. He gave her hand a quick squeeze instead. "Sweetheart, I'm really sorry about your dad. He was a great guy."

Morgan's features turned somber, her gaze drifting to the dock where the water taxis were moored as the ferry moved toward the open water of the harbor. She shifted toward him on the bench, her floral print skirt fluttering around her tanned legs. "Thanks, Ryan. And thank you for the sympathy card. I know I should have acknowledged it, but... well..." She paused to breathe a low, heartbroken sigh that practically killed him. "I just couldn't stand to go through them all again, and then it seemed too late."

Cal Merrifield had keeled over dead of a heart attack in late April. Ryan had been stunned when Aiden Flynn e-mailed him the shocking news. Morgan had lost her mother to cancer about three years ago, and now her father was gone at just sixty years of age. Cal had owned the Lobster Pot bar and restaurant for years before selling it to buy the island's only B&B. He was truly one of the good guys, and Ryan knew that his sudden loss had devastated Morgan and her younger sister, Sabrina. According to Aiden, it had pretty much rocked the entire island of Seashell Bay.

"I heard you left your teaching job," he said, not wanting to force her to dwell on the details of her dad's death.

Her face scrunched up in a grimace that would have been comical if the subject weren't so awful. "Yes, for now. I took a leave of absence."

"I assume that was for your sister's sake?" No way Sabrina Merrifield could manage the B&B. Though she'd been Cal's steadfast helper, poor Sabrina had always had enough trouble just managing her own life.

"Yes. That and my guilt."

He frowned. "Guilt?"

Morgan's gaze skittered off to the side as the ferry captain tooted his horn, drowning out the squawking seagulls. "That was a stupid slip of the tongue. Just forget I said it," she finally replied.

Because Morgan was as upfront and honest as anyone he'd ever known, her response surprised him. But then she smiled, and even though it looked to him like it might have been forced, it brought her quiet beauty blazing back to life.

Simply put, Morgan was a babe, with eyes as blue as a June sky, a clear, honey-smooth complexion, and a cute nose with a slight tilt that gave her face character. She also had the most thoroughly kissable lips he'd ever seen. But though the island guys now all agreed she was a first-class hottie, it hadn't always been that way. Growing up, she'd been a bit nerdy, slightly overweight, and naturally shy.

But by the middle of high school, she'd started to blossom into a very sexy girl. Morgan and Lily and their friend Holly Tyler had made one hell of a triple threat back then, and almost every teenage guy in Seashell Bay had spent considerable time and energy circling them like a pack of overeager puppies.

"Let's go up to the top deck," he said. "It's too nice a day to be stuck down here in the cabin." Morgan had probably sat on the lower deck because she didn't want to haul all her crap up the stairs, but he figured they both could use some fresh air.

"Good idea," she said, getting up.

"Want me to bring your stuff?"

She scoffed. "Boy, pal, you've been away too long. You know it's safe to leave things on the boats. Besides, there's nothing valuable in there."

"Except for the beer," he joked. Still, he decided to keep an eye on people getting off the boat at the two stops they'd make before Seashell Bay. He'd learned not to be fully trusting—not even here.

As he climbed the staircase behind Morgan, Ryan gave her rear view a thorough, if discreet, inspection. Damned if she didn't get prettier every time he saw her, with a body that just didn't quit. When she sat down on a bench at the stern, she reached into her purse and pulled out a pair of sunglasses, covering up the baby blues that he could stare into all day. It mystified him that Morgan wasn't in a permanent relationship with some mainland guy, since she'd been teaching school up the coast for years. He doubted that anything would ever happen between her and any of the island guys, though. Everybody knew everybody else too damn well. As kids, they'd played with each other and gone to school together from the time they were knee-high to a fire hydrant.

There were exceptions, but most young people in Seashell Bay regarded their island contemporaries more as annoying brothers and sisters than potential mates. Friends, yes. Soul mates and lovers, not so much.

"If you're a little cool up here," he said, "I've got a fleece in my duffel."

A refreshing breeze usually appeared around the time the ferry cleared the harbor and turned into open waters. On a hot summer day, you could fry an egg on the sidewalk in downtown Portland and be reaching for a sweater before the boat passed the ruins of Fort Gorges in the middle of the bay.

She tipped her face up to the sun for a moment. "Thanks, but I'm fine." Then she looked at him, inscrutable behind her big, movie-star shades. "Ryan, I'm really surprised to see you here in June. You're usually only back for the Blueberry Festival."

He leaned back in his seat and stretched out his legs, going for casual. "Let's just say this isn't going to be my standard, quick in-and-out. I might even stay for the whole summer or most of it."

He heard the sharp inhalation of her breath. "Well, that'll be a first," she said after a pause. "Your mom and dad must be so happy. And heck, that means people might actually get a chance to know the real you, not just the mysterious tough-guy front you put on." She smiled and gave him a friendly poke on the arm. It wasn't the first time Morgan had teased him about what she called his "strong but silent" act.

"What are you talking about? I'm an open book."

"An open book with blank pages, maybe."

"Wow, that didn't tickle," he said, adopting a wounded look.

Morgan laughed, a light, melodious sound that Ryan had always found insanely sexy.

"Okay, I take that back," she said. "Maybe not blank, but written in some unbreakable code. Mr. Enigma, forever wrapped in mystery."

Yeah, and that's the way I like it.

Ryan had never much liked folks poking into his business, and poking into other people's business was pretty much a team sport in Seashell Bay. "Maybe I just don't have a very interesting story to tell."

She stared at him. "Seriously? We need to play poker sometime, dude, because that's a big, fat lie if I've ever heard one."

"Come on, Merrifield, how many times have we hung out at the Pot drinking beer and playing darts?" he said with a taunting grin. "Or danced at the festival social? Hell, it's not like I hide out in a cave when I come back to the island." Damn, he'd almost forgotten how much he enjoyed kidding around with her.

Morgan's expression went serious on him in an instant, surprising him again. "In a way, you do hide, Ryan. You hardly ever talk about yourself and never about what you actually do. All anybody knows is that you were in the military for years and then you left. Trust me, we've spent many a long hour on the island speculating about what nefarious things Ryan Butler might be up to. Some people even think you were part of the raid on Bin Laden's compound, and maybe what happened there made you decide to leave the army."

That theory was completely bogus, though Ryan had been part of operations every bit as hairy as SEAL Team Six's mission to Abbotabad. "Not even close. Besides, SEALs are navy, and I was army. Who was the wing nut that came up with that stupid idea?"

Morgan made a zipping motion across her lips. "I never reveal my sources. But if you don't like rumors, you could try to be a little more forthcoming. Inquiring minds want to know."

"You mean *nosy people* want to know. Okay, here's the deal—I was in the army, I left, and now I work for a private military contractor called Double Shield."

She rewarded him with an encouraging smile. "That's a start. Now what exactly do you do for Double Shield? Which, by the way, sounds like a condom ad."

Ryan was torn between laughter and irritation. He didn't like people pressing him for details of his life, but he knew Morgan was just kidding around. "I protect people who need protecting."

"Holy cow, you mean like movie stars and rap artists?" She batted her eyelashes in a *golly-gee* imitation of someone who was actually impressed with what he did.

"All kinds of people," Ryan said with just enough edge to signal the topic was closed for discussion.

Morgan blew out a sigh. "See what I mean? Getting information out of you is like digging for gold in Seashell Bay. Totally pointless."

"Now that's an incisive little nugget of analysis."

She groaned at his lame joke. He was really hitting them out of the ballpark today.

The boat pulled up to the Little Diamond Island dock, and a few passengers started to gather up their things.

"Call me paranoid," Ryan said, "but I'm going to head downstairs for a few minutes to make sure nobody gets ideas about your stuff." Maybe they could talk about something else besides his life when he came back.

She smiled. "If it makes you feel better, go for it. They'd be crazy to try with you playing watchdog. Dude, you look more ripped every time I see you."

"Right, a regular man of steel." Ryan flexed a bicep like Popeye to make light of her comment and then headed for the stairs.

As she watched Ryan disappear below, Morgan told herself that her rapidly beating pulse was simply a coincidence. Most übermasculine guys in their early thirties tended to swagger, especially around women. Ryan, though...he moved with a quiet yet powerful grace that was a wonder to behold. His body was pretty damn wonderful too, with broad shoulders tapering to the classic six-pack and long, muscular legs. His Red Sox T-shirt hugged his brawny chest and showcased his cut biceps. That amazing body was the product of years of military training and his beloved kayaking, and it was all too easy to imagine how it would feel wrapped around her.

She breathed a tiny sigh and slumped against the back of the bench, turning her face up to the warm June sunshine. She'd spent hours rushing around Portland to pick up supplies. Normally she gave herself enough time before the boat's departure to use the cargo service for her goods, but too many errands today and a fender-bender near the parking garage had delayed her. Thank God that after her mad dash, Ryan had appeared to help her. The fact that he liked to rattle her chain spoke to the easy friendship that still existed between them.

Her thoughts about Ryan had often strayed from friendship into fantasy territory over the years, and their encounter at last summer's festival dance had done nothing to change that. The two of them had ended up in a slow dance at the end of the evening, egged on by their friend Laura Vickers. A little drunk by then, Morgan had found it all too easy to melt into the dangerous shelter of Ryan's embrace.

It had been a culmination of a stressful evening, brought on by a horrible and very public confrontation between Lily Doyle's father and his longtime enemy, Sean Flynn. Morgan had been so rattled and worried for Lily that she'd responded by drinking more than she normally did, which had lowered her staunch defenses against her supersecret crush on Ryan. Her heart had pounded like a battering ram as he held her close—too close. His bristled jaw had rubbed gently over her cheek, and she'd thought he was going to kiss her right there on the crowded dance floor. Under the influence of alcohol and nerves—and, yes, sheer lust—her smarts had evaporated in the heat in Ryan's mysterious gaze.

At precisely the same moment, they'd both snapped out of it. By some sort of unspoken but clear mutual agreement, she and Ryan had derailed the makings of a runaway train. Even in her instinctive relief, Morgan had been shaken to realize how good it had felt to be held by him. How thrilling the moment had been in its raw sexual power.

And how insanely stupid it had been to let it go that far. While in theory, she loved the idea of having hot sex with Ryan Butler, she was not going to be a one-night stand for a hard-ass soldier who flitted on and off the island, not even stopping long enough to make a ferry pass economical. And Ryan had clearly felt the same, because they'd quickly parted ways after the dance, never speaking a word about what had happened during those few electrifying minutes.

Dammit, though, one look at him today had sent her right back into the grip of an emotional—and hormonal—tsunami. Whatever that dance at the social had stirred up, she obviously hadn't managed to bury it deep enough. Morgan knew her traitorous body would happily straddle Ryan's lap for a hot make-out session right now, in full view of a bunch of islanders who knew them both. But surely all that told her was that it had been way, way too long since she'd had sex.

Yeah, sure, that has to be it.

Ryan came back up the stairs, taking them two at a time as the boat pulled away from the dock. He sat next to her and said, "So, tell me about Golden Sunset. How are you and Sabrina making out with the place?"

She mentally winced, hating the idea of voicing her struggles with the inn. Should she be honest with Ryan or put on the brave face she maintained for all but her closest friends? Uncertain, she gave a little shrug.

"Not too good, huh?" His gaze looked both sympathetic and concerned, and she could tell he wanted an honest answer.

She capitulated. "It's been rough. An awful lot of our regular guests came back year after year mostly because they loved Dad. You know what a big personality he had, and he really knew how to make people feel welcome and wanted."

"Cal was a stand-up guy. One of the best."

Morgan took a deep breath, the grief almost choking her. "Quite a few couples canceled their summer reservations after they heard Dad had passed. I don't know whether they didn't want to come if he wasn't there or they thought the place might be too depressing after we lost him."

Hell, despite her best efforts, the inn's atmosphere *was* depressing. It still seemed impossible that it should carry on without her dad.

"Maybe a little of both," Ryan said, frowning a bit. "It's too bad they didn't look at it as an opportunity to keep supporting the place. And you."

"Amen to that. Anyway, unless business somehow picks up, it looks like we could wind up in the red for the summer. And I think you remember how dead the rest of the year is for tourism in Seashell Bay."

The B&B's bread and butter had always been the summer vacation crowd. While most of that revenue came from tourists, a lot of island residents didn't have room in their homes and cottages for all the family and friends that descended on them in the summer, so those folks often ended up at Golden Sunset. That kind of business would continue at various levels all year, but only during Christmas was the inn ever close to full during the off-season. If Morgan didn't manage to pull in some good summer business, her father's B&B was headed for disaster.

Ryan glanced at another ferry, the *Maquoit*, as it passed them to starboard on its way back to Portland. At least a dozen people waved at them, as always happened when boats passed each other. She forced a little smile and waved back.

"Have you given any thought to selling?" Ryan said. "Or will you be able to ride it out?"

Oh, I think about selling every freaking day.

"I'm not sure anybody would buy the place at this point. Everything was up in the air even before Dad died. Aiden and Lily and their partners are building that new resort...and, well, who really knows how it'll impact our little place?" Morgan was, of course, happy that Aiden Flynn had returned to the island for good. But she had some worries about the effect of his upscale ecoresort on her small business.

"Most of your regulars should stay loyal," Ryan said. "A lot of people prefer the atmosphere of smaller inns. From what I hear, Aiden's place is going to cater to a different crowd."

Morgan gave him a wry smile. "Yes, a crowd that likes lots of comforts and the latest in modern conveniences. Our place is short on both, I'm afraid. Heck, Dad even hemmed and hawed before finally putting in Wi-Fi last year. And our rooms are pretty...well, basic."

She almost said *run-down*, but that felt disloyal. Facing an increasingly tight financial squeeze, her father had let things slide over the past couple of years, and now the place needed a lot of work, both structural and cosmetic. "Anyway, I have to try to make a go of it for my sister's sake. She'd fall apart without the B&B."

Though he'd been mostly away from the island for more than a dozen years, Ryan would know Sabrina well enough to understand. When she was a preteen, she'd been diagnosed with a learning disability. While she was a hard worker at the B&B, cooking and cleaning and doing other chores that were familiar territory for her, there was no way she could manage the operation. Most normal administrative tasks were simply beyond her, which meant they all fell on Morgan.

"So it sounds like you're putting your teaching career on hold for the foreseeable future," Ryan said.

Whenever Morgan thought about that, it felt like someone had punched her in the gut. Though she'd told her principal that she intended to be back in her grade five classroom in September, the low number of confirmed reservations at the inn had made that an increasingly remote possibility.

"I've been hoping I could get the place operating efficiently enough this summer to let me hire a part-time manager to run it with Sabrina after I leave, but that seems more like a wish at this point than a plan. So I'm just taking it one day at a time and trying to figure things out." Morgan didn't want to surrender to pessimism, but she refused to bury her head in the sand either. The stakes for both Sabrina and herself were too high to engage in self-delusion.

"One day at a time is never a bad idea." Ryan leaned back on the bench and stretched out his long legs. His feet reached all the way to the opposite bench. "I guess I'm going to be doing something like that myself for a while."

Morgan welcomed the shift in conversation. "So, what are you going to do with yourself on the island? Kayak all over the place and drink beer? Or will your dad need a sternman this summer?" Like a lot of people on the island, Ryan's dad was a lobster fisherman.

"Actually, I was thinking that if I end up spending the whole season here, I'd try to kayak to every one of the Calendar Islands. Give myself a little challenge to pass the time."

The islands of Casco Bay were sometimes called the Calendar Islands, a reference to the fact that there were supposedly 365 of them. Some, however, were barely big enough to stand on.

"Well, that'll be a heck of a workout." Morgan's brain, which refused to behave itself, easily conjured up the image of Ryan's half-naked, ripped form gleaming in the sun as he paddled through the chop of the bay.

"Just a walk in the park if I stick around for a couple of months. As for helping Dad out, yeah, if he needs me to sub while his sternman takes some time off, I'll be on the boat."

"That's nice of you, since you hate lobster fishing," she said, scrunching her nose in sympathy. Like Ryan, many of Seashell Bay's younger generation had no desire to follow in their fathers' footsteps when it came to the hard slog of hauling traps from sunrise to sunset.

Ryan shrugged. "I don't much like a lot of things I have to do. Doesn't mean I won't answer the call."

She smiled at the typically cryptic Ryan Butler statement. "Your parents will be happy to finally have you at home for more than a few days."

"Yeah, but I'm not going to stay with them. I want a place of my own, a place to..." He paused for a couple of moments, his gaze distracted. "Anyway, I'm going to rent a cottage or a house, hopefully one on the water."

Morgan raised an eyebrow. "Renting isn't going to be easy. Almost everything is booked by this time of the season."

"I know, but it can't be helped. I only made the decision to do this a few days ago. I figure there should be something out here, even if it's a bit of a dump. I don't need anything fancy. As long as it's got indoor plumbing, I'm good to go."

Dump. On some of her worst days, Morgan had silently used that harsh word to describe the current state of the B&B. But on his lips, the word had sparked a pretty interesting, though kind of crazy, idea. She toyed with it for a few moments, testing it out in her head. Sure it might be dangerous, at least for her, but it seemed worth a try.

As the ferry made the turn toward its next stop at Diamond Cove, Morgan mentally put on her big-girl panties and got ready to proposition the sexiest man to ever come out of Seashell Bay.

Fall in Love with Forever Romance

SOULBOUND
by Kristen Callihan

After centuries of searching, Adam finally found his soul mate, only to be rejected when she desires her freedom. But when Eliza discovers she's being hunted by someone far more dangerous, she turns to the one man who can keep her safe—even if he endangers her heart...

WHAT A DEVILISH DUKE DESIRES
by Vicky Dreiling

Fans of *New York Times* bestselling authors Julia Quinn, Sarah MacLean, and Madeline Hunter will love the third book in Vicky Dreiling's charming, sexy, and utterly irresistible Sinful Scoundrels trilogy about a highborn man who never wanted to inherit his uncle's title or settle down...until a beautiful, brilliant, delightfully tempting maid makes him rethink his position.

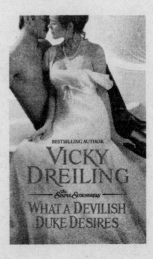

Fall in Love with Forever Romance

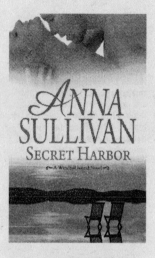

SECRET HARBOR
by Anna Sullivan

Fans of *New York Times* best-selling authors JoAnn Ross, Jill Shalvis, and Bella Andre will love the last book in Anna Sullivan's witty contemporary romance trilogy about a young woman who left her beloved home in Maine to become an actress in Hollywood. Now a star, and beset by scandal, she wants nothing more than to surround herself with old friends...until she meets an infuriating—and sexy—stranger.

MEET ME AT THE BEACH
by V. K. Sykes

Gorgeous Lily Doyle was the only thing Aiden Flynn missed after he escaped from Seashell Bay to play pro baseball. Now that he's back on the island, memories rush in about the night of passion they shared long ago, and everything else washes right out to sea—everything except the desire that still burns between them.

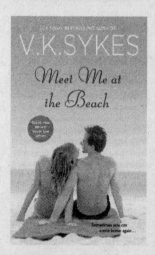

Fall in Love with Forever Romance

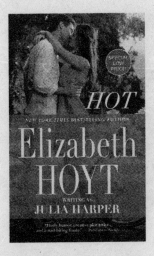

HOT
by Elizabeth Hoyt
writing as Julia Harper

For Turner Hastings, being held at gunpoint during a back robbery is an opportunity in disguise. After seeing her little heist on tape, FBI Special Agent John MacKinnon knows it's going to be an interesting case. But he doesn't expect to develop feelings for Turner, and when bullets start flying in her direction, John finds he'll do anything to save her.

FOR THE LOVE OF PETE
by Elizabeth Hoyt
writing as Julia Harper

Dodging bullets with a loopy redhead in the passenger seat is not how Special Agent Dante Torelli imagined his day going. But Zoey Addler is determined to get her baby niece back, and no one—not even a henpecked hit man, cooking-obsessed matrons, or a relentless killer—will stand in her way.

Fall in Love with Forever Romance

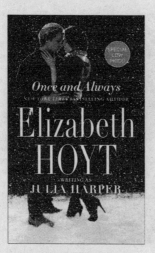

ONCE AND ALWAYS
by Elizabeth Hoyt writing as Julia Harper

The newest contemporary from *New York Times* bestselling author Elizabeth Hoyt writing as Julia Harper! Small-town cop Sam West certainly doesn't mind a routine traffic stop. But Maisa Bradley is like nothing he has ever seen, and she's about to take Sam on the ride of his life!